White Christmas

KATIE FLYNN

White Christmas

CENTURY

1 3 5 7 9 10 8 6 4 2

Century
20 Vauxhall Bridge Road
London SW1V 2SA

Century is part of the Penguin Random House group of companies whose
addresses can be found at global.penguinrandomhouse.com

Penguin
Random House
UK

First published in Great Britain by Century in 2021

www.penguin.co.uk

A CIP catalogue record for this book is available from the British Library.

ISBN 9781529135404

Typeset in 13/16.5 pt Palatino LT Pro
by Integra Software Services Pvt. Ltd, Pondicherry

Printed and bound in Great Britain by Clays Ltd, Elcograf S.p.A.

The authorised representative in the EEA is Penguin Random House Ireland,
Morrison Chambers, 32 Nassau Street, Dublin D02 YH68.

Penguin Random House is committed to a sustainable future for
our business, our readers and our planet. This book is made from
Forest Stewardship Council® certified paper.

MIX
Paper from
responsible sources
FSC® C018179

In memory of Sir Nicholas Winton, who organised the Kindertransport.

December 1938

Rozalin Sachs – Roz to her pals – woke with a start to find her father's hand clamped firmly over her mouth. Fearing the worst, she swivelled her eyes to meet his, and her heart sank when he whispered the words she had been dreading. 'They're here ...'

Nodding in mute understanding, she pushed the bedcovers aside and slipped her feet into her shoes before tiptoeing over to her mother who stood waiting by the back door. Samuel – Roz's father – placed his well-worn dark brown fedora onto his head then pushed it into place. He cast a final glance over his shoulder before addressing his wife and daughter. 'Ready?'

The women exchanged a glance and Roz slipped her hand into her mother's before giving a brave nod.

Though they had hoped this night would never come, they knew the odds were stacked against them, so Samuel had put a plan into place months before, just in case.

Even before the dreadful night of destruction, which the Nazis had proudly referred to as Kristallnacht, Roz and her family had witnessed synagogues being purposely set alight. Anyone who dared object was taken away, arrested as though they were criminals. Roz had had friends who had been in school one day but not the next, and rumours were rife that the soldiers were arresting Jewish people in the middle of the night without explanation. Indeed, they had been woken on more than one occasion by people shouting as their loved ones were taken from them.

Samuel Sachs, a partner in a firm of accountants, had done his best to keep his head down, doing most of his work from home so that he didn't draw attention to himself. He had only ventured out to join his wife and daughter as they, like many others, queued hour upon hour for a visa in the hope that they might leave Germany and start a new life, somewhere far away from the Nazi regime which was rapidly gaining in strength.

The visa had been granted a few days earlier and Samuel had secured a post, working as an assistant accountant at an insurance firm in the Liver Building in Liverpool, England. His wife Inge, an English teacher, had yet to find a job, but they had been assured by the head of the accounts department at Samuel's firm that she would have no problem finding work as a private tutor once they reached English shores. Consequently, they planned to take a train to Holland, where they would catch a ferry to England.

'We're close, but we're not there yet,' Samuel had told his daughter over supper as she examined the visa. 'We must remain vigilant, and only go out if absolutely necessary. We won't be leaving for a few days yet, and we can't afford for anything to go wrong.'

Roz, who was excited at the prospect of a new start, looked up from the visa. 'You'd think they'd be glad to see the back of us,' she said. 'They want us gone, and that's what we're doing.' She furrowed her brow. 'It must be costing them a lot of money to look after all these people they're arresting – you'd think they'd make it easier for people to leave.'

The dark look her mother and father exchanged didn't go unnoticed. 'What?' Roz asked innocently, but her father shook his head.

'Eat your supper, then off to bed, only don't forget, you're not to get changed into your nightie. Put on your bed clothes, just in case we have to leave in a hurry.'

By bed clothes her father meant day clothes which they now wore to bed. Roz used her bread to mop up the gravy from her plate. 'I'm sure they'd understand if we showed them the visa. Like I said, we're—'

Inge cut her daughter short. 'They don't care, Roz, they're cruel, heartless, vicious ...' She held a hand to her forehead. 'You can't reason with someone who's so full of hate, they're too blind to see.'

Roz's cheeks flushed; her mother rarely raised her voice.

Samuel placed a hand gently over his wife's, then reached across and placed his other hand over Roz's. 'A few more days and we'll be gone, and this will all be behind us.' He glanced at Roz's plate which she had wiped clean. 'Off to bed, bubala.'

Roz kissed her parents goodnight and headed across the hallway to her bedroom where she quickly washed, then changed from one pinafore dress into another. Bowing her head, she prayed for a peaceful night and for someone to stop the Nazis and their evil ways. Yawning, she climbed between the sheets, never for a moment thinking that she would be woken just a few hours later.

Now, with the soldiers banging their fists even harder against the front door, she gave a final look around their stylish townhouse apartment, wondering what would become of the possessions which were too big for them to take. Her father announced that the coast was clear and she found herself being manoeuvred to one side so that he might lock the door behind them, muttering that this would help to hinder the soldiers' progress.

As they stepped out into the night, Roz kept her fingers crossed that they wouldn't be spotted. The last thing they needed was for someone to raise the alarm and alert the soldiers to their movements. Using the cover of the buildings, they made their way to where her father had parked his car a couple of streets away. Looking over his shoulder as he unlocked the doors, Samuel ushered his family inside, whilst he took the crank handle from under the driving seat. He placed it into the slot just below the grill and gave it a few turns, but the engine was cold and didn't want to start. With a look of grim determination, Samuel continued to crank the handle until the engine eventually roared into life. Relieved that they were finally on their way, he took his place behind the wheel. He turned to his wife, who nodded, then his daughter, but as he did so, to his horror, he saw several soldiers running towards

4

them. Assuming that they must have been alerted by his starting the engine, Samuel thrust the car into gear and pulled away from the kerb. His mouth went dry as he called out to Roz, who had turned in her seat to watch the soldiers who had doubled their efforts to catch up. But they were no match for a car and several of them had already given up and turned back. Grinning, Roz made a rather rude gesture at the last soldier, before settling back in her seat.

'We're free!' she cried, a relieved smile spreading across her face.

'Not yet, we aren't,' hissed Inge. 'We'll not be free until we're on that ferry.'

'They'll not catch us now,' Roz said confidently, 'not on foot.'

Inge arched her beautifully shaped eyebrows. 'Do you not think they also have cars?'

Fear flooded Roz. Of course they had cars, and what's more, she had just made the sort of gesture which would shock her parents, and probably cause the soldier to be more determined than ever to catch them. She looked over her shoulder, but it was impossible to see anything in such darkness. She turned back to stare out of the windscreen. 'Where will we go? We're too early for a train ...'

Her mother turned to face Roz, a reassuring smile on her lips. 'We can park near the station. Your father scouted the area the other day, and he found a wonderful spot where we can sit nestled behind some trees, out of sight from prying eyes. We should be safe there until the train arrives.'

Roz relaxed a little. 'What about the car?'

Her father shrugged. 'I'm sure they'll discover it sooner or later, but we'll be long gone by then and there won't be anything they can do about it.'

'But they'll take it as their own, maybe even use it to arrest more of our people,' Roz cried indignantly. 'I'd rather you set it alight than that.'

'And alert every Nazi for miles around to our existence?' Samuel wagged an admonitory finger. 'You have to start thinking with your head, bubala, not your heart.'

Roz wanted to retaliate by suggesting they find a river and push the car into it, or set it alight just as the train arrived and then make a run for it, but she knew she was being childish, and at fifteen years old she should know better than to make petulant comments. Frowning, she leaned forward as they passed the turning to the station. 'How far is the hiding place from the station?'

Inge turned to face her daughter again. 'We're not catching the train here; we're going to Berlin. No one knows us there, so we needn't fear someone telling the authorities where we are.'

Roz's jaw fell. 'But that's *hours* away!'

Samuel nodded. 'The Nazis will assume we've gone to the station here in Frankfurt.'

Roz looked at him uncertainly in the reflection of the rear-view mirror. 'You're *sure* they won't follow us to Berlin?'

Samuel shook his head. 'No, they believe they're catching people unawares, so they'll expect us to go for the nearest station.' He tapped his left temple with his forefinger. 'They're soldiers, they're not paid to think, but rather do as instructed without question.'

'So, we're safe!' said Roz.

Her father grinned. 'As safe as we can be, and certainly a lot safer than if we'd stayed at home.'

Inge gently squeezed her husband's hand and smiled lovingly at him. 'Having our things ready in the boot of the car was a good idea.'

Samuel glanced back at his daughter. Her eyes were drooping and she had linked her hands together, laying her cheek against them as she slowly drifted off to sleep. He turned back to Inge. 'I shouldn't have had to hide our things in the car, because none of this should be happening.'

'I know, but it is, and at least we're safe, which is more than I can say for others.' She wiped away a tear as it touched her cheek, then pointed out the windscreen. 'Snow.'

He nodded. 'Luckily it's only just starting. I wouldn't like to think what could have happened had we tried to escape with a blanket of snow on the ground.'

The snow continued to whirl down, slowing their journey considerably, and when they finally reached Berlin the roads were covered in a thick layer of white. Samuel, who had only visited during fine weather, was having difficulty recognising the road layout. In fact, he was so busy peering at a street sign that pointed the way to the station, he completely failed to see the pedestrian step into the road in front of them.

Inge screamed in alarm and Samuel automatically swerved, but with the snow and ice beneath its wheels, the car spun violently out of control before hitting a lamppost and coming to rest on its roof.

With the wind knocked out of her, Inge struggled to breathe. She tried to see how her husband and daughter were, but she could barely see for the thick flurry of snow engulfing her.

Roz had come to, but instead of sitting in the back of the car she found herself lying on a bed of snow. Bleary-eyed, she looked around her as she tried to work out where she was, but it was no use, she hadn't the strength to keep her eyes open, let alone think for herself.

Hearing shouts of alarm, she knew that people were rallying round. Whatever had happened, help must be on its way.

Chapter One

Roz shifted in her seat, then winced as a pain shot down her side. Grimacing, she guessed she must have fallen asleep in an awkward position, so she readjusted herself and tried to drift back to sleep. Only this time something else was keeping her awake. It was the sound of children chatting, singing songs, and, in the case of some, crying softly. Roz peered out through her eyelashes as she tried to work out where she was. She appeared to be in some sort of corridor, surrounded by children. Not wishing to draw attention, she continued to peek between her lashes, but her parents were nowhere in sight. Opening her eyes fully, she became aware of a boy sitting opposite who was staring at her with great interest. Roz, who didn't like the idea of being stared at whilst she slept, shot him a stern glare before looking around the corridor. It was at this point that she saw she wasn't in a corridor at all, but rather on a train, and judging by the swiftly moving scenery outside the window, they were travelling at speed. The realisation as to what this meant filled her with joy. They were on their way to Holland! Wondering where her parents might be, she started to crane her neck in order to see further, when the carriage fell so quiet you could have heard a pin drop. The reason for the deathly silence soon became clear. Two German soldiers had stepped into their carriage from the corridor. Roz felt her heart plummet. What on *earth* were Nazi soldiers doing on a train bound for the coast? Did they know about the Sachs' attempt to flee the country? Were they here to stop them at the final hurdle?

One of the soldiers halted abruptly and pointed at Roz. Speaking in German he asked her what had happened.

Roz stared back at him blankly. What was he talking about? And *why* had he singled her out in particular? Could he know of her escape from Frankfurt?

Growing impatient, the other soldier demanded that Roz answer the question.

Roz's heartbeat quickened in her chest. Her father had told her not to speak to soldiers, but to let him or her mother do the talking for her instead, only they weren't here.

As the first soldier stepped towards her, the boy who had been staring at Roz came to her rescue. He quickly explained that Roz had been hit by a car, which was the reason for her injuries, and that the shock must be causing her silence.

The soldiers, as well as Roz, glanced down at her side. A small gasp escaped her lips. So *that* was why she was in such discomfort! Only why was the boy saying she had been hit by a car? She had no memory of an accident. She wanted to object, to say he had got it wrong, but as she examined her forearm swathed in bandages, she thought better of it. After all, something had clearly happened, even if she couldn't remember it. As she continued to examine her injuries, she remembered her necklace and quickly checked to make sure it hadn't come off. A wave of relief swept through her body as her fingers curled around the treasured gift from her parents.

Looking around, the soldier demanded to see her belongings as proof she had a right to be on the train.

Roz frowned. She assumed he must be referring to her suitcase, but seeing as she couldn't remember boarding the train, she certainly couldn't tell him the whereabouts of her belongings. Much to her relief, the boy came through for her again when he bent down and pulled out a suitcase from under the bench she was sitting on.

The soldier picked it up, flicked open the latches and looked inside, then tipped the contents onto the floor and stirring them with the toe of his jackboot. Having found nothing of interest, he stared at Roz in a derisive manner and barked at her to pick them up, before striding off with his accomplice, both of them laughing at Roz's obvious discomfort.

Gasping in pain, she knelt down to gather her belongings, glancing shyly at the boy who had spoken up on her behalf.

He had sparkling dark eyes and they were smiling kindly down at her. She looked around at the other children in the carriage, all of whom were watching them with keen interest.

'Do you speak English?' she asked the boy, who nodded.

'I don't understand how I got here, or what's going on,' she explained as he held the suitcase open for her. 'And I'd rather people didn't know my business, until I know what's going on myself.'

He smiled grimly. 'I don't blame you. I was there when they brought you into the waiting room at the station, and I rather suspected you'd be all at sea when you woke up. I was hoping you'd wake up so that I would have the chance to explain what was going on before the soldiers made an appearance. Rumours spread fast on the train, and I knew they were checking the carriages. It was only going to be a matter of time before they got to us.'

Roz snapped the clips shut and tucked the suitcase beneath her seat. She held out a hand. 'I'm Rozalin Sachs, but you can call me Roz.'

Grinning, the boy pushed his brown hair from his eyes, before taking her hand and shaking it gently. He apologised as Roz winced with the pain. 'I'm Felix Ackerman.'

Roz glanced down at her forearm. 'You said I was hit by a car, but if that's true then where were my parents and why aren't they here with me now?'

Felix looked shocked. He leaned closer and spoke in hushed tones. 'You have parents?'

Surprised by his reaction, Roz became aware of the prying ears around them. Getting up she looked pointedly in the direction of the corridor, then back at Felix who nodded his comprehension. Something was wrong, very wrong indeed.

Closing the compartment door behind them, Roz leaned back against the carriage wall. 'I know we're talking in English but I daresay we aren't the only ones who can speak or understand another language.'

Felix glanced over her shoulder to the children in the carriage, who had now turned their attentions elsewhere. 'I'd like to say that you can speak freely amongst your own, but nothing's certain any more.' He eyed her curiously. 'You mentioned your parents?'

Roz nodded. 'My parents and I escaped the Nazis last night. We were in our car driving to Berlin when I fell asleep ...' Deep lines furrowed her brow as she tried to recall what had happened. 'I remember lying on something cold and wet – I think it was snow – but that's all I can recollect before waking up just now.'

Felix tapped his forefinger against his chin as he described the moment Roz had been brought into the railway station. 'I was looking for the toilets when a woman brought you in. She said you'd been hit by a car which had crashed just outside ... Someone else said they'd seen the crash, and that the driver had tried to avoid you, then spun out of control.'

Roz's cheeks bloomed. 'How dreadful! Is he alright?'

Felix shrugged. 'No idea – apparently he fled the scene.'

Roz looked cross. 'Oh, charming! He might have killed me, but he didn't even stop to check if I was okay!'

'They think he might have been on the run from the Nazis, and that's why he legged it.'

'Oh ...' said Roz quietly, 'well, that's a bit different. I know what it's like to be on the run, because we were also running away, but it still doesn't answer the question as to my parents' whereabouts. Surely they must have witnessed the accident?'

Felix looked at her blankly. 'I'm afraid I can't help you. I was busting for the toilet, and I knew I didn't have much time before the train left – in fact I only just made it back in time.'

'They must be on the train,' Roz concluded, but to her annoyance, Felix was shaking his head.

'Not this train.'

She attempted to fold her arms across her chest, but the pain in her arm stopped her. 'Why not?'

He nodded his head at their carriage, then, taking her by the elbow, he led her down the corridor, stopping momentarily to look in at each carriage they passed. After the third carriage he released her elbow. 'Now do you understand?'

Roz shrugged dismissively. 'Not really. Where are all the parents, or are they following on a different train?'

He pushed his hair back with one hand. 'There aren't any parents on this train and they aren't following either.' He tried to smile sympathetically. 'This train is for orphaned children.'

Roz clutched her stomach. 'But I'm not an orphan!' she wailed. 'I don't belong on this train! Where are they taking us?'

Felix desperately signalled for her to quieten down. 'Steady on, you don't want to go broadcasting it. Goodness knows what the Nazis will do if they think you're a stowaway. As for where they're taking us? To England!' He grinned. 'You're on the Kindertransport; it's a rescue mission to get all the Jewish children whose parents can't afford a sponsor out of the country.'

Roz shook her head, then stopped as pain coursed up her neck. 'I'm sorry, Felix, I understand this is wonderful news for you, but it's not for me. I should be with my parents; they must be frantic with worry. I don't understand why they weren't with me when I was hit by the car ...' She faltered. 'The car that hit me?'

'What about it?'

'Do you know what sort of car it was?'

He nodded. 'One of those new Volkswagens ... hey!'

Roz was walking away from him, peering into each carriage as she went. Finally she burst into the last one and approached a man with round spectacles resting on the brim of his nose as he read a copy of an English newspaper. He looked up as she approached. 'Fräulein?'

'I need to speak to whoever's in charge,' Roz said bluntly.

He folded his paper and placed it on the seat next to him. 'That would be me. I'm Reggie Jones, one of the chaperones. How can I help you?'

Feeling that she had no other choice than to confide in the Englishman, Roz spoke out. 'There's been a mistake. I wasn't hit by the car, I was in it.'

The man placed a finger to his lips and beckoned her to follow him into the corridor, where Felix stood waiting.

He looked at Roz from over the rim of his spectacles. 'Name?'

Roz introduced herself, then listened as the man explained that he had been present when she had been brought into the station. 'I can assure you, I heard the woman with my own ears, and she clearly stated you had been hit by the car, so what on earth makes you think you were in it?'

Roz briefly explained her escape from Frankfurt, finishing with falling asleep in the car and then waking up in the snow.

Sighing, the man rubbed his forehead between his fingers then stared soberly from Roz to Felix for a few seconds before speaking. 'Tell no one.'

'Why?' asked Roz.

'Because of what I said about this being a train for orphans,' Felix whispered hastily.

The man nodded briefly. 'If the soldiers find out you're not meant to be on the train, they'll send you back to Berlin, and if they can't find your parents – and you'd better hope they can't ...' he eyed her thoughtfully from over the top of his glasses, '... they'll send you to one of the camps.'

Roz's face fell. 'But I can't just leave them—'

He folded his arms across his chest. 'I don't wish to be blunt, but they left you ...'

Roz rounded on him. 'No, they didn't! They'd never leave me!'

Reggie exchanged a rueful glance with Felix before turning back to Roz. 'Then where are they?'

Angry tears ran down Roz's cheeks. 'I don't know!' she said, stamping her foot. 'But I do know that they wouldn't leave me, or at least not intentionally. Perhaps my dad needed the hospital, or maybe my mum did, or ...'

He smiled kindly at her. 'Maybe, and perhaps I put it badly, because your story sounds plausible.'

'You should be careful what you say,' Roz said reproachfully.

He nodded. 'You're right, and I apologise. I'm feeling a little fractious right now. God only knows it's hard enough getting children with permission across the borders, but stowaways?' He looked down the corridor. 'It was touch and go as to whether the Nazis would pull out at the last minute, and even now we can't be certain until we're on the ferry – only then will I be able to truly relax.'

'What about my parents?' asked Roz. 'They don't know where I am, and—'

He held up his hands in a reassuring fashion. 'Don't worry, we'll send word back to Berlin that your parents are missing, and that you believe you were in the car when it crashed. We have people who can look for your parents without arousing the suspicion of the Nazis. When you get to England, you'll be assigned a foster family, so if we find your parents, we'll be able to keep you informed, and hopefully reunite you.'

Roz relaxed a little. 'Do you really think you'll be able to find them?'

He eyed her shrewdly. 'We have more of a chance at finding them than you do.'

She breathed a resigned sigh. 'Then I suppose I've done all I can.'

He nodded. 'Go back to your carriage and keep your head down. The last thing you need is to attract any attention,' he glanced at her cuts, bruises, and bandaged forearm, 'although I suspect you already have?'

Felix nodded. 'I told them she'd been hit by a car and they searched her belongings, but they seemed content with that.'

Reggie pushed his glasses back up his nose. 'They're bullies who like to throw their weight about and frighten children. If you prove to be of no interest they'll leave you alone, but if they think there's more to you than meets the eye ...' He looked meaningfully at Roz.

She nodded her understanding. 'Like my father always used to say, keep yourself to yourself.'

'Your father sounds like a wise man.'

Roz smiled fleetingly. 'He is.'

'I'll speak to you again when we're safely across the Channel.'

Roz gave him a small smile of gratitude. 'Thank you, and I'm sorry to be causing you all this trouble—'

'Hardly your fault, and I daresay it must have been very frightening waking up in one place, when you expected to be somewhere else.'

'It was.' She glanced at Felix. 'I'm so glad you were there. I don't know what I'd have done without you, but I rather suspect I'd be on a train back to Berlin with an armed Nazi escort by now!'

A blush tinged his cheeks. 'Don't mention it.' He jerked his head back in the direction of their carriage. 'Come on.'

As they walked, Roz told Felix about her parents and their plan for a new life in Liverpool working as a tutor and an accountant. They stopped outside their carriage and continued talking. 'Now you know all about me, but I know nothing about you,' Roz finished.

Felix shrugged. 'My story's nowhere near as exciting as yours. My father was English which is why I can speak it so well. Everything was grand until a few years ago when he had an industrial accident.' A shadow crossed his face. 'He never recovered from his injuries, which left Mum a widow. Up until this morning, the two of us lived in a bedsit just outside Berlin. Mum went off to work as usual, and a few hours later our rabbi came to the door, saying the Nazis had arrested her. No explanation as to why, or where they'd taken her. He strongly advised me to get myself onto the Kindertransport in case the Nazis came for me. He said the people who ran the Kindertransport might consider me an orphan seeing as how my father had died when I was twelve and my mother was now gone ... and here I am.'

Roz stared at him agog. 'Weren't you worried?'

He nodded fervently. 'Of course I was, still am, but what can I do? I don't have a clue where they've taken her, and even if I did, she'd not thank me for getting myself arrested.'

'What about when all this is over? How will she know where to find you?'

'Our rabbi will let her know that I'm in England, alive and well.' He patted his trouser pocket. 'I've got his address so we can keep in touch. He's been helping out with the Kindertransport, which is how he knew about it. He said he'd do his best to find out where they took Mum and get word to her.'

'You're lucky to have him,' said Roz. 'We had to keep everything quiet. No one knew about our plan to leave, so no one will know we had an accident, or that I've been separated from my parents.'

'I reckon that man you spoke to, Reggie Jones, is a good sort. He'll do his best to reunite you ...' He eyed her quizzically. 'I must say, I've never seen you in our synagogue. Did you say you came from Frankfurt?'

Roz looked downcast. 'That's it, we don't live in Berlin. We drove there ...'

He looked surprised. 'What were you doing in Berlin? Surely they have railway stations in Frankfurt?'

She nodded grimly. 'Dad worried that the soldiers might head for our local station and cut us off before we had a chance to board a train, so he thought we should leave from Berlin instead.'

'Forward thinking – pity it went wrong at the last minute, although who knows? If you had tried to catch a train from Frankfurt you might be on your way to one of the camps.'

Roz felt an unpleasant sensation in her stomach. 'A scary thought indeed. I'm so lucky that woman came to my rescue ...' A line furrowed her brow. 'Only, she couldn't have seen me getting run over because I wasn't, was I?'

Felix opened the carriage door and sat back in his seat. 'I've been thinking about that. There's more than one Volkswagen in Berlin – perhaps you and your parents were waiting to cross the road when another car just like yours knocked you down?'

Roz shook her head and winced. 'Only that *can't* be right. I don't remember getting out of the car, or ... or anything! The last I remember was driving away from Frankfurt; I don't think it was long after we left before I fell asleep.'

He shrugged. 'You've taken a fair crack to your head; it would be understandable if you'd forgotten some of the events leading up to your coming round.'

Roz sank down into the seat beside Felix's and turned to face him. 'Just supposing you're right, and the bash to my head caused me to have some sort of lapse in memory. Where are my parents now? They couldn't have been run over, the woman would have said so, so why aren't I on a train with them?'

Felix mulled this over, but try as he might he couldn't think of a reasonable explanation. 'You're right, it doesn't make sense.' He frowned. 'Only why would that woman say you'd been run over if you weren't?'

'I do remember lying in the snow. I've no idea how I got there, unless I managed to crawl out of the car.'

Felix leaned his elbow on the armrest between their seats. 'If you had been thrown clear of the car perhaps she assumed you'd been run over?'

'Made the whole thing up in her head?' mused Roz. 'That's possible, especially if ...' She fell quiet as she thought things through, then looked up sharply as a solution presented itself. 'Perhaps Dad swerved to avoid someone, which would explain why we crashed in the first place. If the woman saw that, she might have assumed Dad didn't miss the person, and that I was the victim!'

Felix sat upright. 'Now that makes sense! These things happen so quickly, it's easy to get muddled, and she couldn't possibly have seen how many people were in the car prior to the accident because you don't take notice of that sort of thing until afterwards.'

Roz smoothed her pinafore down. 'I'm no better off, though, am I? I still don't know what happened to my parents, whether they're alive or ...'

Felix placed his hand over hers and gave it a reassuring squeeze. 'They will be! Or at least as far as I know the dead don't walk.'

21

She eyed him inquisitively. 'Sorry?'

'The car was empty, they said there was no one to be found, and that's why they assumed the driver must have been on the run.'

Roz's eyes filled with tears. 'So they *did* leave me ...' she said, her voice barely above a whisper.

Felix opened his mouth to object, but found it impossible to do so. Leaning forward so that the children around them might not overhear, he spoke in a quiet, reassuring manner. 'If they did, it wasn't because they wanted to, but because they had to.'

She gave him a wobbly smile. 'Thanks, Felix.'

'What for?'

'For being here, sitting with me, trying to help me work out just what happened. It's good to have someone with a different perspective, because it stops you from thinking the worst. I'd be a real mess if it weren't for you,' she said truthfully.

'I'm glad I can help. It must be awful not knowing what happened to your folks. At least I know my mum has been taken to one of the camps.'

Roz averted her gaze from Felix. She didn't know what happened to the people who ended up being taken to the camps, but when her father had come back from work with reports of associates being taken, his face had been etched with worry, and the dark looks he had exchanged with his wife hadn't reassured her. Roz had tried asking why they were taking people of Jewish descent to the camps, and whether it was like a holiday camp, but her mother had burst into tears and her father had hushed her angrily, then apologised when he saw his daughter's face.

'Sorry, bubala, I didn't mean to lose my temper.' He had beckoned her to join him and her mother in their embrace, kissing the top of her head. 'You needn't worry about the camps because you will *never* be going to one, I don't care what I have to do.'

Aware that she hadn't responded to Felix's explanation, Roz gave him a fleeting smile. 'How about we make a pact to help each other get our folks to England?'

He smiled back, although Roz could see uncertainty in his eyes. 'My mum wasn't like your parents; she doesn't have a job waiting for her in England. I can't see them letting her leave the country. I think it's going to be a long time before I see her again.'

Roz took his hand in hers. 'Someone will stop Hitler, probably someone like Reggie Jones – he's already getting children out of Germany, so other countries must realise what Hitler's doing. They can't let him carry on.'

Felix looked at their hands, then back at Roz. 'I'm sure you're right, and when they do, we'll get our families together and have a party to celebrate.'

Roz was distracted by a movement outside the door. Reggie Jones opened it purposefully.

'Get your things, we're in Holland. Spread the word.'

Roz and Felix retrieved their suitcases as the children around them cheered in unison. Felix winked at Roz. 'No one can hurt us now.'

They stepped down onto the platform and waited for the others to join them. As they watched the children spilling out of the carriages Roz noticed the soldiers who had entered their carriage earlier marching up and down the train, checking under seats and giving the train a thorough inspection. Reggie arrived at her side and jerked his head in their direction.

'They're checking for stowaways; they're dying for an excuse to shut us down.'

'You'd think they'd be glad to see the back of us,' said Roz, remembering the conversation she had had with her parents only the night before. 'Why would they want to stop us leaving?'

Reggie stared down at her, stony-faced. 'Doesn't make sense, does it?' His voice was flat, but looking up into his expressionless eyes, Roz felt herself drawing a breath which didn't seem to end. She clapped a hand to her mouth as sudden realisation dawned. She searched his face for a flicker of confirmation to her suspicions, but he remained wooden. He briefly glanced at Felix to make sure he wasn't listening before speaking again. 'Just be thankful that you didn't end up in one of their camps.' And with that he turned on his heel and walked away.

Swallowing hard, Roz turned to find Felix engaged in a conversation with a girl who'd also been in their carriage. Seeing him chatting so happily, Roz found herself wanting to take him in her arms and tell him how sorry she was about his mum, but she couldn't do that without proper explanation, and the truth was she couldn't justify her suspicions when she didn't have the facts.

Felix turned round and introduced her to the girl he had been talking to.

'Roz, this is Adele, Adele, this is Roz ...' His expression turned from friendly to concerned. 'Is everything alright? You look as though you've seen a ghost.' He looked over her head towards Reggie who was walking away. 'It wasn't bad news, was it?'

Roz forced her mouth into a smile. 'No, nothing like that, I'm just tired.' She looked past Felix to Adele, grateful to divert the attention away from herself, and held out a hand. 'Hello, Adele.'

Taking Roz's hand, Adele glanced at Felix. 'Felix was just telling me that you were the girl in the crash. I think you were awfully brave not talking to those awful soldiers, they scare the life out of me.'

Roz gave a mirthless laugh. 'I don't know about brave, I think the cat had got my tongue, as my mother would say.' She eyed the other girl quizzically. 'Your English is very good.'

Adele gave a shy smile. 'That's because I'm English. My parents moved to Germany in the hope of a better life ...' She grimaced. 'I've got no family back in England which is why I'm on the train—'

She was interrupted by a middle-aged woman who was calling for attention. Roz listened as the woman explained that they were to stay together as they boarded the ferry for England. A cheer went up amongst some of the children, but others looked fretful.

Roz, Felix and Adele boarded the ferry together and made their way to an empty cabin.

'I was only little when we came to Germany,' Adele confided. 'I can't remember much about the journey, save that I was queasy when we were below deck.' She looked sympathetically at the children being taken below. 'I hope my tummy's stronger than it used to be.'

'I'm sure it will be,' smiled Roz. 'I used to get awfully sick on boats, but I'm much better now.'

Felix settled into the seat next to Roz. 'Have you been on a boat before, then?'

She nodded. 'Dad's passionate about sailing—'

Felix frowned earnestly at her whilst placing a finger to his lips. 'We're not out of the woods yet ...'

Only it was too late, Adele had heard every word. She stared at Roz. 'My parents couldn't afford a dinghy, let alone a proper boat. Your father sounds very rich – how come you're on this journey?'

Roz briefly explained her circumstances to Adele, who listened in awe. 'You poor sod! Talk about bad luck.'

'You won't tell, will you?' Roz asked anxiously. 'I would have given anything to be back in Berlin looking for them, but after speaking to Mr Jones I realised that might be a huge mistake.'

Adele placed a hand over her breast. 'I promise I won't say a word, and I reckon Mr Jones is right, especially if your mum and dad have had to go into hiding ...'

Roz's head whipped up. 'Hiding?'

Adele nodded. 'A car crash like that is bound to draw all sorts of attention, and it's not as if the soldiers were miles away. We know four of them accompanied us on the train to Holland; they could easily have heard the commotion and come out to see what was happening. Perhaps your parents saw the woman taking you into the station and thought it best to lie low until the dust had settled. Although, as I remember, the train left within minutes of you being brought in. In fact, if the accident had happened five minutes later you'd have missed the train altogether.'

Roz could have kissed the other girl. For the first time since leaving Frankfurt, a broad grin lit up her face. 'If that's true ...' She looked at Felix, her eyes dancing. 'I bet Adele's right, I bet my mum and dad were about to get me when this woman turned up and took me away. They probably waited close by, keeping out of sight, only they didn't know anything about the Kindertransport, so didn't realise I was being whisked off to England!' She turned to Adele gratefully. 'I've been so worried, but this makes perfect sense. My parents are bound to ask in the station about a girl who was involved in a car crash, and then they'll know that I was taken to England, and they can catch their train and meet me there!' She gave a small squeal of excitement. 'I'll go straight to the Liver Building and tell them where I'm staying – that way Mum and Dad will know where to find me. They might even be there waiting for me!'

'There you go,' said Felix, his eyes twinkling. 'All's well that ends well. I told you they'd be alright.'

Adele started as the ferry blew its horn, signalling their departure. 'What was that? Should we go and see? Did we hit something?'

Roz laughed. The knowledge that her parents might well be on their way to England had lifted her spirits. 'It's the ferry's way of telling its passengers as well as other boats that we're about to leave.'

Adele relaxed. 'The sooner we get to England the better.'

'In a few hours we'll be far away from Hitler and his nasty Nazis. A new country, and a fresh start, amongst people who want us ...' agreed Roz.

'I don't understand what happened,' Adele said solemnly. 'I was so happy living in Berlin, with lots of friends; we never had money, but that didn't bother us. What was so bad about that?'

As they pulled away from the quayside, Felix looked out of the cabin's small window. 'Goodness knows. My mother says it's because Hitler's jealous. He thinks the Jewish are a strong, wealthy, successful community, and he wants to destroy it.'

'But you're German . . .' said Adele softly.

'Not as far as he's concerned,' said Felix. 'That's why he's arresting everyone.'

'Then what?' said Adele. 'Does he intend to keep them in prison for ever?'

The colour drained from Roz's face as she remembered the look her parents gave each other when talking of the camps.

Felix rested a hand on her shoulder. 'Are you okay? You've gone pale.'

Roz gave a weak smile. 'I'm feeling a bit queasy,' she lied, 'probably that seasickness Adele mentioned.'

Adele furrowed her brow. 'I thought you said you'd gotten over that—'

Felix cut her short. 'Or perhaps it's the conversation that was making you feel unwell?'

Roz stared out the window. 'Perhaps,' she said quietly.

Felix squeezed her shoulder. 'Then we shall change the subject. Why don't we have a bet for fun?'

Grateful that he had sensed her discomfort, Roz nodded. 'What were you thinking?'

'Which of us will get fostered first?' he suggested.

'That's easy,' said Adele. 'Roz will go first because she's the prettiest, and she speaks English beautifully.'

Roz blushed as colour returned to her cheeks. 'I don't know about being the prettiest, but my mother would be happy to hear you think I speak English beautifully, as she was the one who taught me. However, if you want my opinion, I think Felix will get fostered first because he's a boy and he looks strong enough for all manner of jobs. He's clever too.'

Felix beamed. 'I'd like to think I'm quite the catch, but I agree with Adele, I think you'll be the first to be picked.'

Adele chuckled. 'Looks like I'm not the only one who thinks you're the prettiest.'

Just as Roz thought she would die from embarrassment, one of the chaperones entered the cabin. 'Hello! Just come to check that everyone's alright, and nobody's feeling sick?'

All three nodded. 'Where's everyone else?' asked Roz, grateful for the interruption. 'I thought there'd be more of us in here.'

The woman rolled her eyes. 'On deck, feeding the fish.'

Adele jumped to her feet. 'Can we feed the fish too?'

The woman laughed loudly. 'I hope not.' She glanced at Roz, who had gathered her meaning. 'Can I leave you to explain?'

Roz nodded and the woman left them alone. 'She means they're being sick over the side.'

Adele pulled a face. 'That's disgusting!'

'I wish we'd asked how long it will be before we reach England,' said Felix.

'It'll be some time yet.' Roz yawned. 'Probably a good idea to get some sleep.' She stopped mid-stretch and gently lowered her bandaged arm back down. 'I think I must have landed on my arm, as that's what hurts the most.'

'You might have broken something,' said Felix, but Roz was already shaking her head.

'I broke my arm years ago when I was learning to ride my bicycle. I remember that it hurts like billy-o and you can't wiggle your fingers, but mine are fine,' she said, wriggling them to prove her point.

'I think I'm too excited to sleep,' said Adele. 'Billy-o's a very British saying – your mum must have been an excellent tutor!'

'She is; she lived in England for a while so that she could perfect her English.' A thought suddenly occurred to Roz. 'Where are your parents? I know you said you got aboard the Kindertransport because you didn't, but what happened to your mum and dad?'

'They're hoping to come over at a later date, but in the meantime they're doing what everyone else is, keeping their heads down and hoping for the best.'

'Surely you could all come back?' said Felix. 'With you being British in the first place?'

Adele dropped her gaze to her fingernails. 'That's what I said, but my mother worried they might think we'd come over to spy.' She shrugged helplessly. 'Who knows what goes through their heads?'

'I'm afraid she's probably right, but at least they know where you are,' said Roz, 'and you can always write.'

Adele smiled. 'I have faith in mankind. The rest of the world can't stand back and do nothing, and us being sent to another country is just the start. You watch, this next time year, Hitler will be in prison and everything will be back to normal!'

The children from the Kindertransport had been in Dovercourt Holiday Camp, Harwich for two weeks. Roz's injuries had healed well, but despite Adele's prediction of her being the first to be fostered because she was the prettiest, it seemed that the British public preferred the younger refugees.

Adele walked into the canteen, her hands on her hips. 'Someone's just taken the twins! They can hardly speak German, never mind English!'

Roz laughed. 'But they're delightful angels—'

'No, they're not!' snapped Adele. 'They're positively evil! The little devils put mashed potato in my shoes last night.'

Roz grinned. 'I know they can be mischievous, but you can't blame them. The poor things are bored to tears, they have to keep themselves entertained somehow.'

A wicked smiled tweaked the corners of Adele's mouth. 'Their new parents are in for quite the surprise – serves them right for picking youth over experience.'

Reggie Jones entered the canteen and waved to Roz, who immediately left her seat and went to join him. 'Any news?' she asked hopefully.

'I'm afraid not, although some say that no news is good news,' he said, resolutely upbeat.

'Has anyone heard back from the people who work in the Liver Building? My father might already be there.'

He pushed his hands into his pockets. 'We have, and I'm afraid not, although they have said they will get in touch should he make an appearance.' He laid a reassuring hand on her shoulder. 'Chin up. We're pretty sure your parents haven't been arrested or taken to one of the camps, because we'd have heard about it, what with the accident and all.'

'I know, and I'm so grateful for all your help, but if they're not there, then where are they?'

'Safe, or at least we hope they are, and hope is all we have until they choose to surface.' He glanced around the canteen at the children who were sitting there making paper chains to use as Christmas decorations. 'I must say, I'm disappointed to see so many of you still here.'

'Us too,' replied Roz plainly. 'But we're not six years old with faces full of freckles.'

'I'm afraid you're probably right, although you could look at it another way – you could say they were saving the best 'til last.'

Roz laughed. 'You certainly could.'

As he left the canteen, she went back to join her friends who were looking hopeful. 'You're smiling,' said Felix, 'does that mean you've had good news?'

Roz shook her head. 'Afraid not, but he did manage to raise my spirits.'

Felix placed an arm around her shoulders. 'Well then, that's good enough for me.'

Adele giggled. 'I reckon it's just as well you've not been picked yet, Roz, because I don't think I could put up with Felix moping and whinging about how much he missed you.'

Felix shrugged, but didn't deny it. 'We've become great friends – it's only natural that I should miss Roz when she goes.'

'Bet you won't miss me as much,' said Adele, with a wry smile.

'Only because you take the ...' He glanced at Roz, searching for the right word. The children had taken full advantage of their time with Adele, and had begun to speak English as well as any child who had been born and brought up in the country.

'The Mickey Bliss,' Adele said easily.

'Yeah,' said Felix, 'only because you take the mickey out of me all the time.'

Adele grinned. 'You make it so easy for me!'

Roz shook her head with a chuckle. 'Honestly, you two! You bicker like brother and sister.'

The door to the canteen opened and Reggie reappeared. He signalled to Roz. 'Looks like today's your lucky day.'

Leaping to her feet, Roz rushed over to join him. 'My parents?'

His face fell. 'Sorry, dear, I didn't think. I meant it's your lucky day because we've found you a foster family.'

Roz looked doubtful. 'But they haven't even seen me!'

'They didn't need to. They're after an older child, a girl, and the best part ...' he beamed at her, '... they hail from Liverpool.'

Roz gave a whoop of excitement. Grinning, she turned to Adele and Felix. 'Back in a mo.'

Adele put the glue brush she'd been using back into the pot and placed an arm around Felix's shoulders. 'Cheer up. It's not as if it's the end of the world – you can easily keep in touch.'

Felix stared glumly at the door which closed behind Roz. 'I can't help worrying about her. I think it's because I've been there since the start, watched over her, made sure she's alright, but I won't be able to do that if she leaves.'

Adele rested her head against him. 'You really like her, don't you?'

He nodded. 'I feel as though she's my responsibility.'

She withdrew her arm and rested her elbow on the table. 'I know you do, but Roz is a big girl, far more capable than me. I'm sure she can look after herself – she's a little too mature for mollycoddling.'

His eyes met Adele's and he smiled shyly. 'I know she can, and you're right, I know I'm treating her like a child, it's just …'

A smile tweaked Adele's lips. 'You really worry about her …' she gazed at him, '… you're smitten.'

A slight frown creased his brow. 'Are you being rude?'

Adele burst into laughter. 'No! It simply means you like her a lot, an *awful* lot. You know what I mean, like you can't stop thinking about her, like she's …'

'The only girl in the world.' He hung his head as Adele nudged him playfully.

'That's the ticket!' She tilted her head to one side in the hope of gaining his attention.

Felix gave her a sidelong look. 'Please don't say anything to Roz – I wouldn't want to frighten her off.'

'I think it's rather sweet,' said Adele, and seeing the wry smile which crossed his face she added, 'and before you start, I'm not being sarcastic. I really do think it's sweet, and I think she's lucky to have someone like you looking out for her. I don't see why you think it would frighten her off; I'm fairly sure she must realise how you feel.'

Felix wasn't altogether certain he understood his feelings for Roz, let alone Roz's feelings for him. The only thing he could say for certain was that his feelings had gone way beyond being fond, and whilst he'd never been in love before, he knew from his mother that being in love meant you put the other person before yourself, and if that was the case … He looked at Adele. 'I'll miss you too when you go.'

'Not like you'll miss Roz, though, eh?'

He grinned. 'Possibly not.'

'It'll be nice for her to spend her first Christmas in England with a proper family.' Adele glanced at the other children who were sitting at different tables, making decorations from bits and bobs that the chaperones had given them. 'I know it's kind of fun being with so many people our own age, but Christmas is about family, and even though I don't really celebrate Christmas, it doesn't mean to say I wouldn't appreciate being part of someone else's Christmas and the comfort that comes from being in a real family.'

'There is that,' agreed Felix as he looped a piece of coloured paper around another before fixing it in place with glue, 'and above anything else I just want her to be happy.' Which was also true, but he just wished they could be happy together.

*

Roz approached the family who were waiting in the office. The grandmother – at least Roz assumed it was the grandmother – had hair as white as cotton, and her features were those of a woman who had led a hard life. Roz cast an eye over the woman's attire and tried not to grimace; the woman's clothes were too large for her and well worn. The man next to her, who Roz assumed was her son, wore a tight-fitting shirt, the top two buttons of which were missing, and his waistcoat didn't match his trousers, both of which were equally snug. Roz's father had always said you could judge a man by his shoes. She glanced down and wasn't surprised to see that the man's shoes were unpolished and that the laces looked as though they had broken a few times since they were only using half the eyes. As her gaze met his, he looked away swiftly. She knew she shouldn't judge him by his appearance, but it was hard not to when his hair was so thick with Brylcreem it was positively shining, and his face was disfigured with acne scars.

Realising she was staring, she turned her attention to the girl who sat beside him. Roz guessed her to be a similar age to Roz herself, but that was where their similarity ended. Roz was always impeccably turned out, and she had rosy cheeks, wavy, dark hair neatly pinned up, and smiling brown eyes, whilst the girl who sat opposite her had the sort of pallor which could be mistaken for unwashed skin, and her mousy hair was lank and dull. As for her clothing, Roz assumed they must be hand-me-downs from her mother, as the skirt waist was rucked up from being turned over so many times to prevent the hem from dragging along the ground, giving her a thick middle. The shawl that was draped around her shoulders was as dirty as her shoes, which, like her father's, were short on laces, and the bottom of one of the soles hung limply.

Once again, Roz became aware that she was staring, so she lowered her gaze rather than offend her new family, because even though they were obviously rough around the edges, they were offering Roz a home, and for that she should be grateful. She looked at Mr Jones, wondering how he thought they could possibly be described as 'good news'. She could see however that he was just as doubtful as she, but beggars couldn't be choosers, and if Roz turned this family away, she might not get another opportunity, especially one that hailed from Liverpool. She shrugged inwardly. Perhaps all people from Liverpool looked like this, and just because they looked rough around the edges didn't mean that they were bad people. If anything, it might mean that they were hard-working and honest ... Her mother had always taught her not to judge others, but Roz couldn't help it when it came to the man. There was something decidedly shifty about his manner, as though he couldn't wait to get out of there.

Reggie indicated the family. 'Roz, this is Lilith Haggarty, her son Callum and his daughter Susan ...' He stopped mid-sentence as the younger girl shot him a withering look.

'It's Suzie, not Susan!' she snapped sullenly.

'Sorry,' said Reggie, his eyes flickering towards Roz briefly before correcting himself. 'Suzie.'

Roz smiled doubtfully at the small ensemble. 'Hello.'

Callum grunted a response as he locked eyes with her briefly before turning his attention outside.

The older woman scowled at Suzie, obviously willing the girl to converse, but Suzie clearly wasn't interested in making small talk, and only said 'hello', after receiving a sharp nudge in the ribs from her grandmother.

Roz's gut feeling cut in, and she was just opening her mouth to say that whilst she was grateful for the offer, she thought it would be better if she stayed at Dovercourt, when the grandmother started to speak.

'My son and granddaughter are a little shy, but they'll soon come out of their shells once they get to know you better.' She gave Roz an encouraging smile. 'We're all very much looking forward to you coming to stay with us.'

Roz eyed Callum and Suzie with some uncertainty. They didn't look shy, especially Suzie who hadn't been afraid to correct Reggie when he got her name wrong, and if they were looking forward to Roz coming to stay, they were certainly hiding their feelings very well.

Lilith glanced briefly at Reggie before continuing. 'Mr Jones says you're eager to move to Liverpool because that's where your folks are going?'

Roz nodded. 'The Liver Building, have you heard of it?'

The woman's grin broadened. 'Heard of it? Why, we don't live more than five minutes' walk away.'

Reggie looked at her in surprise. 'Really?' He gave Roz a look of approval as he continued, 'It's very grand around there. I've only been to the city a few times myself, but I must say I'm very impressed.' He eyed

Callum quizzically. 'I don't remember you saying what you did for a living?'

Callum glanced at his mother, who gave him an approving nod. He turned to Reggie. 'Coal.'

Reggie nodded slowly; perhaps that explained their rather unkempt appearance. He had encountered many people on his travels, and whilst some of the wealthier ones were impeccably turned out, wearing only the best, the more eccentric ones quite often looked as though they hadn't two pennies to rub together. Obviously the Haggartys fell into the latter category.

'My goodness,' said Reggie. 'They say where there's muck there's money, and that's certainly true in the case of coal.'

Callum Haggarty pulled a pocket watch from his waistcoat, glanced at it then spoke directly to his mother. 'We'd best be off if we're to make the train.'

Lilith nodded. 'So, are we agreed?'

Whilst every fibre of her being wanted to say no – and not just because of the way they looked; Callum hadn't said or done much, but it was the way he held himself: there was an air to him that she found most unpleasant – Roz knew that it would be ludicrous for her to pass up the opportunity to move to Liverpool. She came to a decision. 'I'll get my things and say my goodbyes.'

Lilith Haggarty beamed. 'Splendid!'

Roz was about to walk away when she remembered something. 'My friends will want to keep in touch, what will be my new address?'

'Fourteen Ranelagh Street,' Lilith replied promptly.

Roz shot Suzie a sharp glance; the other girl was frantically coughing into her hand. 'Are you alright?'

Suzie nodded as tears ran down her cheeks. 'Fine,' she gasped before giving her grandmother a furtive glance, which, Roz noticed, was returned with a steely glare.

Roz had no idea what the secretive glance meant, but if she were to guess she would say that Suzie and Callum had no desire to be in Harwich and had only accompanied the older woman so that she wouldn't have to make the journey on her own. She made her way back to the girls' dormitory and gathered her belongings. She would miss Felix and Adele, there was no question about that, but the prospect of being re-united with her parents filled her with glee.

She entered the canteen to see an expectant Felix and Adele waiting for her.

'Well?' asked Felix, before his eyes fell to her suitcase. 'Oh,' he said, the disappointment clear in his voice.

Roz smiled apologetically. She knew Felix would miss her as much as she would miss him. 'They're a little unorthodox, but they live very close to the Liver Building.'

'What do you mean, a little unorthodox?' said Felix suspiciously.

Roz shrugged. 'They're not like the other families who've come by, and if you went by appearance alone you'd think they were paupers, but they're far from that, if their address is anything to go by. It's more the way they present themselves. The father and daughter are ...' she paused whilst she came up with a kind description, '... preoccupied, but the grandmother seems pleasant enough.'

'How do you mean, preoccupied?' Felix asked.

'It's hard to explain,' said Roz after some thought. She knew if she were to show any doubts, Felix would try to talk her out of it. She was already teetering on the edge of staying at Dovercourt as it was, and that would ruin her chances of being reunited with her parents sooner rather than later. 'If I were to guess, I'd say this was the grandmother's idea.'

'I think you should stay here with us until someone better comes along,' said Felix protectively, 'someone who'll appreciate you.'

Roz smiled kindly. 'Felix, we've been here for a couple of weeks, and this is the closest I've come to a foster family. What's the likelihood that someone else will come along who lives as close to the Liver Building as they do?'

Felix looked down at his shoes. 'You don't *have* to live close in order to find your folks again. As long as Mr Jones knows where you are, I'm sure he'll tell the people at the Liver Building and ...'

'And you can't rely on other people,' said Roz frankly. 'This may not be my ideal, but I'd be silly to turn it down.'

Adele nudged Felix gently. 'She's right, you know, and even though I'll miss her as much as you, I think this is what's best for Roz. Besides, we can always write.' She looked to Roz, who nodded.

'Fourteen Ranelagh Street, Liverpool,' said Roz. 'According to Mr Jones, it's in a very smart part of the city.' She looked towards the door which had opened behind her.

'Are you ready?' asked Reggie.

She smiled. 'As I'll ever be.'

'We'll walk you out,' said Felix, who wanted an excuse to see the foster family for himself as well as spend as much time with Roz as he could.

As they approached the foyer, Lilith, Callum and Suzie were waiting by the entrance.

Felix cast an eye over each of them separately before muttering from the corner of his mouth to Roz, who smiled at his comment. 'I see what you mean.'

Roz put her suitcase down and hugged Adele first, then Felix. 'Don't forget to keep in touch, and thanks for everything.'

He looked over her shoulder to where Suzie Haggarty was eyeing him with interest.

'Time we were off,' said Callum gruffly.

Roz picked up her suitcase and made her way to the entrance, calling back to her friends, 'Good luck with everything, and don't forget to write.'

She gave a last wave, then turned and followed the Haggartys out of Dovercourt to her new life in Liverpool.

Roz found the journey to Lime Street Station arduous, not least because of the multitude of changes they'd had to make, but mostly due to the company, or rather lack of it. Apart from when Callum had asked Roz if she had anything valuable she would like him to look after he hadn't contributed to the conversation, pointedly placing his cap over his eyes as soon as he sat down, whilst Suzie seemed to keep choosing the seat farthest away from Roz. Only Lilith made an effort to talk, and even then she had steered the conversation away from the Haggartys, asking questions about Roz's life before she left Germany. It was something Roz wasn't keen to talk about, since she felt as though the older woman was asking for the wrong reasons. Lilith wasn't sympathetic when Roz spoke of the Nazis and how they were treating the Jews. It seemed to Roz that the older woman was only interested in knowing what sort of house Roz and her parents had lived in, whether they owned or rented, how they had made their living and the lifestyle that they had led, which seemed irrelevant to Roz given her current situation. Lilith wasn't keen to hear about the accident, or Roz's opinion on what had happened to her parents, dismissing any idea of Roz being reunited with them out of hand.

'You may as well get used to the idea of living with us for the rest of your natural,' she said casually, removing her shoe with one hand and massaging her bunions with the other, something she did each time they changed trains. 'I don't know much about this lot, but the last lot were evil tyrants. If your folks aren't in Liverpool by now, I doubt they ever will be. From what I hear, that Hitler is ruthless.

Roz stared at her in horrified disbelief. How could anyone be so cruel with their opinions? No one else she had met had expressed such a belief, even if they had thought it secretly.

'You don't know my dad,' she said defensively. 'He's resourceful and clever, not like the Nazis – that's why we were in Berlin in the first place, because my dad outsmarted them!'

For the first time since they had begun their journey back to Liverpool, Suzie joined the conversation with a short, mocking laugh. 'Oh yes,' she said derisively, 'very smart indeed, I don't think! If he was that smart he'd not have smashed his car up, leaving his daughter to face the Nazis on her own.'

'He didn't mean to!' snapped Roz. 'That's why they call it an accident! Otherwise it would be known as an "on purpose".'

Suzie shrugged dismissively. 'Perhaps it was.'

Roz stared at her in disbelief. 'Are you really saying he'd crash our car on purpose?'

Lilith swiftly intervened before Suzie had a chance to answer. 'Now, now, girls, let's not argue.'

Roz glared at Suzie, daring her to reply, but Suzie turned to face the window.

The rest of the journey had been spent in relative silence, only interrupted by Suzie whining that she hadn't wanted to go to Dovercourt in the first place, and how much longer would it be before they were back in Liverpool.

Stepping off the train, Roz told herself that Suzie might well be jealous that her grandmother had suggested they take in a refugee, and that could be why she was being so spiteful, fearing that Roz might take attention away from her.

They walked from the station, albeit rather slowly due to Lilith's hobbling gait, probably, Roz suspected, caused by the enormous bunions which the older woman suffered from. They passed many grand buildings, some of which Lilith pointed out to Roz, even stopping briefly outside the Liver Building, which was in Roz's opinion the grandest building of them all. Every street they passed after that, Roz expected the Haggartys to turn off and present her with her new home, but as they continued it struck Roz that the area they were coming to was more industrial, and she was just beginning to wonder how much further they had to go when Suzie turned down a lane and headed towards a row of warehouses.

Roz wrinkled her brow, until she saw a sign above one of the sheds proclaiming it to be a coal merchant's, only the name above the door wasn't Haggarty's. She looked at the street sign, which read Crooked Lane, and breathed a sigh of relief, grateful that it didn't read Ranelagh Street. She watched Suzie climb some rickety steps which ran up the side of the coal merchant's building.

'Where's Suzie going?' Roz asked Lilith.

'Home!' said Lilith promptly.

'Oh!' said Roz. 'I assumed Suzie and Callum lived with you.'

'They do.'

Roz stared at the building in confusion, before turning to Lilith. 'This isn't Ranelagh Street. I can read English, you know.'

'I daresay you can,' replied Lilith, who was now following her granddaughter up the steps.

Roz gaped at Suzie who was kicking the bottom of the door at the top of the steps with the toe of her boot. 'Damn thing's sticking again,' she muttered as she scraped the door open and went inside.

Lilith looked down at Roz. 'You can sleep down there or up here – the choice is yours,' she said bluntly.

Roz took in the buildings that surrounded her. They were old, dirty, and clearly used for industrial purposes; they weren't what Roz would call homes. With no alternative, she reluctantly climbed the steps and followed the Haggartys into the building, hoping against hope that it would look different once she got inside. But her hopes were in vain; if anything the inside was worse. The room was large enough, but the floor itself was both unswept and uncarpeted. There was no kitchen, nor sink, just a single paraffin stove which she supposed was used for cooking as well as heating. On the floor at the far side of the room lay three grubby-looking mattresses. Roz could put up with a lot but there was no way she would sleep side by side with this family who had lied and deceived both Mr Jones and herself in order to bring her back to this place. Shaking her head, she backed towards the door.

'You lied!' she said, pointing an accusing finger at Lilith, then the beds. 'You made out like you had your own business, but it's not yours. I read the sign; it said "Colin Partington – coal merchant" and that's *not* you! And you said you lived on Ranelagh Street, yet this is Crooked Lane . . . is this some sort of joke?'

Callum threw his coat down onto one of the mattresses and scowled at his mother. 'I said this would happen, that you were making a big a mistake, but oh no, you had to get one who could speak English.'

'How was I to know she could ruddy well read it?' snapped Lilith. 'Besides, how were you intending

46

on getting her to do your bidding if she couldn't ruddy well understand a word what come out of your mouth?'

'Take her back,' Suzie said eagerly, a suggestion which was echoed by Roz, but to both girls' dismay Lilith shook her head.

'She can still work, and that's why she's here, or had you forgotten?'

Callum shook his head. 'We don't need anyone else ...'

'It's alright for you!' said Lilith scornfully. 'What about me? I can't keep lugging sacks of coal around, not at my age, and as for my bunions ...'

Roz stared at them incredulously. 'I am here, you know, I can actually understand what you're saying!' adding *more's the pity* in the privacy of her own mind.

Lilith shrugged. 'And?'

'And you're talking about me as though I'm to be used as some kind of slave ...'

Lilith's brow shot towards her hairline. 'Surely you're not suggesting we give you a wage as well as room and board?' she scoffed. 'I think you need to get down off that high horse of yours and take a look around you.'

Roz cast an eye around the room. 'You're telling me that it'd take all my wages to pay for this – this *hovel*?'

Lilith hobbled over to the door, and, after several attempts, opened it wide. 'Off you go, then, don't let us keep you.'

Roz was about to walk out the door when she realised that she had no idea where she was in relation to the railway station, and not only that, but she had no money to pay for a ticket. This much she said to Lilith.

'Not my problem,' said Lilith, 'you're the one who reckons she's too good to live here.'

A thought struck Roz: she may not know where she was, but a policeman might, and once he heard her story, he'd be sure to help. 'I'll go to the police, they'll ...' She got no further. Callum strode past Roz to the door and slammed it shut, then leaned his back against it, giving her a menacing look.

'They'll what?'

Roz folded her arms across her chest. 'They'll take me back to Dovercourt and arrest you, that's what.'

He stepped forward so that he was just inches from her face and stared down at her tauntingly. 'And just *why* would they do that?'

'Because you lied, because ...'

Callum raised a finger to his lips, indicating Roz should fall silent. 'Only we didn't lie. We never said that we owned our own company – that was the assumption the old feller came to – and we never said we'd look after you for nothing.' He made a sweeping motion with his arm, indicating his mother and daughter, 'No one lives here for nothing. We all pull our weight in one way or another, so why should you be any different?'

Roz furrowed her brow as she thought back furiously over the conversation the Haggartys had had with Mr Jones. As she remembered their words her face dropped. He was right, they hadn't said they owned a company, but they hadn't put Mr Jones right on the matter either, which was, as far as Roz was concerned, a form of lying, not to mention the outright lie concerning their address.

She eyed him in a confrontational manner. 'Ranelagh Street? You can't stand there and tell me that wasn't a lie.'

He looked at his mother. 'You can't expect an old lady to give her address out to just anybody – we didn't know that man from Adam.'

Roz balked at the idea of anyone referring to Lilith as a lady. 'Rubbish!' she snapped. 'And you know it.'

Sighing wearily, he stepped aside from the door. 'Do you know what? I've had enough. Get out.'

'Thank God for that!' muttered Suzie. 'I never wanted her in the first place. I still don't see why we couldn't have had a boy, like that one who come to see Miss High and Mighty here off.'

'Because I ain't havin' some nasty thievin' little Jew livin' under my roof. No doubt he'd do his best to charm his way into your bloomers,' said Callum nastily, adding, 'not that he'd have to try very hard if you're anything like your mam.'

'Dad!' cried Suzie, blushing to her ears.

Roz stared at him aghast. She assumed he must be referring to Felix, which was ludicrous. Felix was a good, honest, kind young man who wouldn't dream of taking advantage of any woman, but especially not one like Suzie. She immediately chided herself – it wasn't Suzie's fault she had been born into such a dreadful family. She had yet to meet the mother, but it sounded as though she was as bad as the rest of them.

As this thought ran through her mind, she was gazing at the three mattresses. She whipped her head round to look at Suzie, surprised it hadn't struck her before. 'Where's your mum?'

Suzie's blush deepened, but Callum answered for her, and judging by the look on his face, Roz had touched a nerve.

He wrenched the door open. 'I told you to get out and I meant it.' Grasping her suitcase by the handle, he threw it out of the door.

Roz raced after her case, just managing to catch it by the handle before it plummeted over the steps to the ground below. As she stood at the top of the steps staring out over the River Mersey, it dawned on her that other than the Haggartys, she knew no one in Liverpool, and whilst going to the police and accusing them of lying was one thing, going to the police and admitting they'd thrown her out might put a completely different spin on the matter. She wasn't local to the area, and for all she knew, the police might take the Haggartys' side, and if that was the case she could end up in real trouble. Back in her home town, she had never had cause to speak to the police, but her father had always warned her that they weren't to be trusted as he suspected most of them to be corrupt. She wondered now if that applied to all police or just the ones in Frankfurt. She had no desire to beg her way back into the hellhole that the Haggartys called home, but at this moment it seemed to be her only viable option. She was just wondering what to say, when Lilith Haggarty beat her to it, ordering Roz back inside.

Roz walked through the door, clutching her suitcase in her hands.

Lilith wagged an admonitory finger at her son. 'The whole reason we brought her here was to help me out, what with my bunions and my lumbago giving me gyp, and the fact I'm getting older, which all means I can't pull my weight like I used to. I know you were never keen on the idea, but needs must, and, besides, this one's bright, which means she has other uses.' She turned to Roz. 'You need to be damn grateful that somebody took you in; you're a burden, the lot of you. Do you really think the people of Britain need any more mouths to feed? We've barely enough work for our own without a load of foreigners coming in, all expecting to be fed, watered and housed. So I suggest you stop causing trouble and do as you're told, and just remember, if it weren't for folk like us, you'd be at the mercy of the Nazis, where you'd be treated no better than pigs.'

Roz stared back at the detestable woman. Of course she was grateful that people like Reggie Jones had stepped in to help rescue the children, but there was a big difference between what he'd done and what the Haggartys were proposing, and she reckoned Lilith knew it too. That's why she'd led them to believe she was a woman of means.

'Where's she going to sleep?' snapped Suzie. 'I told you there wasn't room for no one else, but you wouldn't listen. Instead you go and get some holier-than-thou, stuck-up—'

'Enough!' growled Callum. 'She'll have to share your bed.'

'No way!' cried Roz and Suzie in unison.

'You'll ruddy well do as you're told,' snarled Callum, 'the pair of you. If you don't like it you can sleep on the floor.' He pointed at Suzie. 'And that goes for you too!'

Lilith picked up some old sacks which were currently being used to keep the draught from coming in under the door. 'You can use them as a blanket.'

Placing her suitcase down, Roz took one of the sacks from the woman, her mouth falling open as she read the lettering on the outside. 'Coal sacks?' she cried. 'I'll be filthy ...'

'Then don't bother,' roared Callum. He looked at the three women. 'Living with two of you was bad enough, but *three*? I need my bleedin' head examined!' Noticing Roz move towards the door, he called after her. 'Oi! Where d'you think you're going?'

'If I'm going to live here, I may as well get to know the area,' said Roz simply. 'I take it you don't object to my going out and having a look around?'

'Not at all!' said Suzie spitefully. 'Whilst you're at it, how about a wander down the docks, mebbe a swim ...'

Callum clicked his fingers to gain Roz's attention. 'You can get out of that lot before you go,' he said, indicating the clothes which Roz was currently wearing. He turned to Suzie. 'Fetch her one of your skirts and a blouse.' Glancing at Roz's shoes, he added, 'Some of your old boots too.'

'Why should I?' Suzie stared at him in disbelief. 'What's wrong with the stuff she's got on?'

'Because I ruddy well told you to!' snapped Callum. He turned back to Roz who was staring at him, open-mouthed. 'Don't just stand there, strip.'

Roz, still gawping at him, shook her head. 'I'm not getting undressed in front of you, and as Suzie said, what's wrong with what I'm wearing?'

Callum had had enough of being questioned. He strode towards Roz, grasped her suitcase and threw it behind him, then grabbed her clothing by the collar.

Scared that he was going to wrench her clothes from her body, Roz held up a hand. 'I'll do it myself!' she said hastily, taking the skirt and top Suzie was holding out.

Callum let go of her, giving her a shove as he stepped away. Turning her back to the Haggartys, Roz stripped down to her vest and knickers before hastily donning the scruffy clothing she'd been given. Once she had fastened all but the top button of the blouse, she turned back to see Callum pointedly staring at her feet. Roz fastened the remaining button, then stooped down to remove her shoes and replace them with the awful, threadbare plimsolls which Suzie had handed her.

Thanking her with a sarcastic smile, Callum gathered her clothes off the floor and shoved them into the suitcase. 'You won't have no need for these,' he said, patting the side of the case. He glanced towards the door. 'Off you go!'

As Roz left she could hear the Haggartys bickering furiously with each other. She carefully climbed down the unstable steps and made her way through the warehouses towards the docks.

She had been determined not to let the Haggartys see how upset she was, but now that she was out of sight, she allowed the tears to fall freely. She knew her instinct had been right; they weren't wealthy, but worse than that, they weren't even nice. They had only come to her so-called rescue so that they might get her to work for nothing. As she reached the quayside, she looked out over the Mersey, to the land which lay on the other side. If only she had listened to Felix and declined the Haggartys' offer of a home, she would still be with him and Adele, playing cards, making the little children crowns out of tinsel, and helping the staff with each new influx of refugees. Her bottom lip trembled as she remembered how everyone had been gearing up for Christmas, which was only a couple of weeks away now. They had said they were going to make an extra effort so that the refugees would have something to look forward to. Whether they celebrated Christmas or not, it helped lift their spirits, and made everywhere look warm and welcoming. An image of the Haggartys' home entered her mind. She couldn't imagine that they would bother with a tree or decorations, or presents come to that.

She closed her eyes and breathed in the salty sea air. She toyed with the pretence that Felix would arrive outside the Haggartys' door on the 24th of December and whisk her away to a lovely house deep in the heart of the countryside, with a babbling brook running along the bottom of the garden, and a fireplace so big you could stand up in it, and moments after their arrival, there would be a knock on the door, and their loved ones would walk in … She quickly dismissed such fantasies from her mind. It was futile ... Her stomach lurched unpleasantly as another thought occurred to her. Felix didn't even know where she lived because the Haggartys had given her the wrong address to share with him, so he couldn't possibly come to her rescue. Not only that but he wouldn't be able to keep in touch either, so she probably wouldn't ever see him again.

The thought was too much to bear. Tears cascaded down her cheeks. In just over a month she had lost all that was dear to her. Her beautiful home, her loving parents, and the best friends a girl could ever wish for. Only her feelings towards Felix were more than those of a friend. She had often found herself daydreaming that he would walk up behind her and wrap his arms around her, kissing her softly on the cheek. She felt her tummy flutter. She had never felt or looked at a lad before, as she did Felix. He was special, and not just because he had come to her aid when the soldiers had entered the carriage, but because of the way he looked at her, as though she were the only girl in the world. A half-smile twitched her lips. Even Adele had noticed that Felix paid Roz more attention than anyone else. Her smile faded. He didn't know where she was, and she doubted the Haggartys were about to fess up to the people at Dovercourt any time soon. She would have to see if she could find some way of earning a few pennies to pay for a stamp so that she might write a letter to Dovercourt, letting them know of the Haggartys' deceit, and of her new address. She brightened. There was always a way out, and once again, it was Felix who had shown her the way, even if he hadn't been there to do so in person. It didn't matter, though; just thinking of him had been enough. Wiping the tears from her cheeks, she turned away from the river and back towards the Haggartys'. She would keep her nose clean, do as she was told, and wait for Felix to come to her rescue.

Chapter Two

It was Christmas Eve and little had changed at Dover-court. Adele had been the next to leave, having been chosen by a farming family who were after companionship for their elderly mother, as well as someone to keep an eye on the little ones.

'I'm sure they would have picked you in a heartbeat had they been after a farmhand,' she had assured Felix as she packed her suitcase. 'There's bound to be someone out there after a big strong lad to help out. You mark my words, you'll not be here much longer.'

It had been a few days since Adele's departure and Felix was in the canteen toying with a plate of kippers when he saw a grim-looking Reggie Jones striding towards him, brandishing a letter.

Felix opened the letter and read its contents, then looked up sharply at Mr Jones.

'This is from a firm of solicitors,' he stated, nonplussed, before handing the letter back to Mr Jones, who cast an eye over the address at the top of the letter.

'I'm afraid so,' he said, folding the letter in half and placing it into his blazer pocket.

'I don't understand,' said Felix, genuinely perplexed. 'Does she live in a flat above the solicitors, or ...'

Mr Jones took a seat opposite Felix. 'I've made a few enquiries and it seems that fourteen Ranelagh Street is split over two levels. The solicitors are based on the ground floor, with a tailor's above.' His lips formed a thin line. 'I'm afraid nobody lives or indeed has ever lived there.'

'Next door?' suggested Felix.

'I doubt it,' said Mr Jones. 'I think we've been spun a yarn.'

This was a new expression to Felix, who stared blankly at the older man. 'What do you mean?'

'Told a fib, a tale if you will,' explained Mr Jones. 'The Haggartys deliberately told us the wrong address so that we wouldn't be able to contact them.'

Felix's jaw dropped. 'And why would they do that?'

'Because some people just aren't honest. I couldn't say for certain what their motives are, but if I were to hazard a guess, I'd say free labour.' He gave Felix an apologetic glance. 'Sorry, son, I know you were keen on Roz.'

Felix was furious. 'How could this have happened? Didn't you check?' Another thought occurred to him, 'What about Adele? Has she gone to the right address, or didn't you bother checking out her family's information either?'

Reggie looked up sharply. 'There's no need for that. You know full well how hard it is to rehome you older ones. We don't have the time or resources to check out everyone who walks through those doors; sometimes you just have to take folk at face value.'

Felix waved an exasperated arm. 'Face value? If you'd checked properly then you'd have sent the Haggartys packing! A blind man could see they hadn't two pennies between them.'

'I thought they were eccentric,' Reggie admitted wearily. 'They said they owned a coal business, and to be fair they looked as though they did.'

'Working down the mine, maybe, but owning one? Come on!' snapped Felix.

'So why didn't you question it, if you thought something was up?' Reggie said levelly.

'I did,' said Felix, 'but Roz seemed certain that they were telling the truth, and she wanted to be near the Liver Building. Who was I to stop her?' He looked quizzically at Reggie who was holding his head in his hands. 'What?'

Mr Jones sat down heavily in the chair opposite Felix's. 'They never specifically said it was their business, just that they worked with coal. I assumed they owned the business because they lived in Ranelagh Street, and you'd have to have pots of money to be able to live somewhere as grand as that ...' He heaved a sigh. 'You're right, I should've asked more questions. I knew something wasn't right, but I was so grateful that *someone* ...'

Felix cut him short. 'It's not your fault,' he conceded. 'They came here with one thought in mind, and that was to get free labour, someone to do their dirty work for them; you weren't to know that.'

'That's very good of you,' said Reggie, 'but I should've asked them to be more specific with details, only I was so relieved that someone had come who wanted

59

an older child, and the fact that they lived in Liverpool ...' He fell silent; there didn't seem much point in continuing.

Felix pushed his plate of kippers to one side; he was no longer in the mood for food. 'There's no point in crying over split milk ...'

'Spilt,' corrected Reggie.

Felix shrugged. 'Spilt milk, then. All I want to know now is how we go about finding where she really is.'

'Well, we know that her father was going to work for an insurance company in the Liver Building,' Reggie said. 'We could write to them so that they can give her your forwarding address – when you get one, that is.'

'How will they know where she is?' said Felix.

'She's bound to go in asking questions about her parents, and whether they've been in touch. If we write a detailed letter, explaining who you are, and that we're expecting Roz to contact them, I'm sure they'll pass along your details.'

'Why don't we do it now?' said Felix. 'We can give Dovercourt as the address ...'

Reggie's eyes widened. 'No! Not everyone approves of what we're doing. If they thought we were making mistakes, it might be the excuse they need to shut us down, and that can't happen, not yet. We still have thousands of children to get out, and not just Jews – Hitler's turned on the gypsies now too.'

Felix looked grave. He would have asked why, but he knew that question would prove futile, so instead he asked, 'How bad do you think it's going to get?'

Reggie shook his head. 'So far no one's saying no to him, and that's not a good thing. We've no idea how far he intends his power to extend, but ...'

'But what?' said Felix, his voice hollow.

'He's building up his army, and he's only doing that for one reason ... war.'

Felix sat back in his chair. 'Who with?'

'That's the question which I fear we may soon have answered.'

They stared at each other, and Felix could clearly see the fear and dread in the other man's eyes. 'I need to get to Liverpool,' he said. 'There must be someone who needs an older boy to help out.'

Reggie ran his tongue over his bottom lip. 'We're meant to wait for people to come to us, but I reckon if I asked around to see if anyone wanted a live-in farm-hand or groom, we might have more success. How would you feel about that?'

Felix shrugged. 'I don't care, as long as it gets me there. To be honest, I didn't think anyone would want a boy of my age to stay with them for free; I expected to work for my keep.'

'You're a good lad. I'll make some calls and see what I can do.' Mr Jones stood up. 'Just for the record, Adele's foster family are absolutely fine. I've spoken to her since she left, and she's very happy. Did she give you her address?'

Felix nodded. 'The three of us said from the start that we'd keep in touch, so I shall write to her letting her know what's what with Roz. I daresay Adele's already written, and she'll be happier knowing that we know

61

things aren't right and we're doing something about it.' He tutted under his breath. 'Adele so was eager for Roz to have a good Christmas, hoping that it might cheer her up. She'll be dreadfully disappointed to find out that Roz's new family aren't all they made themselves out to be.' He gazed at the heavily decorated Christmas tree. 'I very much doubt the Haggartys will have the beautiful decorations we do.'

'Chin up,' said Reggie. 'This may not be the Christmas you'd wish for your friend, but hopefully next year things will be different.' He pushed his chair back into place before walking away.

Felix picked at the kippers again with his fork. How could they have been so careless? Especially after everything Roz had been through. He dreaded to think what life was like for her right now, but no matter what, he was determined to find her and make everything better.

March 1939
Christmas had not been acknowledged by the Haggartys in any way, shape or form. Not that Roz had been surprised, as she had soon learned their only concern was to make money, not spend it.

When she had first arrived she had been under the impression that she was only at the Haggartys' to take over Lilith's share of the work, but it seemed that Callum and Suzie's revenge for having to put up with her was to make her do all the work they didn't like doing as well as take Lilith's place on the coal rounds. Her chores started before daybreak, when she was expected to be up and dressed with the kettle on and the porridge simmering whilst the Haggartys had a lie-in. Only once everything was ready was she expected to rouse Callum and Suzie, leaving Lilith to get up when she pleased. After they'd had breakfast and Roz had finished the washing-up, they would load the coal onto the back of the wagon before starting the rounds. The first morning they had taken her to work, Roz had learned that the Haggartys merely delivered the coal and that they didn't own the lorry, nor the home they lived in, and when it came to getting paid, Callum was the only one who got to see the fruits of their labour. By the time they finished it was late in the afternoon, and just when Roz thought it would be time for a break, she and Suzie had been ordered to go to Paddy's market and see what was left that they could scrounge for free. Roz had never had to beg for anything in her life, and whilst she found it hard to believe that they hadn't earned enough to buy food, Callum had soon put her in her place when she had tried to question the fact.

'We live in a city and that don't come cheap,' he had snapped. 'Then there's unforeseen eventualities to set aside for. Such as doctors, and coal for the stove and ...'

'Beer,' muttered Suzie under her breath, although not quietly enough to go unnoticed by her father, who clipped her round the back of her head. 'Ow!' she protested.

'Keep your smart mouth shut!' growled Callum. 'Maybe I do have the odd tipple but if I do it's because you and your grandmother drive me to it.'

Roz had stared open-mouthed. Her father wouldn't dream of raising his hand to a woman, and she couldn't believe Callum had struck his own daughter.

Rubbing the back of her head, Suzie scowled at Roz. 'Don't just stand there gawping, we've work to do.'

Roz followed Suzie. She wanted to say something, to show Suzie that she didn't agree with Callum's actions, but she didn't think Suzie would appreciate her input, so instead the two girls walked in silence.

When they reached the market it was immediately apparent that Suzie was well known to the stall holders, some of whom turned away as soon as they saw her approaching, whilst others sighed heavily before rooting through the worst of their stock which they handed over without comment.

One of them nodded his head at Roz. 'She's new,' the man muttered as he went through his apples, picking out the ones that were heavily bruised. 'Supposed to feed her an' all, are we?'

'Not my fault,' Suzie muttered sullenly.

He gave a snort of disapproval. 'I daresay not, but that don't change things. Don't that old man of yours believe in spending money?'

'Not if he can help it,' said Suzie plainly.

A woman tutted loudly as she packed away her wares. 'There's some of us who earn a living so that we can buy us food, not go begging.'

'Bully for them,' said Suzie, adding, 'maybe they earn more money than us, and haven't got an old lady to look after.'

'Ha! There's nowt ladylike about Lilith Haggarty!' said the woman who had made the comment about begging. 'And she don't go short on food neither by the looks of her belly.'

Roz's cheeks turned scarlet. How could Suzie stand by and let people talk about her grandmother in such a manner? She looked at Suzie who appeared quite unperturbed by the woman's comments. *She's used to it*, Roz thought to herself, *it's like water off a duck's back*. Roz didn't imagine she could ever get used to people viewing her in such a way. On the other hand, she wouldn't dream of begging. Roz's own father would never have expected his daughter to beg for scraps; indeed, he would have moved heaven and earth to make sure it never came to that. Yet Callum hadn't batted an eyelid at the thought of sending his daughter out to beg. Roz wondered how Callum would react if he heard the way people spoke about his family, then chided herself for even questioning it. Men like Callum wouldn't give two hoots what people said or thought, because if they did, they'd not ask their family to do it in the first place.

Suzie turned and gave Roz an accusing look. 'Come on, I didn't bring you along to stand there like you haven't got a brain in your head.'

Blushing to the tips of her ears, Roz approached a stallholder who was packing up for the day. She opened her mouth to speak but the words stuck in her throat. 'Have ...' She cleared her throat and tried again. 'Have you any stale bread or cakes you're going to throw away?'

The woman paused whilst placing some iced buns into a large wicker basket. She glanced at Suzie before looking back at Roz.

'Where'd you come from?' she asked, keeping a keen eye on Suzie who was approaching an unmanned stall.

'I'm living with the Haggartys,' said Roz quietly.

'I can see that,' said the woman, 'but where do you *come* from? I know you ain't one of them 'cos as far as I know, that Callum only ever had the one child, and I can't think another woman would've been foolish enough to lay down with him, even if her mother did.' She jerked her head in Suzie's direction. 'And you certainly don't sound like a Scouser, more like a German if I'm any judge.'

'I'm from Frankfurt,' said Roz absent-mindedly. She was wondering whether the woman was going to say any more about Suzie's mother.

The woman stopped looking at Suzie, turning instead to concentrate on Roz. When she spoke again her words came out slowly. 'Are you one of them refugees I've seen and read about in the papers?'

Roz nodded uncertainly. 'Maybe, but they took a lot of photographs ...' She stopped speaking, for the woman had raised a hand to her mouth, her eyes tearing up. She gave Roz a look of deep sorrow.

'Oh, you poor, sweet child. I can't believe the Haggartys would stoop so low, not after all you've been through ...' She immediately snapped up a paper bag and placed a large loaf of bread and four iced buns inside, before handing it over to Roz. Then, checking that Suzie was still preoccupied, she handed Roz a fairy cake topped with icing sugar. 'Get on the outside of that before that one sees you ...' she whispered, looking meaningfully in Suzie's direction.

Roz frowned at the cake. 'Sorry, but I don't under-stand quite what you mean?'

'Hmm?' said the woman, distracted by keeping an eye on Suzie. 'Oh, I see,' she laughed. 'Get on the out-side of that means eat it!'

'Oh,' said Roz. She bit into the soft sponge, and smiled as the sugary sweetness of the icing engulfed her tastebuds. 'Thank you,' she said, her voice muffled through the thickness of the sponge. This was the first friendly act that Roz had experienced since arriving in Liverpool, and it felt good to know that not everyone was as awful as the Haggartys.

The woman's eyes twinkled kindly at her. 'Not to worry, just you make sure they treat you right, and if you have any bother with that Callum, just you come and see me. I'm Mrs McGregor, but you can call me Phyllis.'

Roz swallowed the mouthful of cake before speak-ing. 'Thanks, Phyllis. I'm Rozalin Sachs, Roz for short.'

Phyllis beamed at Roz, then, seeing Suzie taking an interest in the two of them, she quickly leaned forward and spoke in a conspiratorial fashion. 'I'd best be quick before she comes nosing. Word has it that Callum has a quick temper when he's had a drink, so if you take my advice you'll keep out of his way if he's been down the pub.'

Roz nodded, then asked the question that had been preying on her mind since her first night at the Hag-gartys'. 'What happened to Suzie's mother?'

The woman's eyes grew wide and a haunted look came over her. Looking around to make sure they weren't being overheard, she lowered her voice. 'Don't know, no one does. She was there one minute, gone the next ...' Standing up, she nodded at Suzie who was finally ambling over, before hissing, 'Like I say, he's got a mean temper.' Her eyes swivelled to meet Roz's. 'And they do live by the docks.' She raised her eyebrows meaningfully, before breaking her gaze and addressing Suzie. 'I've given your pal all I have to spare, so you can push off.'

Ignoring Mrs McGregor, Suzie addressed Roz directly. 'Come on, I reckon that'll do us.' She held up some cheese which looked more like rubber, and a couple of bruised apples.

As they walked back to Crooked Lane, Suzie took the bag which Phyllis had given to Roz and peered inside. 'Blimey!' she breathed. 'What did you say to get all this?'

Roz shrugged. 'Nothing.'

Taking two of the buns, Suzie hesitated before holding one out to Roz. 'You can have one, but only if you promise not to tell the others.'

Roz frowned. 'She gave us four, that's one each. Shouldn't we wait and give them their share?'

Suzie withdrew her hand as Roz attempted to take the bun. 'No, we damned well shouldn't. They never give me owt if they have anything nice, so I don't see why I should give them owt.' She arched an eyebrow. 'Promise?'

Roz nodded. 'Promise.'

Satisfied, Suzie handed the bun to Roz, before taking a large bite out of the other she'd removed from the paper bag.

Roz ate the iced bun, although in truth, she'd rather have waited until she had eaten something savoury first, as eating two cakes, one after the other, was beginning to make her feel quite nauseous, not that she was about to admit that to Suzie.

When they arrived back at the docks, Callum was impressed with Roz's efforts. 'They obviously like a pretty young Jew,' he said to his mother, before turning back to Roz. 'From now on you'll do all the askin'.' He glanced at his daughter. 'You still have to go along to keep an eye. She might be popular with them lot down the market, but that don't mean we can trust her.'

For someone like Callum Haggarty to suggest that she was untrustworthy was laughable, but Roz knew better than to make any comment, so she held her tongue.

From that day on, Roz was expected to visit the market every day, and when she came back with far better produce than Suzie had ever managed to acquire, Callum instructed her to go further afield, visiting places that Suzie had never been asked to go, such as the Chinese laundry.

'Ask them if they've any scraps of material, or odd bits of clothing that nobody wants.' He hesitated before adding, 'Even soap, everyone wants soap.'

Roz had automatically looked at Suzie, but Callum shook his head. 'You do this one on your own, I need Suzie to help me down the coal.'

'Why can't she help you?' whined Suzie. 'Why do I get all the dirty work?'

'Because they don't like you!' snapped Callum, shooting her a withering glare. 'They like a pretty face, one that's capable of smiling.'

Horrified that Callum would be so mean to his daughter, Roz hurried off before there was another argument. This would be the first time she had been allowed out on her own since the day she arrived at Crooked Lane, and she was determined to make the most of it.

When she arrived at the Chinese laundry, she nearly collided with a young girl who was just leaving.

'Here, do I know you?' asked the girl, eyeing Roz intently.

Roz shrugged. 'No, but I deliver the coal in the mornings, so you might have seen me round and about.'

She clicked her fingers. 'That's it! You're the girl who's living with the Haggartys. Word has it you're a refugee?'

Roz nodded, a half-smile twitching her lips. 'I'm glad people realise I'm not related to them.'

The girl leaned back against the door to the laundry. 'Word soon gets round the courts, especially when it comes to the Haggartys.' She smiled. 'I'm Mabel Johnson, I live in Mercer Court, not far from Crooked Lane.' She knitted an eyebrow. 'How on earth did you wind up living with them? No one in their right minds would place a refugee with the likes of the Haggartys.'

Roz introduced herself, before briefly relaying the story of her escape from Germany and how she had ended up in Liverpool living with them.

Mabel tutted beneath her breath. 'People like them are always out to take advantage of someone else's misery.' She gave Roz a brief once-over. 'I know they send Suzie out begging, but what are you doing here?'

Roz told her that Callum had decided to broaden his horizons from just Paddy's market to the laundries.

'Honest to God, is there nothing that man won't do to avoid spending money?' Before Roz could answer, Mabel briefly disappeared before reappearing a few moments later with a handful of soap slivers, which she gave to Roz. 'I'm afraid that's all we have. People don't bring their things in to wash and then leave them behind.' The corners of her lips twitched into a smile. 'Although I daresay they wouldn't know that, having never come to the laundry themselves.' She looked at the soap in Roz's hand. 'They won't know what to do with it; none of them look like they've ever had a wash.'

Roz gave her a grim smile. 'They won't,' adding hastily, 'but I do.'

Mabel eyed Roz curiously. 'What do they do with all the stuff?'

Roz checked over her shoulder to make sure that no one was listening. 'The food is for us, but anything else Callum sells down the pub.'

Mabel rolled her eyes. 'Or rather he barters for beer.'

Roz shrugged. 'All I know is he takes whatever I manage to get down the Pig and Whistle and comes back stinking drunk.'

Mabel looked down at the soap in Roz's hands. 'He really is the lowest of the low, and it's a damned disgrace he asks a nice girl like you to go out begging.' She pursed her lips. 'Has he ever ...' she gave a little nod, hoping that Roz would catch her drift, but Roz just stared blankly so she finished her sentence, '... you know, got nasty if you refused to do summat?'

Roz jutted her chin out in a determined manner. 'I need the Haggartys for a roof over my head, and so that I can be close to the Liver Building, but that's where it ends. If he starts throwing his weight about, I shan't be scared to give as good as I get.'

Mabel stared at Roz open-mouthed. 'Blimey, I can see you're made of stern stuff, but I'd be careful if I were you – Callum's not the sort of feller to mess around.'

Roz shrugged. 'He's nothing but a bully and a coward; I've faced bigger than him.'

'Oh?' said Mabel, who couldn't imagine anyone nastier than Callum.

Roz nodded. 'The SS – that's Hitler's private army – boarded the train when I was running away. They searched through my things, and everything, but I didn't buckle.'

'Golly!' said Mabel, clearly impressed.

Feeling proud of the impression she was creating, Roz continued. 'There's far worse than Callum Haggarty in Germany. Take the Gestapo, for instance – Callum's a pussy cat compared to them.'

'Who, or what, are the Gestapo?' said Mabel.

'They're like the police, only much, much worse,' said Roz. 'People are really frightened of them, so much so that my father said I was never to approach them no matter what.'

Mabel blew her cheeks out. 'Our scuffers aren't like that ...' Seeing Roz's look of incomprehension, she explained that scuffers was the Liverpool slang for police. 'They're the first people you turn to if you're in trouble or lost. I'd never be frightened of them, unless I'd done summat wrong, of course.'

Roz shook her head sadly. 'I wish the Gestapo were like the scuffers.'

Mabel eyed Roz quizzically. 'It must be *very* different over there.'

Roz nodded fervently. 'It certainly is. You can't do anything without being questioned. We weren't even allowed to go into some of the shops, and if you're Jewish you have to wear the Star of David so that everyone knows what you are. But it never used to be like that. When I was little Frankfurt was a wonderful place to live – we had lots of friends, and everyone liked everyone else. It's only since Hitler came to power that things started to go wrong.'

'Crikey! I can see why you're not scared of Callum Haggarty. I guess living with the Haggartys must seem heavenly after what you've been through.'

Roz gave a short, mirthless laugh. 'Well, it's safer at least, but I intend to get out of there as soon as I can, though it won't be easy when I don't get paid for any of the work I do.'

'That's why,' Mabel said authoritatively. 'It's his way of controlling you, keeping you under his thumb as it were.'

'He's not as stupid as he looks,' agreed Roz. 'What was Suzie's mum like? When I asked where she was, Callum threatened to throw me out!'

'I never really saw much of her,' said Mabel reflectively. 'She was quiet, kept herself to herself; I don't even know her name.'

'When was the last time you saw her?'

Mabel thought about it. 'Must be a few years ago. I remember seeing her walking from Mercer Court to Crooked Lane the night before she disappeared ...'

Roz's eyes widened. 'She disappeared?'

'Here one minute, gone the next,' Mabel confirmed.

'Someone must know something ... What did the police say?'

Mabel pulled a face. 'I don't know. The Haggartys aren't what you'd call a sociable lot, unless you count Callum getting legless down the pub.'

'People certainly seem to do their best to avoid him,' said Roz. 'I've noticed that on the coal round.'

'You ask anyone around here and they'll tell you the same,' said Mabel. 'When it comes to the Haggartys they're best kept at arm's length.' She stood in silent thought for a moment, then changed the subject. 'Earlier on, you said summat about having to put up with the Haggartys so that you could be near the Liver Building. Why's that?'

Roz told her new friend about her father's offer of work and how she hoped to find him there.

'Have you been and asked?' said Mabel.

Roz shook her head. 'I've not had the time. The Haggartys keep me busy from dawn to dusk, and apart from today, they never let me go anywhere without Suzie tagging along. He's only letting me come alone today because he needs Suzie to help him with the coal, plus he knows people are more likely to give me handouts than her.'

'You're free now though ...' Mabel pointed out.

Roz shook her head. 'I've still to go to Paddy's market, to see what else I can get.'

74

'Who's to say you're not there now tryin' your hardest to get summat decent?' said Mabel. 'Callum won't care how long you take, as long as you don't come back empty-handed.'

'Are you suggesting I go to the Liver Building right this minute?' said Roz.

'Can't see why not. I could come with you if you like. I was just on my way home, but I don't mind taking a slight detour.'

Roz brightened. 'That would be wonderful, but are you sure you don't mind?'

'Nah, it's no bother to me, and I'd like to hear more about your exciting escape from the ...' she hesitated, '... SS?'

Roz beamed. She felt as though a huge burden had been lifted from her shoulders. She had finally found a friend, and a good one at that. Life at the Haggartys' had been hard without someone to confide in.

Mabel pushed her arm into the sleeve of her raincoat. 'If you ever wanted a job where Callum can't take your wages, Mr Woo would take you on.'

Roz felt as though she were floating on cloud nine, but she soon came back to earth when a thought occurred to her. 'Only how do you know he'd take me on? He's never met me.'

Mabel smiled. 'He's always after girls to do the laundry.'

'I'll have to see what I can do,' said Roz, 'think things through.' Inside she was beaming. Things really were beginning to look up. All she needed now was to find her father working at his desk and her world would be complete.

As the girls made their way to the insurance offices, Roz retold the tale of her life in Frankfurt and her escape to Holland then to Liverpool.

'You're like Emily Davison!' breathed Mabel. 'She wasn't afraid to stand up for what's right, although she did die doing it ...'

'Who?'

'Emily Davison was a suffragette who fought for women's rights at the beginning of the century. She died when she threw herself in front of the King's horse.'

Roz was flattered, but hesitant to accept the comparison. 'I'm not sure I'm that brave. There's a great deal of difference between keeping quiet and throwing yourself in front of a horse!'

'Either way it's standing your ground,' said Mabel. 'If I'd seen one of them soldiers, I think I'd've wet myself!'

Roz blushed. She was beginning to think she might have slightly overexaggerated her escape. 'I was rather confused at the time, and I wouldn't like you to get the wrong idea, because I was scared. If it wasn't for Felix ...'

Mabel gave her a lopsided grin. 'The fantastic Felix! He sounds like a real hero.'

Roz's blush deepened. 'He is. I really don't know what I'd have done without him, but thanks to the Haggartys I'll probably never see him again ...' She explained how the Haggartys had lied about their address.

'Ranelagh Street!' scoffed Mabel. 'As if they could afford anywhere as swanky as that!' She shook her head decidedly. 'I know you said Callum wasn't keen on having a refugee come to live with him, but he

76

certainly knew what he was doing when it came to fooling your chaperones.'

'To be honest, he didn't say anything; it was Lilith who did all the talking. He made it clear he didn't want a refugee, but if he had to have one he wanted someone without a brain of their own, someone who'd do as they were told without question, and who couldn't really understand, let alone read, English,' said Roz.

'Well, he didn't get that with you!' chuckled Mabel. 'You weren't in his house more than five minutes and he wanted to chuck you out.'

'I asked too many questions,' agreed Roz, 'the one concerning the whereabouts of Suzie's mum being the one that tipped him over the edge!'

Mabel raised her brows fleetingly. 'That's what men like him need, a strong woman to stand up to them. Suzie's mam was very mousy, the kind of woman that'd lower her head rather than make eye contact.'

'I know the sort,' Roz said. She remembered how some of her non-Jewish friends had started to shun her by walking the other way if they saw her coming down the street, or no longer sitting next to her in school, and all because they feared the Nazi regime. Or at least Roz hoped that's what it was – she wouldn't like to think they actually agreed with Hitler and his views.

They reached the Liver Building and Mabel made her way up to the main entrance, only stopping when she realised Roz wasn't following her. She turned to face her new friend. 'What's up?'

'I might not be scared of Callum Haggarty, but I am scared of going in there and finding my father isn't inside.'

Mabel held out a hand. 'Come on, chuck. You can't stand out here on the pavement, you'll catch your death. No matter what happens you need to know the truth, and the sooner the better.'

Roz reluctantly followed Mabel into the building. Once inside they looked about to see who they might be able to speak to, when Mabel caught the eye of a woman who was sitting behind a desk watching them inquisitively. 'Can I help you?'

Mabel nudged Roz and they headed towards the woman, who smiled up at them from her seat.

'I'm looking for Samuel Sachs,' said Roz. 'Do you know if he's here?'

The receptionist, a fashionable, smartly turned-out woman in her early twenties, shook her head, causing her platinum blonde curls to bounce around her shoulders. 'Sorry, never heard of him. Were you meant to meet him here?'

Roz exchanged a glance with Mabel. 'Kind of,' she said slowly. 'He was supposed to start work for Mr Garmin – have you heard of him?'

The receptionist smiled brightly. 'Yes! He works on the fifth floor. If you'd like to take a seat I'll see if he's available.' She indicated a row of chairs against the far wall. 'Who might I say is calling?'

'Rozalin Sachs, Samuel Sachs' daughter,' said Roz before taking the seat next to Mabel.

'Well, that's a good start,' said Mabel cheerfully. 'She might not have heard of your father, but at least she'd heard of Mr Garmin.'

'I suppose so,' agreed Roz, although she couldn't help feeling it would have been far better had the lady

78

heard of her father, or at least recognised his name. She looked up as the lift doors opened and the young woman reappeared accompanied by a kind-looking man with greying hair. He walked over to Roz and Mabel. 'Which one of you is Rozalin?'

Getting to her feet, Roz held out a hand. 'That would be me.'

He shook both girls by the hand before inviting them into a meeting room where they could talk in private. He invited them to take a seat before sitting down himself. 'We were expecting your father weeks ago,' he said, a worried frown creasing his brow. 'When he didn't show up, I telephoned the company he worked for in Frankfurt but they couldn't help me, except to say that your father, as far as they were aware, was no longer in Frankfurt. Not long after that we received a telephone call from a Mr Reginald Jones ...' He stopped short, seeing the look of recognition on Roz's face. 'You know of him?'

Roz nodded. 'Mr Jones helped bring me to England.' Realising an explanation was needed, she told him of the accident, finishing with: 'I never saw them after that, but I know he'll come here as soon as he arrives in England.'

Mr Garmin smiled reassuringly at both girls. 'Your father worked really hard to get everything sorted so that you could leave the country; there's not a doubt in my mind that he would have a back-up plan.'

Roz breathed a sigh of relief. It was good to hear someone who actually knew of her father, albeit from a distance, confirming that they had as much faith in him as Roz had. 'You're right, he had all eventualities covered – apart from the accident, of course, but no one could have foreseen that.'

Mr Garmin pulled a piece of paper towards him and looked expectantly at Roz, pen in hand. 'Where can I get hold of you?'

As Roz read out the address, he looked at her with surprise.

'I must admit, I didn't know there were any houses on Crooked Lane,' he said.

Roz glanced at Mabel. 'It's not a house exactly …' She hesitated as she thought of the best way to describe the loft where she was residing.

'It's more like a flat,' Mabel explained, much to Roz's relief.

'I see, well, you learn something new every day.' Mr Garmin retrieved a piece of paper from his jacket pocket and handed it to Roz. 'This came for you a few days back.'

Roz held an envelope that was addressed to her. She didn't recognise the handwriting. She looked up at Mr Garmin and Mabel who were both eyeing her expectantly. Her heart racing, she opened the envelope and quickly read the contents of the letter. When she got to the end, she looked up, a broad smile stretching across her cheeks.

Mabel was watching her eagerly. 'Is it from your father?'

Roz shook her head. 'Felix!' Handing the letter to Mabel, she explained who Felix was to Mr Garmin.

'Good to know someone's looking out for you,' he said, getting to his feet.

'He's been wonderful,' said Roz, as they followed Mr Garmin out of the room.

He led the way to the front door of the building. 'If I hear anything I'll be sure to get in touch, but should anything change in the meantime please let me know.'

'I will, thank you. I'm sure we'll hear something soon,' said Roz, trying to remain positive.

Saying his goodbyes, Mr Garmin turned and headed back to the lift.

'Fancy Felix thinking to write to you here,' said Mabel as they left. 'I can't wait to meet him.'

'I can't see that happening any time soon,' said Roz. 'I've no idea where Scotland Road is, but I do know where Scotland is.'

Mabel grinned. 'The Scottie's not far from us. In fact, we could go there now if you like?'

Roz stopped dead. 'Really? Scotland Road is here, in Liverpool?'

Mabel nodded. 'Yes, unless you're worried about getting back to the Haggartys?'

'Blow them!' said Roz firmly. 'It only means Callum will have to wait a bit longer before he can go to the pub.'

Mabel grinned. 'You're like a breath of fresh air, but I still worry you might push him too far. We all know Suzie's mam disappeared, but none of us ever did find out what really happened to her.'

Something in Roz caused her to hesitate. She really wasn't scared of Callum – he might cuff his daughter, which was unacceptable, but that was a million miles away from beating her to a pulp, or worse. Was Callum

81

really capable of murder, accidental or otherwise? She didn't think so, but there was definitely something odd about his wife's disappearance, and his reaction when she had brought the matter up.

'Without proof we're clutching at straws,' she said simply.

'Fair enough, but where is she?' challenged Mabel.

'I don't know. All I can say is, I'm not her, and I'm not afraid to stand up to him, or to be on my own. If he looks like he's losing the plot I'll leave, simple as that.'

Mabel had to admire her new friend's tenacity, and hoped that she would stay true to her word. 'If it gets too much you can always come and stay with us for a few days.'

Roz gave her a sidelong glance. 'Thanks, Mabel. I'm hoping I won't need to, but it's always good to have a back-up plan.'

'Like father, like daughter.' Mabel linked arms with Roz and they continued on the relatively short trip to Scotland Road, where they soon came across the house where Felix was staying. Roz knocked a brief tattoo against the blistered paintwork of the wooden door, then stood back in anticipation. Hearing footsteps approaching, her heart began to beat faster in her chest, only to drop like a stone when an old man with barely a hair on his head answered the door.

'Not interested—' he muttered as he began closing it again.

'We're not trying to sell you anything. We're looking for Felix Ackerman,' Roz said hastily. 'I believe he's staying with you?'

He opened the door wider, a gappy grin spreading across his deeply wrinkled face. 'That's right! Only he's not here at the moment, he's still at work.'

Roz's face fell. 'Will he be back soon?'

He pulled back his sleeve and squinted at the large watch face which adorned his wrist. 'Not for a long time yet. They were late leaving this morning,' he added conversationally.

'Where does he work?' asked Mabel.

'Down the docks – don't know which one, mind you. It could be any, it depends on what needs doin'.'

Mabel clicked her tongue. 'Like looking for a needle in a haystack then.'

He nodded.

'I could always call back tomorrow,' suggested Roz.

'And why not!' said the old man amicably. 'It's a free world.'

Roz gave a hollow laugh. As far as she and her family were concerned, it was most definitely *not* a free world. 'What time would be best?'

He pursed his lips in thought. 'They're normally gone at the crack of dawn and not back until after dark. So before or after, it's up to you.'

'How about if I call back around teatime? Say sometime after six?'

'Right you are ...' He hesitated. 'Who should I say came calling?'

Roz smiled. 'Tell him Roz, and this is my friend Mabel.'

He gave them a cheeky wink. 'He's a handsome feller, that's for sure. I can see why he's such a hit with the ladies.' He chuckled to himself softly. 'I wish I'd had half his luck, back in the day!'

Roz and Mabel thanked him for his help before bidding him goodbye.

'Thanks for coming with me,' said Roz. 'I would never have found the address on my own.'

Mabel waved a dismissive hand. 'Happy to help. It can't be easy moving here from a foreign country, especially on your own. I think you've done marvellously, all things considered.'

'I haven't had much choice,' said Roz truthfully, 'and if I'm to have any hope of getting away from the Haggartys there's only me that can do it.'

'Does that mean you'll think about coming to work at the laundry?' said Mabel, smiling brightly. 'You'd be making your own money; you'd be free!'

Roz knew that Mabel meant well, but she hadn't thought her proposal through. 'I won't be welcome at the Haggartys' if I stop working for them. And would Mr Woo really pay me enough to afford rent elsewhere?'

Mabel's face fell. 'Oh drat, I hadn't thought of that.'

Roz gave her a friendly nudge. 'It's a nice thought, and with Felix here maybe it's possible. He always seems to find a way around things.'

Mabel gave her a wry smile. 'You're lucky to have found a friend like Felix, especially one who's a boy, and handsome too according to that old feller. Is he right, is Felix handsome?'

Roz lowered her face to hide her blush. 'What's that got to do with anything?'

Mabel looked at her in astonishment. 'Everything! For a start it makes the difference between a friend and a boyfriend.'

'I don't know about that. Just because he's hand-some, that doesn't mean he's my boyfriend.'

Grinning, Mabel tapped the side of her nose. 'Just a matter of time. Trust me, I've five sisters and—'

'*Five*?' gasped Roz. 'How many are there of you altogether?'

'Eight, including my two older brothers.' She began ticking their names off on the tips of her fingers. 'Robin, Richard, Nicky, Karen, Kerry, Heather, and Louise.'

Roz gaped at her. 'How big is your house?'

'Two rooms, and it's not exactly a house – we live in the courts.'

Aware that she was staring, Roz tore her gaze away from Mabel, who continued to grin. 'They must be big rooms.'

'We manage,' said Mabel. 'You can come and see it if you like.'

Roz shook her head sadly. 'I'd like to, but I think I've pushed my luck enough for one day, although I'd like to see you tomorrow if you're about?'

Mabel nodded enthusiastically. 'Why not meet me after I've finished work, say around four? You can come and meet my family, then we could go and see Felix. Unless you'd rather see him on your own, of course,' she said with a sly smile.

Roz rolled her eyes. 'And why would I want to see him on my own? No, you're very welcome to come too.'

'Good!' said Mabel. 'You may not see him as a suit-able boyfriend, but I might.' Seeing the muscle twitch in Roz's jaw, Mabel pointed an accusing finger. 'See! You might not admit it, but there's more than just friendship brewing here; you'd not be so vexed otherwise.'

'I'm not vexed,' Roz snapped.

'You should try telling that to your face,' laughed Mabel, quickly adding, 'I'm only teasing.' She indicated a narrow alley. 'This is me.'

Roz craned her neck for a better look, but the passage went on for quite a way.

'It might not be much, but it's home,' said Mabel cheerfully as she turned up the alley. 'Ta-ra, chuck, I'll see you tomorrer!'

'After work,' Roz confirmed. As she made the short journey back to Crooked Lane, she remembered the meagre offering of a handful of soap. She knew Callum wouldn't be pleased, but making a new friend, visiting the Liver Building *and* learning that Felix was in Liverpool, was worth the row. She opened the door and peered inside. Callum swore as soon as he saw her, then grabbed his coat and made his way to the door. He looked at her expectantly, his hand held out.

'Well?' he snarled. 'Hand it over.'

Roz slapped the soap down into the palm of his hand without explanation. He stared at the slivers before looking at her. 'What the hell is this and where's the rest of it?'

She looked past him to Suzie and Lilith who were sitting on the only two chairs. 'That's it,' she said simply.

'You'd better not be holding out on me.'

Roz eyed him levelly. 'Why would I do that?'

Grabbing her roughly by the wrist with one hand, he used the other to clutch at the pockets of her skirts. Roz tried to object, but he twisted her wrist painfully. When he had finished frisking her skirt he pushed her aside and strode to the door. 'Bloody useless, you haven't even tried. I'd have got more if I'd sent *her*.' He turned to Suzie. 'You will go with her tomorrow, make sure she pulls her finger out.'

Roz's face fell. She couldn't have Suzie tagging along because Callum would know what she was planning. 'No!' she said, rather too hastily for Callum's liking. Suspicion rising, he pushed the door to.

'And why not?'

'Because I don't ruddy well want to,' Suzie butted in from the far side of the room. But Callum ignored her, waiting for Roz's response.

'She puts people off,' Roz said quickly. 'I'll get even less if she comes with me.'

Callum continued to stare at her in a calculating fashion, certain that Roz was lying, but on the other hand ... He nodded slowly. 'I can see that.' Ignoring Suzie's protests, he continued, 'But if you come back empty-handed again—'

Roz pointed at the soap. 'I don't call *that* empty-handed,' she said defensively.

'As good as!' he said, shoving the soap into the pocket of his overcoat.

Roz was about to retort that he should be grateful he got anything at all and he was welcome to go out begging himself, when she thought better of it. He had agreed to let her go out the following day without Suzie accompanying her; if she gave him cheek now, he might revoke that and then Roz really would be stuck.

'I'll do better tomorrow,' she muttered quietly.

'You better had,' said Callum. He turned the collar of his coat up and headed outside, closing the door behind him.

'Where've you really been?' asked Lilith, who wasn't as easily fooled as her son.

Roz felt her heart drop. She had thought the conversation had ended when Callum had left, but obviously not. So she continued the pretence. 'It's not my fault people are getting fed up with handing stuff over for nothing,' she said, although she was careful not to make eye contact with the older woman, who was a lot shrewder than her son. She walked to the kitchen area of the room.

'I don't buy it,' said Lilith simply. 'But it doesn't matter what I think, it's Callum you need to worry about.'

Roz gave a short, mocking laugh. 'I'm not frightened of your son, Lilith, even if you are. He's already taken everything I own; I've nothing left for him to take.'

Lilith arched her brow. 'Then you underestimate him.'

Grasping the kettle from the stove, Roz made her way to the door. 'I don't think I do,' she said evenly, 'but he hasn't a hold over me, not any more ...' As soon as the last words left her lips she rued saying them, fearing it would arouse suspicion.

She took the kettle to the communal water pump, filled it and returned to the room, where she was unsurprised to see the two women – who had instantly fallen silent upon her entry – staring at her suspiciously.

'What did you mean by that?' Lilith asked.

'By what?' Roz said, radiating false innocence.

'You know full well what,' said Lilith. 'Where did you go today? Or more to the point, who did you see, 'cos there ain't no way you've been on your own all this time.'

Roz faltered mid-step. Surely the old woman couldn't know? She chided herself inwardly. Of course the other woman didn't know, she was guessing. 'No one!' she said calmly, making sure to keep her back to them as she replaced the kettle on the stove.

'Liar,' said Lilith. She leaned forward on her chair, giving Roz the benefit of a scrutinising stare. 'You've met someone what's offered to take you away from the nasty Haggartys and Liverpool.' The sneer left her face as a thought entered her mind. 'Your parents ...' she said softly, then shook her head. 'No, if they were here, you wouldn't be. It can't be them, but then who?'

Roz lit the stove before turning to face the old woman. 'You're right on one thing. If my parents were here, then I wouldn't be, but my father would, and he'd want to know what your son had done with my clothes.' She gave a short, mirthless laugh. 'I shouldn't imagine they'd fit anyone at the pub, and I've never seen him wearing them ...'

Lilith's eyes narrowed. 'You've allus had a gob on you, but you're more cocky than usual. What's give, or rather *who*'s give you such courage, I wonder?'

Suzie wrinkled her nose disapprovingly. 'She's a right mouth on her, that one; she don't need no one to hold her hand.'

Roz's heart was beginning to race in her chest. Lilith was getting too close to the truth for comfort. She tried to remain casual, changing the subject. 'Just because I stand up to your bully of a father, doesn't mean to say I'm mouthy. If your mother had ...'

Lilith, normally slow moving, shot to her feet and thrust the end of her walking stick at Roz. 'Don't you dare!' she hissed angrily. 'You know nothing, and if you know what's good for you, you'll keep it that way.'

'I know I've touched a nerve,' replied Roz, but she was watching Suzie who looked anxious.

'Rubbish!' snapped Lilith. 'No one likes someone stickin' their nose in where it's not wanted, jumpin' to assumptions what aren't true!'

Roz wrinkled her brow. 'I don't remember making any assumptions, you didn't let me get that far.'

Lilith tutted irritably. 'You're biting off more than you can chew, don't say I didn't warn you.'

Roz took the kettle from the stove and poured the warm water into a small bowl which she used as a basin to wash in. She had hoped that her attempt to divert attention from herself to Suzie's mother would mean that they stopped questioning her, and it looked as though it had worked, which was just as well because she couldn't afford to arouse suspicions. Tomorrow she would work twice as hard down the market so that Callum would have no complaints. Tomorrow. A small smile crept to the corner of her lips. Tomorrow she would see Felix and explain everything that had happened since leaving Dovercourt, and see what his thoughts were on the matter. She had no doubt he would want to help get her out of the Haggartys', but how? She imagined Felix standing toe to toe with Callum. Felix was thicker set than Callum, but a shade smaller, not that that would matter to someone like Callum, who undoubtedly didn't believe in fighting fair.

Felix led Coconut, the piebald gelding, into his stable. It had been a long day, and he could smell the saucepan of scouse that Bill had prepared whilst they were out working.

When Reggie Jones had told Felix he had found him a job and somewhere to live, he had been delighted. That was until he heard that the job included a horse. Felix had never had anything to do with horses but knew that they could be dangerous and unpredictable after having witnessed a Percheron bolt through Berlin, leaving a trail of destruction in its wake. From that day on Felix had vowed to keep his distance whenever he saw a horse, so to be told he would have to work with one had unsettled him somewhat. Finding out that the horse also lived with them in a stable just at the back of their house didn't improve matters, especially when he learned he had to lead the large gelding through a very small opening, which nearly touched the horse's sides, in order to access the stable. The only good news was that he would be working as a carter in Liverpool, not far from the Liver Building. When he first laid eyes on Coconut, he had approached him as though he were a ticking bomb, ready to explode at any moment, but he quickly learned that he was docile, with no greater goal in life than to do his work, plodding from one place to another before heading home for a bucket of mash, a freshly laid bed of barley straw, and a warm stable to shelter from the wind and rain.

Alan, Felix's employer, had been impressed with how quickly Felix had overcome his fears.

'You'd never know you hadn't grown up around horses,' he said, watching Felix as he deftly removed the harness and handed it over.

Bending down, Felix grabbed a handful of straw and began to rub the horse down. 'Coconut knows his job inside out; it wouldn't surprise me if he could tack himself up.'

Alan laughed. 'You're not wrong there. I suppose you could say he taught you everything he knows.'

Felix nodded. 'He's certainly shown me that not all horses are wild and reckless.'

Alan passed Felix a bucket of warm mash. 'Too bloody lazy, that's why,' he said, closing the stable door behind them and sliding the bolts into place.

'Far better that way,' said Felix as he followed Alan into the kitchen where they received a cheery greeting from Alan's father, Bill, who was sitting by the table.

Bill got to his feet and grabbed a ladle. 'Ready for your supper?'

Yawning, Felix sat in the chair opposite Bill's. 'I was ready hours ago.'

Bill grinned as he ladled the stew into three bowls. 'A carter's life ain't an easy one, that's for sure.' Taking a loaf, he began cutting thick slices of bread. 'You've taken to it like a duck to water, mind you.'

Felix beamed. As a small boy he'd always wanted a pet, but his parents wouldn't allow it. Coconut might not be a pet but he was the next best thing, and truth be told, Felix was smitten. He loved everything about his new life. Looking after Coconut was very important to him, and he was proud of the praise he got from his fellow carters about how he handled the gelding. He leaned back as Bill placed the bowl of scouse in front of him, taking a moment to savour the wonderful smell of stewed lamb and vegetables before digging in. 'Great scran as always, Bill.'

Bill grinned an almost toothless smile. 'Got you talkin' like a native already.' He indicated Felix with his spoon whilst addressing his son. 'This one's been holding out on us, Alan.'

Felix looked confused. 'I have?'

Beaming, Bill wriggled his eyebrows suggestively. 'You never told us you was a hit with the lasses.'

Felix smiled uncertainly. 'I thought lasses were women?'

Bill nodded. 'You had a couple of callers this afternoon. I hope you ain't got neither of them into trouble.' He chuckled.

Felix paused, a spoonful of stew poised before his lips. 'You must have got it wrong. I don't know any women in Liverpool.'

Bill took a slice of bread and tore the crust off and dipped it into his stew. 'No mistake, the taller one asked for you by name ...' he paused, deep in thought, '... only I can't remember her name for love nor money!'

'What did she look like?' asked Felix curiously.

'Bit smaller than you, long dark hair, big brown eyes, and a smile what could light up the Adelphi.'

Felix looked up sharply. 'Roz!'

'That's her!' confirmed Bill. 'So you do know her then!'

'She was on the train with me from Berlin,' said Felix, 'only the people that took her in gave the wrong address, so I hadn't a clue where she was – until now.'

'Ah ...' said Bill, 'you still don't. She never gave an address, just said she'd call back tomorrer, sometime after six.'

Felix looked hopefully at Alan. 'Will we be back in time?'

Alan, who had been spooning down stew with one hand whilst holding a copy of the *Liverpool Echo* with the other, peered at Felix from over the top of the pages. 'Looks like we'll have to be 'cos I can see that wild horses ain't goin' to stand in your way, only we've still a full day's work to do, so it'll mean an earlier start than usual.'

'Fine by me,' said Felix, enthusiastically scooping the scouse onto his spoon and wolfing it down.

Alan winked at Bill as he folded the paper and placed it on the table. 'I'd like to see this Roz for myself – she must be a real beaut to get this boy out of his pit before time.'

Blushing to his roots, Felix tried to hide his smile behind a piece of bread. 'She's just a friend.'

'Oh aye, I bet you'd not be that enthusiastic if it were some feller what had come callin',' said Bill with a mischievous chuckle.

Felix shrugged nonchalantly. 'She's been through some hard times, and I'm trying to help her find her parents back in Berlin. They went missing the day she boarded the train.'

Bill and Alan exchanged a dark glance. 'If that's the case,' said Alan, 'you might well be all she's got.'

Nodding, Felix stared gloomily at the pieces of lamb in his bowl of scouse. Ever since arriving in Liverpool he had kept the truth about his mother's arrest to himself, but seeing the expressions on Alan and Bill's faces, and hearing their opinion on the Nazis when it came to the Jewish people, he turned his thoughts to his own mother, where she might be and what might have happened to her. Up until now he had convinced himself that he was in a better position than Roz because he knew his mother was in one of the camps, but whilst no one knew for a fact what happened once you were there, anyone with an ounce of common sense could see the outlook wasn't good. He spooned up a particularly large piece of meat and stared at it. His rabbi had said his mother had been arrested, but surely you took people who'd been arrested to jail, not a camp? Weren't camps for holidays? He felt his heart sink because deep down he knew the truth. The soldiers were calling it a camp because they knew there would be mass hysteria otherwise, the same as the parents whose children had boarded the train told them that they were going to join them later on. Felix knew they were lying, he was pretty certain other children did too, but no one had questioned it.

'No point lookin' at it ...' Bill's words cut across his thoughts.

Smiling briefly, Felix popped the spoon into his mouth.

'You alright, boy?' said Alan, his face full of concern.

'I will be,' replied Felix.

95

Alan clapped a hand on the table. 'You're here now, and that's all that matters. You can put your old life far behind you – you needn't worry about no Nazis whilst you're living in Britain.'

Standing up, Felix gathered the empty bowls and took them over to the sink. 'You don't think he'll try and invade Britain?'

Alan shook his head decidedly, but Bill didn't seem so sure. 'I was in the first lot, and I seen what them Germans are like first-hand. If it wasn't for the Americans we would have been well and truly scuppered. But if I thought that lot were bad, they ain't nothin' compared to Hitler and his Nazis. They're a different kettle of fish altogether, and I can't see him lettin' the Americans get in his way, not this time around. They'll have learned their lessons from the last lot, which makes them ten times more prepared and a hundred times more dangerous.'

Felix stared open-mouthed at the older man. 'Then what was the point in sending us here?'

Bill gazed into space, deep in thought. 'Hope,' he said after some consideration, 'as well as buying time.'

Alan joined Felix at the sink and spoke directly to his father. 'You really think we'll be going to war?'

Bill eyed the pair shrewdly. Alan might be much older than Felix but he looked just as scared. 'They got beat just over twenty years ago, yet they're back for more.' He began ticking the list off on his fingers. 'That's twenty years of reviewing their mistakes, seeing where they went wrong and how they could have done things differently, and twenty years of planning and preparing for a war to end all wars, but this time with them as the victors. I've seen the newsreels, I've seen how that maniac can bend his own people to his will no matter how twisted it might be.' He took a deep breath before letting it out slowly. 'The night of the long knives, that's what they called it.' He looked from Alan to Felix. 'Imagine killing your own army just to gain more power. They know what he's done, yet they're treatin' him like a god. All standin' there chanting his name over and over. I would never have believed anyone could be so stupid, yet they follow him like lambs to the slaughter!'

'Fear,' said Felix simply. 'They don't worship him, they fear him. Don't forget, I lived in Berlin the whole time Hitler's been in power, and I've seen the way he can turn people against each other, just because of a different belief or religion. The Germans have seen what he can do to his own people, so they've no doubt he can do it to the rest of them if they disagree with what he says ...' He glanced at Alan, who was looking quite unwell. 'Your father's right when he says Hitler's ten times worse than the last lot.'

'So what do we do?' asked Alan, going back to his seat and sinking into it. 'Keep our fingers crossed and pray they don't turn their attention on us?'

'That's all we can do for now,' said Bill, ''cos we don't know what they've got in the pipeline.' He glanced at Felix, adding for clarification, 'What they've already got planned.'

'They're taking Jews to camps,' said Felix, 'thousands of us, yet no one seems to know where these camps are. How can they not know? Surely they must be huge to accommodate so many people? They must have been built in secret in the dead of night.'

Bill nodded. 'Like I say, twenty years to prepare. If they've got us in their sights, first we'll know about it is when they start droppin' bombs.'

Felix swallowed hard. 'You don't know how lucky you are to have the Channel between them and you.'

'Oh yes we do,' said Bill with verve, 'but even the Channel won't stop them. It didn't last time, so why should it this, when they've got better planes, boats, and ammunition?' He stood up to help Felix with the washing-up.

'Better prepared ...' said Felix softly.

Alan rested his head in his hands. 'How long do you think we've got?'

'How long's a piece of string?' said Bill. 'But I reckon we'd best get our skates on, 'cos we're goin' to be playin' catch-up as it is.'

Felix passed the dishcloth over a bowl then handed it to Bill who wiped it dry. 'We can't let him win,' said Felix. 'He's a maniac.'

'I know, son,' said Bill, 'and we won't, 'cos even though he's had longer to prepare, we're British, and he'll never take us over, not whilst there's breath in our bodies.'

'And don't forget the Americans,' added Alan. 'They'd stand by us, and no matter how prepared Hitler thinks he is, he's no match for them.'

'I'm sure you're right,' said Bill, nodding slowly, 'but don't you think Hitler's thought of that already?'

'He's arrogant,' said Felix, 'he probably thinks he can persuade them to be his ally.'

'Then he don't know diddly squat,' said Alan, much to Felix's amusement.

'Diddly what?'

'Squat,' said Alan. 'It means he don't know nothin', because there's no way the Americans would side with the likes of Hitler, not after last time. You wait and see, if the proverbial hits the fan, they'll be by our side before you can say knife.'

Chapter Three

The next day was Roz's intended rendezvous with Felix and she was determined to make everything appear as normal as possible so as not to arouse suspicion, but on the other hand she wished to look her best for Felix so she had made an extra effort with her hair, and had tried to scrub the filthy plimsolls. This hadn't interested Callum in the slightest, but Suzie had been quick to pick up on Roz's extra attention to detail.

'Why all the effort?' she asked suspiciously.

Roz glanced at Callum, who was looking lazily in her direction. 'I've been scrounging down the market for a while now. If they don't think I'm beginning to look any better, they may not see the point in giving me anything.' She shot Callum an accusing glance. 'I don't think the stallholders would be too happy if they knew all their stuff ended up down the pub, do you?'

Callum's eyes flickered over her appearance. 'Not too good, mind,' he muttered, ignoring her last question, 'else they'll think you don't need nowt no more.'

Roz glanced at Suzie but she wasn't as easily swayed as her father.

'My arse!' scoffed Suzie. 'A girl only goes to that much trouble if there's a feller involved.'

Callum's head snapped up. 'What's that?'

Roz made sure her eyes never left his. 'I don't know what she's talking about. Besides, what feller's going to be interested in me?'

Callum ran his tongue around the inside of his cheeks. If it had been Suzie they were talking about he'd have agreed, but Roz was different. She was taller, prettier, and there was a certain air about her that Suzie didn't possess. Without breaking eye contact he addressed his daughter. 'P'raps you should go with her when she goes out.'

Roz opened her mouth to protest, then thought better of it. If she did, then their suspicions would definitely be confirmed. She tried to appear nonchalant. 'Fine, but don't blame me if we come back empty-handed ...' She continued to stare at him. *Would* he take the bait?

'Why would we come back empty-handed because of me?' snapped Suzie indignantly.

'Because no one around here trusts you,' said Roz, trying to keep the smugness out of her voice. She was rather enjoying telling Suzie the truth without fear of repercussion. 'You were always on the scrounge, whining that no one gave you enough, threatening to curse them if they didn't cough up ...' She paused to quickly banish the smile which was tweaking the corners of her lips, in case Callum realised she was embellishing the truth.

'I never!' cried Suzie. 'I'm not a soddin' tinker!'

'Whereas I,' cooed Roz, happy in the knowledge that Callum was now glaring at his daughter, 'ask them nicely. I tell them that whatever they give will be for me and me alone, and that's why I get so much stuff, because I don't threaten people.'

Suzie pointed an accusing finger at Roz. 'She's lyin', it's written all over her face!' She looked beseechingly at her grandmother. 'Tell him!'

The old woman subjected Roz to a long, calculating stare, and Roz prayed that the lighting in the room was too dim for anyone to notice the betraying blush that was sweeping her neckline.

'I daresay she's tryin' to snare some poor soul, but who's going to be interested in a scrawny little Jew? Hardly summat to boast about, is it? Take no notice of her.'

Far from being offended, Roz felt a wave of relief sweep over her. The last thing she needed was for Suzie to follow her around – and she could hardly take her to meet Felix. So she ignored Suzie's sniggers and looked at Callum for approval.

'Just get out there and do your duty,' he said sullenly. 'I don't care how you get the goods, as long as you get 'em … only mind you don't get yourself banged up, 'cos I ain't havin' no Jewish sprog in this house. One of you is bad enough.'

At first, Roz had thought Callum meant for her not to get arrested, but the mention of a sprog, which Roz knew to be Liverpudlian slang for a child, and hearing the shrieks of laughter coming from Suzie, she knew exactly what he was implying. If she were not so keen to go and meet Felix, Roz would have told Callum that, perhaps unlike the other women in his house, she was not the sort to sell herself for favours.

But she knew that to say this now would only cause outrage from Suzie and Lilith and she would be delayed even longer, not to mention the fact that she would be saying it out of spite, as she didn't think any man would consider bedding the other girl no matter how low the price.

Roz collected her string bag from behind the door and left without a word. As she climbed down the steps outside the warehouse, she could hear Suzie congratulating her father on how he had hit the nail on the head when it came to Roz's character.

You're meeting Felix, Roz told herself. *It doesn't matter what the likes of Suzie and the other Haggartys think. They don't know you, nor have they tried to get to know you. If it weren't for the fact that you had nowhere else to go, you'd never share the time of day with any of them.* Keeping this thought in her mind, she hastened to Paddy's market. She was so focused on the task at hand that she never noticed Suzie stealing silently down the steps behind her.

Her trip to the market had been a success and her string bag was getting heavier with each step. As she made her way to meet Mabel, her thoughts turned to Felix. He knew that the Haggartys had lied because he had said so in his letter. She wondered what he must have thought when he found out the truth, then marvelled at how clever he had been to remember the Liver Building and to think to write to her there. He had just taken it in his stride, which was one of the things she liked about him, his ability to remain cool and level-headed when things went wrong. As she walked, the loose sole of her plimsoll caught on the uneven paving, causing her to trip. Cursing under her breath, she heard her skirt tear as she landed on her knees. Having let go of the bag in order to break her fall, the contents were now rolling freely across the pavement. Getting to her feet, she hastily gathered the items she had managed to scrounge and placed them back into the bag before looking at the damage to her skirt. She sighed heavily. It hadn't looked good before, being three sizes too big and in desperate need of darning, but now it had an almighty rip from the knee to the hem which hung down by her toes. She rolled the waistband of the skirt over several times, and looked down at her plimsolls. The one which had tripped her up now had a huge hole and you could clearly see her toe poking through. Dusting herself down, Roz continued on her way to the Chinese laundry. There was no sense in getting annoyed, accidents happened, although this one could have been avoided had she been wearing her own shoes instead of Suzie's cast-offs which were at least one size too big.

She wondered what Felix would think when he saw her. Would he even recognise her? Roz knew how much she had changed in the short time she had been living with the Haggartys. The skirts she had been given to wear were big when she had first tried them on, but they were even bigger now, due to the weight she had lost. Living on such a meagre diet had presented other problems. She no longer had a clear complexion, and her hair was dull and lifeless. Her cheekbones, which had once been nicely defined, were now gaunt, and Roz knew that she looked ill. She felt it too. Working on the coal was hard, physical labour, which meant that you were permanently dirty no matter how hard you tried to get clean, and the dust got everywhere, under your nails, in your hair, even in your ears. The Haggartys didn't have a bathtub, so a strip wash was the best she could manage. She hesitated. Did she really want Felix to see her like this? The answer to that was no, but it was either that or she might as well give up all hope. Besides, Felix had seen the Haggartys for himself, so he probably had a good idea by now that things weren't going so well for Roz.

She was swapping the heavy bag onto her other shoulder when another thought entered her mind. She knew that Felix was keen on her, and whilst she hadn't admitted it to Mabel, she was sure she liked him as more than a friend or brother, but how would he feel when she turned up dressed in the Haggartys' hand-me-downs?

This brought her mind back to the time she had found a suitable-looking dress in the pile of unwanted clothing which the Haggartys kept to use as rags, or to block up holes in the walls. She had been waiting for the water for the porridge to come to the boil when she came across the dress. Holding it up against her she had thought it to be about the right size. With the family still fast asleep, she slipped it on and was pleased to see that it fitted nicely. Thinking no more of it, she had returned to her duties, and called for Suzie and Callum to get up. Suzie had been the first to rise. Half asleep, she had soon woken up when she clapped eyes on Roz wearing the dress. Her finger shaking, she demanded that Roz take the dress off.

'No, it's not yours and it certainly isn't Lilith's,' said Roz, who couldn't see a problem. Suzie looked anxiously over to where her father was still asleep then back to Roz. 'Take it off!' she hissed, only this time her voice was trembling.

Frowning, Roz looked to where Callum was beginning to stir. Why was Suzie worried about Callum seeing Roz in a dress which had been left on the rag pile?

She soon found out. As Callum's eyes settled on her, he was out of bed and across the room in a flash. Gripping her by the neckline of the dress, he practically tore it from her.

Roz was so shocked that she reacted with her gut. Pushing him off, she deflected his hand which had come up in a sweeping motion.

With both Haggarty women now wide awake, she had heard them gasp in unison at her actions. Her heart thundering in her chest, Roz had waited for Callum to strike again, but it seemed he had second thoughts. Backing away he kicked the kettle off the stove, causing boiling water to spray across the room. She had been about to wag her finger and say 'temper, temper', but the look of warning on Suzie's face made her think twice. 'It was me mam's,' Suzie whispered quietly.

Realisation dawning, Roz spluttered an apology and hastily stripped down to her vest and knickers. 'It was on the rag pile,' she murmured as she quickly donned her dungarees.

There was one thing about the incident that still puzzled Roz. As Callum had aimed his blow, Roz saw from the corner of her eye that Lilith Haggarty had begun to scramble out of bed, looking to Roz as though the older woman was getting ready to intervene. But why? Roz knew she was hated by all the Haggartys, but Lilith in particular was always pushing Roz roughly out of the way, or throwing things at her rather than passing them to her. If anything, Roz assumed that Lilith would have applauded Callum's behaviour, but her actions had spoken very differently. If Roz were to make a guess, she would say that Lilith was scared – of what, Roz couldn't be certain. The only logical explanation she could come up with was that Lilith had been worried that Callum's actions might leave Roz with a black eye and that would cause tongues to wag down at the market. Callum was known for his hot temper, so people would know he had been the one to strike Roz, but would that really have bothered the old woman? She thought of Suzie's absent mother, and the dark looks she had been subjected to whenever she had dared bring the matter up. Mabel had said that there had been a lot of speculation over the years as to what had happened to Suzie's mother – maybe Lilith had suspicions of her own? Roz shuddered. What did she think her son had done that would make her want to defend someone she positively hated?

As Roz rounded the corner towards the laundry on Stanley Road, she chided herself inwardly. Why had she spent the last few minutes thinking about her miserable life with the Haggartys when she had people like Mabel and Felix waiting for her?

Blissfully unaware that she was being watched by Suzie, Roz waited for Mabel to appear.

*

107

Moments after Roz had left to go to the market, Lilith had addressed her granddaughter sharply.

'Follow her, you stupid child, before she gets away!'

Utterly perplexed, Suzie looked from her grandmother to her father and back again. 'I thought you said not to pay any attention to her.'

'I only said that so that she wouldn't get suspicious,' hissed Lilith, hobbling over to the window where she could see Roz carefully climbing down the stairs. She held up a halting finger as Suzie went to open the door. 'Not yet, she's not clear of the building. Wait until she's halfway across the yard before you go. We know she's heading to Paddy's market first, but I'd wager she's a destination in mind after that. I don't believe that cock-and-bull story she gave us yesterday. I could tell by the look in her eye she weren't tellin' the truth, and her behaviour this morning makes me believe I was right to doubt her.' She brought down her finger in a sweeping motion. 'Off you go, child, before you lose her, but make sure you ain't seen. I want to know exactly where she goes, and what she's up to.'

Grinning deviously to herself, Suzie slipped out of the room.

Callum joined his mother by the window. 'Why're you so bothered where she goes?'

She raised her brow in surprise. 'Aren't you?'

Callum shook his head. 'Even if she is seein' some feller, what skin is it off of our nose? Worse comes to the worse, she leaves and moves in with him, makes no odds to us.'

'Unless she's gettin' paid for her services ...' said Lilith, who had left Callum and was now poking her stick through the sacking that Roz used as her bedding. She hooked it by the end and brought it up so that she could examine it more closely.

Callum pushed away from the window frame. 'You think she might be holdin' out on us?'

Lilith shrugged. 'Could be, but if she is, she's taken the money with her, or hidden it elsewhere.' She cast a shrewd eye around the room, before giving up and throwing the sack back on the floor.

'Sneaky little bitch!' cursed Callum through thin lips. 'And on my time too.'

'See what I mean?'

Callum nodded. 'You wait 'til I get my hands on her—'

Lilith paled. 'No! Wait until we hear what Suzie has to say first, but no matter what, you're not to raise a hand to that girl, do you hear me? I know what your temper's like, and I won't see you hang for some silly little tart.'

Suzie had found trailing after Roz to be fun at first, but waiting outside the market for what seemed to be an eternity had soon put a dampener on things. She had been relieved when Roz reappeared and she could follow her to the next destination, hoping against hope that it would be somewhere warmer this time. She was disappointed when she saw Mabel Johnson come out from the laundry and link arms with Roz. *All this sneaking around*, thought Suzie bitterly, *just because little Miss High and Mighty had befriended one of the girls from the courts? I don't know what Gran thought she was up to, but she'll be disappointed to hear it's nothing more than knocking around with the likes of Mabel Johnson, stuck-up cow that she is.* Assuming that the two girls were going back to Mercer Court, Suzie was about to head home when to her surprise the girls turned onto the Scottie Road. Why on earth were they going in that direction? Unless Roz was going to go into one of the shops and ask for some leftovers ... She shook her head dismissively. Roz had objected to asking the stallholders in the market; she'd hardly approach shopkeepers, especially not off her own bat. Curiosity getting the better of her, Suzie abandoned her plans for an early dart home, and continued to follow the girls.

Out of earshot from her unknown spy, Roz confided in Mabel that she was feeling nervous at the thought of seeing Felix again when she wasn't looking her best.

'He sounds like a grand chap to me,' said Mabel. 'I doubt he'll be bothered by your appearance, although I daresay he won't be best pleased when he hears Callum sold your clobber down the Pig and Whistle.'

'Clobber?' enquired Roz, who had not yet mastered all the Liverpudlian slang.

'Clothes,' explained Mabel. 'It was a downright mean thing to do if you ask me. They might just be clothes to the likes of him, but they were things your parents had bought you, the only thing you have left to remind you of them ...' She stopped short, seeing the wry smile cross Roz's face.

'Is there something else?'

Nodding, Roz told Mabel about the gold Star of David necklace which she had been given at her bat mitzvah.

'Can I see?' asked Mabel, eyeing Roz's neckline.

Roz shook her head. 'I've left it back at the Haggartys' ...'

'You've what?' cried Mabel.

Roz smiled. 'Not to worry, I've hidden it where they'll never think to look – in my bedding.'

Mabel frowned. 'What makes you think it's safe in your bedding?'

Roz's grin widened. 'You think they'd make my bed for me?'

Mabel emitted a shriek of laughter. 'When you put it that way, your necklace is safe as houses! Only why not wear it?'

Roz shook her head. 'There's no privacy in that place. I have to strip down to my undies in the same room as everyone else, although Callum hangs up a curtain between us and him, which is a bit of a relief, and I do my best not to see old Lilith Haggarty in her bloomers ...' She shuddered. 'I should imagine it's not a pretty sight!'

Mabel pulled a revolted face. 'Me too! I think it's a crying shame you can't wear it, though.'

'You know what you were saying before, about how Callum shouldn't have got rid of my clothes because they were personal reminders of my parents?'

'What of it?' asked Mabel.

'I've been wondering why Callum reacted so badly when he found me wearing a dress which had belonged to Suzie's mother. At the time I thought it was a bit strange, but maybe he was angry for a different reason?'

Mabel's eyes widened. 'When you say he reacted badly, just what do you mean exactly?'

111

Roz quickly relayed the story, as her friend listened patiently.

'You really are brave, Roz. I don't think I'd have dared stand up to him the way you did, and I very much doubt you upset Callum emotionally. I think he reacted the way he did because you scared him, like raking up the past type of thing, maybe even made him feel guilty.'

'Do I look like her?' said Roz, praying the answer would be no.

Mabel spluttered on a cough. 'Good God, no! Nothing like her, so you needn't worry about that!'

'Good,' said Roz. She stopped walking as they arrived outside the door of Felix's new home.

Her stomach fluttered wildly as she glanced at Mabel who knocked without hesitation. She smiled and said, 'Good luck ...' before slipping her arm out of Roz's and standing to one side.

Roz tried to usher Mabel back but there was no time; the door opened and Felix stood in the doorway. His eyes locked with hers, and a slow smile spread across his face.

'Hello,' he said, as Roz smiled back.

'Bet you never thought you'd see me again,' said Roz, before glancing in Mabel's direction and beckoning for her to join them. 'This is my pal, Mabel, she lives just round the corner from me.'

Felix raised his brow. 'Where do you live?'

'Crooked Lane, above a coal merchant's – and no, they don't own it in case you're wondering. That was another lie – and the only reason why they wanted me to move in with them was so they could use me as free labour.'

Felix nodded slowly. 'We guessed as much.'

Roz looked past him. 'We?'

'Mr Jones. I'll admit I tore a strip or two off him when I found out he'd had his suspicions that they weren't all they cracked themselves up to be, but like he said, sometimes, when you've got little choice, you have to take folk at face value.'

A voice called out from within the house. 'Close that bloody door or come in! I'm not payin' to heat the Scottie!'

Felix grinned. 'Do you want to come in?'

Roz looked at Mabel who nodded. 'Better than standin' out here,' she glanced up at the sky which was threatening rain, 'it looks like the heavens are about to open.'

The girls followed Felix into the house where he introduced them to Alan and Bill, who gave them a welcoming, gappy grin.

'Can't stay away, eh?' Bill chuckled. 'Just as well, mind. He was chuffed to bits when he heard you'd come callin'.'

'Bill!' objected Felix, though the girls could see he wasn't too bothered by the older man's words.

Alan, who had got up from his chair, gestured for the girls to take a seat. 'Stop teasin' the lad. We'll leave you to make these girls a cuppa.' He touched his forelock as he ushered his father out of the room.

Roz took the seat nearest the range where Felix was putting a kettle on to boil. 'Looks like you've landed on your feet, as my mother would say.'

Felix looked to the door which had closed behind the men. 'They're grand, really nice fellers, would give you the shirt off their back ...'

Mabel tutted loudly. 'Not like the bleedin' Haggartys, then, who *literally* took the clothes off our Roz's back.'

He looked at Roz, his face clouding over. 'Why did they do that?'

'To sell down the pub,' said Roz simply.

He shook his head as he added a couple of scoops of tea to the pot. 'They're even worse than I imagined, and I didn't think that was possible.'

'They got her workin' for nothin',' Mabel volunteered, 'not to mention beggin' for stuff down the markets.'

Roz, who had been wondering how to tell Felix of her embarrassment, frowned at Mabel, with both relief and annoyance. Seeing the look on Roz's face, Mabel apologised, adding, 'Maybe I spoke out of turn, but it's not your fault. You told them you didn't want to go, but they forced you anyway.'

Roz mellowed. 'I know, I just find it a bit embarrassing. I've never begged for anything in my life, never had to, and it's not as if we even keep the stuff for ourselves ...' Seeing Felix's look of incomprehension, she explained how Callum took everything she brought back and sold it down the pub.

'I knew he was shifty from the moment I clapped eyes on him,' snapped Felix. 'Not to mention the rest of his family. Not that I said anything, of course, because I trusted the staff at Dovercourt to know what they were doing, and you seemed happy enough.'

Roz shrugged. 'I never trusted them either, but at the time they were my only option, and like you, I thought the staff would know if their intentions weren't honourable. It never occurred to me that someone would take in a refugee to use as free labour.'

Felix collected three mugs from the cupboard beside the sink and placed them on the table in front of them. 'Why didn't you leave when you knew what their intentions were?'

'I thought about it,' Roz admitted, 'but I couldn't face going back to Dovercourt to start from scratch, not to mention, how would I have got there with no money? And also Crooked Lane's only a stone's throw from the Liver Building. I might not like living there, but at least I have a chance of finding my parents. Who knows where I'd end up if I left?'

'I take it you've had no luck finding your parents?' said Felix, pouring boiling water from the kettle into the chipped earthenware teapot.

Roz shook her head. 'Not a dickie bird, as my mother used to say. I've left my details, though, so if they turn up at least they'll know where to find me.'

Felix gave a mirthless chuckle. 'The Haggartys will be in for a shock that day!'

Roz glanced around the snug little kitchen. 'I wish I'd ended up somewhere like this.'

A loud whinnying sound came from the back of the house, startling Mabel. 'What on earth was that?'

Felix stopped swilling the teapot round and set it down. 'Come with me and I'll show you.'

Intrigued, Roz and Mabel followed him through to the back of the house. As they proceeded, Roz sniffed the air. 'I don't mean to be rude, but it smells like a ... oooh.' She stopped short as her eyes focused on a horse. Its ears pricked, it whinnied again as they neared the stable.

Felix stroked the horse's muzzle. 'Roz, Mabel, this is Coconut.'

115

A giggle escaped Mabel's lips. 'Coconut? What a strange name for a horse!'

Felix lifted the horse's muzzle. 'He's got a real whiskery chin, which reminded Bill of a coconut, so ...'

Roz was smiling dreamily as she gingerly patted the horse's cheek. 'I don't think he looks like a coconut; I think he's beautiful.' She cooed softly. 'Is he yours?'

Felix half nodded. 'He belongs to Bill and Alan, but they've taught me how to tack him up, pick out his hooves, prepare his mash, the works. Alan says I'm a natural.' As he spoke he smoothed Coconut's forelock between his fingers. 'I've even ridden him – not far, mind you, and we haven't got a saddle, so it's a bit uncomfortable—' He got no further.

Roz's eyes were shining with admiration. 'Felix Ackerman, you are a lucky boy and I am very envious!'

'You can sit on him if you like?' said Felix, eager to please. 'I'm sure Alan wouldn't mind ...' He looked down at her skirt. 'You can sit side-saddle as it were.'

'What about me?' said Mabel, anxious not to be left out.

'Before we go any further, let me ask Alan, see what he says to me letting the two of you have a sit on him.'

Mabel nudged Roz excitedly as Felix disappeared back into the house. 'You wait 'til the others find out I've sat on a horse!'

'I shan't be bragging to the Haggartys, they'd scold me for wasting time,' said Roz.

'Miserable blighters,' huffed Mabel, 'just as well they can't see you.'

Felix returned and unhooked Coconut's halter from the peg outside the stable door. 'Alan said yes, although

116

I knew he would.' He slid the bolts back on the door and disappeared inside. 'We haven't long come back from work, so he said we could only go up to the butcher's and back.'

'Actually ride him? Out on the street?' gasped Mabel. 'Where people can see us?'

He nodded. 'That alright with you?'

Mabel was beaming. 'I should say so! I just wish my family could see me riding a horse.'

Felix swung the stable door open and stood beside Coconut. 'Who wants to sit at the front?'

'We're going to ride him together?' said Roz. 'Will he be able to take our weight?'

Grinning, Felix cast an eye over the two girls. 'He could carry four of you without batting an eye! He's as strong as an ox is our Coconut; besides, I bet neither of you weigh more than seven stone, soaking wet!'

'How about if one of us goes in front up the road, and we swap on the way back?' suggested Mabel, who was jiggling with excitement.

'Go on then,' said Roz, 'you can go first if you like.'

Mabel shook her head. 'Felix is your friend, so it's only right you go first.'

With no need to be asked twice, Roz allowed Felix to give her a leg up. She noticed how deliciously warm Coconut was, something that Mabel commented on when she was placed into position behind Roz.

Felix instructed the girls to hold on tight, as he led him out of the yard and onto the Scottie. Mabel held tightly onto Roz's waist as Felix led them along the road. He looked up, his eyes twinkling as they met Roz's. 'Having fun?'

Roz nodded, and there came a muffled 'The best ever!' from Mabel.

Breathing in the horsey scent, Roz smiled happily. It felt typical that as soon as Felix arrived back in her life, all seemed well with the world once more. She was so focused on her first riding experience, she didn't notice someone quickly ducking out of sight behind a couple who had stopped to admire the girls being taken for a ride.

Before the happy group had a chance to turn around, and perhaps discover that they were being spied on, Suzie had slunk off into the darkness.

The nerve of the girl! She fumed as she tried to stamp the feeling back into her ice-cold toes – it might be March but spring was still a long way off. Parading round like she hadn't a care in the world, when she knew she should be out there working for the Haggartys! Well, her father would soon wipe that sickly grin off Roz's chops when she returned home later that evening. He wouldn't be at all happy to know that he'd been kept waiting, when he could be having a drink down the Pig and Whistle, all because Roz was more interested in having her own fun.

A malicious grin crossed her face as she imagined Roz's horror when she was outed in front of the Haggartys, not to mention the other girl's dismay when Callum forbade her from seeing Felix or that stuck-up cow Mabel again! *Serve her bloomin' right*, thought Suzie, *and as for that Mabel and her snotty sisters, too good to be friends with me, but they'll smarm up to a stinkin' Jew what nobody else wanted, that's typical of that lot ...* She cast her mind back to the row her family had had with the Johnsons when they had accused the Haggartys – unfairly in Suzie's eyes – of trying to break into their house. Whilst it was true that Callum had been caught halfway through their kitchen window, he had explained that he thought he'd seen an intruder and was only trying to apprehend what he believed to be a burglar. Not that they'd believed him for a second, oh no, they scoffed at his suggestion, told him to get out, and didn't even try to give him the benefit of the doubt. Yet they'd believe the word of a Kraut without question. Well, she'd soon put an end to that!

Roz and Mabel, oblivious of their spy, had swapped places and were slowly making their way back down the alley to the stable. 'I feel like Lady Godiva,' beamed Mabel, much to the bemusement of Felix and Roz who had never heard of her. When Mabel briefly explained the naked woman's history, Roz shrieked with laughter.

'Thank goodness you've got your clothes on!' she said once she'd regained her composure.

'I don't mean the naked bit,' giggled Mabel, 'but riding through the streets with everyone gawping at us.'

Felix led Coconut back through the yard and brought him to a halt. 'Time's up. Do you need a hand to dismount?'

His words had barely left his lips before Roz was standing next to him. Feeling a tad disappointed that she had not needed his help, he looked at Mabel who was still astride the horse. 'Mabel?'

Leaning forward, she placed her arms around Coconut's neck and gave him a hug. 'I think I'll stay here for the rest of my life.'

Felix chuckled. 'I don't think the two of you will fit through the stable door.'

Pouting, Mabel kissed Coconut's neck, before gently sliding down from his back. 'I think I'm in love.' She sighed happily, watching Felix slip the halter from the horse's head and come back out to join them.

'Me too,' agreed Roz. 'I've never ridden a horse before. I'd like to do it again sometime, if that's okay with Alan, of course?'

'Me too, me too!' jabbered Mabel excitedly. 'I don't mind doin' a bit of work to help out, maybe clean his stable or brush him, fill his water, anything!'

Felix smiled affectionately at the girls. 'I can see you're just as smitten with Coconut as I am, and I'm sure Alan wouldn't mind us taking him for the odd ride now and then.'

They said their goodbyes to Coconut and headed back into the house, where Roz gasped as her eyes fell on the clock above the mantel. 'I'd better have my tea then think about making a move.'

Felix took the tea which had been warming on the Aga and poured it into three mugs before adding milk and sugar at the girls' request, and handing them round. 'When can you come and see me again?' he asked. 'Or could I come to you?'

Roz shook her head immediately at his latter suggestion. She had no desire for him to see her living conditions, for even though they weren't her choice, she would be thoroughly embarrassed for him to see the ... she hesitated in her thoughts; she couldn't call it a house, or apartment, or flat, it was a loft space above a warehouse. Not wishing to appear rude, she spoke quickly. 'I'll come to you. How about tomorrow?'

He nodded slowly. 'It's a shame you have to leave so soon. Will there be a frightful row if you stayed longer?'

Roz glanced at Mabel. 'Yes, Callum'll be wanting to get down the pub.'

Felix's jaw tightened. 'If I had a place of my own ...' He hesitated. 'That's the answer!'

Roz, looked at him, perplexed. 'Sorry?'

'I'll save my money and rent a flat of my own, and you can move in with me,' hastily adding, 'as friends, of course, and I wouldn't expect you to pay rent, but it would mean you could get a proper job, earn your own wages and ...' He stopped abruptly as Roz jumped up from her seat, flung her arms around his neck and kissed him on the cheek.

'Thanks, Felix, and it's a lovely idea, but will they let you rent a flat on your own at your age?'

Felix's cheeks tinged pink. 'Probably not until I'm eighteen, which won't be until next year, and whilst I know it's still quite a way off, it's still better than nothing.' He eyed her expectantly before continuing. 'Of course I hope you'll have been reunited with your parents long before then, but call it Plan B if you will.'

'Something to fall back on,' said Mabel, who was smiling encouragingly at Roz. 'Everyone hopes you'll be back with your parents by then, but if not ...'

Roz nodded slowly. 'That's very kind of you, Felix, but it's a big undertaking and I wouldn't like to see you put yourself out. If you're sure, then I'd have to insist on paying my way.'

Felix gave her a reassuring smile. 'Whatever you want, and you'd not be putting me out. I like living with Bill and Alan, but this place is only one bed, and three of us in one room is a bit cramped. I'm very grateful to them for taking me in, really I am, but it's about time I started thinking of making my own way in this world.' He gave a little chuckle. 'Not to mention Bill's snoring is enough to wake the dead! And I dread to think where the noises Alan makes are coming from!'

Roz shot him a wry glance. 'Try living four in a room without proper mattresses, let alone bedding.'

His lips twitched in a disapproving fashion. 'Is that how you're living?'

Realising she'd revealed more than she'd intended, she shook her head. 'Ignore me, it's not as bad as I make it sound.'

'Nope,' said Mabel, 'it's worse.'

Felix gave Roz a sympathetic look. 'Don't they realise you've lost everything – your home, your parents, your country?'

Roz laughed. ''Course they do, but they don't care. The way they see it, they're doing me a favour and I should be grateful for any scraps they throw my way.' She shrugged. 'I keep my head down and get on with things because I don't want them to kick me out. Believe me, Crooked Lane might not be paradise, but it's a lot better than the gutter.'

He removed his cap and scratched his thick thatch of brown curls. 'I wish I could do something to get you away from them sooner.'

Roz laid a hand on his arm. 'You've thrown me a lifeline, Felix, something to look forward to, and that in

122

itself has brightened my day.' She waved a dismissive hand. 'I can put up with the likes of the Haggartys for now, and who knows? My parents could be on a train making their way to Liverpool as we speak.'

'That's the ticket,' said Mabel happily, 'always look on the bright side.' She flashed Felix a cheery smile. 'And don't worry about our Roz – she's already put that beast of a man, Callum, in his place.'

Felix threw Roz a startled glance. 'I hope he didn't try anything ...' he looked both shy and awkward, '... *you know* ...' he finished lamely.

Roz looked aghast. 'God, no! He might be a lot of things, but he's not that. Mabel just means that Callum knows I'm not afraid of him, so he tends to leave me alone – bosses me around, but that's about it.'

Felix gave a heartfelt sigh of relief. 'Glad to hear it!'

Roz smiled shyly. 'I'm sorry, Felix, but I really am going to have to get back. Callum wouldn't try and raise a hand to me, but I can't afford for him to throw me out.'

'Supposing he did, though?' mused Felix.

'The scuffers would send me back to Dovercourt,' said Roz simply, 'and they might try to send me back to Berlin ...' She held up a hand as Felix tried to speak. 'Charity only goes so far, Felix, and I could end up with a family a lot worse than the Haggartys, and a lot further away from Liverpool too.'

Felix nodded dejectedly. 'Well, you'd best be off then, but are we still on for tomorrow?'

Roz grinned. 'You bet we are!'

*

123

Back at the Haggartys' Suzie was filling Callum and Lilith in on Roz's deceit.

'Didn't I tell you!' said Lilith smugly, sitting up. 'I knew she was up to no good!'

Callum looked doubtful. 'Apart from the fact she's had me waiting here when I could've been down the pub, I'm not sure I see the harm in it.'

Suzie pouted obstinately. 'She lied! She made out that she was doing your messages whereas she's been riding on a horse and slathering all over this Felix feller.'

Callum cocked an eyebrow. 'Remember his name, do you?'

Suzie blushed. 'I heard them giggling and calling him Felix.'

He eyed her shrewdly, as though searching her thoughts, before looking away. 'Well, she ain't beggared off with him, she still comes back here, still does her chores, so apart from her being late ...'

'And the fact she lied!' snapped Suzie. 'Not to mention that soddin' Mabel – God only knows what lies Roz is telling her.'

Callum pulled a nonchalant face. 'Who cares? I don't.'

Suzie stared in disbelief at her father. How could he sit there as calm as you like, as if all was well? Roz was lying, and hanging round with their sworn enemies, and her father was acting like he couldn't care less! On the other hand, Callum had never been that keen on taking Roz on in the first place, so he'd probably prefer it if she slung her hook.

Still cold from her excursion, Suzie walked to the stove, kicking Roz's bedding angrily out of her way. As

124

she did so, she saw something small skid out from inside the sacking and under the stove. Suzie was just about to draw attention to the mystery object when she thought better of it. Her father probably wouldn't care that Roz was hiding things in her bedding, and her gran had done little to change his mind. Bending down, Suzie pretended to tie her lace whilst fishing the small gold-coloured object from under the stove. Standing up, she glanced at the gold chain in her hand. A slow smile spread across her cheeks. Roz was holding out on them; surely this would make her father see sense? She turned the piece of jewellery over between her fingers and saw, on the end of the chain, a small gold star. It twinkled in Suzie's hands as it caught the light. She was about to turn and show her find to her family when a thought crossed her mind. The necklace could be Roz's, and if it was, her father wouldn't shout at Roz, or throw her out, but take it down the pub and swap it for something more to his liking. She rolled her eyes – probably a few pints of beer. Coming to a decision, she quickly pocketed the item. Lifting the kettle off the stove she gave it an experimental shake. 'Empty,' she announced out loud, 'I'll fetch more water.' Not expecting a response, she slunk out of the room and down the stairs, carefully carrying the kettle, which was actually half full of water, to the communal pump which stood in the square. She looked around to make sure no one was watching, then pretended to fill the kettle whilst examining the necklace in greater detail. As she admired the star, she thought back to something she had overheard in the market when rumours of the Kindertransport had first begun, about the Star of

David, and how Hitler made all the Jews wear it on their clothing so that they could be easily identified. She nodded slowly to herself; the necklace was Roz's personal possession, which was why she'd hidden it. After all, none of the stallholders would give her something so fancy, especially for free. Her mouth curled in a malevolent grin. The jewellery would be real gold; everyone knew Jews were loaded. Probably a present from her precious parents! Personally, Suzie hadn't believed the story of the car crash for one minute. It was an obvious ruse to get Roz out of the country so that she could start a new life for her family in Britain, and they would follow later on expecting handouts from the government. Suzie pushed the chain deep into her pocket. People like Roz didn't deserve nice things, not when they came over here, expecting everything for free, not when they had fancy bits of jewellery, and probably a stash of money hidden somewhere. No wonder the Germans wanted rid of them. No, she thought decidedly, Roz didn't deserve special things at all. Suzie had lived in Britain all her life; if anyone deserved nice things it was *her*! The best part of it was Roz wouldn't be able to accuse Suzie of taking the jewellery, because that would mean admitting she'd had it in the first place, which would alert the Haggartys to her wealth, something she was obviously trying to keep secret. What fun Suzie would have, watching Roz search for her necklace in vain. Oh yes, she would enjoy that *very* much!

*

126

'Are you certain you've not hidden it elsewhere?' asked Mabel as Roz blinked back tears.

'Positive,' said Roz miserably. 'When I got back the Haggartys were really quiet, as if something had happened. At first I wondered whether they knew about me meeting Felix, but I dismissed that straight away, because there's no way they'd keep quiet about something like that – quite the opposite, in fact. Callum was annoyed that I was late, but happy with the things I'd managed to bring back. He said I wasn't to be late again, or he'd send Suzie out instead. I know that's an empty threat because no one likes or trusts Suzie, and I very much doubt they'd give her anything, even if it were destined for the bin. Lilith kept giving me daggers, but she remained tight-lipped, and Suzie wouldn't even look at me. I was tired so I couldn't be bothered trying to work out what was up with those two, so I had a wash and went to bed. That's when I found it was missing.' She shrugged helplessly. 'I looked at Lilith expecting to see her grinning, but she wasn't even paying me attention.'

'What about Suzie?' asked Mabel.

Roz remained silent, deep in thought, before answering. 'She was unusually quiet. I'm certain she was watching me, I could see her from the corner of my eye, and whenever I looked at her, she looked away quickly.'

'It was her then,' said Mabel simply.

'Well, that's what I thought at first, but if it were, surely she'd have said something? Gloated about how she'd found a necklace, knowing I wouldn't be able to say it was mine? She'd have been on cloud nine watching me squirm, but nothing!'

'Why couldn't you admit it was yours?'

'Because on the train to Liverpool, Callum asked me if I had anything of value, and that if I had, I should give it to him so that he could look after it for me.' She gave a scornful laugh. 'He must have thought I had rocks in my head! I may not have known the extent of their deceit then, but I know better than to hand my things over to a complete stranger.'

Mabel blew her cheeks out. 'Good job too, else your Star of David would have been long gone.' She frowned in confusion. 'Only if one of them's got it, why not say summat?'

'That's why I'm wondering if it's fallen out of my bedding and slipped between the floorboards somehow. I couldn't search for it too thoroughly last night, in case I aroused suspicion, but from what I could tell, there simply isn't a big enough gap for it to have fallen through.'

'You'll have to find some excuse to get them out, so that you can have a proper look,' said Mabel decidedly. 'Are you going to tell Felix?'

'No,' said Roz, 'I don't see the point. It's not as though he can do anything to help.'

'Well, he might be able to think of a way to get them out the loft so that you can search for it properly,' said Mabel, 'because I'll be darned if I can think of a good enough excuse.'

'Me neither,' Roz admitted. 'Perhaps it would be a good idea to run it past Felix.'

Having already taken the things from the market back to Callum, Roz had made an excuse that she wanted to get some fresh air. Lilith and Suzie had exchanged knowing glances but neither had objected, so Roz had met Mabel and the two were heading down to Albert Dock to find Felix. Roz scanned the area looking to see if she could spot her friend, but all the men were wearing similar clothing – dark jackets, trousers and caps. It was like looking for a needle in a haystack, until she spotted Coconut, who was the only dapple-grey horse there. She went to point him out to Mabel, but judging by the smile on her face, Mabel had already seen him.

They took great care crossing the busy quayside, which was hectic with men transferring goods down from the ships, whilst others loaded them onto the back of lorries or carts. The noise was tremendous with people shouting orders, trying to make themselves heard above the sound of engines and seagulls, as well as each other. As they neared Coconut, they heard a cry from above. Looking up, Roz gasped as she saw Felix standing on top of a pile of sacks which were being craned from the ship to the quay. As the driver carefully rested the pallet onto the ground, Felix unhooked the crane and gave the driver the thumbs up, signalling that the load was free.

He grinned at the girls who were both looking awestruck. 'I want your job!' cried Mabel. 'You get to work with Coconut *and* ride on the biggest swing I ever saw!'

'It's not all fun and games,' said Felix, seconds before a warning cry came from further down the dock. Turning, they saw a load which was being craned off one of the ships break free from its ropes and crash down onto the people below. Within moments dozens of dockers, including Felix, had run to the scene.

'Did you see what happened?' Roz asked Mabel, who had been facing the right direction when the cry went up.

'Kind of – it looked as though one of the ropes snapped. No one was riding it like Felix, thank goodness, although there were a few men guiding it down when it went.'

Roz grimaced. 'I hope they're alright.'

'Felix was right when he said it's not all fun and games,' said Mabel. 'Do you think we should help?'

'We'd only get in the way, and they look like they know what they're doing.' Roz stroked Coconut's cheek. 'You didn't bat an eye, did you?'

'He's probably seen it all before,' said Mabel.

Seeing Felix jogging towards them, Roz called out, 'Is anyone hurt?'

'A few cuts and bruises – quite lucky really, as those crates are heavy. Not sure what's in them, but there's a fair bit of broken glass and a strong smell of alcohol.'

'Sounds expensive,' said Mabel.

'Possibly, but that's what insurance is for!' Felix turned to Roz. 'Did you get into trouble last night? I know you were worried about being late.'

Roz quickly explained the events of the previous evening, looking at him curiously. 'What do you think?'

He shrugged. 'If Suzie's as devious as her father, I'd put money on Suzie having found your necklace and not told the others.'

'But why?' said Roz. 'She's got no need to search my bedding; it would be quite an odd thing for her to do.'

'Perhaps she came across it by accident,' said Felix, 'or, maybe you're right, maybe it has slipped between the floorboards.'

'How do I search for it without raising suspicion?' said Roz. 'If they know what I'm after, or even if they see that I'm looking for something, they might wait until I go out and search themselves, and they might have more luck than me.'

'Couldn't you wait until they go out?' Felix suggested.

'They never go out together; in fact, Lilith hardly ever goes out, so no.'

'What we need,' said Felix, rubbing his chin, 'is an excuse to get them out, and by the sound of it, Lilith is your biggest problem, so we need something that will make her leave too.' He eyed Roz quizzically. 'Am I right in saying that it's you, Callum and Suzie who do the coal round every morning?'

Roz nodded. 'There's no way Lilith would join us, she's too old and frail.'

'What about if she were to think there'd been an accident?' said Felix slowly. 'Do you think she'd leave if she thought her son or granddaughter were in danger?'

Mabel stopped stroking Coconut and frowned at him sharply. 'What are you suggesting?'

Felix laughed. 'Not a real accident! But if someone told her there'd been an accident, what then?'

Roz looked at Mabel for the answer, but Mabel shrugged. 'I'd like to say she'd go to their aid, but who knows with that lot?'

Roz tapped her finger against her chin as she weighed up the possibilities. 'If she thought one of them was so badly hurt they couldn't do the deliveries, therefore they wouldn't get paid ...'

Mabel nodded, a grin forming on her face. 'Now that would get her hobbling!'

'But if I'm with them, I can't look for the necklace,' said Roz reasonably.

'That's where I come in,' said Felix.

'Oh no!' said Roz vehemently. 'I'm not having you get involved.'

'Too late!' said Felix. 'You've lost enough as it is, I won't see you parted from something so special.' He held up his hands to quieten Roz who was about to protest. 'I'll pay one of the messengers a penny to tell Lilith that you've broken down. Then when she's out the way, I'll nip in and check it out.'

'And what if you get caught?' asked Roz, who wasn't at all convinced by Felix's plan.

'Who by?' said Felix. 'Lilith will be on a wild goose chase, and from what you've told me it doesn't sound as though their place is full to the brim of furniture and clutter.'

Roz sighed impatiently. She really didn't want Felix seeing her living conditions; she had no doubt that he would be understanding, but she still found it embarrassing. On the other hand, there was no point letting pride get in her way, and without Felix, she might never find her necklace, which was more than she could bear. She thought over his plan. What Felix said made sense, but the thought of any of the Haggartys catching him snooping around their home was an idea she didn't relish. She looked at Mabel for help, but it seemed Mabel agreed with Felix.

'From what you say there's nothing in there – it's not as though there's lots of drawers and cupboards for Felix to search through!' reasoned Mabel. 'I know you're worried that Felix will get into trouble, but he's only going to be inside for no more than five minutes, right?'

Felix nodded.

Roz still looked doubtful. 'And what about when Lilith realises she's been lied to?'

Felix shrugged. 'Everybody makes mistakes, and good luck to her if she wants to seek out the boy who brings her the message. There's loads of young lads down the docks, and lots of coal merchants; the Haggartys will most likely think there's been a mix-up, and seeing as they won't find anything amiss when they return, they won't have reason to suspect anything's up.'

'I think it's a good idea,' said Mabel. 'Especially if it means you get your necklace back.'

'Okay then. When shall we do it?' said Roz, much to Felix and Mabel's delight.

'We've got early deliveries for the next few days,' said Felix. 'How about next Wednesday?'

Roz nodded reluctantly. 'Alright, but promise me you'll only be inside for five minutes?'

He placed his hand over his heart. 'You have my word.'

'And if you think Lilith suspects anything?' asked Roz.

'I'll give up on the whole idea.'

'It would be nice to get my necklace back ...'

Mabel clapped her hands together 'I feel like Miss Marple!' she said, before realising she'd better explain who Miss Marple was.

Roz grinned. 'But you're not doing anything!'

'Oh yes I am!' said Mabel with grim determination. 'I'm going to be the lookout; I shall hoot like an owl to warn Felix if someone comes.'

'I take it you can actually hoot like an owl?' laughed Felix.

'My grandpa taught me.' Mabel cupped her hands together and blew between her thumbs, emitting a very lifelike owl hoot.

'Gosh,' said Roz, impressed by her friend's talent.

'Impressive,' agreed Felix.

'Good, isn't it?' said Mabel.

Felix and Roz exchanged glances. 'I don't know what an owl sounds like,' admitted Felix. 'I've only ever lived in the city.'

Mabel looked expectantly at Roz, who gave her a rather embarrassed smile. 'Me too, although I bet you sound just like one.'

Mabel rolled her eyes. 'Good job we tested it out first, or I could've been hooting myself hoarse!'

The following Wednesday, they put their plan into action. Mabel waited until she saw Callum drive the lorry past the end of Mercer Court before slipping out of the house and positioning herself out of sight. Having been given clear instructions on how to get to the loft above the coal merchant's on Crooked Lane, Felix had left his home far earlier than he normally would and made his way to the docks, where the night shift was still going strong. He slipped one of the messenger boys a penny to go to the Haggartys' and tell Lilith that a man had just seen a terrible accident involving Partington's coal lorry, and that she was needed quickly. The boy raced off and Felix strode idly behind, his hands deep into his pockets. He didn't wish to arrive before Lilith had had time to get out. When he reached Crooked Lane, he saw Mabel standing outside the merchant's waiting for him.

Without as much as a word, she stuck her thumb into the air and went to her hiding place across the road. With the coast clear, he took the unstable steps two at a time and entered the sparsely furnished room. As he stood looking around him, it took him a moment or so to get over the extreme poverty in which his friend was living. How could Roz wonder where her necklace had got to? There was hardly a chance of it slipping down the back of the sofa, as there wasn't one, not even a bed frame. Realising that he was wasting precious time, he walked over to what he assumed must be the sleeping area. His eyes came to rest on a bed – if you could call it that – which had sacks in place of blankets. That must be where Roz slept, he thought bitterly, for it was the only bed that had been neatly made. Taking the sacks, he pushed them to one side and looked at the floorboards beneath. Nothing, not even the narrowest of gaps. He lifted the mattress next to it, and peered beneath, but again there was nothing to suggest a necklace could fall between the boards. He picked up the pillow, which turned out to be two very flat pillows inside one case, and continued to search.

*

On the other side of town an argument was breaking out.

'How the hell should I know?' roared Callum. 'If you ask me you either dreamed it or you're going doolally in your old age!'

'Waste of bloody time,' said Lilith, as she bent over trying to get her breath back.

'Just what did the lad say?' asked Roz, radiating innocent concern.

'That there'd been an accident, coal everywhere,' snapped Lilith, glaring at Roz. 'I'd wager a pound to a penny that this is your doing.'

Much to Roz's surprise, Callum spoke on her behalf. 'Don't be so bloody wet! How the hell could she do that? She's been with us the whole time.'

Lilith glared at Roz, whose face remained impassive. 'Probably her idea of a joke.'

'And why,' sighed Callum, who was clearly regretting having to live with three women, 'would anyone do that?'

'To get me rushin' around like a headless chicken!' hissed Lilith.

'Perhaps one of the other lorries has had an accident, and the boy made a mistake,' suggested Roz, as nobody else seemed to be coming to that conclusion.

'There you go,' said Callum, his patience wearing thin. 'Seeing as you're here you may as well come with us.'

They spent the rest of the journey in steely silence, with Lilith quietly seething in the passenger seat, and Roz fighting the urge to laugh out loud. She relaxed a little knowing that it would be a good few hours before they returned to the yard. She smiled to herself. Wouldn't it be wonderful if Felix found her necklace!

Chapter Four

Felix sat on the wall outside the tobacconist's, swinging his legs to and fro as he waited for Roz. He slipped the gold chain complete with its Star of David from one hand to the other, watching the spring sunshine catch the points of the star as he did so. He had thought that finding the necklace would be the best outcome, but now he wasn't so sure. Roz already knew that she lived with immoral liars, but this? This was something else. His head snapped up as he heard her hail him from across the road. Smiling, he slid down from his perch and walked over to greet her.

'Well?' she asked, her tone laced with hope.

In answer he held up his hand and released the star so that it slid down the chain.

Roz let out a cry of delight as she cupped her hands to receive the precious piece of jewellery. 'You clever, clever man! Where on *earth* was it?' Her smile vanished when she saw the rueful look on his face.

Felix explained that he had found the necklace stuffed in between the pillows of the bed next to Roz's own. He ran his tongue over his bottom lip. 'I'm afraid it couldn't have got in there by accident; I had to remove both pillows from the case before I saw it.'

Roz stared at him in dismay. 'I can't say I'm surprised because I know what Suzie's like, but to steal from someone who lives with you?' She shook her head. 'I don't reckon even Callum would do that.'

'I daresay she's never seen anything like it before,' Felix said, then added hastily, 'and I know it's not an excuse, but she probably couldn't help herself.'

Only Roz knew better. 'She'll have taken it out of spite, just to hurt me. She knows I can't ask for it back, so she was relishing the idea of having power over me.'

'Question is,' said Felix, glancing at the necklace, now in Roz's hand, 'what are you going to do now? Suzie will know you've found it, and if she uses her brain, she'll soon realise that this morning's shenanigans were a ruse for someone to search the loft.'

'Oh bother,' sighed Roz, 'I hadn't thought about that.' She looked at him from under thick lashes. 'What do you think I should do?'

Felix rested his chin against his knuckles. 'I'll look after the necklace for you, then you needn't worry about it going missing again. As for Suzie, knowing or even suspecting what we've done is one thing, but proving it? That's another matter entirely. Especially when she can't produce the necklace, and as you've never been seen with it, it would be her word against yours. Whilst I daresay they'd believe her, she'd have to explain why she kept the necklace for herself rather than hand it over to her father.' Pausing, he looked at Roz who appeared doubtful. 'They'll know she must have had it at least overnight, because you can't plan something like we did at the drop of a hat, so she won't be able to squirm her way out of that one.'

Roz tried to get it straight in her mind before running it past Felix. 'So, she'll know that I know that she knows, but she won't be able to do anything about it?'

A smile twitched the corners of Felix's lips. 'That's about the size of it.'

'Do you think she'll try and confront me when no one's looking?'

Felix raised an eyebrow. 'And say what exactly? That you stole back the necklace that she stole from you in the first place?' He shook his head in a chiding manner. 'From what you've told me, not even Suzie would be that stupid.' He placed his hands into his pockets. 'No, she'll have to bite her tongue for a few days, and you'll be grateful that looks can't kill, but other than that, she can't do a damned thing.'

A slow, satisfied smile formed on Roz's lips. 'Serves her right, and perhaps it'll teach her that she's not as smart as she thinks she is.'

'It'll certainly let her know that you've got friends,' agreed Felix.

'The best friends a girl could have,' said Roz, still smiling at Felix. 'I do appreciate what you and Mabel have done for me. I'm very lucky to have people like you in my life.'

Beginning to blush under such praise, Felix dropped his gaze. He liked Roz an awful lot, and if he were to have his way, they would be far more than friends. He glanced back up. 'I wish I could get you out of there today. I hate the thought of you having to live with people like them in a place like that.'

Leaning forward, she gently caressed his arm. 'Knowing I have friends like you watching my back makes it all worthwhile.'

Felix felt a warm glow enter his body under her delicate touch. He glanced down at her, wondering if she was aware of the effect she had on him, but by the look of innocence etched upon her face, she hadn't got a clue.

'It's important that those of us who came across on the Kindertransport look after one another,' he said, tucking a lock of Roz's hair behind her ear, 'but I'd like to think that you and I have a special bond, because we spent the whole journey together.'

'And Adele,' said Roz. A reminiscent smile played on her lips. 'Whatever happened to her?'

'She went to a farming family to be company for their elderly mother. We made doubly sure it was all alright after we realised the Haggartys had lied.'

'You've heard from her?' said Roz. 'How is she? Is she far from here?'

'She's fine, doing well in fact. I'd give her your address, but it wouldn't be a good idea for her to write to you at the Haggartys'.'

'You're right there, the less they know about me the better,' Roz agreed.

'Do you fancy a cuppa?' said Felix. 'We could nip into town and catch up, maybe have a treat in Blacklers.'

'Don't see why not,' said Roz. 'Is it far?'

He raised his eyebrows. 'You've never been?'

141

Roz looked intrigued. 'No, should I have?'

He gave her a sympathetic smile. 'Everyone should visit Blacklers at least once in their life, or so Alan and Bill say, but I guess you haven't because of who you've been living with. I daresay the only time they'll ever have gone in, is to see if they can steal something.' Taking her arm in his, he began to lead the way into town.

'I don't think they'd bother going into a cake shop just to steal—' Roz began before Felix put her straight.

'Blacklers is a huge department store; the restaurant is only a small part of it. They sell fancy jewellery, things for your home, dresses, anything and everything you can think of.'

'Ah,' said Roz, nodding wisely, 'that makes more sense. The Haggartys have got a real reputation around Liverpool; I can't see the staff letting the likes of them in.'

'True.'

He walked her over to an impressive-looking building and led her inside.

Roz gazed in wonder at the beautiful chandeliers which hung from the ceiling. 'I've not been anywhere like this since we left Germany.' She leaned forward to examine an intricate glass ornament in the shape of a swan and saw the female sales assistant give her a sideways look of disapproval as she served another customer. Roz felt quite annoyed at this unprovoked judgement until she glanced down at her attire. Dungarees, plimsolls with no socks, and a jumper which had been patched and knitted back together so many times, it had lost most of its shape. Feeling a wave of humiliation engulf her, she spoke hastily to Felix. 'Can we go?'

Felix looked surprised. 'Don't you like it here?'

Roz glanced shyly around her. 'Yes, but,' she looked pointedly at her clothes, 'I think I might be a tad underdressed.'

His brow creasing ever further, Felix looked around to see the reason for Roz's sudden insecurity, and caught the woman serving behind the counter subjecting Roz to a long, disapproving look. 'I see,' he said softly.

'You can't blame her,' Roz hissed. 'She's right in thinking I don't belong in here, because I don't. I haven't got two pennies to rub together.'

'It's a free country,' said Felix, 'and whilst you might not have money to spend, I have.' Sliding his arm out of Roz's, he took her hand and led her to the restaurant. 'Let's have a cuppa and an iced bun. I bet the folk in the restaurant won't be so snooty.'

Roz didn't want to go, but neither did she want to disappoint Felix, so she allowed him to take her through. It was odd, because had she been on her own, or with Mabel, she reckoned she would have turned around and walked straight out, but Felix made her feel as though she had as much right to be there as anyone else, and that it didn't matter how she looked.

They shared a pot of tea, and Felix treated them to an iced bun each. He had been right when he said the women in the restaurant wouldn't be so snooty, as they'd hardly given Roz a second glance.

'I bet you did things like this with your parents all the time back in Frankfurt,' said Felix.

Roz licked the icing from her fingers before replying. 'Every day after school my mother would take me to Sophia's, a café on the corner of our street; it sold the most delicious cakes and milkshakes.' She smiled wistfully. 'We would buy a loaf of bread, or buns, or whatever Mum needed, and on a Friday, to celebrate the end of another school week, Mum would treat me to a chocolate milkshake and a pastry of my choice.'

'Do you think you'll ever go back there? Once it's all over, I mean?'

She shook her head sadly. 'The Nazis, Kristallnacht ...' she placed the remainder of her bun back onto the plate, '... they were forced out, nothing left, and no one's seen the Abrahams – they were the owners – since.'

'Perhaps they tried to escape, like you and your family?' Felix suggested.

'Maybe,' agreed Roz, before polishing off the rest of her bun. Feeling fuller than she had in a long time, she gazed around her. Blacklers was very much like many of the department stores she once knew in Frankfurt, or at least how they used to be before the soldiers and their dominating presence took over. 'They've got no idea, have they?' she said, looking at their fellow diners. 'What it's like to live under the Nazi regime, I mean.'

Felix followed her gaze to a group of women, chattering away and laughing happily. 'Let's hope they never do,' he said solemnly, before turning his attention back to Roz. 'They're lucky, and I don't know what will happen to our friends or family, but I do know that I'm very grateful to be here, with you.'

Roz blushed a little. 'Me too, and stuff that silly sales-woman. I've dealt with Nazi soldiers, so the likes of her don't even register,' adding, 'or at least, not when you're with me.'

He grinned at her. 'That's how it should be. Ignore the ones who look down their noses at you, their opinion is worthless.' He drained the last of the tea in his cup and stood up. 'Ready?'

Roz nodded. 'This has been lovely, Felix, thank you.'

Taking her arm in his, he placed his hand over hers. 'My pleasure. We'll have to do this more often, and next time you come it won't be in dungarees but a pretty frock.'

Her brow furrowed with uncertainty. 'I haven't got a pretty frock.'

He patted her hand. 'You will have. Come on, I'll take you to the market on Great Charlotte Street.'

Roz shook her head. 'There's no point. How will I explain to the Haggartys where I got it from? Besides, Callum'll only make me hand it over and go and sell it down the pub.'

Felix stuck his chin out in a determined manner. 'No, they won't! Because I'm coming back with you, and I shall tell them that I bought it for you, and if they even think about taking it from you, they'll have me to answer to!'

Roz looked doubtful. 'I appreciate what you're saying, but Callum's not the sort to scare easily, and I wouldn't want to see it comes to blows over a dress.'

'You could always keep it at mine, or at Mabel's. I'm sure she wouldn't mind.'

Roz placed her hand over his. 'I'm fine as I am, Felix, honestly I am. If there's one thing I've learned today, it's not to care what others think, and you taught me that.'

'I really don't mind—'

She shook her head decidedly. 'I'm not embarrassed about who I am, and my clothes shouldn't be a reflection on that. Besides, I rather like having you and Mabel as my little secret, something the Haggartys know nothing of.'

Felix looked down at her, his eyes twinkling affectionately. 'I think I like the idea of being your secret! Makes me feel special.'

'You *are* special!' Roz cried. 'Goodness me, Felix, you've been with me since the beginning of our journey. You're the only one who knows what it's like to flee your home and country just so that you might be safe ...' she cradled his hand in hers, '... and you're the only one who knows what it's like to have family still in Germany, and that makes you very special indeed.'

When Roz had begun to tell Felix how special he was to her, he had hoped she was going to say that he was special in the romantic sense of the word, but as she continued to speak it became apparent – to Felix at any rate – that Roz saw him as nothing more than a friend. Albeit a very good one who had experienced the same traumas as herself. He sighed inwardly. Sometimes, when people are thrown together through a twist of fate, things can become so intense that a deep-rooted friendship forms, similar to having a sibling. We came together at the wrong time, he thought dejectedly. Roz will only ever see me as an older brother. He sighed audibly. She might never see him the same way he saw her, but he was still determined to look after her.

Hearing him sigh, Roz looked up expectantly. 'What's up?'

'Just mulling over what life could have been like had we met under different circumstances.'

She shrugged complacently. 'We wouldn't. I lived in Frankfurt, you in Berlin. Had it not been for the Nazis, our paths would most likely have never crossed.'

Typical, thought Felix: no matter which way he looked at it, the woman he loved was always going to be out of his reach. It obviously wasn't meant to be.

Roz watched Felix deep in thought. She wondered whether his silence was a result of her rejecting his offer to buy her a frock. She hoped not, as the last thing she wanted to do was cause offence, and she meant it when she said he had taught her to not be bothered by what others thought, but in truth, she also felt as though she were taking advantage of him. When they had been at Dovercourt, she had begun to suspect that Felix had fond feelings for her, but since seeing him again in Liverpool, she felt as though things had changed, not from Felix's point of view, but from hers. She might say she wasn't bothered about what others thought, and that, to a certain extent, was true, but she was still embarrassed for Felix to see her as she was now. True, he knew it wasn't her choice, but she felt as though it showed a weakness on her part, that she might not be the woman he once thought her to be. A beggar, she thought – no matter how much she dressed it up, that's what she had turned into, and whilst Roz did not regret swallowing her pride in order to try to find her parents, there was still a small part of her that thought she should have tried harder to find an alternative; just what, she couldn't say. Looking at Felix, another thought occurred to her. Perhaps he had offered to buy her the frock because deep down he was embarrassed to be seen out with her? She instantly chided herself. Felix wasn't like that. After all, the first time he had met Roz she hadn't exactly looked her best having just being thrown from a moving vehicle. *Too much on your plate*, she thought to herself. *You need to concentrate on one thing at a time, and let everything else sort itself out.* Besides, if Felix remained true to his word, and she had no doubt that he would, he was going to find somewhere for the two of them to live once he'd turned eighteen, and he wouldn't have made that suggestion had he had any romantic thoughts towards her, he was too much of a gentleman for that. She nodded slowly to herself. He might have been keen on her in Dovercourt, but things had certainly changed since then.

When Roz returned to Crooked Lane later that evening, she wasn't surprised to find that Suzie was in a foul mood, far worse than normal, but refusing to tell her grandmother why. Roz was pretty sure she knew the answer was the missing necklace, but of course she couldn't say so. Instead she watched Suzie with mild amusement as the other girl pouted, huffed and sulked the evening away. As they got into bed that night, Roz watched Suzie carefully, to see if she checked her pillowcase, and when she didn't Roz smiled. She was right in her assumption that Suzie had already checked and found the jewellery missing. Well, it served her right. Suzie had taken what wasn't hers in the first place, and now she was having to suffer in silence. *Now she knows what it's like to live with people you can't trust*, Roz thought with smug satisfaction.

Suzie was feeling far from smug. Her grandmother had been in a vile mood ever since being called out to the non-existent accident, and Suzie now thought it might be all down to her own actions. She would love to spill the beans on Roz, but she couldn't without admitting she had kept an item of value from her grandmother and father, who would believe Suzie worse than Roz for holding out on them. She longed to tell them that Roz was not all that she appeared, and that she believed Roz had asked her friends to help retrieve the necklace, but again, she was unable to do so. She had briefly wondered whether her father or grandmother had found the necklace, but knew that if this was the case, they would have given her a clip round the ear for not handing it over, believing she had either found or stolen it. As they had been getting ready for bed, Suzie was certain that Roz was trying to swallow a smile. *I'll get my own back*, Suzie thought bitterly, *and then she'll be sorry she ever messed with the Haggartys*!

September 1939
Roz sat on the steps outside Mabel's family home hugging her legs close to her chest, staring at the entrance to the court. Mabel and her family were attending

church like they did every Sunday, but this Sunday they were staying on to hear the announcement by Neville Chamberlain.

Six months had passed since the incident with Roz's necklace and little had changed at the Haggartys', save that Suzie had doubled her efforts to get rid of Roz, her latest being that Roz was German and that they were living with the enemy. Callum had taken no notice of his daughter until she said that the people in the market might feel differently if war was declared.

'Handouts to a Kraut?' she taunted. 'I reckon they'd rather slit their own throats first! You mark my words, they'll turn their backs on her and us, and if people decide they don't want a Nazi delivering their coal, they can easily get it elsewhere.'

Roz had had to bite her tongue harder than she ever had before. The temptation to point out that the people of Liverpool had already turned their backs on the Haggartys well before Roz had arrived on the scene was almost overwhelming, but she knew there was no point. Suzie was ignorant; the only reason she wanted Roz out of their home was jealousy and spite.

Now, Roz got up and massaged the life back into her backside. Cold stone steps do not make comfortable seats. She looked to where Mabel and her family were walking through the alley. She raised a hopeful eyebrow, but the look on Mabel's face said it all.

Roz's heart sank. 'Is that it, then?'

Mabel nodded morosely. 'They wouldn't get out of Poland, so we're at war.' She turned to her mother who was chatting with one of the neighbours. 'Is it alright if I go with Roz to see Felix?'

Nodding, her mother waved a hand to acknowledge Roz's presence. 'Mind you take a bit of toast or summat, else you'll not have owt to eat 'til tea.'

'Thanks, Mam.' Mabel ushered Roz inside and into the kitchen, then grabbed the loaf of bread which sat in the middle of the table and cut a thick slice, glancing at Roz she raised an enquiring eyebrow. 'Fancy a slice?'

Roz nodded. 'Yes, please, I've not had anything since last night ...' She shook her head as Mabel pulled a disapproving face. 'Not because of the Haggartys but because I've not been able to eat; I've been too worried about this announcement.' She slumped into a chair. 'I've got no hope of my parents coming over now.'

Mabel pulled a face. 'I'm afraid you're probably right. They're not going to let people cross the Channel willy-nilly.' She handed Roz a toasting fork and the two girls knelt in front of the fire, gently warming their bread. 'What do you reckon the Haggartys will say when they find out?'

Roz shrugged. 'Callum won't care unless the business suffers, Suzie will be in her element – she's already started making the Hitler salute whenever I walk in the room –' she rolled her eyes, 'and Lilith will want me gone.'

Mabel examined her toast before placing it back over the smouldering coals. 'How can Suzie be so bloody stupid? Doesn't she know anything?'

'She doesn't care,' said Roz simply. 'She never liked me much before, but after that business with my necklace she's been more determined than ever to get me

151

out, and this is the best chance she's got.' She handed her toast to Mabel for her to butter.

'Now we're at war, you might be able to leave the Haggartys and find work in one of the factories,' suggested Mabel. 'I'd certainly give it a go if I didn't already have a job.'

'Thanks,' said Roz, as Mabel handed her back the slice of buttered toast, 'but do you really think they'll want to hire someone with a German accent to make their bombs?'

Looking slightly embarrassed, Mabel giggled. 'When you put it like that, maybe not, which is silly because you'd do anything to get rid of Hitler.'

'I know,' said Roz, speaking thickly through a mouthful of toast, 'but others might not see it that way, and I don't blame them.'

'Well, at least the folk down the market and around here know better,' said Mabel, licking her fingers free of butter and toast crumbs.

Roz got to her feet and rinsed her fingers in the sink. 'I wouldn't bet on it,' she said. 'Back home, in Frankfurt, friends and neighbours that we'd known all our lives turned their backs on us. If they can do it, so can the folk round here.'

'I'd like to think not,' said Mabel. 'Come on, let's go and see Felix.'

Roz followed Mabel out of the court and together the girls walked towards the Scottie. 'I wonder if he's heard,' mused Roz.

'Oh, he'll know alright, because this is going to affect everything, especially the dockers and carters. The shipping routes will have to change, and not only that, but they'll want the men to go and fight,' Mabel said knowledgeably.

Roz gasped. 'Not Felix!'

Mabel waved back at a couple walking down the opposite side of the road. 'I shouldn't think so, he's too young. They'll want the men to fight, not boys.'

Roz frowned in annoyance. 'He's not a boy!'

Mabel waved her hands in a placating manner. 'I meant he's not old enough. They'll want men who are old enough to join up, and Felix isn't eighteen yet.'

Roz quickly apologised for her outburst. 'Sorry. I suppose I'm a little tetchy because I'm worried about him.'

Mabel gave a nonchalant shrug. 'Don't worry, it's a hard time for all of us. Mam's worried the men in our family might get called up, but that won't happen 'cos they're all in reserved occupations, thank God.' She eyed Roz. 'If it's any consolation, I don't think they'll send Felix off to war whether he's old enough or not, because of his accent.'

Roz had had another thought, which chilled her to the bone. 'What if they send him back?' she said, her voice just above a whisper. 'What if they send us all back?'

Mabel looked horrified. 'They wouldn't do that! You're refugees. They wouldn't,' she repeated, her voice fading doubtfully.

'People do strange things when they're scared,' said Roz. 'I know what the Nazis are like, and believe me, people have good reason to fear them.'

As they hurried towards Felix's house, Roz was pleased to see that he was outside chatting to Alan, who waved a hand as he saw the girls approaching.

'Have you heard?' Alan asked, taking the cigarette he had been rolling and placing it between his lips.

Both girls nodded.

'What's going to happen, Alan?' said Roz.

He took a deep drag of the cigarette before blowing the smoke out in a series of rings. When he had finished, he glanced at the three of them. 'I reckon it's not good news for any Germans living in Britain,' he said pragmatically, 'but at least you kids came over official like. You've got all your documents, and a good reason for being here, and of course your age goes for you.'

Roz let out a sigh of relief. 'So we'll be alright? They're not going to ask us to leave?'

He shook his head, although Roz noticed he did so hesitantly. 'It's still early days, but I can't see them doing that, not with you kids, though they might with some of the older ones. I suppose it'll depend on the individual. I will say this, though, you're damned lucky you came over when you did, because there won't be any more refugees let out of Germany now we're at war with them.' Although he couldn't possibly have known it at the time, Alan had hit the nail on the head, for the children aboard the last train to leave Germany on the 3rd of September were sent to Prague.

Roz couldn't help wondering whether her parents would have been sent back had they made it to Britain. She'd like to hope not, but who knew? She turned to Felix. 'What about you, how do you feel?'

He rubbed a hand across the back of his neck. 'Nervous, I think we'd be fools not to. We know how people can change their feelings towards you, and whilst I know Alan and Bill would never do that, some of the lads down the docks might.'

'What will happen if they do?' said Roz, anxiously eyeing Alan.

He sucked hard on the last of his cigarette before throwing it to the ground and grinding it under his heel. 'Then they can ruddy well go take a flyin' jump,' he said gruffly. 'Ain't no one goin' to tell me who I can or cannot hire, but I don't think it'll come to that. The lads trust Felix because Coconut does.'

Mabel couldn't help herself: she burst into laughter. 'You mean they'll take the word – or rather, the feelings – of a horse over another human?'

He nodded seriously. 'Animals can sense whether a person is a wrong 'un or not, and Coconut took to our Felix straight off the bat.'

Mabel grinned at Felix. 'Never mind a seal of approval, looks like you've got the hoof of approval.'

Alan clapped a hand down on Felix's shoulder. 'I'll leave you youngsters to it.' Bidding the girls goodbye he disappeared into the house.

Felix turned to Roz. 'How have the Haggartys taken the news?'

'I don't know,' she admitted. 'I've not seen them yet, but I reckon Suzie'll probably be crowing from the rooftops as she'll see it as a good opportunity to get me out of the house.'

'I can't see Callum chucking you out,' said Felix. 'He'll be busier than ever now that war's been declared.'

Roz frowned. 'How do you work that one out? From where I'm standing, people won't be giving anything away for free any more because of rationing.'

'Black market,' said Felix simply. 'For people like Callum, war can be an opportunity to make money at the expense of others.'

'That's Callum to a T,' said Mabel. 'he's a spiv ...'

'He's a what?' giggled Roz, who had never heard the word before.

'It's someone who deals in the black market, a criminal if you will, who sells stolen goods and stuff like that. Everyone knows Callum sells hooky gear when he's deliverin' the coal.' Mabel continued thoughtfully, 'What with the war, he'll have more customers than he had before, which means he'll be too busy to drive the lorry, and seeing as Lilith's too old to do any of that stuff, and Suzie's too stupid,' she nodded at Roz, 'he'll want you to do it.'

'Drive the lorry?' exclaimed Roz.

'Why not?' said Felix. 'It doesn't look that hard.' He gave her an encouraging smile. 'You'd soon pick it up, no problem.'

Roz looked flattered. 'I must say, it would be fun. Do you think Mr Partington would approve?'

Mabel laughed. 'He won't know! Callum's not that stupid; he'll drive the lorry out of the yard to the first customer, then after that it'll be up to you.'

'What'll happen to me if I get caught driving a lorry containing black market goods?' Roz asked anxiously.

Mabel waved a dismissive hand. 'Nowt. Everyone knows it'll be all down to Callum, these things always are.'

'Only she's German,' Felix pointed out, 'and that might not look so good.'

Roz held her hands up. 'Hold on, hold on, we don't even know if Felix is right. We could be worrying over nothing!'

Mabel grinned. 'Suzie would be mad as fire if she thought you were going to drive the lorry instead of her.'

Despite the possibility of getting caught out by the police, Roz couldn't help but smile. It would be lovely to see Suzie squirm when Callum handed Roz the responsibility instead of her. Suzie could have welcomed Roz into her home and befriended her, but she'd made up her mind that she didn't like her before getting to know her, even stealing the last memento she had from her parents. If Callum asked Roz to drive the lorry, she would say yes, not to help him out, but to annoy Suzie!

December 1939

They were three months into the war, and so far very little had changed. As suspected, a lot of Germans living in Britain had been interned as enemy aliens, but not Felix or Roz – much to Suzie's disappointment.

'Madness!' she had exclaimed as Roz took her place behind the wheel of the lorry. 'They should've locked you and all them in Dovercourt up and thrown away the key! I bet all them what come over on the trains are Nazis – it's their way of sneaking them into the country under false pretences. They probably train them young over there, and we all know about the parachuting nuns in jackboots.'

Just as Roz's previous discussions with Felix and Mabel had predicted, Callum had seen the declaration of war as a nice little earner, and he had hit the ground running, getting Roz behind the wheel of the lorry that very same day and teaching her how to drive, something which Suzie had objected to strongly, but as Callum had pointed out, Roz's feet could easily reach the pedals whereas Suzie might struggle. Not only that, but he had said he wanted Roz up front and out of the way where she couldn't interfere with his dealings. As they knew she would, Suzie had put up a fight, saying that driving the lorry was fun whereas standing round keeping a lookout for scuffers was boring. This comment alone had awarded her a clip round the ear off her father, who stated that if he couldn't trust her to keep her mouth shut, he could hardly trust her to drive the lorry.

Now, as Roz waited for Callum to give her the signal to move on, she watched Suzie with mild amusement. It was clear from Suzie's tone of voice that she didn't believe herself to be in any danger from Roz, and had only brought the matter up because winter was now upon them and she had no desire to stand around in the freezing cold acting as a lookout for her father whilst Roz sat in the comfort of the cab which was warm and cosy.

Before Roz had a chance to reply, Callum, who had noticed two policemen turn the corner of the road, hissed through his teeth. 'I told you to keep an eye out for scuffers but you're too busy bloody arguing!' He hastily stuffed the tins of fruit he was about to deliver back between the sacks of coal.

158

Suzie muttered something about the best Christmas present she could have would be to see Roz behind bars, which made Roz laugh.

'Why would they arrest me?' Staring fixedly at the other girl who had come nearer the front of the cab to keep an eye on the policemen, Roz leaned forward out of Callum's hearing. 'I'm not the thief around here.'

A glint appeared in Suzie's eye. 'Are you calling my dad a thief?'

'If the cap fits!' said Roz. 'Or does he have a receipt for any of that stuff?'

Suzie glowered at her. 'My dad does those what can't afford stuff a favour. If it weren't for him, they'd have nowt.'

'It goes against the war effort,' said Roz. 'He's helping the Germans.'

'That should please you, then,' said Suzie churlishly.

Hearing Callum thump the top of the cab, which was his signal for Roz to move on, Roz put the lorry into gear and pulled away quickly, grinning at Suzie who was getting left behind. 'You really don't know anything, do you, Suzie?' she called out. 'I must say I rather envy you. It must be lovely to be so ignorant.'

Without fear of consequence, Suzie ran and jumped onto the running board. Leaning through the open window, she grabbed the steering wheel, pulling it hard over.

'What are you doing?' cried Roz, desperately trying to get the vehicle back on course whilst applying the brakes. There was a muffled scream as Callum, who had been sorting through his wares, fell from the back of the lorry.

Suzie looked petrified. 'He's going to go mental!' she squealed.

Roz pulled a carefree face. 'You shouldn't've pulled the steering wheel ...' She fell silent as a furious-looking Callum appeared next to Suzie.

'What the bloody hell do you think you're playing at?' he roared. 'You could've killed me.'

Suzie pointed a trembling finger at Roz. 'It was her, she called you a thief, said you ...'

'I did not!' protested Roz. 'I called *you* a thief. It was you who assumed I was talking about your father!'

'Enough!' roared Callum. Grabbing Suzie by the neck of her jumper, he hauled her off the running board so hard she slipped as her feet touched a patch of black ice. 'If the two of you don't learn to keep your mouths shut, I'll ...' His voice was trembling with rage.

'You'll what?' asked Roz, much to Suzie's horror.

His jaw flinched as he tried to get a hold on his temper. 'I've had enough of the pair of you, allus taking snipes at each other, and now this!' He indicated his trousers which were covered in some kind of liquid.

Resisting the urge to laugh, Roz challenged Suzie. 'It was your fault, you were the one who pulled the wheel ...'

Callum had had more than enough for one day. He stared fixedly at Roz. 'If I tell the authorities that I have reason to doubt your being here, and that I've seen you talking to folks you shouldn't ...'

Roz spluttered a laugh of disbelief. 'You?' she said, her tone incredulous. 'Go to the scuffers? Do me a favour! You're the last person who'd turn to the police, and even if you did, I'm sure they'd be interested to hear about your little side ...'

Callum seized Roz by the neck and pulled her over the seats towards him, then struck her across her cheek with the back of his hand. 'Don't threaten me!' he hissed viciously. 'I don't have to put up with women that don't do as they're told, and *you* are beginning to get on my nerves. I don't have to put a roof over your head, and you won't get anywhere else, not with that accent.' He heaved an impatient sigh. 'You're getting to be more trouble than you're worth, and as I can't be asked wondering what trouble your gob is capable of creating, let's make this simple, shall we? One more word out of your mouth which displeases me, and you'll be joining the rest of the filth in the Mersey, do I make myself clear?'

Roz's instinct was to push him away, to tell him to take his hands off her, but there was a murderous glint in Callum's eye that she'd never seen before and it had scared her into silence, so she nodded feebly.

'Good!' said Callum. Pushing himself off Roz with one hand, he cuffed Suzie round the back of her head with the other. 'You can sit in the back with me.'

Suzie opened her mouth to complain that it would be cold and uncomfortable, then changed her mind. Today was not the day to question her father.

Roz was glad that Suzie had been banished to the back of the lorry because it meant she could allow the tears to flow, and she didn't want Callum or Suzie to know how much he had scared her. Showing a sign of weakness would be a very bad idea indeed with people like the Haggartys.

Hastily wiping the tears from her cheeks, she pushed the lever into gear and gently pressed her foot against the accelerator until the wheels of the lorry stopped spinning and gained traction on the tarmac beneath the ice. Snow had started to fall, so she turned the wiper blades on to clear the windscreen.

As the lorry trundled forward she looked at the houses around her. It wasn't an affluent area and people tended to buy their coal by the scuttleful, or individual lumps, rather than a sack, but every house on the street had made an effort to bring some cheer to the festive period. Fires burned in the grates, causing a warm glow which glinted off the coloured glass baubles and strings of gold and silver tinsel hung from the branches of even the poorest looking Christmas trees.

Thinking of Suzie sitting on top of the coal in the back of the lorry, Roz felt a small pang of pity for the girl. She imagined it couldn't be easy being Callum's daughter. He never showed her any sign of affection, far from it. He was cold and unloving, the complete opposite of Roz's father who doted on his daughter.

Roz wondered whether it had been any different when Suzie's mother had been around, but then thought probably not. Callum ruled the roost in the Haggarty house; he obviously had no respect for women.

Callum banged the top of the cab with his fist, indicating Roz should pull over. She slid down from the driver's seat and carefully made her way up the path to one of their customer's houses. She rapped her

162

knuckles against the door and waited for someone to answer. The door swung open and a child of no more than five years old stood before her, a black scuttle gripped firmly in his hand. He beamed up at her. 'Merry Christmas, Miss Coalman! Mam says only half full, please.'

Roz smiled down at him. 'Merry Christmas to you too, Jimmy.' Taking the scuttle from his unresisting fingers, she made her way back to the lorry, climbed in and filled it half full. She was about to jump back down when she glanced at Jimmy. He was hopping from toe to toe and rubbing his arms in an effort to keep warm. She might not have a good Christmas herself, but she'd be damned if she'd see a child go cold. Glancing around to make certain that neither Callum nor Suzie were looking in her direction, she quickly filled the scuttle as well as stuffing some coal into the pockets of her dungarees. Once she'd climbed down from the lorry, she followed little Jimmy through into the back of the house. Passing through the parlour, she noted the fireplace which stood empty. The house itself might be cold, but the bright decorations and the cheerful characters that lived within its walls brought their own kind of warmth.

'Miss Coalman's bringin' the coal through, Mammy, we can warm us toes now.'

A merry-looking woman with hair pulled tightly into a bun greeted Roz.

'I swear it doesn't last as long as it used to,' she sighed as Roz set the scuttle down and waited for payment. 'And I daresay things'll only get worse now we're fightin' the Hun.' Remembering that Roz was German, she hastily apologised. 'I don't include you in that statement, luv, yous not like them Nazis.' She hesitated as her eyes fell onto the full scuttle of coal. 'Jimmy! I said only half . . .' She looked at Roz who was holding a finger to her lips.

'I'm certain they won't miss a few extra lumps, and I won't tell if you won't,' Roz said, a half-smile twitching the corner of her mouth.

'I don't want you getting in any trouble,' said the older woman, looking past Roz to the Haggartys outside.

Roz took the payment for half a scuttle. 'Don't you worry about me, Mrs Gardener, I can take care of myself.' As she made her way back through the house she nipped over to the grate, pulled the coal from her pockets and placed it inside, something which did not go unnoticed by Jimmy's mother.

'God bless you,' she said, a tear forming in her eye. 'You can tell you're no relation to them Haggartys.'

Roz stood up from the fireplace. 'I'm glad to hear it, and as for the coal, believe me, they won't miss one or two lumps,' she said, wiping her fingers absent-mindedly on her dungarees. Roz knew this was true, because Callum was always siphoning coal which should have gone to the customers to sell to his associates down the Pig and Whistle. He was always careful never to take too much, maybe a couple of lumps from each sack, but it soon mounted up to what was probably a hefty profit when sold as a backhander.

She left the house and made her way to the next one.

*

164

Being Jewish, Roz and her family didn't celebrate Christmas, but that hadn't meant she didn't enjoy going round to her friends' houses, where she would help put up their decorations and enjoy the delicious treats, whilst singing festive songs.

The Haggartys didn't celebrate Christmas either, but not because of their religion. They were a mean, miserable family who had, in Callum's own words, 'no time for such childish nonsense'. Last year Roz's Christmas had been dull and lifeless, but with friends like Mabel and Felix, she already knew that this year was going to be different and had jumped at the chance to help decorate the Johnsons' tree. Roz couldn't remember when she had last had so much fun. The family had taught her the words to the carols they were singing, and she very much enjoyed feeling part of Mabel's family.

When they had finished there, she and Mabel went to see Felix, who was giving Alan and Bill a hand hanging paper chains along the picture rails. The girls had joined in and Mabel had offered to sit on Alan's shoulders rather than use the ladders, reasoning this would be faster, although every time Alan moved Mabel would squeal, followed by a fit of the giggles, which the others found contagious, and Bill wagered they'd have been far quicker using the ladders.

When they eventually pinned the last chain in place Felix asked the girls if they'd like to help him decorate Coconut's harness with tinsel. They jumped at the chance and enjoyed this the most.

Going back to the Haggartys' after that had been soul-destroying and now, as Roz filled yet another scuttle, she vowed that no matter what happened, this would be her last Christmas at Crooked Lane.

It was Christmas Day and Roz was on her way to meet Felix. Since his arrival in Liverpool she had not managed to see him very often, mainly because of the long hours he worked down the docks, but also because of the demands placed on her by the Haggartys. So busy was their work life, they were rarely free at the same time, but with neither of them working Christmas Day, they had agreed that no matter what, they would spend the day together. She had risen early as usual and made herself some breakfast, then slipped out whilst the Haggartys were still fast asleep.

Determined that she would see both her friends on Christmas Day, Roz now made a slight detour. She had half expected that she would need to be quiet when calling on Mabel, but to her delight she entered the court to find it a hive of activity. It seemed the residents were as excited about Christmas as Roz herself. Many of them had gathered in the courtyard and they were sharing food and drink, and the air was filled with laughter. Seeing Roz approach, Mabel waved her over.

'Merry Christmas!' she called, handing Roz an iced bun.

'Iced buns for breakfast?' said Roz, her voice muffled by the sticky treat.

'Why not?' said Mabel. 'If we can't spoil ourselves at Christmas, when can we? Besides, it's not as if we've money to burn.' She waved a vague arm at the people around her. 'We can't afford fancy prezzies, but between us we can make a banquet fit for a king – as long as he likes pasties and jam sarnies – and what better way to spend the day than sharing it with your family and friends?'

'I think it's marvellous!' said Roz, as someone pressed a glass of lemonade into her hand. 'The Haggartys are still in bed, the miserable so-and-sos, and when they do get up I doubt they'll do much more than sulk and whine the day away until Callum and Lilith head down the pub like they did last year.' She pushed her hand into the pocket of her dungarees and pulled out a small package which she handed to Mabel. 'Merry Christmas, Mabel.'

Her friend's face was a picture of astonishment as she carefully removed the wrapping, and her face split into a wide smile when she drew out the bar of chocolate from within. Flinging her arms around Roz's neck, she kissed her on the cheek. 'Thanks, Roz! It's my favourite!' A thought suddenly occurred to her. 'Only … how … ?'

Blushing, Roz glanced shyly at those who had stopped to look. 'How did I afford it when the Haggartys don't pay me? I was given it by the lady who runs the tobacconist's.'

Mabel shook her head. 'You shouldn't have given it to me, Roz. You never have anything of your own, so to give away the only thing that was yours …'

'I want you to have it because you're my bezzie, and I want you to be happy.' Roz giggled. 'And I know chocolate will make you happy.'

Mabel clasped Roz's hand in hers. 'Thank you so much, and you're right, chocolate makes me very happy!' She opened the chocolate and broke two pieces off, one of which she handed to Roz. 'Wait here, I won't be a mo.'

Roz allowed the piece of chocolate to melt slowly in her mouth whilst Mabel disappeared into her house only to reappear a few moments later with a small package. 'It's the only thing I could think of that the Haggartys wouldn't nick off you.'

A frown furrowing her brow, Roz opened the package and burst into laughter. 'Soap!'

Mabel beamed. 'I know Callum takes the laundry soap, but I doubt he'd manage to shift rose-scented soap down the pub, not to those great hairy men he drinks with.'

'You clever girl!' said Roz. 'And if they ask where I got it from, I shall say a friend! That ought to set the cat amongst the pigeons!'

'You don't half like to stir things up,' chuckled Mabel. 'I don't think I'd want to antagonise the Haggartys.'

Roz looked around to see if she could see a clock anywhere. 'I don't suppose you know what time it is?'

'We've a clock on the mantel,' Mabel told her.

Following Mabel into the house, Roz bade Mabel's brothers, Robin and Richard, who were sitting at the kitchen table, a merry Christmas.

'Blimey, don't say the Haggartys have let you out to enjoy yourself?' asked Robin, his tone a mixture of sarcasm and surprise. 'Wonders will never cease.'

'Not exactly let me out,' Roz confessed, 'considering they're still asleep.'

He winked at her. 'That's the way. Where's that pal of yours – Felix, isn't it?'

'I'm going to his now,' said Roz. 'We thought we'd go for a walk to Princes Park, see if anybody's singing carols, enjoy a bit of Christmas spirit.'

'You can bring him here if you like,' said Robin. 'The more the merrier, isn't that right, Mabel?'

Mabel nodded enthusiastically. 'Oh, please say you will! He'll really enjoy it. After lunch we all get together and play blind man's buff, Duck Duck Goose, musical chairs, all sorts of parlour games.'

'Sounds like great fun, and I know Felix will be up for it. I did say I'd have my Christmas lunch at Bill and Alan's, but I can't see why we couldn't come after that.' She glanced at the clock. 'Although I'd best get a move on.'

Giving a small whoop of joy, Mabel followed Roz out of the door. 'Don't forget to come back with Felix – Bill and Alan too, if they fancy it.'

Roz kissed Mabel on the cheek. 'Thanks, Mabel. This time last year I was dreading the thought of another Christmas with the Haggartys, but you've changed all that.'

Blushing, Mabel waved a dismissive hand. 'Go on, get you gone, and we'll look forward to seeing you later.'

With a spring in her step, Roz headed to Felix's at a brisk pace. She couldn't wait to tell him they'd been invited to a party.

When she arrived at the Scottie, she was pleasantly surprised to see that a few of the residents were out on the streets, much the same as they were in Mercer Court. She knocked briefly on the door before entering and calling out 'Merry Christmas!' as she stepped into the kitchen.

Felix jumped up from his seat, a broad smile etched on his cheeks. 'Merry Christmas to you too!'

Bill laughed knowingly. 'He's been like a cat on a hot tin roof all morning, waiting for you to arrive.'

'Sorry!' said Roz. 'I had to call in at Mabel's first and, well ...' She went on to explain how they had all been invited to the court party after lunch.

Rubbing his hands together enthusiastically, Bill was grinning like a four-year-old. 'I'm a cracker at blind man's buff!' he said, his eyes shining with anticipation. 'Musical chairs too, but I ain't played that in years, and I daresay I'll be a bit slower than I used to be, but it's not allus the hare what wins the race!'

'Duck Duck Goose,' said Alan, shaking his head with a wry smile. 'I remember it well, along with What's the time, Mr Wolf!'

Bill was beside himself with excitement. 'After Chamberlain's announcement I didn't think we'd have much of a Christmas, but this ...' his grin broadened, '... this is the sort of Christmas I remember having when I were knee high to a grasshopper!'

'So you'll come, then?' asked Roz, with a wry smile.

'Yes!' said Bill, before anyone else had a chance to answer.

Felix collected his coat from behind the door. 'If we're to make it to Princes Park and back, we'd best get a wriggle on.'

'Are you sure you don't need a hand with lunch?' said Roz, but Alan shook his head, despite Bill's hopeful face.

'No, we don't, but thank you for the offer.'

Roz waited for Felix to lace his boots, then, bidding the men goodbye, they left for the park.

'What did the Haggartys say?' said Felix as he held his arm out for Roz, who slipped her hand through the crook of his elbow.

Much to his amusement, she did an impression of someone snoring.

'They're still asleep?' Felix laughed. 'I bet they'll wonder where you are when they wake up.'

'Couldn't care less if they do!' said Roz. 'I'm not spending Christmas Day with Suzie whilst Callum and Lilith get bladdered down the pub.'

Felix roared with laughter. 'My word, Miss Sachs, you really are doing well with your English!'

She giggled. 'How proud my mother would be to think that her daughter knew what the word bladdered meant!'

Felix gently squeezed Roz's hand. 'Your mother will be very proud of her daughter, as will your father.'

Roz looked doubtful. 'You still think they're out there somewhere, and not in a camp like your mother?'

He nodded fervently. 'I think you'd have heard something by now if they'd been arrested. No news is good news, as they say.'

She sighed wistfully. 'I hope you're right, Felix, but it's easy to think the worst when you're so far away.'

'You've got to remain positive,' said Felix. He decided to change the subject. 'So tell me about Christmas in Mercer Court – what are they up to?'

'It's a world away from Christmas in Crooked Lane. I think the residents of the courts are marvellous, Felix. Most of them haven't got two pennies to rub together but that doesn't stop them; instead they make Christmas special by sharing what little they do have.'

'I don't know whether you'd call that Christmas or Scouse spirit,' replied Felix.

'A bit of both, I'd say,' said Roz. 'The only spirit the Haggartys have are the ones down the pub.'

'Let's forget about them,' said Felix, 'today is Christmas Day – *our* day!'

They had reached the park, and Roz was delighted to hear a band strike up as they entered the gates. 'Christmas carols!' she exclaimed, as she and Felix headed over to join a group of people surrounding the band.

'Does it remind you of home – before it all went wrong, of course?'

She nodded. 'The only tradition we had was to go and listen to the band playing carols. I used to love the camaraderie, singing with complete strangers, all those happy faces. It hasn't been like that in Frankfurt for years.'

Felix patted her hand. 'At least we can still have a good Christmas.'

As the band struck up 'Good King Wenceslas', Roz and Felix were grateful when someone handed them a piece of paper with the words.

Some twenty minutes later, after having sung their hearts out, they headed back to the Scottie. 'Thanks, Felix.'

'What for?'

'For taking me to the park, and reminding me that life goes on, no matter what.' She glanced anxiously at him. 'What do you think will happen now that Britain is at war with Germany?'

Felix shrugged. 'I know Bill's pretty pessimistic, but I see a difference between the British and Germans.'

She nodded. 'It's their spirit; they're determined that he won't win, no matter the cost.'

Felix heartily agreed. 'They certainly won't go down without a fight, not like the Polish. For God's sake, Hitler just walked straight in, and they didn't do a damned thing to stop him.'

'Be fair, they couldn't!' said Roz. 'It wasn't as if he announced his intentions or gave them a chance to prepare – he just turned up with tanks!'

Felix stopped as they reached the door to his house. 'You're right. For some reason we keep talking about things over which we have no control and I say we stop, so let's forget about the war, the Nazis and the Haggartys and have us some fun.'

Roz nodded and followed him inside, her nostrils flaring as the smell of home cooked food wafted towards them.

The day was one that Roz would never forget. Bill had cooked the most wonderful lunch with all the trimmings, and for pudding they enjoyed jam roly-poly with custard, something that was new to Roz, but she very much liked. After that the men dressed up in their warmest clothes and headed to Mercer Court where they whiled away the afternoon playing games which took Bill back to his childhood.

'I've not seen my father run in years!' said Alan, who had been most surprised and impressed by his father's ability to claim the last remaining chair in the latest game. 'I didn't even know he *could* run any more!'

Roz laughed. 'It's lovely to see Bill having fun.'

'Mam would've loved seeing him have such a good time,' agreed Alan.

Roz regarded him shyly. 'I've not liked to ask before, but what happened to your mum?'

Alan flicked his eyes from his father to Roz. 'Tuberculosis,' he said simply. 'She's been gone a few years now, but there's never a day passes that we don't miss her.'

'What was she like?' asked Roz, who was curious to learn more about the missing piece of Alan and Bill's jigsaw.

'The life and soul, and she'd have loved you,' said Alan. 'Felix, too. Mam loved people, she had a big heart and she wore it on her sleeve.' He laughed as his father did a victory jig after winning the game of musical chairs. 'Daft old sod.'

'He's lovely,' said Roz, 'you're very lucky to have him.'

A sloppy smile on his face, Alan began to walk towards his father. 'They're about to play another game, are you coming?'

They spent the remainder of their time in Mercer Court playing all manner of games until it became too dark to see. Calling it a day, they all headed for home, wishing each other all the best as they went.

'I'll see you home,' said Felix, when Roz announced her toes had started to go numb.

Smiling sweetly, she shook her head. 'There's really no need ...'

But Felix wouldn't take no for answer, so she allowed him to walk her to the corner of Crooked Lane.

'Thanks for giving me such a lovely day,' she said, smiling up at Felix, whose eyes glittered in the moonlight.

'My pleasure,' he said. 'I wish every day could be like today.'

Roz nodded then clapped a hand to her mouth. 'I nearly forgot!' Plunging her hand into her pocket, she withdrew a small bottle of aftershave.

Felix gaped at her. 'Where on earth did you get that from?'

She beamed. 'I've been holding out on the Haggartys. There's a loose floorboard under where they keep the stove; they'd never think of looking there because they never do any cooking. In short, I've done some bartering of my own.'

Felix looked both grateful and anxious. 'I love the aftershave, but I'm not worth the risk.'

Roz smiled up at him. 'I think you are.'

He took something out of his pocket and handed it to her. 'Merry Christmas, Roz.'

She peered into the paper bag, a smile playing on her lips. 'A present that the Haggartys will never find.'

He grinned. 'Not if you eat them before they get the chance.'

She offered him one of the Liquorice Allsorts, but Felix declined. 'I think I'll burst if I eat another morsel!'

Smiling, Roz popped a sweet into her mouth. 'There's *always* room for sweets!'

Felix looked at Roz as she savoured the taste. If he were brave enough he would take her in his arms and kiss her, and he couldn't think of a better time to do so, but doubt clouded his mind. Roz was too dear to lose, and if she spurned his advances what would become of their friendship? Deciding he couldn't take the risk, he kissed her softly on the cheek. 'I've had a wonderful day. We must do it again soon.'

Roz nodded. 'Goodbye, Felix.'

She was just about to leave when Felix suddenly remembered something. 'Wait!'

Roz turned back. In her heart she rather hoped he might find the courage to kiss her more firmly, but he was holding out an envelope for her to take. 'It's a letter from Adele. She sent it with mine seeing as she can't write to you here.'

'Oh, how wonderful!' said Roz. 'Will you please explain that it's difficult for me to write back with no paper or pencils at the Haggartys'?'

He nodded. 'Don't worry, she knows.'

Putting the epistle into her pocket, Roz began to climb up the stairs to the loft, then looked back to see Felix waving to her from the pavement. Waving back, she headed through the door. Inside, Suzie was already in bed, snoring softly, and there was no sign of Callum or Lilith. Roz assumed they must still be down the Pig and Whistle. Glad that she didn't have to face an inquisition, she padded over to the table and pulled Adele's letter from her pocket.

Dear Roz,

I do hope you're having a better Christmas this year. Felix said it was pretty rotten for you last time, which is such a shame as I was really hoping the Haggartys would give you a proper Christmas. As you know, I was really lucky with the family that took me in, and they have a huge tree, so big they have to use ladders to put the star on the top!

Roz continued to read the letter which told of her friend's happiness and her wishes for Roz to get away from the Haggartys sooner rather than later. Once finished, she slipped out of her clothes and got into her bed beside Suzie. She couldn't explain why, but she had a feeling that things were soon going to get better.

It was the summer of 1940 and Hitler had stepped up his bombing campaign. Anyone who lived near docks or train lines lived in constant fear of being bombed. Liverpool had, so far, been lucky, with the main targets being London and the south.

Despite the imminent danger, Callum refused to move his family away from the docks.

'It'll be another false alarm,' he'd snap at Lilith, who invariably complained about the long trek down the rickety steps to the air raid shelter in Mercer Court.

'Then why are we bothering to leave?' Lilith would retort. 'You can't see a damned thing in this blackout – I'm in more danger of breaking me bleedin' neck getting to the air raid shelter than I am of actually getting bombed.'

Callum never bothered to reply – not that he needed to, for Roz knew only too well why they bothered to leave. It was so that Callum could take them down to the shelter, make a big show of ensuring his mother was comfortable, have a good look to see who was already there, then make himself scarce. Often he would use the excuse that he had to keep an eye on the coal to stop would-be looters from helping themselves, which in Roz's opinion was laughable. Not because people weren't looting, but because Callum was one of the ones doing the looting. At first she had only suspected this to be the case, but after hearing a family talking of how they'd been looted the last time they'd had a false air raid, she knew her suspicions were valid.

'Took my gran's mink stole, the thieving blighters!' one woman had told the woman next to her. 'I wouldn't have minded so much, 'cos I can't stand the bloomin' thing, but it meant a lot to me gran. She had it for her weddin' anniversary off me grandad.'

Roz had pricked up her ears. She had come across some sort of animal stole stuffed down beside Callum's bed when she had been sweeping the floor that very morning. It had scared her half to death, and believing it to be a rat, she had given it a severe beating with the broom, until she realised it was already dead. She listened as the woman described the fur in detail, and had come to the conclusion that it had to be the same one.

When the siren had given the all-clear, Roz and the two Haggarty women had returned to their shared abode, and Roz had rather unwisely mentioned the stole to see if Callum would react. He did, and not in a positive manner. He asked her if she had been snooping around his things, which of course Roz denied, but he didn't believe her, and had ended up threatening her with a one-way trip to the Mersey, and the others with a belting should he find them near his things.

Lilith and Suzie had objected to being included in this threat but Callum didn't care. He said he didn't trust any of them, and they were to keep their noses out of his business. From that day on, things had changed. Callum was out of the house far more than he was in, which suited not only Roz, but Lilith and Suzie as well, since life with Callum in the house was like walking on eggshells. If Lilith asked him where he had been, he would snap at her, saying it was none of her business, and she shouldn't question her own son. Suzie rarely spoke to her father, save to ask if he needed her help when he went out, to which he would reply that she would only get under his feet. Roz would have found life much improved, except for the fact that Suzie and Lilith held her responsible for Callum's constant bad mood.

'You shouldn't have accused him of nickin' stuff,' Lilith muttered after a run-in with her son. 'He gets his knickers in a twist at the slightest thing these days and that's down to you.'

Roz looked at the woman in disbelief. 'I never accused him of anything; I just mentioned a conversation I had overheard. If anyone jumped to conclusions it was Callum, not me.'

'You knew full well what you were saying,' said Suzie petulantly. 'You done it on purpose 'cos you knew ...'

'That's enough, Suzie!' snapped Lilith.

'Don't shout at me!' wailed Suzie. 'Everything was fine 'til she come along. We never wanted her, it was you who wanted her 'cos you're a lazy old—'

She had ducked out of the way just as one of Lilith's shoes came careering towards her. 'You nearly had my bleedin' head off!'

Her grandmother spoke through pursed lips. 'If you don't hold your tongue, I'll make sure I don't miss next time.'

As time wore on, things became more and more fractious, with everyone blaming each other for the bad atmosphere. The only escape Roz had was Felix and Mabel, and she made sure she was with them as much as possible.

Now, as Mabel and Roz approached Felix, they were pleased to see that he had finished work early and was already leading Coconut away from the docks. Seeing the girls approach, he grinned at them like the cat that got the cream.

'What's put such a smile on your face?' asked Roz, smiling back.

'I've found a place above the ironmonger's on the Scottie Road. It's perfect, two beds – I'll have the smallest – and it's dry, warm and ours if we want it.'

Roz stared at him, temporarily lost for words, but she quickly found her tongue. 'You mean it?'

He nodded. 'I've spoken to the landlord and explained our circumstances, and he said he doesn't care who moves in as long as they pay the rent on time, and don't make a mess.'

'But I've got no job, not a paid one at any rate...' said Roz doubtfully.

Mabel had been fiddling with some Everton mints which had got stuck to the paper bag they were in, but now she looked up. 'You can start at Mr Woo's as soon as you like. He's got women leavin' left, right and centre to go and work in the munitions factories.' She carefully pulled the paper off one of the sweets before popping it into her mouth and stowing it in the side of her cheek. She offered the bag to the other two, then added, 'Not that I'd fancy workin' in one of them places. Dad says it's ruddy dangerous work, and you turn yellow.'

'Phosphorus,' said Felix as he declined the proffered bag of sweets, 'that's what makes your skin and hair turn yellow; it's also what causes the explosions.'

Roz grimaced. 'Far safer in the laundry, although I wouldn't mind doing my bit if they ask me to.'

'Like joining one of the services?' Mabel asked.

'Yes, if they'd have me,' said Roz, 'but I've a while 'til I'm eighteen and I'd rather hope it would all be over well before then.'

'So are we agreed?' said Felix. 'I can't legally rent until I'm eighteen, but seeing as it's my birthday soon ...'

Roz couldn't stop the smile from creasing her cheeks. 'You really are a marvel, Felix Ackerman.'

He shrugged dismissively. 'You'd do the same for me.'

Mabel nudged Roz in the ribs. 'Are you going to tell the Haggartys or are you goin' to just get up one mornin' and walk out?'

Roz hadn't given this any thought until now. She really didn't care about telling them as she knew they wouldn't be interested if she were to leave. It wasn't as if they'd worry something had happened to her and go to the police and local hospitals, but on the other hand to not go back would be leaving them in the lurch because neither Lilith nor Suzie could drive the lorry. 'I shall tell them I'm leaving so that they have time to sort themselves out. I may not like them, but Lilith is old, and I don't think she could drive the lorry, so they'll have to teach Suzie – either that or Callum will have to give up his little sideline.'

'He won't like that idea,' said Felix. 'If you give notice do you not think they'll make your life hell in the meantime?'

Roz laughed. 'What on earth could they do to make it any worse than it already is? Besides, I should think Suzie and Lilith will be whooping for joy when they hear I'm leaving.'

Felix wasn't so sure. 'They might not like you, but you do a lot of the work. You said yourself that the folk on the market used to give more because it was you doing the asking, and Callum will have his hands full driving the lorry again if you're not there. I think you're worth more to them than you think.'

Mabel crunched her mint with satisfaction before speaking. 'He's right. They'd have chucked you out long since, had you not been needed. The only reason why you get to spend more time with me and Felix is because you can't go scrounging down the market any more.'

'True,' Roz conceded, 'but they can't stop me, and if they do, I'll tell Callum that I know what he's been doing every time the siren sounds – that should change his mind.'

Mabel's eyes grew wide. 'Ooh, I don't think that's a good idea. You know what an evil temper he has when he feels threatened, and he's already said you'll be sleeping with the fishes should you say summat he doesn't like – and he won't like that!'

Felix nodded fervently. 'I think Mabel's right. You start throwing threats around, and he might decide to take you for a dip—'

'Like he did Suzie's mam,' Mabel hissed. She was looking around to make sure no one could overhear her. ''Cos it wouldn't surprise me if she said summat out of turn, and ...' she drew her finger across her throat whilst making a slitting sound.

'Do you really think he murdered her?' Roz asked. 'I know he could quite cheerfully have choked me on more than one occasion, but there's a deal of difference between thinking and doing.'

Mabel looked exaggeratedly around. 'Where is she then?'

This was a good point. No one, including Suzie, from what Roz could gather, knew where her mother was. But surely Suzie and Lilith would have heard or seen something? She said as much to Felix and Mabel.

'And you think Lilith or Suzie would grass him up?' asked Mabel, her tone incredulous. 'Not a chance! If anything, they were probably in on it.'

This was something that Roz refused to believe. 'Maybe Lilith, but not Suzie,' she said determinedly. 'I may not like the girl, but I can't believe she'd have played a hand in covering up her own mother's murder.'

'Unless it was an accident,' said Felix, who had been deep in thought up to this point. 'I mean, say he hit her and that was that? He might not have meant to kill her, but the right punch in the wrong place, and bam, it's all over.'

'Sounds plausible to me,' agreed Mabel. 'You've felt the back of his hand before now, and you said yourself that when he went to strike you before, Lilith turned white, like she was frightened – possibly a case of déjà vu?'

'That's terrible,' whispered Roz. 'Poor Suzie …'

'And she has still had to live with him, knowing what he's done. That must be tough, even if it was an accident,' Mabel added.

'Explains why she didn't want you coming to live with them,' said Felix. 'She was probably jealous that your mum and dad are still together, and fearful that her father – who didn't want you to go there – might lose his temper with you too, only this time it would mean jail because the people of Dovercourt would eventually find out, and that way she'd have lost both parents.'

Roz shook her head sadly. 'Never in a month of Sundays did I think I'd feel sorry for Suzie Haggarty.'

Felix regarded Roz with a concerned frown. 'Don't poke the bear, that's what Alan says. I think you leave with as little fuss as possible, whilst at the same time being reasonable. Tell them you've found somewhere else to live, and that they're expecting you in a few days' time.' He nodded wisely. 'That way, they'll know you've got someone waiting who'll ask questions if you fail to show up.'

'Good idea!' said Mabel approvingly.

'I should have the keys to the flat this Wednesday, which is only three days away, so if you tell them tonight it gives them plenty of time to make alternative arrangements.'

'More than fair,' said Mabel, 'because I'd tell them as I was walking out the door if it were me.'

'Me too,' said Roz, 'but I have to do what's right, if not for me then for Lilith; she's too old to be beggared about.'

'Then that's that settled,' said Felix happily. 'Tell them when you get back, and we'll get everything put into place for Wednesday.' He raised an eyebrow at Mabel. 'I take it Roz will be able to start work at the laundry at a moment's notice?'

She nodded. 'We're desperately short on women as it is. When I first ran the idea past Mr Woo he wanted her to start there and then, so as far as he's concerned the sooner the better.'

'All you have to do now is break the news to the Haggartys,' said Felix. 'I can come with you if you like, for moral support.'

She smiled gratefully. 'I'd love that, but this is some-thing I really should do on my own. Besides, I've stood up to the SS; the Haggartys are nothing in comparison.'

Felix wasn't exactly sure he'd call sitting in stunned silence, standing up to the SS, but if Roz felt that this applied, then he wasn't about to discourage her.

When Roz returned to the Haggartys' later that evening, a hundred thoughts ran through her mind as she stood, her hand poised, ready to push the door open. The first one being, did she really have to tell them before she left? She knew it was the coward's way out, but saying these things with Felix and Mabel standing beside her had seemed a lot easier than facing them on her own, on their turf, as it were. She was still summoning the courage when raised voices coming from within interrupted her thoughts. She cocked an ear. Callum was saying something about the docks, that something had been found there. She was about to enter when all went quiet, and the door swung open.

'Told you someone was spyin' on us ...' said Suzie, with a look of triumph. 'Now do you believe me?'

Glaring at Roz, Callum strode past her and looked outside before pushing her in and slamming the door shut. 'Well?'

Feeling thoroughly confused, Roz blinked at him. 'Well what?'

'How long have you been stood out there listening?'

'Spying,' corrected Suzie with malicious satisfaction.

Roz shook her head. 'I haven't been listening, I was thinking about something else.'

'Liar!' accused Suzie, her voice filled with vengeance. 'Caught in the act, and you can't even come up with a reasonable excuse.'

Having no idea what the Haggartys were talking about, Roz felt it best if she explain why she had been lingering outside. 'If you must know, I was wondering when it would be best to tell you that I was leaving.'

Suzie glanced at her father, a look of disdain etched on her face. 'What a coincidence! You're caught listening in on things that don't concern you, and all of a sudden you're leaving – how convenient!'

Callum hadn't taken his eyes off Roz, and when he spoke his tone was menacing. 'I'll ask you this once, and I want the truth. How long were you out there and what did you hear?'

Roz could feel her heart begin to race in her chest. She really had no idea what they were talking about, but judging by the look on Callum's face it must be something bad, so rather than admit she'd heard some comment about the docks she decided to pretend she'd heard nothing at all.

'I swear I didn't hear a word any of you said,' she stated. 'I'm starting a new job in the laundry on the Scottie Road on Wednesday and I've been offered a new place to live. I knew I'd be leaving you in the lurch, so I was thinking about the best time to tell you so that you had time to prepare.'

'As if you'd give two hoots about dropping us in it!' scoffed Suzie. 'As if anyone would give you a job let alone a place to stay.'

Roz stared at them. She had no idea what to say, and she wished she knew exactly what they had been saying, because at least then they'd all be on the same page. She shrugged helplessly. 'I can only tell you the truth. It's up to you whether you believe me or not.'

Much to Suzie's delight, Callum had caught hold of Roz by her hair, although Lilith quickly leapt to her feet. 'Now, son, take it easy. Let's not go jumping to conclusions.'

The look of fear on the older woman's face frightened Roz more than Callum's reaction. She looked terrified, and after the conversation Roz had just had regarding Suzie's mother, she began to think that Felix's suspicions were true.

But Callum wasn't listening to his mother, and his fist was trembling against the side of Roz's cheek. She would have put it down to anger, but when she looked into his eyes, she could see something she had never seen before in Callum. He was scared. Something her father had said a long time ago entered her mind. *Never approach a dog that's scared. Fear can make them dangerous, so always take a step back and let them come to you.* That was exactly how Callum looked, like a dog which had been cornered and was about to fight for its life. Her heart raced as he hissed in her ear, his voice trembling. 'Maybe you're telling the truth, and I hope for your *boyfriend*'s sake that you are, because if I ever find out you've been spreading lies, it won't be you that suffers, but that horse, the one our Suzie seen you riding like you was Lady Muck. You mess with me, and the only thing he'll be fit for is the knacker's yard, understand?'

A feeling of complete and utter dread filled Roz. She had expected Callum to threaten her, yes, but to hear that he knew all about her time with Felix had come as a massive shock. She managed to look at him from the corner of her eye, and there was no doubt in her mind that he meant every word. Tears pricking her eyes, she nodded and tried to speak but her mouth had gone dry. Still holding her by her hair, he marched her back to the door, opened it and shoved her through.

She heard Lilith emit a scream as she nearly went over the side of the steps.

Ignoring his mother, Callum gave his final warning. 'Don't you forget what I said. Go blabbing and you'll only have yourself to blame for the consequences,' he growled before slamming the door behind her.

Roz didn't need telling twice. Without so much as a backward glance, she ran down the steps and didn't stop running until Crooked Lane was far behind her. As she ran, she wondered where was best to go. Callum had mentioned Felix, but nothing about Mabel – could it be that they knew nothing of their friendship? Or was Callum wary of Mabel's brothers? She noticed he hadn't threatened Felix, but instead focused on a defenceless animal. As for Mabel's brothers, well, they were more than capable of taking on the likes of Callum. On the other hand, she had no wish to drag Mabel into her trouble, and despite Callum's threats, there was no way she was going to keep her friends in the dark. Felix needed to know what had been said so that he could keep a careful eye on Coconut. Her mind made up, she continued until she reached the carter's house on the Scottie Road.

Back at Crooked Lane, Callum sank heavily into a chair.

'Do you think she was telling the truth?' asked Suzie, as she stared out of the window after Roz.

'I don't care as long as she keeps her gob shut,' said Callum sullenly.

'What happens now?' said Lilith. She was sitting in the chair opposite Callum's, a stern expression etched into her wrinkled face.

He shrugged. 'Nowt. We keep our heads down and carry on as normal until we hear different.'

Suzie looked from her father to her grandmother. Her father had heard rumours that a body had been found down the docks, but that was all. He had come tearing back to Crooked Lane and told them of his news just before Roz had arrived back. Suzie hadn't thought much about the discovery until her father's reaction to Roz having turned up just at that same moment. *Why* had he reacted so violently? Even if they had discovered a body down the docks it had nothing to do with the Haggartys. Or at least that's what she had thought until Callum's outburst. Now, she wasn't so sure, and with old rumours stirring in her mind, she had to ask herself the question she wouldn't have dared to ask her father. Could it be her mother? A shiver ran down her spine and she tried to dismiss the idea from her thoughts, but found it impossible to do so. Bodies were often found down the docks, so why had her father reacted so badly to this discovery? Surely there could only be one reason. Keeping her back to her elders, Suzie felt a tear trickle down her cheek as she stared out the dirty window in the direction of the docks.

*

Felix had been surprised to see Roz so soon, but not surprised to hear of Callum's threats. 'And you say you didn't hear a single word?' he said as he poured the tea.

She pulled a face. 'Not really, just something about the docks.' Taking the mug of tea which Felix offered her, Roz blew gently on the surface before taking a tentative sip. 'He was so angry, more so than usual.' She thought for a moment then added, 'Scared too, I could see it in his eyes, and I've never seen Callum look scared about anything.'

Felix sat down opposite her. 'Had he found it or had someone else?'

Roz furrowed her brow as she tried her hardest to remember the half-heard comment. 'I really couldn't say.' She looked up sharply. 'Perhaps they've found his stash of stolen goods from all the looting he's been doing, and he's scared they're going to put two and two together and realise it was him.'

Felix gave her a dark look. 'Or perhaps they've found a body.' Seeing her incomprehension, he added, 'Suzie's mother?'

Roz stared wide-eyed at Felix and opened her mouth to speak, but words failed her.

Felix continued with his theory. 'She's been gone for a few years. If he dumped her in the docks, I should imagine identification would be pretty difficult, but it wouldn't stop him worrying he'd been found out.'

Roz grimaced at the thought of dredging up a body that had been underwater all that time. She looked at Felix. 'So you think he was telling them what he'd heard, so that they could get their stories straight before the scuffers came calling?'

Felix nodded slowly. 'Prepare for the worst but hope for the best. Only of course he didn't count on you over-hearing what he'd been saying. He's probably worried that if the police ever did come asking questions you might repeat what you'd heard. Let's face it, it would look decidedly iffy if Callum was overheard discussing his story *before* his wife's remains had been identified.'

Roz stared at him, open-mouthed. 'That's why he threatened me.'

Felix's jaw flinched. 'He knew you'd keep quiet if he threatened Coconut ...' He eyed her thoughtfully. 'Yet you still told me. Why, when he told you not to?'

She snorted her contempt. 'If he thinks I'd not tell my friends they might be in danger, then he doesn't know me at all. Forewarned is forearmed.'

Felix winked at her, and Roz felt her tummy flutter. 'Loyal to the core, that's my Roz. Callum wouldn't know the meaning of the word loyalty, so he probably thinks you'll keep shtum. Question is, what if it does turn out they've found Suzie's mother's body?'

Roz drew in a deep breath before letting it out. 'That's what worries me. Rumours will fly. What if someone says something and he thinks it's come from me?'

'He'll only come after you if someone says you've been spreading rumours, so I think you'll be fine, because I'm not going to say anything, and neither will Mabel.'

'It's ridiculous!' Roz exclaimed. 'I *couldn't* say any-thing incriminating because I never heard anything.'

'Only he doesn't know that, and that's why he's scared,' said Felix.

'Good! Because if he did murder her, accident or not, he deserves everything he gets.' Roz quickly fell silent as the door to the kitchen opened.

Alan strolled into the kitchen and glanced at the clock above the door before turning his attention to Roz. 'Cinderella's cutting it fine – you not afraid your coach'll turn into a pumpkin?'

Felix explained her predicament, although he left out the bit about their theory surrounding the dock findings.

'So, you've outstayed your welcome at the Haggartys',' said Alan, expertly rolling a cigarette between his fingers. 'Well, you're welcome to stay here for as long as you need, although from what Felix says, the two of you are going to share a flat above the ironmonger's?'

Roz nodded. 'Thanks for letting me stay. Mabel said I can start work whenever I like at the laundry, so I'll be able to pay my way.'

He waved a dismissive hand. 'You don't look like you eat more than a sparrow ...' he hesitated, '... although you will need your ration book. I don't suppose you've got it?'

Roz quickly patted her dungarees, and pulled it out to show Alan, who nodded approvingly. 'Callum's never been interested in paying for food, rationed or not.'

'Good job, because I daresay you wouldn't want to go back to the Haggartys cap in hand.'

Roz rolled her eyes. 'I'd rather go without than go back there.' She glanced guiltily at Felix, but Alan appeared not to notice.

He pointed at the sofa. 'I'm afraid you'll have to kip down on the sofa, but you should be warm enough. Felix here can fetch some blankets and pillows.' He nodded at Felix, who took this as his cue to do as Alan suggested.

The difference between Alan and Callum's attitude towards her was so great, Roz felt the tears well up. 'I wish I'd gone to a nice home like yours, instead of the Haggartys'.'

'You're here now, that's all that matters.'

Roz smiled happily. She could forget all about the past and concentrate on a brighter future with Felix.

Felix came back laden with pillows, blankets and a duck feather eiderdown, all of which he placed on the sofa.

Alan nodded approvingly. 'I'll leave you to get settled, queen.'

She waited until he had left the room before beckoning Felix to join her on the sofa. 'I'd forgotten all about this,' she said, pulling out a second ration book and handing it to Felix, 'mainly because I didn't intend using it.'

Felix looked at the ration book, a frown creasing his brow. 'Who's Sheila Derby?'

Roz took it back and pushed it into the pocket of her dungarees. 'I don't know. Callum gave it to me a couple of days ago. He asked me to try and use it down at the market, but there was no way I was taking that kind of risk – for all I knew, any of the stallholders could be Sheila Derby, and I would be caught red-handed trying to use a stolen ration book.'

Felix scowled. 'He really is a piece of work!'

Roz placed her hand over Felix's. 'There's something else.'

He raised an eyebrow.

'When he gave it to me, just like you, I wondered where he'd got it from. After all, if he'd stolen it from someone then surely they'd have reported it missing?' Felix nodded so she continued, 'But what if they were none the wiser?' Seeing his blank expression, she pressed on, 'What if he stole it off a *dead* person?'

Felix's eyebrows shot to his hairline in horror. 'Steady on. I know he's a real scoundrel, but stealing from the dead?'

'He loots houses during the air raids, Felix, the man's got no scruples.'

'So what do we do about the ration book?' asked Felix. 'Hand it in to the police?'

Roz looked doubtful. 'If we do that, they'll want to know where we got it from, and even though I'd happily tell them, what if they don't believe me? Or worse still, what if Callum talks his way out of it? I've got no proof he gave it to me.' She shook her head. 'He'd kill me, Felix, I know he would, or Coconut.'

Felix wiped away the tear which fell down her cheek. 'Don't worry, we won't go to the police, but I do think we should keep it just in case.'

'In case of what?'

'In case he starts throwing his weight around or making accusations. If he does, we could use the ration book against him, because if your hunch is correct, and he has stolen it from a dead person, he'd be in real trouble, the sort of trouble that winds you up on the end of a noose.'

'Collateral,' said Roz.

He nodded solemnly. 'We may need to cover our backs, and that book could be the very thing.'

'By God, queen, you can stay as long as you want!' exclaimed Bill the next morning. 'Especially if you can knock up grub like this. There's nowt better to wake you up than a bowl of hot porridge and a strong cup of tea.'

'Glad you approve,' said Roz, giving a mock curtsy.

'You really didn't have to make breakfast,' said Alan, adding hastily, 'although I'm glad you did, 'cos me dad's right, this kind of grub sets a feller up for the day.'

Roz watched the men eat their breakfast with a sense of satisfaction. In all the time she had been at the Haggartys' none of them had ever thanked her for preparing their breakfast. Far from it; they'd either whinged that it wasn't creamy enough, despite the fact they never had any milk, or complained that the toast was too dry, even though they never had any butter either. It was a welcome change to have praise instead of constant put-downs.

As the men continued tucking into their porridge, Roz gathered her coat and shoes. 'Mabel doesn't know what happened last night, so I thought I'd go and see her, and I can explain as we walk to work.' She grinned as she tied the laces of her plimsolls. How wonderful was it that for the first time since arriving in Liverpool she was going to be working in a laundry – a nice, warm, clean environment – rather than scrambling over the top of the coal, and using her bare hands to pack the various containers she was handed? Her grin broadened as she imagined the arguments that would be raging in the Haggarty household at present, and she had to wonder just who would be cooking breakfast now that she was gone.

Resting his spoon in his bowl, Felix got to his feet as she made her way to the front door. 'Aren't you having anything to eat?'

Roz smiled. 'I had some toast whilst I was waiting for the porridge to cook.' She looked over Felix's shoulder to Alan and Bill. 'There's some toast keeping warm in the oven. If you leave the pots to soak in the sink, I'll do them when I get home.'

'Right you are!' called Bill, only to be reprimanded by his son.

'I needn't remind you that Roz is our guest, and it's your job to do the cooking and the dishes in this house, whilst me and Felix do the paid work.'

'I don't believe in a free ride,' said Roz. 'Think of it as a holiday, Bill.'

Bill grinned at his son, who shook his head and laughed. 'You're spoiling him, queen.' He waved his spoon at his father. 'Don't get used to it. Roz'll be moving out in a few days and it'll be back to normal.'

Felix stepped through the door behind Roz and pulled it to behind them. 'I'll call for you after work – I believe Mabel usually finishes around four?'

Roz nodded. 'She does, or rather, we do!'

Fighting the urge to kiss her goodbye, Felix shoved his hands into his pockets. 'I'll see you later.'

Waving goodbye, she headed along the Scottie, the smile of freedom etched across her face.

When she had woken that morning, she'd been confused because instead of lying on rough straw-filled sacks with dirty ones as bedding, she was lying on a cushy sofa with a feather eiderdown keeping her cosy and warm. As the memory from the evening before swept over her, she couldn't help but sigh happily. She was finally free from her terrible life with the Haggartys and her future was looking up at last.

As she neared Mercer Court, she felt her tummy lurch unpleasantly. What if she bumped into one of the Haggartys? She immediately chastised herself for being so silly. If she came across the Haggartys she would ignore them and continue on her way. She had nothing to do with them any more, and she need not explain herself either.

She knocked briefly on Mabel's front door and waited to be invited in, as was always the case whenever she went round.

'Come in!' bellowed Mabel's father.

Roz opened the door and stepped through. 'Hello, Mr Johnson, Mrs Johnson. Is Mabel here?'

Mrs Johnson looked at her with surprise. 'Yes, she is, but what are you doing here? I'd have thought you'd be doing the coal?'

Roz beamed. 'I've been sacked, so I don't live or work with them any more.'

'About bloody time too,' said Mr Johnson.

'Language, Donald!' scolded his wife.

Roz waved a dismissive hand. 'He's right.'

Hearing Roz's voice, Mabel entered the kitchen. 'Roz!'

Roz smiled. 'The one and only!'

'What happened?' Without waiting for a reply, Mabel continued, 'I take it they weren't exactly cock-a-hoop to hear your news? Did you tell them when you got home last night?'

'I certainly did. Callum was so angry he threw me out on the spot.'

Mrs Johnson gaped at her daughter and Roz. 'What news is this and where on earth did you spend the night?'

Leaning against the dresser, Roz told the Johnsons the whole story, finishing with the unknown discovery at the docks. Mrs Johnson lowered her gaze before casting the girls a warning glance, and when she spoke her tone was leaden. 'Keep out of their way. That goes for you too, Mabel; that family is bad news.'

Mabel eyed her mother suspiciously. 'You knew Suzie's mam better than anyone else round here. Do you think this has something to do with what they found down the docks?'

Mrs Johnson glared at her daughter. 'I think you should keep your nose out of other people's business. If the Haggartys hear that you've been poking round asking questions, they won't take kindly to it. Take my advice and steer clear.'

Mabel gave Roz a knowing look, before snatching a piece of toast from the rack and spreading it with jam. She took a large bite. 'Do you want some?' she asked Roz, her voice muffled with toast.

Roz shook her head. 'I ate breakfast before I came round.'

Turning to her parents, Mabel kissed them both on the cheek. 'Ta-ra, Mam, Dad, I'll be back after work.'

Waving farewell, Roz followed Mabel out of the house. Once they were clear of Mercer Court, Mabel turned to Roz. 'Whenever I ask about Suzie's mam, she gets all tetchy. I reckon she thinks Callum's done her in, and she's scared he'll do the same to anyone who goes snooping.'

Roz threaded her arm through Mabel's. 'Can we not talk about the Haggartys? This is my first day without them, and I want to keep it that way.'

Nodding apologetically, Mabel asked Roz about her evening with Felix.

'Alan and Bill invited me to stay for as long as I liked,' said Roz. 'They're marvellous, they really are.'

It took the girls no time at all to make the short journey from Mercer Court to the laundry. When they arrived, Mabel introduced Roz to Mr Woo, who was delighted to meet her.

'Told you he was nice,' said Mabel. 'Follow me and I'll show you what's what – not that there's a lot to it – and I'll introduce you to the girls whilst I'm about it.'

Roz's first day in the laundry simply flew by and she couldn't believe it when Mabel came to tell her that it was time for home.

'It can't be!' said Roz. 'It doesn't seem like five minutes since we had lunch!'

Mabel grinned. 'They say time flies when you're having fun! Come on!'

Getting their coats, they bade the rest of the girls goodbye. As they made their way outside Roz was delighted to see that Felix was waiting for her. He held up a bag and grinned.

'What's that?' she asked, eyeing the bag inquisitively.

'A picnic!' said Felix. 'I thought we could take it to St George's Hall, and you could tell me all about your first day in the laundry.'

'What a lovely idea,' said Roz.

Mabel tied the belt on her coat. 'I wish someone would whisk me off for a romantic picnic. See you tomorrow, Roz; ta-ra, Felix!'

Roz very much wanted to correct her friend, to reaffirm that she and Felix were just good friends, but Mabel had gone, and Felix was holding out the crook of his arm expectantly. With no one to explain to, she threaded her arm through his, and together they made their way through the streets of Liverpool.

'So,' said Felix, 'how was your day?'

'Wonderful!' replied Roz. 'The girls are so friendly and cheerful, and everyone has a good natter whilst they work. It's completely different to working with the Haggartys. I don't think I stopped smiling the whole time I was there, and I couldn't believe it when Mabel came to tell me it was time to go home.'

'Good. You deserve a break after all you've been through, and whilst you live with me I'm going to make sure that you smile every day.' Felix indicated the gates leading into the grounds of the hall. 'Do you remember the first time I brought you here?'

She nodded. 'It was after all that business with my necklace. We'd been to see *Goodbye, Mr Chips* – it was the first film I'd seen since I left Germany – and when it finished you treated me to fish and chips, and after that we went for a stroll through the grounds. I remember thinking how sad it was that Suzie would probably never go to the cinema, or enjoy a moonlit stroll.'

'Always thinking of others,' said Felix, 'that's what I lo … like about you.'

Roz faltered mid-step. It sounded very much as though Felix had been about to say love then changed it to like. She looked up at him, but his face remained impassive and she decided that she must have misheard and allowed him to lead her over to the bench by the stone lions where they sat down. Felix opened the bag and shot her an inquisitive glance. 'Sarnie or pasty?'

Roz wrinkled her nose in disgust. 'I don't know how anyone can eat those things, they're full of gristle.'

He laughed softly. 'Sarnie it is!' He held out two sandwiches. 'Cheese and pickle or pickle and cheese?'

Laughing, Roz pretended to mull it over. 'It's a tough decision, but I'll take pickle and cheese, please.'

'Wise choice,' said Felix, handing one of the sandwiches over.

As Roz bit into it she pondered over how much her life had changed in such a short space of time, and how very different it would be again, in a few days' time. She gave Felix a sideways glance to see what he was looking at and blushed as their eyes met. Felix hastily averted his gaze, as though embarrassed that he had been caught staring. This, and the suggestion from Mabel that they were going for a romantic picnic, caused Roz to think about the question that she had been avoiding ever since Felix first said he would find a place of his own so that they could live together. What would people say? She knew it shouldn't bother her because it was none of their business, but she also knew they would be right to question it, because even though they both insisted they were just friends, she felt it increasingly obvious that if it weren't for their circumstances, as likely as not they would be a lot more than friends.

She wondered whether she should say something, but suppose she did, and he confirmed her thoughts, what then? They couldn't live under the same roof in sin, and even if they didn't become lovers, Roz would still know that it was the wrong thing to do, as would the rest of society, something she could well do without. Living in Liverpool as someone of German origin was bad enough as it was without being judged for who she lived with.

Felix's voice cut across her thoughts. 'Penny for them?'

Roz placed her sandwich on her knee. 'Do you think people will talk when they see that two young people of the opposite sex are living together?'

Felix shrugged nonchalantly, but Roz had seen his bottom jaw clench. 'Who cares if they do?'

'Me for one,' said Roz truthfully, 'not because I take heed of gossip, but I know the harm it can do, and I've had enough judgement because of my religion. I don't want to set tongues wagging because we'll be living together.'

'We're not doing anything wrong,' said Felix, although Roz noticed he was quick to avert his gaze as he spoke. 'It would be different if we were romantic-ally involved.'

'I know that, but they don't, do they?' she said, think-ing that they would only have to see the way Felix looked at her to question the relationship.

It appeared Felix had had the same thought. 'Alright, so we're close, much closer than others, but that's because of the journey we've shared. I'll also admit that I have strong feelings for you.' He looked at her, and as their eyes met, Roz could see the adoration in his, and even if it was just the love of a friend it didn't really matter: others would see the same look she had.

'People aren't stupid, Felix, they have eyes in their head, as do I,' she said quietly.

He put his sandwich back in its wrapper and placed his hand over hers. 'It doesn't matter how I feel, I'm not having you out on the streets, and if you're won-dering whether my feelings are more than those of a friend, then yes they are, but they're going to be. We've been through so much together, it's only natural we have a strong bond, but that isn't necessarily a bad thing.'

Roz allowed him to slip his hand into hers. Why on earth was she letting herself worry over what others thought when she had a real gem like Felix by her side? She came to a decision. 'Thanks, Felix, I appreciate your word as a gentleman, and as for the gossips, well, I'm used to that after living with the Haggartys.'

When they had finished their picnic, they went for a walk past the Liver Building, where they popped in to see if anyone had heard from her parents, and to give Roz's new address. Disappointed to hear there had still been no contact, Roz told Felix that while she was not surprised, it felt good to hand over her new address.

Strolling arm in arm back to the Scottie, Felix wondered just how long he could keep up the pretence that he only saw Roz as a very dear friend. He knew that she had seen through him, and so would others. He drew a deep breath. If he wanted the best for Roz, which he did, he would keep up the pretence for as long as necessary, because even if he couldn't express his love for her, this was the next best thing and he wasn't going to do anything to jeopardise that.

Chapter Five

July 1940

Roz sat on the steps to the flat above the ironmonger's, tears seeping between her lids. How could it have all gone so wrong at the last minute? They had started the day in celebration of Felix turning eighteen. Roz had made an eggless sponge cake as her gift which, despite her reservations, had turned out well. She had gone off to work with a spring in her step, knowing that when she returned she would be moving into her new home with Felix. Or at least that had been the plan. In reality it had been very different. She thought now that she should have realised it wasn't going to be a good day when Mabel's mother had come to say that Mabel wouldn't be able to work as she was laid up with a tummy bug.

It was later that same morning and Roz had been on her tea break, telling the girls what she intended to make for their first supper at the flat, when Robin, Mabel's oldest brother, had come tearing into the laundry shouting for Roz. Fearing that Mabel had taken a turn for the worse, she had run over and asked for an explanation. Taking her by the hand he had uttered the words 'Felix has been arrested' before turning and running full tilt down to the docks.

As she ran behind him, a hundred questions raced through Roz's mind. What on earth had Felix done that could have caused him to be arrested? Or was this Callum's idea of revenge? Perhaps they really had found a body! She quickly dismissed this, because Callum wasn't the sort of man to go to the police – he'd far rather use his fists.

All became clear when she arrived at the quayside to see Felix sitting on his suitcase, alongside a few other men. As she approached, he stood up to greet her.

Tears trickling down her cheeks, she looked from Felix to the other men, then to a group of British soldiers who stood close by.

'What's happened? Robin said you'd been arrested, but I don't see any handcuffs or police?'

Felix gave her a sad smile. 'Not arrested in the sense you think.' He sighed heavily. 'I'm eighteen, Roz, so the British government have decided to intern me as an enemy alien.'

Her eyes widened. 'But they can't! You've been living and working in Liverpool for over a year. It doesn't make sense, it's obvious you're not one of them ...'

He placed an arm around her shoulders. 'I'm not in any trouble, they're just making sure they keep their people safe. Once the war is over, they'll let me go.' He pressed a key into the palm of her hand. 'I've paid a month in advance, so you've no worries for a bit ...'

'How long do you think you're going to be away?' Hearing movement behind her, Roz looked round to see the first of the men being led up the gangplank to HMT *Dunera*. 'Where are they going?' As the words left her lips, a soldier approached Felix.

'Time to go,' he said, jerking his head in the direction of the ship.

Gripping Felix's hand in hers, she turned to the soldier. 'Please don't do this, he'd never do anything to hurt anyone.' Her voice was getting higher as the soldier tried to lead Felix away. 'You're making a big mistake. Ask Alan or Bill if you don't believe me; they've lived in Liverpool their whole lives.'

Realising that Roz's outburst was beginning to attract unwanted attention, the soldier tried to push her gently to one side, but she was having none of it. Doubling her efforts to keep Felix with her, she wrapped her arms around his waist to prevent them from taking him away.

Felix spoke quietly to the soldier over the top of Roz's head. 'Just give me a minute, mate, you can see the lady's upset.'

Rather than risk Roz making more of a scene than she already had, the soldier nodded abruptly. 'You've got one minute, but that's all.'

Still holding him in a tight embrace, Roz looked up into Felix's face. 'Please don't go,' she said, her voice barely above a whisper.

Pushing her hair back from her tear-stained face, Felix kissed her forehead. 'I'll be back before you know it.' His eyes shone down at her with the same warmth as they had when they first met. 'You know I wouldn't leave you if I had a choice.'

Realising that she was making things worse, Roz put on a brave face. Leaning back, she tried her best to smile, and was pleasantly surprised when Felix took her in his arms and kissed her full on the mouth.

If anyone asked Roz where she would have wanted her first kiss to be, the answer would not have been on a busy quayside, but right now, it was exactly where she wanted it to be. With silent tears falling down her cheeks, she felt herself melt into his embrace. Kissing him back, she noticed the familiar scent of his aftershave.

As they continued to kiss, the soldier cleared his throat before stepping forward. 'Righto, mate, we really do have to go.'

Felix reluctantly broke away from Roz. 'One more minute, please.' Without waiting for the soldier to respond, he turned back to Roz, his eyes twinkling as they locked with hers, and he said the words that Roz realised she had been longing to hear.

'Roz Sachs, will you be my one and only?'

Beaming through the tears, Roz nodded fervently. 'Of course I will.'

Shaking the soldier off his arm, he took Roz in his arms and kissed her for the final time, although this time the kiss was deeper and longer than the first. As he broke away, his lips brushed her cheek and he whispered, 'I love you, Rozalin Sachs, and I don't give two hoots what the neighbours think.'

Roz managed to get the words 'I love you too' out, as the soldier took hold of Felix, slightly more roughly than he had the first time, but before he could lead him away, Felix thrust his hand into his pocket and pulled out an object which he handed to Roz.

'You can wear it now you no longer live in Crooked Lane.'

Roz took the necklace in her fingers and kissed the star. Watching the soldiers lead him up the gangplank, she called after him, 'I'll be right here waiting for you, Felix Ackerman.'

Just before he was led from view Felix managed to turn his head and smile. 'I know you will, my little bubala.'

Roz stopped in her tracks. The only person who ever called her bubala had been her father, and she was almost certain that she had never mentioned it to Felix. Was this a sign? Were they about to be parted for ever? Fishing a handkerchief from her dungarees pocket, she stopped a soldier who was about to move the gangplank.

'Excuse me!'

Turning to acknowledge her, the soldier paused, 'Can I help you, miss?'

'Why do they have to stay on a ship?' she asked, wiping her tears with her handkerchief. 'Surely there're other places they could stay?'

He frowned, looking from Roz to the *Dunera* and back again. 'How else would they get to Canada?'

'*Canada!*' cried Roz. Her knees gave way and she fell against the soldier who caught her before she hit the ground.

Her face white with shock, she looked at the soldier who was frowning with concern. 'They never said he was going to Canada. I just assumed he would be staying here ...' Hearing her own words, she realised now how silly this sounded. She turned pleading eyes to the soldier, who was looking both guilty and embarrassed. 'He's the only person I have left. I've lost my parents, and now the man I love most in the world. Couldn't you make an exception, turn a blind eye? I swear I won't tell a soul.'

Smiling sympathetically, he looked back at the ship. 'I'm afraid not, queen. The most I can do is promise to keep an eye on him.'

Realising that there was nothing more that could be done, Roz stood on the quayside until the ship set sail. Even then she refused to leave until it was lost from sight, when she turned and walked home to the empty flat that should've been called home.

Feeling unable to go into the flat without Felix by her side, she sat on the steps. At the sound of approaching footsteps, she lifted her head. Hope ever present, she called out to her unseen visitor. 'Felix?'

Bill rounded the corner, shaking his head sadly. 'I'm afraid not, queen.'

Roz looked at Bill. He was ashen-faced, and the look of dread said it all. She placed her fingers to her lips, trying to stop the words which she feared to speak. 'What's happened?'

'Torpedo,' said Bill simply, adding hastily as Roz grabbed the stair banister for support, 'only a glancing blow, no one's been hurt, but they've had to change course.'

Sinking onto the step, Roz placed her head in her hands. 'Honestly, Bill! I thought something even more terrible ...' She shook her head as relief swamped her.

Bill sat on the step next to her and placed a comforting arm around her shoulders. 'Sorry, queen, I didn't mean to scare you.'

Sniffing, she wiped her nose with her handkerchief and leaned into Bill's shoulder. 'He's alright, and that's the main thing.' She glanced up at him through wet lashes. 'You said they've had to change course?'

He nodded grimly. 'I've a pal what's in the Navy, he serves on board the SS *Malakand*, but he gets to hear all the gossip. Anyway, he reckons the *Dunera* reported a change of course due to the danger she was in, especially after what happened to the *Arandora Star*.' Seeing Roz's blank expression, he continued, 'She got hit by a torpedo, only she wasn't as lucky as the *Dunera*, which is why they've set a new course for Australia ...' He looked at Roz, whose head had snapped up upon hearing the word Australia.

'But ... Australia's the other side of the world ...'

'I know,' Bill said simply.

'How long will it take them to get there?' She shifted to a more comfortable position. 'It took hours just to cross the Channel, and Australia's much further than that!'

'I don't know, queen, and in answer to your question, it'll be weeks, if not months.' He shrugged helplessly. 'I really couldn't say for sure.'

'I'm never going to see him again, am I?' said Roz, her voice hoarse with emotion.

Bill wanted to reassure her, but how could he under the circumstances? Australia was the other side of the world, getting there wasn't going to be easy, and as for getting back ... A lad like Felix wouldn't be able to pay for his passage back to England, and the Navy wouldn't bring him back when he wasn't a British national. He tried to put on a brave face. 'If I know our Felix, wild horses won't stop him coming back to you.' He glanced up the stairwell. 'You've got this place for a month, but what'll you do after that? With the best will in the world he won't be back before the month's up.'

'I suppose I could ask Mabel, although it's pretty cramped at her place.'

Bill got to his feet. 'If all else fails you're welcome to kip on our sofa.' He glanced at his wristwatch. 'I'd better be getting back – Alan doesn't know about the *Dunera* yet.' He gave Roz a warm, friendly hug. 'You must let me or Alan know if you need anything.'

Nodding, she waited until he was out of sight before heading up the steps and into the flat. She had stopped off at the butcher's on her way to work to buy some corned beef so that they might have corned beef and tomato sandwiches for their supper. Taking the net bag she had used to carry the goods, she placed the bread, meat, and tomatoes on a plate, and rooted round in one of the kitchen drawers for a knife.

Having made her sandwich, she wandered over to the window and looked out onto the street below where the people of Liverpool continued with their busy lives. It's as though nothing has changed, Roz thought to herself, yet as far as I'm concerned, nothing will ever be the same again. I got my first boyfriend, and lost him within seconds of him asking me to be his belle. Taking a bite of her sandwich, she chewed thoughtfully. It seemed to Roz that every time she made arrangements to move somewhere else, the people she loved most were taken away from her. Felix was the only one who understood what it was like back in Germany, to have your parents go missing, to not know whether you'll ever see them again. She wiped an errant tear from her cheek. She was on her own. She might have Mabel, but Mabel could never understand what it was like to be a Jewish refugee, in a country which now saw you as the enemy. Not feeling like doing anything much, she finished eating before curling up on the settee and falling asleep, where her dreams turned into nightmares with Felix adrift in the ocean shouting out for help.

It was the morning after Felix's deportation, and Roz was up betimes. Having not had much sleep the night before, she supposed it was better for her to be busy, so she got ready for work at the laundry. Hurrying down the stairs which led to the road, she found Mabel walking up to greet her.

Roz was about to explain all that had happened the previous day, but it seemed bad news travelled fast.

'Our Robin told us everything – poor Felix. I was dying to come and see you last night, but my tummy was still playing cartwheels.'

Roz nodded. 'Thanks, Mabel, and don't worry, I know you'd have come if you could. I hope you're feeling better?'

'Much, thanks, but never mind me – how are you feeling this morning?' said Mabel, falling into step beside Roz.

'Numb,' said Roz simply. 'I don't think it's sunk in yet, and of course I'm ever hopeful that something else will happen that might cause the *Dunera* to turn back.'

Mabel smiled sympathetically. 'I reckon Felix is probably hoping the same.'

'I wish I was eighteen,' said Roz. 'They might have taken me too.'

'What about your mam and dad?' Mabel asked. 'You'd not find them if you were living in Australia.'

Roz looked grim. 'I may not find them living in Liverpool either. In fact, the more time that goes by, the more I start to wonder if I shall ever see them again.'

Mabel walked on in silence before speaking her thoughts. 'Do you really think that?'

Roz hesitated before answering. 'How can I not? It's been over a year now and no one saw my parents after the crash. For all I know, the Germans already have them.' She added hastily, 'I hope not, of course I do, but it does seem strange that they were nowhere to be seen. I know my parents wouldn't have left me on my own, not willingly.'

Mabel slipped her arm through Roz's. 'I know it's not much of a consolation, but you've always got me.' She smiled up at her friend. 'I'm not as handsome as Felix, nor can I understand the same as he does, but I'm a good listener, and I'll help in any way I can.'

Roz squeezed Mabel's arm. 'I know you are, and I'm very lucky to have met you...' A thought occurred to her. 'I'm not going to be able to afford the flat on my own after the month's up. I don't suppose you'd like to move in with me, straight away if you like?

You'd not have to pay the first month, as that's already paid for.'

Mabel looked up excitedly. 'Really? Just me and you? On our own? Girls together?'

Roz nodded. 'Yes, but only if you want to, that is. I must admit, I don't think I could face another night on my own.'

'Well you can count me in!' said Mabel.

'Perfect!' said Roz. 'We'll go and see the landlord straight after work and run it by him, but I can't see him saying no.'

If only Roz had been right, everything might have worked out very differently, but as it turned out, the landlord was not happy at the thought of two young girls staying in his flat on their own.

'I'll get a reputation! God only knows what the iron-mongers would say if they thought I was renting to a couple of adolescents.'

'We won't be any trouble, Mr Andrews—' Mabel had begun, but her words fell on deaf ears.

'Neither of you is eighteen. It was different when I thought Mr Ackerman was going to be here, and whilst I sympathise with your position, I'm afraid his bad luck has transferred onto you.' He held up his hands in a placating manner as Roz and Mabel protested. 'Sorry, girls, the answer's no.'

Sighing heavily, Roz turned to Mabel. 'Looks like I'm going to be on my tod for a bit ...'

Mr Andrews looked up sharply. 'If you're thinking of staying here, you can forget it. Two's bad, one's worse – you'll have to find somewhere else to stay.'

216

Roz gaped at him. 'What possible trouble can I bring on my own?'

He shrugged. 'How am I to know what a young girl will get up to on her own? Wild parties if I know the kids of today.'

'Parties!' echoed Roz, her tone incredulous. 'I hardly think so ...' but it was no good, his mind was made up.

'Well, you can jolly well give her the month's rent back, seeing as you're the one who's denying her access,' said Mabel.

Mr Andrews spluttered in protest. 'I shall do nothing of the sort! It's hardly my fault Mr Ackerman got himself arrested. I'm down a month's rent ...' He wagged a reproving finger at Roz. 'And even if I wasn't, there's no way I'd give you the money. If anyone was to get it, it would be Mr Ackerman.'

'But he's on his way to Australia,' cried Roz. 'How on earth are you meant to give him his money back when he's halfway around the world?'

He shrugged nonchalantly. 'Not my problem. You can get your stuff and post the key back through the door.'

Roz took the key out of her pocket and handed it over. 'I don't have anything to get, I'm wearing everything I own.'

Roz turned to Mabel as they heard Mr Andrews close the door behind them. 'What now?'

Mabel slipped her arm through Roz's. 'You'll have to stay with us until we can get summat sorted out.'

'There's no room at yours,' said Roz. 'I can't ask your parents ...'

'You don't have to; I'm sayin' you can stay, and I know they'd not turn you away, especially not under the circumstances.'

Mabel had been correct, and her parents had welcomed Roz with open arms. 'That bloomin' Mr Andrews is a tight-fisted beggar!' snapped Mrs Johnson. 'Don't you worry your head, Roz, you can stay here as long as need be.'

Roz was grateful for their hospitality, but she knew the Johnsons were already stretched to the limit when it came to providing for their family. After several nights of being woken by a thud as one of Mabel's siblings had been unintentionally pushed out of bed, Roz announced that she intended to find somewhere that might provide a live-in position.

Mr Johnson looked up from his morning copy of the *Echo*. 'Live-in position, you say?'

Roz nodded. 'Like a maid, or a nanny or—'

He turned the paper to face her. 'How about a land girl?'

Roz took the paper and began to read, and Mabel, who was sitting next to her, craned her neck so that she might also read the article. It was an advert for the women's land army, asking women to sign up and dig for victory. It promised clean air and healthy living, all whilst doing your bit for your country.

Roz looked at Mabel. 'What do you think?'

Mabel chewed thoughtfully on her toast. 'I don't see why not. You love Coconut, and I bet they have a lot of horses on farms ...' Her voice faded into silence as Roz's question hit home. She locked eyes with Roz. 'You mean for me too?'

Roz nodded. 'I'm not the only one who loves horses. I was quite surprised when we managed to prise you off Coconut's back.'

Mabel looked at her father then her mother, both of whom seemed to think the idea a good one. 'You've always been one for the animals,' said her mother. 'You're too young to join the services, but this is different. I reckon you should go for it.'

Mabel glanced at Roz, who was nodding encouragingly. 'I think this could be a real adventure for the two of us, and this way we'll be doing our bit.'

Mr Johnson took the paper back from Roz and read the advert again. 'Says here you'll get all the training you need, and that working on the land is the best job of all.'

'I might meet a farmer,' said Mabel wistfully, 'with lots of land and money, and he might ask me to marry him and I can live in a beautiful country cottage and ...'

'Blimey,' chuckled Mr Johnson, 'someone's certainly looking at the bigger picture.'

'I'd love to be a farmer's wife,' said Mabel. 'I'd ride my horse to town, and church, and the market.'

'Are you marrying a farmer or a horse?' said Mr Johnson.

'Both!' giggled Mabel.

'How do we apply?' Roz asked. 'I bet there'll be loads of applicants, so the quicker we get ours in the better.'

Mr Johnson gestured with his pipe at an address underneath the article. 'Tells you all you need to know right there.'

Mrs Johnson took a pair of scissors and handed them to her husband. 'Cut it out for them, Donald.'

Checking there was nothing worth reading on the other side of the page, he did as she asked then handed the clipping to Roz. 'There you go!'

Roz looked at Mabel. 'This could be just what the doctor ordered. I'll be able to tell Bill and Alan where I'm going should Felix get in touch, and of course I'll tell Mr Garmin in the Liver Building, just in case.'

'We won't have time to go before work, but we can nip over straight after,' said Mabel. 'Poor Mr Woo, it seems nobody wants to work in a laundry any more.'

When the two girls finished work, they hurried down to the recruitment office in the city centre. Fearing they may be too late, they were both relieved to find that they were just in the nick of time, although they were dumbfounded to hear that to be a land girl you had to be eighteen. When the lady in charge of recruitment told them this fact, both girls had nodded mutely when asked if they were of the appropriate age. They had expected to be called out, told to go home and wait until they were old enough, and were therefore surprised and delighted when the woman continued without hesitation. It seemed the only problem would come with Roz getting a certificate to confirm she was fit on medical grounds. Once she'd explained that she had come to Britain on the Kindertransport and had no assigned doctor, the recruiting officer said that it could be sorted easily and that they would make an appointment with one of the army doctors.

Mabel turned to Roz as they left the office. 'I can't believe what we've just done!' she said in an excited whisper. 'Do you really think she believed we were eighteen?'

Roz shrugged. 'I had worried that being German and eighteen, she might report me to the authorities, but she didn't seem to care less, but I suppose it's not as if we're going to be doing anything dangerous – how hard can it be to plough a field or dig up vegetables?'

Looking slightly disappointed, Mabel agreed. 'I wonder how long it will be before we get our first posting.'

As it turned out, they only had to wait a matter of weeks before receiving the news they were being sent to the Lancashire Agricultural College at Hutton. Mabel's father had been surprised that the girls were getting such thorough training, as most of the people who applied for the land army were sent straight to a farm, and more or less told to get on with it.

Mabel's mother sobbed gently into her apron skirt, telling her daughter to be careful of the sharp machinery, to never stand behind an animal and to keep away from members of the opposite sex.

'I'll do all bar the last one,' Mabel giggled as she and Roz boarded the train for Hutton. They chose a carriage with an available window seat and took their places, waving goodbye to Mabel's parents and various siblings. The train wheels squealed as they gained traction against the tracks, and Mabel squeaked with excitement.

'This is it, Roz! We're leaving home to make our own way in the big wide world!'

Roz smiled ruefully. 'One of us left home a long time ago.'

Mabel grimaced. 'Of course you did. Sorry, I keep forgetting you're not a Liverpool lass.'

Roz waved her hand dismissively. 'Don't worry, I've lived here for over a year now, and to all intents and purposes this is my home. Even though I've never really belonged anywhere, it's certainly felt like more of a home than Frankfurt did in the last few years I was there.'

'You're an honorary Scouser,' said Mabel, 'and just like the rest of us, you're doing your bit for King and country, helping our boys fight the Hun.'

Roz mulled this over. She had no idea what was going on in Frankfurt, but she suspected that everyone she once knew had either fled the city or been taken to one of the camps. She might have grown up there, but she couldn't call it her home any more. Home is where the heart is, and her heart belonged with her friends and family, wherever they might be. Liverpool was the closest thing she had to a home, and even though the government was interning people as enemy aliens, it was not done in the same manner as the German soldiers when they arrested people. When the Germans did it, you could see the glee and hate in their eyes, but with the British it was fear of the unknown, and knowing what the Germans were capable of Roz didn't blame them. They had welcomed her in and taken her to safety. It was hardly their fault that she had ended up at the Haggartys', and even though she disliked that family intensely, living with them was nowhere near as bad as it would have been had she stayed in Frankfurt. She glanced at Mabel, who was staring absent-mindedly out of the window.

'You're right, I'm doing my bit for my country, helping the British win the war, and helping my family and friends to gain their freedom from the Nazis.'

'You say you wouldn't go back to Germany. Does that mean you'll stay in Britain when the war's over?' Mabel asked, watching as a farmer moved his cattle along from one field to another.

Roz answered without hesitation. 'I would never turn my back on Britain. As far as I'm concerned, it would make me as bad as those who turned against us when we lived in Frankfurt. Some might have feared the Nazis but others didn't – you could see the change in the way they looked at you, as though you were dirt on the bottom of their shoes.'

Mabel grimaced. 'I can't imagine how awful that must have been.'

'A lesson learned,' said Roz, 'that you can never fully trust anyone.'

Mabel looked affronted. 'You can trust me. I'd never do anything like that!'

'Never say never,' said Roz. 'No one knows how they'll react given the right circumstances.'

'But I'm British,' said Mabel stoutly, 'and we don't buckle under for anyone!'

Roz thought about Churchill's warning to the Germans to get out of Poland, and a faint smile crossed her lips. Mabel was right, the British had stood up to the Nazis, and not backed down when their demands weren't met. With this thought in mind, she was determined to be the best land girl Britain had ever seen, to repay them for all they had done for her and her fellow countrymen and women.

'You're right,' she said, 'and seeing as how my family fled Germany – or at least I did – I suppose that makes us more British than German, because just like the Brits we weren't prepared to be bullied into submission.'

Mabel leaned back in her seat. 'That's the ticket! Like I said, you're an honorary Scouser!'

HMT *Dunera* had been at sea for close to two months, which was far longer than she had expected when she left her berth in Liverpool.

When Felix had first boarded, he had wrongly assumed that it was solely for German Jews, and was horrified to find that they were sharing the same space as Italian and Nazi prisoners of war. Being expected to live cheek by jowl with the enemy for weeks had been bad enough, but after the failed torpedo strike, it had been announced that they were changing course for Australia. There had been an outcry from prisoners and internees alike, who were packed into the ship like sardines. Conditions on the *Dunera* were dire, with no room to move and no proper facilities; they were expected to sleep on the floor. Anyone needing to relieve themselves during the night would have to tread on others just to get out.

The water supply, which had only been intended for a much shorter period, had to be rationed to three times a week, and the food had all but run out, not just for the prisoners but for the soldiers who were guarding them. This had led to short tempers and heated exchanges, not so much between the prisoners and internees, but with the guards who thought themselves above the law, and would strike or punish anyone whom they didn't like the face of. Felix's saving grace had been the soldier whom Roz had spoken to on the quayside the day of their departure. It seemed to Felix that he was the only decent soldier on board. He would keep an eye as best he could and call out any guard who was getting over-enthusiastic with their mistreatment of the prisoners.

When Felix complained about the conditions, he had been laughed at by the soldiers, who said it was nothing compared to what the Nazis were doing to their lot. This was the first time anyone had confirmed how bad the Nazis were to those they imprisoned, and Felix couldn't help but wonder what had happened to his mother. Would they really treat a woman like this, or worse?

It was with a huge sense of relief that they eventually docked in Melbourne where he and the others hoped their journey had come to an end, but it seemed that this stop was for the prisoners of war and not the internees. Watching them depart the ship, he thought it a wonder that any of them had got out alive, because they'd certainly lost a few en route. With the prisoners of war gone, they set sail for Sydney.

Life on board the *Dunera* was slightly more pleasant with the absence of the enemy on board. Even so, it still troubled Felix that the British government, who had been sympathetic to the plight of the Jews, had seen fit to mix Nazis and fascists with Jews, as though this was perfectly acceptable.

When they arrived in Sydney a doctor had insisted on boarding the ship before anyone was allowed off. After examining and interviewing the men, he was so appalled by his findings that he made it plain that he intended to take things further, issuing a full investigation into the soldiers' behaviour. It was from this point on that things got better for Felix and his shipmates, who were taken to a proper camp, given food and water, and for the first time in months treated like human beings.

Much later, when the war was finally over, Felix would reason that war did funny things to people, and that the soldiers themselves, although disciplined for their actions, had probably witnessed things which had led to their total disregard for their prisoners. He never blamed them, saying that it was a difficult time all round, and without the British he would have been dead for certain, and that two months on board the *Dunera* was a small price to pay. A statement which showed his depth of character.

After two weeks of training, Roz and Mabel had left the college for their first posting to a hillside farm in the mountains of North Wales. The lecturer had said this was where they sent all new women as it was a wonderful place to learn. What she had failed to mention was that all the signposts were written in Welsh.

'I don't know what any of the signs say,' moaned Mabel as their bus trundled slowly down a heavily potholed lane. She pulled the paper with details of their posting from her pocket and looked at the writing. 'Is this really a word? Only it's all double Dutch to me!' She handed the paper over to Roz, who looked equally perplexed.

'I didn't even know people spoke different languages in Britain,' Roz admitted. 'I thought you were all English ...'

She heard a harrumph of disapproval from the driver.

Mabel giggled. 'Mind what you say. We might not speak Welsh, but that doesn't mean to say the Welsh can't speak English!'

Roz looked out onto the sun-dappled mountainside, which was speckled with tiny white blobs. As they drew nearer, the white dots turned out to be sheep. Marvelling at the higgledy-piggledy stone walls which divided one field from another, Roz gazed dreamily out of the window. 'It's so beautiful, much better than the stuffy city.'

This comment was met with approval from the bus driver, who turned in his seat to address them over his shoulder. 'This is where the real men live,' he said in a sing-song Welsh lilt, 'not like those white-collar workers in the city.'

Roz grinned at Mabel, who was looking impressed at his description of the Welsh men.

'I don't know so much about that,' said Roz. 'Most of the men I know work down the docks.'

Slowing down, he steered the bus around a sheep which had wandered into the road. 'True, but they're not as hardy as a Welsh man. When it snows here, it really snows. The drifts can be up to your waist, and there's no sitting in front of a nice warm fire, no indeed, you have to get out there and see to the animals, break the ice on their troughs, make sure they're fed and cared for.'

Roz and Mabel exchanged worried glances. They hadn't been told any of this in Hutton; in fact the hardy-looking woman giving the lectures had made it sound as if the hardest thing they would have to do was make sure they weren't kicked by a surprised animal, or didn't hurt themselves on the machinery if they weren't paying proper attention. No one had said anything about working in blizzard conditions. Breaking into a whisper so that she would not be overheard by the driver, Mabel said as much to Roz, who shrugged her indifference. 'We're only just heading into autumn, and they did say we'd probably get posted to a few different places at first so that we could get used to all manners of farming – bearing that in mind, it's quite likely we won't be here this winter.'

Mabel wasn't so sure. She imagined it would be hard to get women to agree to work somewhere as remote as the area into which they were heading, and two naïve girls, just starting out, probably seemed like their best bet.

The bus slowed to a stop and the driver turned to address the girls, who were the only passengers on the bus. 'This is your stop.'

Mabel looked anxiously out of the window. 'Where do we go from here?' She was about to hand the paper over to the driver to see if he knew their destination, when he laughed.

'Glasfryn is at the bottom of the lane.'

'Where are all the shops?' asked Roz, who was wondering where they were meant to get supplies.

He grinned. 'You're going to be living on the farm, *that* is your shop.' He pointed to the narrow grassy track. 'It's about half a mile down there.'

'Half a mile!' cried Mabel. 'But what about all my things?' She pulled the kitbag they'd each been given to carry their uniform and essentials.

His grin broadened. 'It'll be good training for when you start the real work.' He glanced at his wristwatch. 'Sorry, girls, but I can't sit around chatting – the folk round here depend on the buses.'

The girls took their bags and disembarked from the bus, then waited until he had pulled away before beginning the long slog towards their new home.

'There's a reason why they don't tell you the ins and outs,' muttered Mabel as she hefted her bag from one shoulder to the other.

'Do you suppose they would have as many volunteers?' said Roz, who was rather enjoying the walk along the hedge-lined track thick with foxgloves and meadowsweet.

Mabel shot her a wry glance. 'No, I do not!'

'I think it will be rather fun!' said Roz. 'We're certainly being thrown in at the deep end.'

The track which led to the farm was winding with a grassy path up the middle, and the walk seemed to take for ever, not helped by Mabel moaning that they were going to be living in the middle of nowhere, with not a man in sight. As they rounded yet another corner the girls were delighted to see a quaint little cottage with white stone walls and a low thatched roof before them. A large black and white collie sauntered across the yard towards them, tail wagging, he gave them a welcoming woof. Deciding that the dog was friendly, Roz patted her knees to coax him over, and fussed him when he arrived by her side.

To one side of the cottage was a row of stables, the doors of which were all painted black. Outside the last stable stood the biggest horse either of the girls had ever seen.

'Blimey!' breathed Mabel. 'Look at the size of his hooves – they're bigger than Mam's dinner plates!'

The horse appeared to chuckle, which alarmed both girls until they realised that a young man in his late teens, with short, curly black hair and a cheerful face, was standing on the other side of the horse. Wiping his forehead with the back of his forearm, he approached the girls.

'I'm Gethin Davies and this is Zeus.' He indicated the horse who was grazing on the weeds growing between the cobbled stones, then pointed down at the dog who was having his ears ruffled by Roz. 'And I see you've already met Jenson!'

'Hello, Gethin, I'm Roz,' said Roz, 'and this is my pal Mabel.'

Mabel was looking dewy-eyed at the handsome young stranger, who was attempting to shake her by the hand. Realising that she was staring, Mabel swiftly took his hand and noted the rough calluses which her father had always said indicated a hard worker. Eventually finding her tongue, she tried to speak, cleared her throat, and started again.

'Hello, Gethin, we're your new land girls.'

He cast an eye over their uniforms. 'I thought as much. I don't think anyone would voluntarily wear those britches.'

Mabel looked down at the baggy khaki britches, which she had completely forgotten she was wearing. 'Not my choice either,' she mumbled, feeling slightly embarrassed, 'but probably more practical than anything I own.'

He gestured towards a small porch at the side of the cottage. 'If you'd like to follow me I'll introduce you to my parents.'

'I'd follow him to hell and back,' Mabel whispered, much to Roz's silent amusement. They entered the porch, where they copied Gethin by removing their shoes.

'Mam won't have outdoor shoes in the house,' he explained. 'Slippers or socks, but no shoes.'

The girls placed their issue boots next to Gethin's and stepped into the house itself, noting as they did so, the immediate aroma of what smelt like some sort of pie with gravy. Gethin's parents, a middle-aged couple, sat either side of a long wooden table which stood in the middle of the kitchen. Looking around, Roz decided she very much liked what she saw. There was an enormous Aga set into the chimney breast, above which hung a pulley airer, laden with clothes. On the opposite side of the room there stood a large Welsh dresser, displaying a beautiful dinner set of white plates bordered with the tiniest blue flowers. As there didn't appear to be a single chip or crack on them, Roz assumed they were probably only used for special occasions.

She looked at Mabel, who was staring, open-mouthed, in complete wonder at her new surroundings. Gethin's father stood up, removed his pipe from the corner of his mouth and smiled warmly at the girls. He cast a shrewd eye over each of them before guessing who was who, indicating each girl with the stem of his pipe.

'Roz and you must be Mabel, am I right?'

They both nodded and Gethin introduced his parents, Howell and Heulwyn.

Heulwyn got up and invited the girls to sit down at the table whilst she made them a cup of tea.

'You've come a long way and I should think you're fair parched, not to mention starving hungry. Have you had anything to eat?' Heulwyn asked, a concerned look etching her otherwise cheery complexion.

'Spam sarnies on the bus down,' said Mabel, pulling a disgruntled face, 'but I wouldn't call that food.'

'Me neither!' Heulwyn bustled over to the dresser, opened one of the cupboards and took out two plates, which were obviously for everyday use. 'I've a shepherd's pie in the oven. It should be just about ready.'

Roz's mouth began to water at the very mention of pie, although truth be known she didn't have a clue what shepherd's pie was, and admitted as much to her hosts, who laughingly reassured her that it wasn't made of actual shepherds, but was in fact a lamb and vegetable stew – sounding a bit like scouse to Roz – with a mashed potato topping.

Heulwyn dished out the hearty food onto five plates and Gethin handed them round, whilst Heulwyn told Roz and Mabel where they could find the cutlery. 'If you're going to be staying with us, you need to know where everything is,' she said reasonably. 'Start as you mean to go on, is what I always say, and this is your home whilst you're with us.'

Roz glanced at Mabel, and her expression said it all. Why couldn't a family like the Davieses have taken her in rather than the Haggartys?

As they ate the first proper meal in what seemed like an age, the Davieses quizzed Mabel and Roz about the life they had left behind in Liverpool. Roz told them all about her journey from Frankfurt, something which they were particularly interested in, as it gave them an insight into life in Europe before the war. In turn they told the girls about life at Glasfryn farm and what would be expected of them.

'We have cattle which we keep in the lower pastures, and sheep which graze on the mountain behind us during the summer months, but in winter we bring them down to the farm,' explained Howell. 'We grow our own hay, which we keep in the Dutch barn, and the pigs and chickens are behind the stables.'

'What do you use Zeus for?' asked Mabel, hoping against hope that they were going to say the girls needed to ride him.

'Ploughing, moving anything heavy like the hay cart, picking up feed from the village, that kind of thing,' said Gethin.

'If you've always lived here, then why do you need land girls?' said Roz, who was failing to see where she and Mabel came into the equation.

Beaming with pride, Howell indicated his son with the stem of his pipe. 'This one's off to train as air crew in the RAF; he should be getting his papers through within the next couple of weeks.'

Mabel's heart sank. In one sentence, Howell had destroyed her dream of marrying Gethin and moving to a farm similar to Glasfryn, where they would keep horses and dogs and have babies galore. She glanced at Roz, who had guessed exactly why her friend was looking crestfallen.

'That makes sense,' said Roz.

Mabel smiled fleetingly at Gethin. 'At least you'll have time to show us what's what before you go.'

'You'll soon get into the swing of things,' Gethin assured her. 'It's pretty simple really, the milking being the only tricky part, but once you've got the knack you'll be away.'

When the meal was over, Roz joined Heulwyn at the sink. 'I can see why you need help, but we're rather green when it comes to farming. The college was alright, but they really only taught us the basics; we didn't do anything hands on with any animals.'

Howell waved a dismissive hand. 'I don't know why they bother. Farming's a practical skill, not something you can learn from a book!'

'Dad's right,' said Gethin 'and as you've a heap to learn, why not start now with a look around the farm?'

'When you've seen where everything is, you can come inside and have a nice hot bath before turning in,' said Heulwyn.

Thanking their host for the wonderful meal, the girls followed Gethin outside, and were surprised to find that the nights were a lot colder here than they were in Liverpool.

Gethin indicated the mountain behind the house. 'I won't take you to see the sheep as you can see them from here. I suggest we start with the yard first.' He took the girls round the stables which were mostly used for storing farming equipment, animal feed and things of that nature. 'We only really use the stables for when one of the stock is sick,' he explained to Mabel, who had rather hoped to find foals, lambs and calves inside them.

Leading them round the back, he pointed to two pigs which he introduced as Bonnie and Clyde. 'They're our breeders, a fine breed called Gloucestershire Old Spots,' he said conversationally, before pointing out the chickens. 'We let them roam free during the day but lock them up at night, safe from the foxes. Come with me, and I'll show you how to round them up. There's ten hens and one cockerel.' He grinned at Mabel, who was looking anxious. 'Don't worry, it's easy to tell which is which.'

The girls spent the next ten minutes chasing chickens around the yard, whilst Gethin looked on in mild amusement. 'Every time I get near one, it flies off!' said Mabel as they herded the last chicken into the enclosure.

Gethin then led them to a field and leaned against the wooden five-bar gate. 'That's the dairy herd,' he informed the girls. 'We've fifteen cows and one bull.' He winked at Mabel. 'Again, you'll know which is which, especially if you try to milk the wrong one ...'

This comment caused Roz to go off into hoots of laughter, whilst Mabel stood looking perplexed. 'I don't get it,' she said, frowning.

Smiling kindly, Gethin laid his hand on her arm, much to Mabel's secret delight. 'You'll see what I mean tomorrow.'

With Roz still giggling, he led them round to another gate, and pointed to the sheep who were grazing in the distance. 'You don't have to do much with the sheep at this time of year, but come springtime, you'll have your work cut out for you with the lambing. I won't be here then but you'll be in good hands with Dad. There's nothing he doesn't know when it comes to lambing.'

By the time the girls had finished their tour they were both yawning widely. 'I'll be asleep before my head hits the pillow,' Mabel told Roz as they followed Heulwyn up to their bedroom at the back of the house. Opening the door, Heulwyn stood to one side, allowing the girls to step through.

'Howell's already brought your bags up, and I've run you a bath,' she indicated a room across the hallway. 'Take all the time you need, girls, and I'll see you in the morning. *Nos da.*'

'Sorry?' said Mabel.

'*Nos da,*' repeated Heulwyn, 'it's Welsh for goodnight.'

Mabel yawned the words '*Nos da*' back to Heulwyn who made her way back down the stairs.

Calling 'goodnight' after her hostess, Roz knelt down next to the low, deep-set window and looked across the yard to the fields beyond. Turning to Mabel she sighed happily. 'We've really landed on our feet here.'

Mabel nodded as she pulled her vest over her head. 'I wish Gethin was staying, but I suppose if he was there wouldn't be any need for us.'

236

Roz grinned at her friend. 'He certainly is handsome, and I gathered by the soppy look on your face that you are rather keen on him.'

Mabel put on a dressing gown and pulled the cord into a bow, before tucking her towel under her arm. 'Can you blame me?'

'Not really, especially when I know how much you want to marry a farmer,' said Roz, 'and if I'm any judge I'd say he was keen on you too.'

Mabel opened the door to their room and the girls could see the steam coming from the roll-top bath in the room opposite. 'Do you really think so?' Mabel's eyelids, which had been drooping sleepily, were now wide open.

'I do. It's the same way Felix looks at me,' said Roz. 'Talking of Felix, I wonder how he's getting on.'

'I don't know much about Australia,' Mabel admitted, 'but I do know it's hotter there than it is here, so at least he'll be getting plenty of sunshine.'

Having heard no more about HMT *Dunera*, the girls had assumed that it must have arrived safely in Australia. Roz knew that Felix would write to Alan and Bill, but she realised that it would take months for any mail to come through. In her heart she knew that it was highly likely she would never see him again, but in her experience fate had a funny way of working things out, so she refused to give up hope – after all, she hadn't given up hope of finding her parents.

*

237

Over the next two weeks Gethin taught the girls every-thing there was to know about stock farming, something which pleased Mabel no end, especially when it came to milking. Roz picked it up straight away with little tuition, but Mabel struggled and it took many attempts, with Gethin placing his arms around her whilst he demonstrated the best method of getting the milk without upsetting the cow, before she finally suc-ceeded. In fact, Roz suspected her friend had got the knack much sooner than she apparently did, just so that she could be close to Gethin.

They found the work far more tiring than they had thought they would. Gethin had made it sound as though milking was the hardest part of the day, whereas in fact, they spent the whole day tending to the ani-mals, feeding the pigs and chickens, mucking out the pens, hunting for eggs, herding the cattle from the field to the shed and back again, and checking the sheep to make sure that they were in good health. For the first few days both girls claimed they ached in places they never knew they had.

Their time on the farm flew by, and before they knew it, it was the morning before Gethin was due to leave the farm and Roz, Mabel and Gethin were herding the cattle into the milking shed.

'You can't beat a sunrise on a clear day,' Gethin said as he closed the gate behind them.

Mabel followed his gaze to the horizon, where the sun's rays were feeling their way across the land. 'Had someone told me this time last year that I'd be getting up before dawn to do the milking, I'd have thought them potty,' she said conversationally, 'especially if they'd told me that sunrise would be my favourite time of day, but not any more! I love being awake when most of the world is still asleep.' She glanced around her. 'No cars, no screaming kids, and no people arguing in the street 'cos they've had a skinful, just cows chewing the cud ...'

Roz, who was not a fan of the farm's cockerel, butted in. 'What about Gulliver? You can't say he's a joy to hear at five o'clock in the morning!'

'He's my alarm!' said Mabel defensively. 'I'd far rather hear him sounding off than that Moaning Minnie.'

Roz grimaced. When they had been living in Liverpool, the air raid siren, nicknamed Moaning Minnie, had been seen as an inconvenience because it had always been a false alarm. But since leaving, the girls had heard from Mabel's parents, as well as Bill and Alan, that the bombing had started in Liverpool. Not as bad as down south, but it had certainly put things into perspective.

'I wonder if Callum is still looting,' Roz mused aloud.

Gethin's eyes widened as he leashed some of the cows, ready for milking. 'Looting?'

Roz explained Callum's air raid shenanigans.

'That's terrible,' said Callum. 'What did the police do?'

'Not a lot they could do,' said Mabel, 'not unless they caught him red-handed, and they've got more sense than to be checking houses for would-be criminals in the middle of an air raid, false or otherwise.'

'People like that make my blood boil,' said Gethin, 'but I'm a big believer in what goes around comes

239

around. Just you wait, he'll get his comeuppance one of these days.'

'Doubt it,' said Mabel, 'people like him get away with murder.' She shot Roz a meaningful glance.

'And yet good men like Felix get taken to the other side of the world for doing nothing!' Roz said ruefully. 'It doesn't seem right, does it?'

Roz had never mentioned Felix in front of Gethin before, and he was curious to find out more.

'Who's Felix?'

'He came over with me on the Kindertransport. Everything was fine until he got interned for being an enemy alien.' She looked up from milking one of the cows. 'I don't suppose you've heard of HMT *Dunera* …' She fell silent as Gethin's eyebrows shot upwards.

'You're kidding?' he said in hushed tones.

'You've heard of it, then?'

Gethin nodded slowly. 'I thought everyone knew of the *Dunera* and what sounds like the voyage from hell.'

Thinking that Gethin was referring to the failed torpedo, Roz waved a vague hand. 'I wouldn't go that far – it's not as if any harm was done,' she said, adding, 'luckily enough.'

Gethin stared at her. 'I wouldn't call being beaten, having your water rationed to three days a week, and all your possessions thrown into the sea, lucky!'

Roz stared back, utterly perplexed. She had no idea what Gethin was on about and could only assume they must be talking about different ships, or journeys. She said as much, but Gethin was resolute.

'I know what I'm talking about, it's been in the papers and on the news. The doctor who boarded the ship in Sydney said conditions were disgusting, and that people had been treated inhumanely.' His eyes searched Roz's for any sign of understanding. 'They were shipped along with Nazis and Italian fascists ... didn't you know?'

Roz stood up sharply, spooking the cow in front of her. 'Of course I didn't know! I thought you were referring to the torpedo which glanced off the ship. When did all this come out?'

'Not long ago, and if you ask me Churchill's been trying to keep it all pretty hush-hush.' He shot her another incredulous look. 'There's been outrage amongst the British people, saying they should bring them back, and that it should never have happened in the first place. I don't know how you couldn't have heard anything.'

'Because I was either in Hutton or here,' said Roz, who was finding all this rather hard to believe. 'Why didn't Alan or Bill say something?' Still convinced Gethin must have his wires crossed, she looked at him thoughtfully. 'Did anyone die, on the voyage, I mean?'

Gethin looked awkward. 'A few,' he said, quickly adding, 'I think they were probably the older men, though. I'm sure Felix will be alright.'

Tears pricked Roz's eyes. There was an honesty and certainty about Gethin which caused her to believe that he was speaking the truth. She looked at Mabel, who left the cow she had been milking to comfort her.

'Felix can hold his own, Roz,' she soothed reassuringly. 'Why don't you go back to the house and write to Bill and Alan? Me and Gethin can finish up here, then perhaps Gethin can take you into town to mail your letter?'

Gethin nodded. 'Just let me know when you're ready.'

Wiping her eyes on the backs of her hands, Roz nodded miserably. 'I'll feel happier once I've written to them, and better still once I've had a reply.'

It was the morning that Gethin was due to leave for the RAF. The whole family had been up earlier than usual so that they could get the work done and see him off at the train station.

Roz had written and sent her letter the day before. Whilst she was at the post office she had voiced her fears to the post mistress who had reassured her that when it came to the deaths on the *Dunera*, no one of Felix's age had been reported.

Standing on the platform, which was a lot smaller than the one at Lime Street, Roz hooked her arm through Mabel's. 'You're going to miss that boy.'

Mabel nodded sadly. 'At first I was annoyed that he was leaving, now I just want him to come back safe and sound.'

Roz glanced meaningfully in the direction of Gethin's mother, who was blowing her nose into her handkerchief, whilst being comforted by her son. 'You're not the only one who's worried.'

Mabel's bottom lip trembled as she fought back the tears which threatened to expose her innermost feelings. 'I dreamed of finding myself a farmer, and now I wish I hadn't, because it's going to be a lot harder worrying where he is, and whether he's safe.'

Roz squeezed Mabel's arm. 'That's what love is. I'm the sa—' She stopped short, but Mabel was no fool.

'I'm what?' she said, cocking an eyebrow. 'I'm the same with Felix, that's what you were about to say, wasn't it?'

Blushing, Roz nodded. 'I was, but then it occurred to me that the only times I've ever been sure of my feelings for Felix are when I've thought him in mortal peril. The first one being when he was arrested and the other, yesterday when I thought he could be dead, but when I think he's safe, I tend to question my love for him, and whether it's more of a kinship than a romance.'

Mabel looked at Gethin who was trying to cheer his mother up. 'I'd say that you love him, and it's the fear of losing him that brings it to the fore. Don't forget you've got an awful lot more on your mind than just Felix.'

'My parents, you mean?'

Mabel nodded. 'You're not free to be in love when you've got the worry of your parents hanging over your head – that's why your feelings only come out when you think that Felix is in danger.'

'The only thing I can say for certain, is the thought of losing Felix is more than I can bear,' said Roz.

Mabel blinked up at her, tears shining in her eyes. 'Whichever way you look at it, you love that boy.' She was looking at Gethin who had turned to face them. 'What a pair we are! Both in love, and both on our own.'

'Like thousands of other women,' said Roz quietly, 'and all because of one hateful little man.'

Gethin was approaching the girls and Roz could tell from his stance that he felt awkward. She slipped her arm out of Mabel's and smiled at him. 'So long, Gethin, good luck with everything, and take care. I'll leave you to say goodbye to Mabel.'

'Thanks, Roz.' He placed an arm around Mabel's shoulders. 'Come now, I can't have my favourite milkmaid in tears!'

Sniffing loudly, Mabel tried not to look at Gethin. She knew her eyes must be puffy from crying and she didn't want him to remember her that way, but Gethin was having none of it. Placing his finger beneath her chin, he raised it up so that he could gaze into her eyes. 'I'll be back before you know it.'

Cursing the tears which fell, she went to wipe them away, but Gethin had beaten her to it. Leaning down, he kissed her forehead, then her lips. Mabel felt as though her feet had left the floor, until she remembered that Gethin's parents were only a stone's throw away. Blushing to the tips of her ears, she broke away hastily and glanced shyly at his parents and Roz, who appeared to be showing great interest in the locomotive.

'What does this mean?' she asked, looking coyly at Gethin who was smiling with amusement at her embarrassment.

'That I'm your beau. If you'll have me, of course …' he said, giving her a cheeky wink.

Mabel felt as though all her Christmases had come at once. 'Of course I will, I just wish …' she heaved a sigh, '... only there's no point in wishing, is there?'

The train whistle shrieked loudly, causing them to jump. 'That's me!' said Gethin. Breaking away from Mabel, he slid his hand into hers and led her over to where his parents and Roz stood patiently waiting. His mother burst into a fresh bout of tears as he heaved his bag over his shoulder and kissed her on the cheek.

Waving a cheery goodbye, he jumped aboard the train, just before the guard slammed the carriage door shut.

It may have only been a couple of weeks, but Mabel and Roz felt as though they had known the Davieses a lot longer.

As the train pulled out of the station, Roz turned to Mabel, who was trying to smile through her tears. 'At least you can write to him; I wish I could do that with Felix.'

'I shall write the moment we get home, and every day after that,' Mabel said firmly.

Heulwyn fell into step beside her. 'I'm glad our Gethin's found a good, honest, hard-working girl to come back to.'

The blush returned with lightning speed as Mabel looked cautiously at the older woman. 'I didn't know he was going to kiss me ...' she began, only to be waved into silence by Heulwyn who was smiling warmly at her.

'Like I said, I'm *glad* our Gethin's got a girl like you to come home to; it might encourage him to take extra care out there!'

Having had the seal of approval from Gethin's parents, Mabel felt on top of the world. She just wished he was here to hear it.

Nearly three weeks had passed since Roz had written to Bill and Alan, and she was beginning to wonder whether they had received her letter when she finally got a reply.

Dear Roz

I'm so sorry we didn't tell you about the Dunera, *but we had no idea whether Felix had been involved in any of the unpleasantness and didn't wish to upset you unnecessarily. With hindsight we should have realised you would find out eventually, which of course is worse than if we had just been straight from the start. We have been as worried as you, but hoped that no news was good news, and as luck would have it, it turned out we were right. We received a letter from Felix just two days ago, saying that he would be returning to serve in His Majesty's army! Of course we were over the moon to hear that not only was he alright, but that he was coming home! I have written back with your address but it's quite probable that he will be halfway back to Blighty before it reaches him. However, he knows where we are, and we're certain he'll pop round as soon as he docks, so we'll pass it on to him then.*

I hope this brings you some comfort, and I'm terribly sorry if we worried you unduly. We know you've heard about the bombings, but thankfully they aren't as bad as they are in other parts of the country …

Having read the most important part, Roz tucked the letter back into its envelope. She would read the rest later in bed. A small, happy smile formed on her cheeks. Felix was coming home!

Chapter Six

December 1940

When Felix arrived at Alan and Bill's house he already knew that Roz was no longer living at the flat, and was hoping he might find her back with the carters, so was disappointed to learn that she was living on a farm in North Wales.

'How far away is that?' he asked, his brow furrowing as he tried to place Wales on the map of Britain in his mind's eye.

Alan laughed. 'Far enough, and Roz is smack bang in the middle of the mountains, so not easy to get to, although I've only ever been to Rhyl myself, so maybe I'm no expert.'

'Do you think I'd have time to get there and back before my training?' said Felix, his voice laced with hope.

Alan looked to his father, who had a better knowledge of the Welsh countryside.

Bill sucked the air between his teeth as he weighed it up. 'Depends on the transport. Getting to North Wales is the easy part; getting to the farm where she's working will be a lot harder. A taxi from the train station will probably cost you an arm and a leg, so you'd have to bus it. Even so, I very much doubt it would take you more than a couple of days from here, so the answer is yes, you could make it there and back. Don't forget you'll have to clear it with the folk she's staying with, only I shouldn't imagine there's a B&B nearby, nor a hotel come to that.'

'I could stay in a tent?' suggested Felix, causing both Alan and Bill to break into laughter.

'In December? You'd freeze yer knackers off!' Bill spluttered.

'An igloo,' chuckled Alan, 'that'd be a better bet.'

'Just how far away is it?' said Felix.

'Like Alan said,' replied Bill, 'she's in the mountains. It's not so much distance as height, if you get my meaning?'

Felix nodded slowly. 'But the mail takes for ever. I never got any of your letters and you only got one of mine. I know Australia's a lot further, but even so, it'll take time, and that's the one thing I've not got.'

Bill was rubbing the newly formed stubble on his chin. 'You could always send a telegram, that'd be a lot quicker.'

Felix beamed. 'Of course! Why didn't I think of that?'

'Because you're too busy gettin' your knickers in a twist, and not thinkin' straight,' said Alan, 'that's what women do to you.' He turned to find he was talking to thin air – Felix had already left.

*

Roz stared at the boy who stood in the doorway to the kitchen. 'A telegram? Are you sure it's for me?'

The young boy waved the telegram at her. 'If you're Rozalin Sachs, then yes, this is a telegram for you,' he said slowly and loudly, as if Roz couldn't understand English.

Too scared to take the telegram, Roz looked at Mabel. 'There are only two people who know I'm here, Bill and Alan. Why would they send me a telegram? I can't imagine it being anything good. After all, we know there's only one kind of news that gets delivered by telegram during wartime.'

Heulwyn took the telegram from the boy and handed it to Roz. 'This lad's got places to be; best you read it quick in case you need to send a reply.'

Roz pulled herself together and read the contents whilst everyone around her looked on with bated breath.

'It's Felix,' she whispered, her heart racing with relief, 'he's back in Liverpool and wants to know if he can see me before he goes off for training.'

Heulwyn, who had feared Roz's assumption that only bad news came with wartime telegrams to be right, sank gratefully into one of the kitchen chairs. 'Of course he can,' she said. 'Tell him he can come as soon as he likes. He can even stay for Christmas if he makes it in time.'

Roz's eyes shone with gratitude. 'Oh, Heulwyn, are you sure?'

Howell spoke up from behind the pages of his newspaper. 'She'd not have suggested it otherwise, especially not after what that poor lad's been through.'

Taking a pencil from his pocket, the boy stood poised to write. 'Is that the message? Come as soon as you can, and stay for Christmas?'

Roz nodded. 'It certainly is.'

Several telegrams later, and the date had finally been set for the 23rd of December, when Roz and Mabel would meet Felix at the station. However, the snow had started to fall a few days before his arrival, and the roads were already impassable by anything other than a horse, so Howell had got the old wooden sleigh they used for such conditions and harnessed it to Zeus.

'I don't know the way,' said Roz as Howell gave her instructions on how to drive the horse.

He gave her a wry smile. 'There's only one road, you can't possibly go wrong.'

Mabel pointed at the bells which Howell had attached to the harness. 'What are they for?'

'So that folk hear you coming. Horses' hooves don't make the same noise in snow as they do on tarmac.'

'What if he runs off?' said Mabel, who whilst eager to take the reins, was also wary of any consequences that might arise from their inexperience.

Howell roared with laughter. 'I'll take my hat off to you if you can get this bloody lump to run.'

'One road all the way?' Roz said tentatively.

He nodded. 'You can't get lost, and even if you did, Zeus'll bring you home when he gets hungry.'

Her heart thumping in her chest, Roz nodded. She didn't have much choice when it came down to it, and she could hardly leave Felix at the station, not when he'd come all this way. She turned to Mabel. 'Are you going to do the driving?'

Mabel's smile said it all. Getting onto the seat behind Zeus's ample behind, she waited for Roz to join her, whilst Howell rooted around for something underneath the driving seat, appearing a few moments later with a thick woollen blanket which he placed over the girls' knees. 'That'll keep you warm.' He walked over to the farmyard gate and, kicking it free from snow whenever it got stuck, he eventually pulled it wide open and grinned at them. 'Off you go.'

Mabel clicked her tongue as Howell had instructed, and just as he had said, Zeus plodded slowly forward. Waving goodbye over their shoulders, the girls snuggled together as fresh snow began to fall.

'Isn't it beautiful?' Roz breathed as they listened to the crump, crump, crump of Zeus's hooves in the thick snow, mixed with the gentle jingle of the bells.

Mabel nodded dreamily. 'I wish my folks could see me now. This is even better than Coconut.'

Roz gave her friend a reproving glance. 'Poor Coconut, it's not his fault he's stuck working down the docks.'

Just as Howell had said, there was only one road all the way to the station, and Zeus didn't stop walking until they arrived some thirty minutes later and saw Felix waiting under the shelter of the station roof.

He waved a greeting as he approached the sledge. 'Well! Talk about arriving in style!'

Roz jumped down to greet him and gave a small squeal of delight as he whisked her up into his arms, before setting her back down. As their eyes locked, they both instinctively leaned in to a kiss. Feeling the warmth from his lips and smelling the familiar scent of the aftershave she had bought him last Christmas, it seemed to Roz that once again all was well with the world. Hearing a small cough behind them, Roz pulled away with an embarrassed giggle. Holding Felix's hand tightly in her own, she looked up at Mabel. 'Sorry, I think we got caught up in the moment.'

'So I see!' said Mabel, who was grinning broadly. 'And whilst I understand you needing to say hello, it's sodding freezing sitting up here on me tod.'

Felix threw his kitbag onto the floor of the sledge and helped Roz up before joining her.

'If we all snuggle under the blanket we'll soon get warm,' suggested Roz.

Mabel turned the horse around with ease, and they set off on the journey home.

As Zeus settled into his methodical gait, Roz told Felix about the farm, and their new lives as land girls, whilst Mabel told him all about Gethin, his life in the RAF and their relationship.

'It's a shame he couldn't come home for Christmas,' said Felix. 'Are you sure the Davieses don't mind my coming?'

Roz waved a dismissive hand. 'Not at all, in fact it was Heulwyn's suggestion that you stay for Christmas.'

As Zeus continued on his way, they talked about the war, what had happened so far, where Felix would be posted, and Australia – the creatures Felix had seen and what life was like in the land down under. Roz asked him about his time on the *Dunera*, but Felix was reluctant to share the tale of his voyage, save to say that it was one he wouldn't wish to repeat.

Mabel chuckled softly as Zeus entered the farmyard with no instructions from her. She turned to Felix. 'Is Coconut driven by his tummy too?'

Felix nodded. 'I think all animals are.' Laughing, he added, 'Me too most of the time!'

'Well, you'll not go hungry here,' said Roz. 'Heulwyn's a wonderful cook and she believes in large portions – me and Mabel have both put on weight!'

'Sounds like a woman after my own heart!' said Felix. Jumping down from the sleigh, he took his kitbag from under the seat and threw it over his shoulder before giving both girls a hand down, just as a voice hailed them from behind.

Mabel waved a hand as Howell approached them. 'Hello, Howell, you were right!' she said, swiftly removing the harness. 'He was a dream to drive, and he knew exactly where he was going.'

Howell greeted Felix with a hearty handshake. 'Hello, Felix, I'm Howell. Come on in, Heulwyn's itching to get supper on the table.'

Felix turned to say that he would give the girls a hand with the horse, only to see that they had already unharnessed and stabled Zeus who was already enjoying a bucket of warm mash.

'Blimey, that didn't take long,' he said, his tone full of admiration.

'Been taught by the best,' said Mabel, indicating Howell with a nod of her head.

'Poppycock! It's the thought of Heulwyn's meat and potato pie that's driving them on,' Howell replied, winking at them.

'Maybe just a little,' Mabel admitted, as she followed the others across the yard.

Roz was about to tell Felix to take his boots off in the porch, but it seemed he was one step ahead of her.

Heulwyn, who was standing by the fire, beckoned them over. 'Hello, Felix, I'm Heulwyn. I expect you're frozen to the bone. Come on over and warm your toes, you can worry about unpacking later.'

The evening seemed to fly by, with the Davieses keen to hear about Australia, and everything else that Felix had to tell them.

'You'd have made a good farmer,' said Howell, after hearing how Felix had taken to working with Coconut down the docks. 'You sound like a natural when it comes to animals. I've seen plenty of folk try to make a beast do their bidding, but an animal has to trust you if it's to do as you ask.'

A proud smile formed on Felix's lips under the farmer's praise.

'We'll see how well he gets on with the milking tomorrow,' grinned Mabel. 'We'll soon see whether he's a natural or not!'

It was Christmas Eve morning and the girls were teaching Felix how to milk, something which caused a great deal of hilarity at first, but despite their teasing, Felix had soon got the knack, and it wasn't long before he was churning out pail after pail.

'Well, I never thought I'd be milking cows on Christmas Eve,' he said, passing another pail over to Roz who was pouring it into the churn, 'but it sure beats working down the docks.'

'And I never thought I'd see you again, let alone spend Christmas with you,' Roz sighed happily. 'It's about time things started going our way.'

He grinned up at her from his milking stool. 'I thought last Christmas was special, but I think it's going to pale in comparison to this year.'

Mabel untethered the cow that Felix had finished milking. 'I think it's a shame Jewish people don't get to celebrate Christmas; it's my favourite time of the year.'

'Mine too,' admitted Roz. 'I don't think my parents would mind me saying that, because even though we're Jewish we're German too ...' she paused, '... or were, because I don't think I am any more.' She glanced at Felix. 'Do you still think of yourself as being German?'

He shook his head. 'If being a German means you have to be a Nazi, then no, I don't think of myself as being German.'

Roz mulled this over. 'I can remember what it was like before we left Frankfurt, and whilst I'd like to believe that there were some Germans who didn't agree with the Nazis, I saw very little evidence of it. Then again, I reckon our neighbours were just as scared of the soldiers as we were, so maybe they were only pretending to like them.'

Felix shrugged. 'Maybe ...' He began to milk another cow that Mabel had brought over. 'It must be lovely being a cow, no religion, no war, just chewing the cud and hanging about with your friends all day.'

'Life certainly would be simpler,' agreed Mabel, leaning against the cow's rump. 'Although I don't think I'd like the thought of sharing my man with a lot of other women.'

Roz began to giggle. 'Bit like one of those sultans and their harems.'

Felix flashed her a dazzling smile. 'Not for me, I'm a one-woman kind of guy.'

Roz felt herself begin to blush. She still couldn't get used to the fact that Felix was her boyfriend, nor that he was back in Britain. When they were together it felt natural, and she was glad that no matter where he was posted in Britain, it could never be as far away as Australia.

Before they knew it Christmas Day was upon them, and after a frantic morning of milking, feeding and mucking out, they all sat down to a glorious roast chicken dinner.

'It'd be a shame to let that hen go to waste,' said Howell, winking at the girls, 'after she got run over by accident.'

Everyone around the table knew full well that the chicken had not died accidentally, but who could prove otherwise? Roz's mouth had watered as she tasted the delicious fare, with thick gravy, sprouts and chestnut stuffing. The meal had been fit for a king, finished off with Heulwyn's bara brith, something which Felix and the girls had never tasted before, but all agreed that it was now a new favourite.

In the evening they played rummy, go fish and draughts. And by the time they were all ready to turn in, Felix remarked that it was hard to believe there was a war on, living in such a wonderful part of the country.

'You don't get sirens out here, I suppose,' he said, much to the amusement of Mabel, who advised him that Gulliver the rooster was probably louder than any air raid siren – something which surprised Felix as he hadn't heard the cockerel since his arrival.

'It's all this fresh country air you've been getting,' said Roz. 'It must be knocking you out like a light.'

They spent the next few days much as they had Christmas Day, working flat out in the morning and taking the afternoons and evenings off to play parlour games, listen to the radio and tell stories. The highlight of Christmas for Mabel was the arrival of a letter from Gethin, telling her all about his life in the RAF and inviting her down to see him as soon as she could find the time, which made her heart sing.

'I did think he might forget all about me when he saw all those pretty Waafs,' she confided to Roz. 'They say absence makes the heart grow fonder, but not when you're surrounded by a bevy of beauties.'

Roz shook her head. 'He's like my Felix, loyal.'

Mabel had giggled. 'You make him sound like Jenson.'

Roz pictured the way the collie looked at her when he wanted fussing, then pictured Felix, and the way he looked at her. She began to giggle. 'I've never thought of it like that before, but now you mention it ...'

Mabel slapped the back of Roz's hand in a playful manner. 'Don't tell him that. He might not like it if he thinks he's got competition when it comes to a dog.'

'No competition,' said Roz, 'Jenson wins every time!'

'It's that shaggy coat and those big puppy dog eyes, isn't it?' laughed Mabel.

Roz cast her friend a wry glance. 'Are we talking about Jenson or ... ?'

Mabel stifled a giggle. 'Poor Felix, fancy losing to a dog!'

Roz shook her head. 'I'm only teasing. Of course Felix wins ...' She jumped as a voice spoke from behind.

'Only 'cos I don't drool on your lap when you're eating your supper,' chuckled Felix.

Blushing to the tips of her ears because Felix had overheard her talking about him, Roz hastily changed the conversation.

'He doesn't sneak up on me giving me a heart attack either. I thought you were helping Howell with the bull?'

'As it turns out, if a bull decides he doesn't want to go somewhere, he doesn't go, but if he changes his mind, he goes there very quickly indeed!'

Roz's eyes widened. 'Oh dear, I hope nobody was standing in his way.'

'Not for long,' said Felix, with a half-smile. 'I can run a lot faster than I thought.'

Mabel shook her head. 'That bloomin' beast's the only thing on this farm that scares me.'

Felix pushed his hands into his pockets. 'He certainly is a big feller, but I don't think he means any real harm – just a tad short-tempered is all, but at least you won't have to deal with him now we've moved him.'

Roz pouted. 'I can't believe you're leaving tomorrow!'

He placed his arm around her shoulders. 'Time certainly does fly when you're having fun. It seems like I've hardly been here any time at all!'

'It's so unfair that you have to join the army,' said Roz, her tone petulant. 'You weren't the one in the wrong, they were.'

'Saving face,' said Felix mildly. 'They know they did the wrong thing but don't want to admit it, and I can't say as I'm surprised, but look on the bright side – I made it back; not everyone on the *Dunera* is able to say that.'

Roz glanced at Mabel. 'Gethin has asked Mabel to go and visit him. Do you think I'll be allowed to come and visit you when you get your posting?'

He nodded fervently. 'Of course you can, you can treat it like a holiday.'

She brightened. 'It will be, won't it?'

The following morning, it was with a heavy heart that Roz took Felix to the train station. Deciding that she could handle Zeus comfortably on her own, Mabel had suggested Roz might like to go by herself, so that she and Felix could spend some time together.

Even though the snow had stopped falling over the past few days, it still covered the roads, so they had decided their best bet was to take the sledge. As Zeus's hooves thudded against the thick blanket of snow, Roz recalled the journey which she and Mabel had taken to pick Felix up, and how different she had felt then from how she felt now. Back then, she had been full of excited anticipation, whereas now she was full of nervous trepidation. She didn't know how long it would be before she saw him again, and she had an underlying fear that something would happen and he would be taken back to Australia, or Canada, or somewhere equally far away. She voiced her fears to Felix, who did his best to reassure her that having already made one such mistake the government would be in no hurry to repeat it.

Now, as they neared the station, she began to think of excuses for him to stay. Perhaps pretend he'd had an accident and was unfit for duty, or that the snow was too bad for them to get through or ... Felix's voice cut across her thoughts.

'Penny for them?'

She gave a heartfelt sigh. 'Just thinking of ways to keep you here.'

He gave a short, mirthless laugh. 'Accidents to forgotten tickets, eh?'

She glanced curiously at him. 'You've been thinking the same?'

Nodding, he placed his arms around her shoulders and pulled her into a hug. 'Of course I have. I'd do anything to stay with you, but it wouldn't be right, and I won't turn my back on the people who saved me in the first place.'

She leaned her head into his shoulder. 'And I wouldn't want you any other way.' Looking up, she nuzzled her face into the warmth of his neck. 'I wish we had a few more hours.'

He kissed the top of her head. 'Me too, but time waits for no man.' He glanced through to the platform and the train which passengers were already boarding. 'I'll be for the high jump if I miss my train.' Lifting her chin, he kissed her softly, his hand cupping the side of her neck as he did so.

Roz opened her eyes and gazed into Felix's which twinkled at her. Breaking their embrace, he jumped down from the sledge and grabbed his kitbag. His jaw flinched as he looked back at Roz, her eyes filling with tears. 'I'll write every day, and once I'm settled somewhere, we'll arrange for you to come and visit.'

A tear fell onto her cheek as she nodded hastily. Wiping it away absent-mindedly, she smiled through lips that trembled as she spoke. 'Look after yourself.'

Nodding, Felix half turned in the direction of the station, before turning back and dropping his kitbag to the ground. Sensing what he was about to do, Roz placed the reins on the driver's seat and jumped down into Felix's arms. Holding her tight, he kissed her with a passion that she had never experienced before. Feeling lost in his embrace, she didn't hear the train whistle and was confused as to why he suddenly broke off, picked up his bag and began running towards the train. He just managed to jump into the only carriage with its door open before the guard shut it behind him. Felix leaned out through the window, waving enthusiastically at Roz. As the train began to pull out of the station, he called out to her.

'I love you, Rozalin Sachs!'

With a beaming smile she called back. 'I love you too, Felix Ackerman.'

Waving until he was out of sight, Roz returned to Zeus, tears of happiness flowing freely. She kissed the horse's soft muzzle. 'He really does love me, Zeus, and that's why he came back to me,' she said quietly, a contented smile lingering on her lips as she mounted the sledge and clicked her tongue for Zeus to move on.

She thought back to the conversation she'd had with Mabel when they'd last stood on the platform waving Gethin off. At the time she had worried that her feelings for Felix were only strong when she thought him in danger. Well, she knew he wasn't in danger any more, yet there wasn't a doubt in her mind that she loved him with all her heart, and what's more he loved her too!

March 1941

Felix had been posted to Lincoln to serve on an anti-aircraft gun, and from his letters it appeared he was very happy with his new role. Mabel's first instinct had been to ask if Felix had seen Gethin, seeing as her beau was also serving on an airfield in Lincoln, but Howell had explained that Lincoln was huge, with airfields dotted all over the place.

Spring was in the air, and the girls were getting to see Glasfryn at its best. The daffodils were in full bloom and they were well into the lambing season.

Mabel was in the kitchen helping Heulwyn bake bread whilst Roz helped Howell check the sheep to see if any of them were close to giving birth. Hearing a brief knock on the kitchen door, Heulwyn called for the unknown visitor to enter.

It was Dewi the postman. '*Bore da!*'

'*Bore da*, Dewi.' She took the envelopes from him and handed him a biscuit.

Grinning, he thanked her for the sweet treat before bidding her goodbye.

Heulwyn looked through the envelopes, most of which were bills, and handed three of them to Mabel.

Wiping her floury hands on her apron, Mabel scanned the writing on the envelopes before taking the one she wanted to read the most – the one with Gethin's handwriting on the outside – and slit it open. Eyes shining as she read the first line, she cried out with joy. 'Gethin's coming home!'

Hastily stuffing her own letters into her pinny, Heulwyn came round to Mabel's side of the table and read the letter which Mabel was holding out for her to see.

'We must make him something special,' she said authoritatively, 'to celebrate him coming home.'

'We've a few weeks yet, but...' Mabel gave an ecstatic sigh, '... oh, I can't wait!'

Taking the next two letters, she slit the first one open and looked down at the familiar signature of her parents at the bottom before stowing it away for later. She looked at the last letter, a puzzled frown creasing her brow. She didn't recognise the writing and the envelope looked rather formal. She glanced at the few letters which Heulwyn had set aside for Roz – one was from Felix, one from Roz's friend Adele and she was fairly sure, ah yes, she also had an official-looking letter just the same as Mabel's. The crease on her brow deepened as she tried to work out who the letters could be from, but she couldn't think of anyone, so she opened hers, crossing her fingers that it wouldn't be bad news. She read the contents, a hand covering her mouth, then looked at the older woman, tears shining in her eyes.

'Oh, my dear, whatever is the matter?' cried Heulwyn. 'Please say it's not one of your brothers?'

Mabel shook her head. 'We're being posted some-where new.'

'Oh, *cariad*,' Heulwyn murmured, taking Mabel in her arms, 'it's not the end of the world. I mean, we've loved having you here, but I suppose it was inevitable you'd move on at some stage.'

Wiping her eyes, Mabel handed the letter to Heul-wyn. 'We'll be leaving before Gethin comes home.'

Tutting loudly, Heulwyn read the letter. 'Well, if that isn't just typical!' she exclaimed. 'Of all the rotten luck!'

'It's not fair!' said Mabel. 'Why now?'

Heulwyn rubbed Mabel's shoulder. 'They don't do it on purpose, although it feels like it at times. They haven't notified us yet, but I expect we'll hear soon, and they'll be sending a couple more girls to replace you.' She glanced at the letter again, when a thought occurred to her. 'How about if I say we can't let you go until *after* Gethin's come home? I won't put it quite like that, of course, I shall say that we need your experience to help with the late lambing. Do you think that would work?'

Mabel brightened. 'Anything's worth a go, but what about Roz? Because I'd bet a pound to a penny that her letter says the same as mine.'

Heulwyn grimaced. 'They did tell us that Glasfryn is the perfect stepping stone for girls coming into the land army, so I suppose we always knew we were going to be seeing a lot of coming and going ...'

At that moment Roz entered the kitchen beaming with happiness. 'Twins ...' she said before adding, 'oh no, what's wrong?'

Wordlessly, Mabel handed her the envelope identical to her own. Roz immediately opened it, then looked up at the other two. 'Looks like we're on the move?'

Mabel nodded sadly. 'I opened Gethin's letter first – he's got some leave and will be home in three weeks.'

'Oh ...' said Roz, the penny finally dropping. 'Oh dear, is there nothing we can do?'

Heulwyn explained her plan to ask the authorities if the girls could stay just until the lambing was over, concluding, 'It would buy us just enough time for Mabel and Gethin to see each other, even if it's only for a few days.'

Roz nibbled the inside of her bottom lip. 'Do you think we'd have more chance if you just asked for Mabel to stay?'

Heulwyn weighed this up before answering. 'Maybe. I certainly wouldn't like to give them a choice out of the two of you, just in case they choose Roz.'

'Then ask for Mabel to stay and I'll go on ahead,' said Roz sensibly. 'You can argue that Howell won't be able to teach the new girls and do the lambing at the same time, so he needs Mabel to do the lambing whilst he shows them how to milk and feed the animals, as well as everything else.'

'When you put it like that, whether Gethin comes home or not, we need at least one of you here to help out with the lambing. I'll have a word with Howell, he'll know what to say.'

Mabel sank into one of the kitchen chairs. 'Thank you, Heulwyn.'

Heulwyn patted her shoulder. 'I'm not just doing it for you. I'm doing it for our Gethin as well, because I know how disappointed he will be if he comes home to find that you're not here.'

A smile twitched the corner of Mabel's lips. In truth, she never wanted to leave Glasfryn, which had come to feel like her home. If Gethin coming home bought her more time then that was fine with her, and who was to say that she might not get to stay longer – if not permanently should the other land girls not make the grade?

The goodbyes had been tearful, not least because Roz felt as though Heulwyn and Howell were like family, but also because she was leaving her best friend behind.

'I know you'll be following me in a few weeks, but I'm really going to miss you!' she said with a loud sniff as they stood waiting for the train to arrive.

'It's been a real adventure, hasn't it?' said Mabel, her bottom lip trembling. 'I bet it'll be strange going back to Liverpool after all this time.'

Roz had been surprised when she had received her posting to Gateacre, Liverpool, because she hadn't thought there were any farms near the city, but Mabel had soon put her right, explaining that Gateacre was just a few miles from the city, and assured her friend that it was a lovely area.

Now, as the train appeared in the distance, Mabel fought back her own tears. 'Make sure you look after yourself. Liverpool's not as safe as it used to be.' She waved a hand as Roz opened her mouth to say that she wouldn't be in the city itself. 'I know you're not going to be down by the docks or anywhere near a transport line, but they make mistakes, so just you keep your wits about you!'

'I know, and I will. Don't forget to say hello to Gethin for me.' Roz looked to Heulwyn and Howell. 'I'm really going to miss you two! Thanks for giving me the best Christmas I ever had.'

'You'll have to see if you can come this year,' said Heulwyn as she fished in her pocket for a tissue, 'see if we can make it a tradition.'

Roz smiled happily. 'I'd like that very much.' She glanced behind her at the passengers who were disembarking from the train to the crowded platform of people all waiting to get on. 'Looks like I'd better step to it if I'm to have a hope of getting a window seat,' she said, although she really wanted an excuse to leave the others before her emotions got the better of her. Hugging them each in turn, she bade them a hasty goodbye before picking up her bag and making her way to the nearest carriage. Finding a seat by the window, she wiped the condensation clear then smiled as her eyes met Mabel's. Her friend had been so pleased when the authorities had told her that she would be allowed to stay on until the end of the lambing season, and Roz knew that Mabel secretly hoped it could go on indefinitely, but Roz wasn't so sure. As the war progressed, more and more women were being called up to serve their country. Glasfryn might have seemed hard work when they had first arrived, but under Howell and Gethin's eagle eyes, they had learned everything there was to know about livestock, as well as a bit about arable farming. It was the perfect learning ground, and Roz felt sure that Mabel would eventually be moved on.

The train whistled to warn of its departure and Roz waved to the trio on the platform. It had been a long time since she had been on her own – in fact, she couldn't remember a time when she had last been by herself. Her thoughts turned to her parents, and where they might be. It was something she tried not to think about because it only upset her, which seemed pointless as she was powerless to do anything about it. Another thought occurred to her – she had left her address in Wales with Mr Garmin in the Liver Building, and even though she had not expected to hear any news, she supposed she should do the same for her new address, just as she had with Adele. For some reason her thoughts turned to the Haggartys. She wondered if Callum was still looting, and then supposed that this was a stupid thing to wonder about as he most certainly would be, especially with all the bombed out houses to steal from. The man would be like a child in a sweet shop. On the other hand, he might have fallen victim to the bombing whilst committing a burglary, and if he had, what would have happened to Suzie and Lilith? They would definitely be better off without him, but Suzie was very immature for a girl of her age, and Lilith too old to do very much. This got Roz to wondering how much longer Lilith would be able to cope with the steep steps that led up to the loft. As she started to mull this over, she chastised herself for worrying about people who wouldn't give two hoots about her. Suzie had stolen from her and Lilith had made it clear she detested Roz. Why waste time caring about people like that? *Because that's who I am*, she thought bitterly, *always feeling sorry for others, especially when I know they're being bullied, and that's what Callum does; he bullies them into doing everything he wants, because he knows they'd be lost without him.* She tutted angrily to herself. It was so unfair that good men like her father were trapped in Germany, whilst bullies like Callum walked around without a care in the world.

When Roz arrived in Liverpool she was shocked by the devastation that met her. She'd heard about the bombings, but there was a great deal of difference between hearing about it and seeing it for herself, and she hadn't imagined it to be anywhere near as bad as it was. Once she'd made her way to the bus station, she asked around until she was directed to the bus heading for Gateacre. Settling in the seat behind the driver, she wondered how long it would be before the bus was due to leave.

She didn't have to wait long before the clippie rang the bell and the bus pulled out of the station. Roz dug around in her handbag, which had been a gift from Heulwyn, and pulled out her purse. A moment later the clippie came over and asked her destination.

'Hollybank Farm?' confirmed the clippie approvingly. 'Very nice. I take it you're a land girl?' she said, glancing at Roz's britches.

Nodding, Roz handed over the money and waited for her ticket. 'Looks like it's been hell on earth whilst I've been in Betwys-y-Coed.'

A sharp-eared passenger behind her leaned forward in his seat. 'So you've been in Betwys-y-Coed whilst we were getting bombed?'

Roz nodded. 'Working on a farm …' She fell silent under the man's accusing glare.

'Is that a German accent? 'Cos it sounds like one to me,' he said sternly.

Roz glanced at the clippie who was beginning to blush.

'What exactly are you getting at?' Roz snapped defensively.

His eyebrows rising slowly, he spoke in low, menacing tones. 'A bloody Kraut buggers off to Betwys-y-Coed whilst we're gettin' bombed then comes back just as the bombin' stops and starts askin' questions? What do you *think* I'm bleedin' gettin' at?'

Roz gaped at him. 'I don't tell the authorities where and when to send me!'

Looking as if he didn't believe a word she said, he leaned back in his seat, muttering, 'Maybe not, but you've probably got friends that can!'

Roz glared at him. 'My parents are stuck in Germany with people who'd see them dead just because they're Jewish. In future I suggest you try asking questions before jumping to conclusions.'

Looking rather embarrassed, but still disgruntled, the man muttered something about his having every right to be suspicious.

'Of course you've every right!' said Roz. 'But you shouldn't go off half-cocked. Try giving people the benefit of the doubt before you accuse them of being Nazis.'

The clippie frowned at the middle-aged man who'd made the accusations. 'She wasn't even asking questions, just stating the obvious – it does look like hell on earth, because it was.' She turned to Roz. 'Ignore him. You'd be a poor spy if you started asking questions on a public bus.'

Roz suppressed a chuckle. 'You're right there.'

Thankfully the journey from the station to Hollybank was mercifully short. The clippie called out to Roz when it was her turn to disembark and wished her luck as the bus pulled away.

Roz stood at the end of a long, grassy driveway. The difference between Hollybank and Glasfryn was immediately apparent. Glasfryn was set on the side of a mountain, whereas Hollybank was acre upon acre of open countryside. As she walked up the drive, she saw a herd of cattle three times the size of Glasfryn's, grazing in the pasture that bordered the drive. In the distance she could see what appeared to be two cottages, causing her to question just how big Hollybank was. She was about three quarters of the way down the drive when a man on horseback appeared. As he neared her Roz realised, with great admiration, that he was riding bareback, and the horse wasn't bridled but wearing a leather headcollar, with a rope acting as the reins.

He pulled the horse to halt and smiled down at her. 'Can I help you?'

Roz stared up at the handsome stranger, with blond hair and a smile so dazzling it practically took her breath away. Finding her tongue, she nodded. 'I'm Roz, the new land girl.'

Leaning down he held out his hand, and as Roz took it in her own, their eyes met, and Roz felt her tummy flip. He really was the most strikingly handsome man she had ever met. 'Hello, Roz. I'm Bernie Lewis, my folks own Hollybank.' He jumped down from the horse, landing lightly beside her. 'Come on, I'll show you where to go.'

Wanting to strike up a conversation in order to take her mind off how incredibly dashing he was, she motioned to the horse. 'Now I know who you are, who's this?'

He smiled, and once again, Roz felt her tummy jolt. 'This is Goliath,' his smile broadened, 'he's a Suffolk Punch. Do you like horses?'

She nodded. 'Very much. We had a beauty in Glasfryn, called Zeus. I think he was a Welsh Cob.'

'Hardy,' said Bernie, 'like this one.'

The driveway opened into a large square stable yard, flanked either side by two cottages, one much larger than the other. Roz assumed the bigger house to be the main residence, which Bernie confirmed. 'That's Hollybank Cottage where me and my folks live, and this,' he gestured to the much smaller cottage, 'is Rose Cottage which is where the land girls live.'

Roz's ears pricked at the mention of land girls, being in the plural. 'How many of us are there?' she asked.

He walked Goliath over to a stable, unhooked the rope from his neck and tied it to a ring. 'Two at the moment, including you, but there's two more to come, one of whom is your pal Mabel, I believe.'

Her eyes widened. 'You must have a huge farm if you need *four* land girls!'

He grinned. 'Eighty acres all told. We've a herd of forty Albions,' seeing her blank expression he elaborated, 'they're cows, and fifty Badger Face ...'

Roz nodded. 'I know they're sheep, I've worked with them.'

He gave her an approving look. 'The rest of the land is made up of arable, ranging from hay to wheat, with a few turnips, sprouts, potatoes and carrots thrown in.'

'Gosh, you really do have it all here,' Roz said admiringly. 'I can see why you need so many girls.'

Bernie knocked briefly on the green door to the cottage, and a woman called out for them to enter.

Once inside Roz could see that it was far more basic than the Davieses' farmhouse, with a range, a few cupboards and a table with at least eight chairs around it. It certainly wasn't as homely as Glasfryn, but she supposed that was because this was being used to house workers rather than a family. She smiled at the woman who appeared to be considerably older than her, judging by her weathered complexion. The woman stood up and went over to the range where she lifted a kettle before taking it to the sink and filling it with water. 'Tea?'

Roz nodded. 'That would be lovely, thank you,' adding, 'I'm Roz, by the way.'

The woman placed the kettle on the hob, took a box of matches and lit the stove. 'Pleased to meet you, Roz. I'm Joyce.' She glanced at Bernie. 'Are you stopping for a cuppa?'

He shook his head. 'I was just off into the village when I came across this one,' he said, glancing at Roz, 'maybe next time.' He left the women to get to know each other.

'Handsome devil, isn't he?' said Joyce as she spooned tea into a pot.

Roz, who was watching Bernie through the cottage window, nodded faintly. 'He certainly is. I bet he's broken his fair share of hearts.'

Joyce shrugged. 'I've not seen him take a shine to a single girl what's come here.' She took two mugs from a shelf and placed them on the table. 'Not that they haven't fallen for him, of course, and I don't blame them – he's handsome, charming and wealthy.' She arched a singular eyebrow. 'Too young for me – not that I'd be interested.'

Roz looked at her with surprise. 'Really? I'd have thought you'd just described every girl's dream, so why not yours?'

Joyce wrinkled her nose. ''Cos I'm old enough to know that all what glitters ain't gold. Bernie's alright, but he's handsome and he knows it.' Leaning back against the cupboard from which she had got the tea, she eyed Roz quizzically. 'It sounds like he's your type?'

Roz went to shake her head then stopped. 'I'm already spoken for.'

Joyce nodded wisely. 'Good-looking girl like you, I'm not surprised. Is he local? Only you don't sound like you come from Liverpool, or Britain come to that.'

Roz explained her situation and was pleased when Joyce took her at her word. 'I've heard about the refugees, we all have, and what they did to them fellers on the *Dunera* – well, you don't need me to tell you, if your Felix was one of them.'

'He didn't say much,' Roz admitted. 'He didn't need to, his face said it all.' She glanced around the interior of the kitchen before adding, 'You mentioned something about Bernie not taking a shine to a single girl that's been here? Is there a large turnaround of land girls at Hollybank?'

Joyce nodded. 'It's hard work and they ask a lot, but if you're prepared to knuckle down you'll get on fine.' She looked out of the window towards the bigger house. 'The Lewises are fair, but they believe in everyone pulling their weight with no excuses.'

Roz smiled. 'I certainly don't mind that; in fact, I'd rather get stuck in than stand idly by.'

Joyce poured the tea into the mugs. 'My personal opinion? The girls that come here are probably alright, until they meet Handsome – that's when all thoughts of work go out of the window, and the daydreaming begins.'

'You mean staring into space and envisaging weddings,' chuckled Roz.

Joyce nodded. 'Milk?'

'Yes, please. Well, you won't have that worry with me, nor my pal Mabel, as we both have men of our own. I can't speak for the other girl, of course – when's she due?'

Joyce shrugged. 'Who knows? They always promise but rarely deliver.'

Roz took a sip of the tea which Joyce handed her. 'Well, I'm here now, and Mabel will be following on in a couple of weeks, when the lambing has finished.'

Joyce brightened. 'It sounds like you've both got quite a bit of experience. It'll be good to have real help for a change and not some soppy girl daydreaming about love and marriage.'

Roz grinned. 'That was Mabel before she met Gethin. He's the farmer's son from Glasfryn.'

'I take it Gethin's Mabel's beau?' Joyce hesitated as Roz nodded, then continued, 'Then she's one of the lucky ones. I reckon most girls sign up for the land army hoping to meet a country gent, and are shocked to find their ideal man actually spends most of his life in wellies, old shirts, flat caps and poo-splattered trousers!'

Roz laughed. 'Not Bernie, though – I noticed he was very well dressed for a farmer's son.'

'He's a rarity alright,' Joyce said. 'Not many farms are like Hollybank; there's money here.'

Roz nodded slowly. 'A proper business.'

'Very much so. Unlike a lot of farmers, they're not renting their property; they own it.'

'Impressive,' said Roz. 'I've only been to Glasfryn – have you been to many other farms?'

Joyce took a sip of her tea before answering. 'I have indeed, and I must say I probably prefer the tenanted farms, but only because they feel like proper farms. I wasn't too happy when I found out I was coming here – it's too close to the city for me. I prefer to be deep in the countryside where it's safe.'

Roz looked at her with surprise. 'We're well out of the city. I know the Luftwaffe make mistakes, but it's not like we're close to the docks or railway lines.'

Joyce opened her mouth to reply, shut it, then tried again after a moment's careful thought. 'You're right, I'm being silly. Besides, I never go into the city, so why worry?'

'What, never?'

Joyce shook her head resolutely. 'Like I say, I'd rather be on the farm.'

Roz cocked her head to one side. 'You're from Liverpool, though? You certainly have the accent ...'

'And that's why I don't want to go back,' chuckled Joyce. Seeing the dubious look on Roz's face, she waved a vague hand. 'I'm only teasing. Liverpool's a grand city for those that want to live there, it's just not for me. Leaving was the best thing I ever did, joining the land army being the next. I love farming. It keeps you fit and you can earn enough to survive, and if you're lucky enough to own one, you're quids in.' She blew on the surface of her tea. 'Without sounding too morbid, there might be a few farms up for grabs when this business comes to an end, and if there are, I'm going to apply for a tenancy, to run my own farm.'

'Gosh!' said Roz. 'That sounds like a fabulous idea, and you'll have tons of experience after working on so many different ones.'

'That's why I'm always the first to offer myself for a move,' said Joyce. 'The more experience I get, the better off I'll be, and one day, I'll be able to run my own farm, safe in the knowledge that I know what I'm doing.'

'I think you're marvellous!' breathed Roz. 'I shouldn't imagine there are many female farmers that own their own tenancy!'

'Paving the way,' said Joyce. She drained her cup. 'How about I take you for a gander – I mean a look round the farm,' she added, after seeing Roz's blank expression.

'Good idea!' said Roz. She drained the last of her tea.

'I'll show you to our room first, though, so that you can put your things away. You're going to need your wellies – I take it you have got a pair? I know the army can be lax on these things.'

Roz followed Joyce through an open doorway into the bedroom, which was sparsely furnished with four beds and two chests of drawers. 'Funnily enough, I do. I think Heulwyn felt sorry for me and Mabel because she gave us wellies, handbags, jumpers, socks, just about anything and everything she could lay her hands on that she didn't need for herself.' She glanced at the beds. 'Which one's mine?'

Joyce sat down on one of the beds and looked at the remaining three. 'Take your pick. The mattresses are diabolical, but you'll be so knackered you won't care.'

Roz laughed as she placed her bag onto the bed next to Joyce's. 'You make it sound delightful.'

Joyce smiled. 'I like it, but I guess I'm a rare breed.'

'You're a farmer,' said Roz as she pulled her wellingtons out from her kitbag. 'That's why you like it, and if you ever need a helping hand on this farm of yours, count me in – Felix too, he loved farming.'

Joyce beamed. 'I'll hold you to that.'

Suitably dressed, Roz and Joyce were about to make their way out of the house when someone knocked on the back door.

Joyce turned to Roz with raised eyebrows. 'Looks like we've got a visitor,' she said, before calling out, 'Coming!'

She opened the door and Roz could hear her talking to someone outside. As Roz joined Joyce, she was surprised to see Bernie standing beside Goliath who was harnessed to a cart.

Seeing Roz arrive, Bernie gave her a small nod of acknowledgement. 'I thought I'd see if you wanted to join me?'

Uncertain as to what she should say, Roz looked at Joyce who was examining her wellies, a broad grin on her face. With no help from the other woman, she smiled pleasantly at Bernie.

'Thank you for the offer, but Joyce was just about to show me around the farm so that I could get a feel for the place.'

Trying to swallow her smile, Joyce looked up. 'Oh, don't worry about that. I can take you around the farm any time, and I wouldn't want Bernie to think he'd wasted his time in harnessing Goliath here.'

Stepping back, Bernie motioned for Roz to climb into the cart. 'It makes more sense for me to take you round the farm in the cart, because it'll take you all day on foot.'

Feeling that she had no other choice but to join her host, Roz allowed Bernie to help her into the cart. Clicking his tongue, Bernie gave the horse the order to move forward. As Goliath strode down the drive, Roz watched Bernie from the corner of her eye. Not only was he handsome, but he was polite, courteous and thoughtful – very much like Felix, only with lots of money, land, and … Roz hated herself for thinking it, but there was no denying that Bernie was conventionally much better looking than Felix.

Bernie's voice cut across her thoughts. 'I've got to drop some mail off for my father in the village, and after that, I'll take you to the far side of Hollybank and we can make our way back to the cottage; it's the easiest way to see the whole farm.'

'I can't even begin to imagine how big eighty acres is!' said Roz.

Slowing Goliath down to almost a halt, Bernie checked the coast was clear before driving onto the main road. 'Enormous. You'll probably still be asking where things are for the next few days, but this way you'll get an idea of the size of the place.'

Roz watched Goliath's ears which kept flicking back as he listened for instructions. 'Glasfryn was set on the side of a mountain, so even though they had a lot of land you very rarely went up it.' She paused for thought. 'In fact, I didn't have the chance to go up because they don't turn the sheep out onto the hillside until they've finished lambing.'

As she spoke they began to pass through the village, and they hadn't got far before Goliath came to a stop. Handing Roz the reins, Bernie jumped down and took the mail from under his seat. 'Won't be a minute,' he said, before disappearing into a shop, which Roz guessed to be the post office. After a moment or so he reappeared. Taking the reins back, he drove the horse up to a crossroads. 'Have you driven a horse before?'

Roz nodded. 'I took Felix back to the station after Christmas.'

He looked at her, raising an eyebrow. 'Felix?'

'It's a long story,' she said.

Shrugging, Bernie checked the road was clear before expertly turning the horse onto the main road. 'We've time.'

Roz told Bernie about her journey so far, including Felix's internment and how he had ended up in Australia.

'Sounds like you've had a rough ride,' he said.

'It's certainly been full of surprises,' Roz conceded, 'not all of them pleasant, but things have started to look up of late.'

'I hope it's not too forward for me to ask if you and Felix are serious?'

'Very much so. Ever since we met on the train, Felix has always been there for me ...' She stopped speaking as Bernie raised his brow as though surprised.

'So you didn't know each other before?'

Roz shook her head. 'If it wasn't for the Kindertransport, we'd never have met. Why?'

He pulled a face. 'I don't mean to question your relationship, but you know what they say about wartime romances.'

'Only we didn't get together during the war,' Roz pointed out.

Bernie looked down at her. 'Same kind of circumstances, though. For a start you were both running away from a common enemy – it's not like you met in the cinema, or out shopping. By the sound of it, you were going through hell when you first met.'

Roz stared straight ahead. 'You're saying you think we're only in love because we shared a bad time in our lives, a bit like a victim and her rescuer?'

He nodded. 'Kind of,' hastily adding, 'I'm not saying that you don't love Felix.'

'Just that, I'm not *in* love with him,' said Roz, who would have felt quite annoyed had it not been for the fact that she'd had this very same thought on more than one occasion. However, after Felix's trip to Glasfryn she had dismissed the idea, but with Bernie more or less echoing her own thoughts, had she been right to question her feelings all along?

'I'm just saying that war does funny things to people,' said Bernie, 'and you did meet under very trying circumstances; it's only natural you should form a close bond.' He pulled Goliath to a halt, jumped down and opened a field gate. Looking at Roz, he asked her to drive Goliath through, which she was pleased to do. He closed the gate and climbed back on board before continuing, 'It's part of the reason why I've never dated any of the girls who come to work on the farm.'

She arched an eyebrow. 'Part of the reason?'

He grinned. 'Well, that and the fact that I've never been attracted to any of them.'

'Attraction certainly helps,' said Roz absent-mindedly as she mulled over Bernie's words.

He turned to face her, his eyes twinkling. 'It certainly does.'

Feeling thoroughly confused as to why Bernie had felt it necessary to question her relationship with Felix, Roz listened as he pointed to the various fields that were being used to grow crops. As she gazed out over them, it occurred to her that she wouldn't need to know any of this until the crops had matured, which wouldn't be for a long time yet.

When they eventually came across the livestock, Roz noticed that they were all in close proximity to the farmhouse. She looked at Bernie as he boasted of the

Badger Face sheep, the Albion cattle, and their prize-winning Saddleback pigs. Why was it that he had taken her all around the farm, something that Joyce could easily have done? Was this something he did with every new land girl that arrived on the farm? If it was, he had only himself to blame for their infatuation. She was pondering this thought when a voice hailed them from one of the sheds. It was Joyce.

'Had the grand tour then?' she asked, as Bernie pulled up beside her.

'Yes,' said Roz, hastily jumping down and joining Joyce outside the stable before Bernie had a chance to help her. She turned to look up at him. 'Thank you, that was a real treat. I can see the farm is going to need a lot of hands when it comes to harvesting the crops.'

Bernie gave Goliath a hearty slap on the rump. 'That's why we have this feller, he's worth his weight in gold come the harvest.' He indicated the cottage where he resided with his parents. 'I forgot to show you the orchard ...'

'No matter,' said Joyce airily, 'I can show her that.' A small smile played at the corners of her lips. 'Unless you'd rather, but it would be handy if one of us could show her round the yard, so she knows where everything's kept.' She glanced quickly at Roz, fighting the grin which threatened to spread across her face.

Looking slightly affronted, Bernie shrugged. 'I'm easy – I've not got much to do at the moment.'

'Lucky you!' laughed Joyce. 'Come on, Roz, I'll show you where we keep the tools. After that, I'll show you where you can get water for the troughs.' She glanced briefly at Bernie. 'Thanks for showing Roz the fields; I can take it from here.'

Taking the hint, Bernie led Goliath around to his stable, waving a hand of acknowledgement as Roz thanked him again for the ride.

Joyce led Roz over to the far side of the yard and into a huge shed where she indicated the various tools that were needed for all the general farmwork. 'You'll find everything you need in here,' she said informatively, 'pitchforks, spades, forks for digging the spuds, wheelbarrows,' she shrugged, 'everything.' She walked out of the barn and over to a stable with a ladder out the front, then glanced at Roz. 'Hayloft,' she said, pointing to an opening above. Looking over her shoulder to check Bernie's whereabouts, she turned back to Roz, a shrewd smile on her lips. 'Not that it's any of my business, but what *exactly* did he show you?'

Roz shrugged. 'The village, the post office, and then the fields where the crops are being grown. To be honest, I don't really know why he showed me the fields – I can't imagine you have much to do with the crops until they're harvested.'

Joyce raised her brow. 'Don't you?'

Roz shook her head. 'No, do you?'

The smile on Joyce's lips was broadening. 'I'd have thought it obvious, but then again, you don't know Bernie like I do.' She leaned against the wall. 'Bernie doesn't usually show interest in any of the girls that come here. He's polite, helps when it's needed, but otherwise he's strictly a lone worker.' She raised an eyebrow. 'There's only one reason why he showed you round the farm – he was laying his cards on the table.'

Seeing the blank look on Roz's face, she elaborated, 'Showing you what he has to offer.' Then, still seeing a look of incomprehension, she cut to the chase, 'He was trying to impress you, so that you would know he was a good catch ... worthy of marriage.'

Roz shot Joyce a sharp glance as the woman's words caught up with her. 'You said he normally keeps himself to himself – does that mean I'm the only girl who's ever had the grand tour?'

Joyce wriggled her eyebrows suggestively. 'Good God, yes! Blimey, Roz, you're the only girl he's ever spent more than five minutes with.'

Roz visibly deflated, although a tiny part of her felt flattered. 'I wonder if that's why he was so interested in hearing about Felix?' Realising Joyce didn't know what she was referring to, she explained further. 'I told Bernie I had a boyfriend, and he suggested that Felix and I are only together through circumstance.'

Joyce eyed her incredulously. 'He *what*?'

Roz nodded. If she was honest, she had also thought Bernie to be out of line with the assumptions he had made, considering they'd only just met. 'He even said that he thought we probably loved each other, but doubted we were *in* love.'

'Of all the ...!' Joyce shook her head disapprovingly. 'Bernie obviously finds you attractive and he's trying to make you question your relationship with Felix ...' Seeing the doubt on Roz's face, she hesitated. 'He didn't succeed, did he?'

Roz looked awkward. 'Not exactly, but I can't help thinking there is some truth in what he said, mainly because I used to have doubts myself. Felix and I have a very close bond, and we share an intimacy that no one else could understand, but does that really mean we're in love?'

Joyce smiled sympathetically. 'Don't take too much notice of Bernie. I think he's placed doubt in your mind for his own gain. Only you know whether you're in love with Felix or not.'

Roz sighed unhappily. 'That's just it! I'm not sure, not any more, and whether Bernie meant to stir things up or not, I've got a lot of thinking to do.'

Joyce patted her on the arm in a friendly fashion. 'Count yourself lucky. There's a lot of women who'd jump at the chance to be in the position you're in.' She began to lead them towards the orchard at the back of the farm cottage. 'You've got yourself the pick of the princes – I wish I had half your luck!'

Roz laughed. 'It does sound as if I'm in an enviable position.'

They continued their tour, and after they had seen everything the farm had to offer they retired to the cottage where they ate a supper of cheese and tomato sandwiches before heading to bed.

'As I'm sure you know,' said Joyce, climbing between her bedsheets, 'farming starts early, so you're going to need your kip!'

The next morning, both women were up before dawn and Joyce was rejoicing at having Roz to help her with the chores.

'You're an absolute marvel. I thought I might have to follow you round showing you what to do, but it's clear you've gained plenty of experience whilst at Glasfryn. Normally I wouldn't be finished until late evening, but at this rate we'll have got the majority of the jobs done by early afternoon.'

'I enjoy the work,' Roz admitted. 'I find it almost relaxing, and it helps to take my mind off my problems, like what might be going on back in Frankfurt.' She glanced up at an approaching figure, which turned out to be Bernie. 'Hello!'

Bernie touched the tip of his cap in response, adding, 'Morning! I thought I'd see if you'd like to come and help me with the milk round?'

Roz looked at Joyce who nodded. 'Don't see why not. We've got most of the work done,' she glanced at Bernie, 'but only if you give a hand when you come back. They've given us a good 'un this time, so don't you go puttin' a spanner in the works.'

He waved a negligent hand. 'You have my word. And you don't need to be concerned about me; our Roz here is spoken for.'

'Mmm,' came Joyce's response, although the look of warning that she cast Bernie made it clear she wouldn't stand for him upsetting the apple cart.

Roz glanced from one to the other. 'Am I doing the milk or not?'

'Go on then,' said Joyce. She wagged a reproving finger at Bernie. 'If she leaves, I'll be holding you responsible.'

He placed his fingers to his forehead and grinned. 'Scout's honour!'

Tutting her disapproval, Joyce mumbled something about 'Scout's honour my eye' before returning to her chores.

Roz trotted to catch up with Bernie who was striding across the yard. 'I've never actually delivered the milk before, but I always thought it looked fun.'

'It is, or at least I enjoy it,' he confessed. 'You get to meet people and catch up on the gossip. Old Goliath here always gets a treat or two from some of the house-wives, and I enjoy the peace and quiet of the journey there and back.'

Roz stopped short. 'Are you sure you want me to come? I wouldn't want to ruin your quiet time.'

He shook his head hastily. 'I'd like the company. I only meant I enjoyed the peace and quiet of getting away from Mam and Dad.' He chuckled. 'Mam's always banging on about me giving her grandkids, and Dad's always asking when I'm going to let him retire.'

Roz wrinkled her brow. 'I didn't think you were in a relationship?'

He collected Goliath's harness and handed it to her. 'I'm not, which is why Mam keeps nagging me to get a move on, but like I tell her, I'll wed when the right girl comes along.'

Roz smiled. 'I've not met your parents yet.'

'It'll happen tomorrow,' he said. 'Dad's got work in the city today, and Mam's gone to keep him company – they won't be back 'til late.'

Roz took the harness over to Goliath who stood patiently in his stable. 'Does he need his hooves pick-ing out?'

Bernie shook his head. 'Already done. He's just wait-ing for his harness and the cart, and after that we have to load him up, then we can be off.'

Roz found Goliath's harness was different to Zeus's, but the principle was the same. Once they'd set the traces and attached him to the cart, they led him round to the milking shed and heaved the churns onto the wagon.

Bernie smiled as he took a seat on the driver's bench next to Roz. She looked at him. 'What?'

He shook his head. 'Most girls want a hand getting on the cart, but you were on here before I had a chance to offer my services.'

Roz raised her brow in a superior fashion; she still hadn't quite forgiven him for causing her to doubt her relationship with Felix. 'I'm not most girls.'

Clicking his tongue, he cast an approving eye over her. 'I've noticed.'

Roz banished the grin that was threatening to break out. He was flirting, which was outrageous considering he had already tried to sabotage her relationship with Felix. On the other hand, knowing that she was the only girl that Bernie had taken an interest in was extremely flattering.

The trip into the city was the best journey Roz had ever undertaken. From the wild flowers adorning the hedgerows, to the sun sparkling off the sea in the distance, she thought she had never been anywhere as beautiful as this.

The houses they delivered to reminded Roz very much of the ones they had delivered to when she had been doing the coal round. The women came out with jugs, bottles, cups, bowls, anything that could hold milk, and Bernie would charge them accordingly, although Roz observed he always gave the women a good deal, unlike Callum who was mean with his portions. She also noticed how these women reacted when they saw Bernie coming toward them.

Like giggling schoolgirls, Roz told herself, *yet some of them are old enough to know better.* She realised that these were the thoughts of a jealous woman, but why on earth was she jealous of someone who had cast doubt in her mind? *It's because you know he's a catch*, she told herself, *and even if you don't want him, it's nice knowing that he might want you!*

By the time they were on their way back from their rounds, Roz felt she knew Bernie a lot better. He lived a carefree life, only really involving himself in anything to do with farming and having little opinion on other matters. They had talked in passing about the war and the refugees, but Roz felt that he was only interested in her story, not in anything that was going on in Germany itself.

'My father said that these people in power should concentrate on what matters,' he told her as he turned onto the road which led to the farm, 'like taking care of those that can't look after themselves and making sure there's enough to go round.'

Roz laughed doubtfully. 'I'm not saying your father is wrong, but I don't think that's the main concern of any government, at home or abroad.'

'That's why I keep away from politics, and do what I can,' said Bernie as he turned Goliath into the yard. He glanced in the direction they had come from. 'Not all those women can afford the milk we sell, so I either make sure they have extra or don't charge them at all. It's not like we can't afford it. And there's no way the government officials can prove how much our cows produce, or whether I've spilt the odd bit of milk by accident,' he said with a wink.

'Perhaps you should run for Prime Minister,' said Roz, 'when all this is over, of course.'

Bernie pulled Goliath to a stop. 'No chance! I'm a farmer to my bones, I wouldn't want to be anything else.'

'Do you want a hand to put him away?' she asked, sliding from her seat.

'No, he does not!' said Joyce indignantly. 'The lazy beggar can do it himself. You can help me with the hens.'

'And there I was hoping to not lift another finger. She's a hard taskmaster is Joyce,' chuckled Bernie. He winked at Roz. 'Go on, queen, I'll be along in a bit, before she comes after me with a pitchfork.'

Watching him through narrowed eyes, Joyce turned to Roz. 'Did you enjoy doing the milk round?'

Roz nodded. 'Very much so. Have you ever been?'

Joyce's eyes grew wide. 'Good lord, no! Like I said, I prefer it in the sticks.'

'I know, but surely you must be curious? When was the last time you visited the city?'

Joyce mulled this over. 'Can't remember, and that's the way I prefer to keep it.'

'What about friends or family?' Roz asked. 'Surely you must miss them?'

Joyce gave a nonchalant shrug. 'None to speak of; besides, I prefer animals to humans, they come with less complications.'

Roz laughed. 'You're not wrong!' She looked over to Bernie who was carrying Goliath's harness to the tack shed. Why did she have to come to a farm that had someone like Bernie living on it? Life had been simple before she met him.

Taking a tray, Felix joined the line in the NAAFI. So far his introduction to army life was going well, and he rather thought he was suited to it. He had made friends easily, and he enjoyed the drills and exercises. Whilst he had felt free when working for Alan and Bill, they had provided a family environment, whereas the army gave him a true feeling of freedom, which was strange considering the constant orders, discipline and routine he had to follow.

'How do,' called a familiar voice from behind him. Felix half glanced over his shoulder to his pal Ronnie, who had joined the queue.

'Not bad, you?' replied Felix as he moved up the queue.

'Ready for a cuppa, I know that,' said Ronnie. 'One of them fruitless scones wouldn't go amiss neither, if there's any left by the time we get there.'

Felix smiled. Ronnie, like most men in the army, thought with his stomach.

'My Matilda makes beautiful scones, fruitless or otherwise,' Ronnie continued. 'Does that Roz of yours make you cakes?'

Felix pulled a face. 'She's never been in a position to, but I reckon she will once we're married.' He gazed at the scones. 'I know she'll be a grand cook.'

'Married, eh?' chuckled Ronnie. 'Don't you think you're rushing into things a bit?'

Felix gave his friend a lopsided grin. 'If you knew her, you'd understand. She's one in a million is my Roz, beautiful, funny, clever, talented and kind.'

'Flamin' Nora, Cupid's stuck his arrow into you good and proper!' laughed Ronnie. 'Good job you're hundreds of miles away, or else you'd be married with a gaggle of kiddies round yer ankles.'

'That,' said Felix with verve, 'would suit me just fine!' Reaching the head of the queue, he smiled at the woman serving. 'Cup of tea and a scone ...' Seeing her about to pick up the last one, he glanced at Ronnie, who was eyeing the scone with a pitiful expression. 'On second thoughts, make that an iced bun,' said Felix, chuckling at the look of relief which swept over Ronnie's face.

Taking the tea and bun, he paid the woman, and waited for his friend to be served. They found a table and sat down.

Taking a large bite of the scone, Ronnie savoured the flavour before swallowing, then raised his scone as if toasting Felix. 'Thanks for reconsidering, you're a real gent,' he said, licking his fingers free of margarine. 'That Roz is a lucky girl.'

Felix was about to take a bite of his bun but paused to answer his friend. 'I like to think so; I certainly try to do all I can to make her happy.' He took a bite of his bun and chewed it thoughtfully before adding, 'If we had met under different circumstances, you know, if Hitler hadn't come into power, and everything had remained as it was, there's not a doubt in my mind that Roz wouldn't have looked at me twice.'

Ronnie's brow furrowed. 'Why on earth not?'

Felix gave a small shrug. 'She came from a well-to-do family, or at least they had a fancy apartment in the centre of Frankfurt, her father's an accountant and her mother a teacher – they weren't short on money. She's way out of my league, so I wouldn't have considered approaching her.'

'Ah, so you don't mean she wouldn't be interested in you, more like you'd not give her the chance?'

'I suppose so,' said Felix, but in his innermost thoughts he didn't really believe this to be true. Someone like Roz wouldn't be with someone like him, because some eligible bachelor would have snapped her up already.

'And in any case,' said Ronnie, 'she's not in Germany now, so she could have her pick of the crop if that's what she really wanted.' He raised a quizzical eyebrow. 'Do you think she will? Or have you nothing to fear?'

Felix didn't even need time to mull this over. Whilst it was true that if he had met Roz in Frankfurt he would have automatically assumed she wouldn't be interested, since getting to know her he knew that she wasn't driven by money or looks, but was a good, honest, down-to-earth girl who loved him with all her heart. There wasn't a question in his mind that he and Roz were destined to be together, and he said as much to Ronnie.

'No rich farmer is going to sweep her off her feet and make her the lady of the manor then?' chuckled Ronnie.

'Nope,' said Felix confidently. 'Roz has made it clear that she wants to be with me, and I believe her. I'm a lucky sod, Ronnie, because I know there's men out there that have more to offer than me, but Roz won't even entertain them.'

April 1941

Roz tutted loudly as she read Mabel's letter. Looking up, she informed Joyce of her friend's news. 'She's staying at Glasfryn indefinitely,' she said miserably. 'She reckons the girls that came were worse than useless so they've been sent somewhere else ... They should give us more training, like they do with the Waafs and the Wrens and the ATS – they wouldn't dream of getting them to do a job without proper training!' she said indignantly. 'Take the ack-acks – they have to train them properly else they'd be shooting down our fellers, and the Wrens would be putting our ships in danger, and the Waafs would be taking the pilots to the wrong planes!'

'I suppose they think you don't need much training to dig up a potato,' said Joyce, a wry smile lingering on her lips. 'Sorry, luv, but you must see that it's not so much the training as the women who apply. They think it's going to be easy, but they soon realise they're wrong.'

'How on earth are we going to cope if we don't get more girls?' said Roz. 'I was counting on Mabel because I know how hard she works, but some of these others sound like they don't like to get their hands dirty.'

'Well, we won't get anything done sitting here gassing about how useless everything is,' said Joyce, getting to her feet. 'Unless we teach the cows to milk themselves, the hens to collect their own eggs, and the sheep to shear each other, it's down to us.'

'And Bernie, thank goodness,' added Roz.

'Aye,' said Joyce with a wistful grin, 'Bernie's certainly helpful these days.'

Roz nudged her friend in the ribs as they donned their wellingtons. 'That's nothing to do with me! He's a farmer, it's his job.'

'Always has been,' agreed Joyce, 'but before you came, he'd deliver the milk and see to the heavy jobs around the farm, whereas now he works with us cheek by jowl, and I'm not the only one who's noticed – his mam passed comment on it the other day.'

Roz blushed to her ears. She had met Bernie's parents, Helen and Arthur, a couple of days after she had moved into Hollybank Farm, and even she had to admit that it was obvious from the way they greeted her that Bernie had been singing her praises. She cast her mind back to that first meeting.

They had finished their work for the day and were heading back to the cottage when a voice hailed them from behind. Turning, Roz was greeted by a rather stout woman with black hair and a rosy complexion, and a man who was a shorter, older version of Bernie.

Stopping, Joyce introduced Bernie's parents to Roz.

'Sorry we weren't here to greet you,' said Helen, 'but our Bernie assures us you're being well taken care of.'

It had been all Joyce could do to stop herself from giggling. The approving looks from Helen and the broad grin of her husband had made it obvious that Bernie had told them all about Roz, and he had obviously spoken highly of her, giving his parents a very good impression indeed.

Now, Roz eyed her friend through suspicious eyes. 'What do you mean, his mam passed comment?'

'Said that since he'd started working with us, he wasn't a miserable so-and-so in the mornings any more.' She grinned. 'I got the impression she put that down to you.'

'Maybe,' said Roz, trying to appear nonchalant, 'or maybe he's discovered he prefers working with people who aren't drooling all over him.'

'Oh-ho! Do I detect an air of envy?'

'Not at all!' scoffed Roz. 'Besides, if what you're saying is true, what have I to be envious of?'

'The fact that you can't drool over him, because you're spoken for?' Joyce suggested.

'*I*,' said Roz loftily, 'wouldn't drool over him whether spoken for or not! It's unseemly.'

'Get you!' laughed Joyce, but to Roz's annoyance she added, 'I'd believe you, only I've caught you watching him ...' She waved Roz into silence as she started to protest. 'I'm not saying you were drooling, but don't pretend you don't fancy the pants off him, because I shan't believe you.'

Roz puffed out her chest to protest, then thought better of it. What was the point? She did fancy him, very much so, but was that such a bad thing? She glanced shyly at Joyce. 'Do you think it's wrong of me?'

'Wrong?' said Joyce, looking surprised. 'Why would it be wrong? You can't help who you're attracted to! If you acted upon your feelings without sorting things out with Felix first, then that would be out of order, but looking? Nah, there's no harm in that.'

'Then why do I feel like there is?' said Roz miserably. She looked up guiltily. 'I remember my mother talking about a woman who lived down our street. Her husband had been having an affair and my mother said he couldn't have loved her in the first place otherwise he'd not have eyes for anyone else. *That's* why it's wrong!'

Seeing tears begin to form in her friend's eyes, Joyce hastened to Roz's side. 'Don't be so silly,' she soothed. 'There's a world of difference between finding someone attractive and being in love with them. I wish I hadn't opened my big mouth; I didn't realise you felt so strongly ...'

'That's the problem,' said Roz, fishing her handkerchief from her trouser pocket. 'I love Felix with all my heart, but every time I see Bernie, my feelings get brought into question. I love being with him, spending time together; he makes me laugh, and he's so caring, Joyce,' she put her head in her hands, 'which is why I'm so confused.'

Joyce eyed her sternly. 'I like Bernie, very much so, but I can't help thinking he has a hidden agenda, first casting aspersions on your relationship with Felix, which was none of his business, especially as he barely knew you, then making sure he spends as much time with you as possible so that he can get his feet under the table as it were!'

Roz rolled her eyes despairingly. 'Only how can he cause me to doubt my feelings for Felix if I really love him?'

'Because he's used to getting what he wants, and he wants you!' Placing her arm around Roz's shoulder, she softened her tone. 'Don't let him get under your skin, Roz.'

'What should I do?' Roz sniffed.

'Stop listening to Bernie for a start.' Joyce jerked her head in the direction of the pigs. 'We can figure this out whilst we see to the pigs.' They got the wheelbarrows and forks and headed for the pigsties. Opening the door, Joyce held up the board which stood beside the wall and herded the pigs into an empty pen so that they might continue their work interrupted.

'Whoever thought having the affections of two men would be so difficult?' said Roz as she sifted the manure out of the straw.

Laughing, Joyce pointed at herself. 'Me!'

'I often wish I'd never met Bernie,' Roz admitted. 'I was happy with Felix before, or at least I thought I was.'

'You're getting your knickers in a twist for no reason,' said Joyce. 'Felix is across the other side of the country, and he hasn't a clue you're questioning your feelings. The way I see it, you've got plenty of time to make up your mind.'

Roz rested her hands on the fork. 'You're right. What Felix doesn't know won't harm him, and as I'm not intending on starting anything with Bernie, I'm not doing anything wrong.' She began forking the manure into the barrow. 'I'm just so confused.'

'Unsurprising with Bernie working his magic,' Joyce said acerbically. 'What you need is time to yourself, and I'd wager you've not had that since leaving your parents behind.'

Roz felt a pang of guilt. Felix had done nothing but think about her wellbeing since he'd met her, yet here she was putting herself first, which in truth was all she had ever done, or at least that's how it felt to her. She said as much to Joyce.

'Better that than being like me,' said Joyce resolutely. 'For years I put everyone else first, which only made me miserable.'

'I wouldn't say I was living in misery exactly,' said Roz.

'But you aren't happy either,' argued Joyce. 'If you want my opinion, you'll forget about men for a bit and concentrate on yourself. If they don't understand that, then you have to question whether either of them really loves you.'

Roz nodded. Joyce was right. Bernie was very keen on her, and whether he meant to or not, he was pressuring her into making a decision. If Roz could stand up to the Nazis then she could stand up to Bernie. She would tell him nicely that he needed to back off and give her space. If he really had feelings for her then he would respect her wishes.

Chapter Seven

May 1941

For most people the May blitz was a frightening time of uncertainty, but for Callum Haggarty it was a golden window of opportunity. And whilst he had been alarmed by the severity of the bombings on that first fateful night, even he hadn't envisaged the bounty that awaited him. All he had to do was pick which house looked the most enticing, then root through the debris until he came across anything that looked promising, and with no one to stop him the world really was his oyster.

It seemed like child's play until the night he had stumbled across the occupants in one of the houses. His first instinct had been to leg it, but on second glance he realised they were in no position to chase after him. If anyone else had entered the property they would have respected the dead and left, but for Callum this was an even more promising opportunity. After all, dead people don't object when you take the rings from their fingers, the earrings from their ears and the watches from their wrists. He didn't see it as being wrong: they were dead, they had no use for their belongings, not any more, and if he didn't take them, someone else would. When he arrived home laden with possessions, neither his mother nor his daughter questioned where he had got them from. If they had, he would have told them the truth. It was a dog-eat-dog world in the lives of people like the Haggartys, and he knew they wouldn't complain about spending the money the items would bring.

It was the third night of the blitz and Callum was taking stock of his previous night's takings. Getting rid of the stuff was easy – no one asked questions, not any more; getting the right price however was another matter. As with the previous two nights, the siren sounded. Callum grinned, gathered his treasure, as he called it, and wrapped the items in an old coal sack, before hiding it up the unused chimney breast, behind a few loose bricks.

'You can't trust no bugger nowadays,' he said to Lilith and Suzie as they watched him stow his goods. 'Them what know I'm in business will know I'm out "bomb-combing", so they might decide to come and help themselves.'

Bomb-combing was Callum's macabre version of beachcombing. He said it was the same principle: no one questioned when you took items found on the beach, so why should it be different if you find stuff lying around a bombed house?

He cursed as some of the items that were too big to fit into the hiding hole fell back down.

'You need to get rid of the stuff faster than you are,' snapped Lilith unhelpfully. 'There's no sense in hangin' on to it, you're just being greedy!'

Callum rounded on his mother. '*Greedy!* I don't see you riskin' your neck every time the siren goes off, oh no, you get your backside down to the cosy shelter and snore your head off 'til the coast is clear! It's me what goes into the danger, it's me what risks his neck with bombs, it's me what risks gettin' caught, to put food on the table, so no, I don't take the first price offered. My life's worth more to me than that!'

'I never asked you to go out,' muttered Lilith, 'and folk won't pay full price when they know the stuff's been nicked.'

'It has not been nicked,' seethed Callum. 'I don't break into anyone's house, I find the stuff fair and square when I'm checkin' to make sure no one's trapped beneath the rubble ...' He closed his eyes as the memory of one of the houses he had been looting entered his mind. He had thought he was alone, when he had heard a noise coming from another room. At first he had suspected another looter, so he had gone to warn them off his patch. He had cautiously entered the next room, a brick raised above his head ready to clout whoever it was should they try to put up a fight, but to his surprise the room appeared empty. Suspecting it to be a cat or some other animal, he let the brick fall from his fingers and was about to leave the room when he heard movement from under some rubble.

'Hello?' he said, his voice full of anticipation.

Again, he heard movement. Bending down, he squinted into the darkness and nearly screamed when he saw an eye looking back at him from under the rubble. The lid blinked slowly. Leaning forward, he peered at the person who lay trapped beneath the debris. A tear had escaped and was carving a clean path down their cheek as they gazed back at him. They were alive, they needed help. He paused. They had seen his face quite clearly. Standing up, he ran his fingers through his hair as he weighed up the options. He could rescue the person from beneath the rubble and be hailed a hero, because no one could prove he was there for any other reason than to look for victims trapped in their homes. But people knew the Haggartys of old, they wouldn't believe him for a moment, they would accuse him of looting, and that might raise a few questions. Some people – the scuffers in particular – might start poking their noses into his affairs; they might find out a few truths which Callum would rather keep secret. On the other hand, the person beneath the rubble had seen him, but had they recognised him? It was likely – he had delivered coal around this area for years, most people knew him by sight. Swallowing hard, he came to a decision. Taking a brick, he placed it over the gap where the person still stared out at him. He heard a soft whimper of objection, so he took another brick then another and placed them over the hole until he heard no more.

Now, with the memory washing over him, he shuddered. His mother knew nothing of his life on the streets, knew nothing of the sacrifice he had made in order to protect them all. Glaring at her, he gathered the rest of the items and thrust them into her arms.

'Just for once, you can feel what it's like to be out there in the middle of things, instead of tucked away down a shelter,' he rasped. 'You can stay here and protect my hard work, whilst I go out and get more. You say I'm greedy but you have no idea what it's like to risk your life – well, tonight you're going to get a taste.' He looked at Suzie. 'You can go down the shelter. I'll see you down myself.'

Suzie gaped at her father. 'You can't seriously be suggesting we leave Gran here on her own? You know she can't manage the steps.' She shook her head. 'I'll stay here.'

But Callum was adamant. 'You'll do as you're damned well told,' he snapped. 'Your grandmother is old enough to look after herself but you aren't, so you'll come with me, and when you go into the shelter, if anyone asks where your gran is you're to tell them to mind their own ruddy business, understand?'

Looking in desperation to her grandmother, Suzie turned pleading eyes to her father. 'I know you're angry, Dad, we both do, and Gran does appreciate what you do for us, don't you, Gran?'

Lilith nodded. 'But your father's right, Suzie, people will come looking if they think there's treasure to be had, and your father's worked too hard to see all this taken away.'

Suzie stared at her grandmother. 'It's just *stuff*!' she cried in anguish. 'It's not even our stuff!'

Gripping his daughter painfully by her elbow, Callum marched her to the door. 'It's nice to know that I risk my life every night for "stuff"!' He spat the last word out as he dragged her down the stairs, Suzie objecting with every step that they shouldn't leave Lilith on her own.

He frogmarched her to the shelter, oblivious to her pleas. 'They're bombing the docks!' she cried. 'It's a miracle we've never been hit before. It's only a matter of time, she's your *mother* ...'

As they neared the shelter Callum spun his daughter round to face him. 'And that's why she's staying behind, because she doesn't want to see her son risk his neck for nowt. Now get in there and keep your mouth shut!'

As he spoke they could hear the bombs begin to fall in the distance. Suzie looked fearfully in the direction of their home, then at the shelter behind her. She was about to try to break free from her father's grip and head back to Crooked Lane when another hand gripped her other elbow.

'Come on now, miss, it's not safe up here. Best you get inside.'

It was the air raid warden. Within the blink of an eye, her father had left her side and vanished into the night. Suzie struggled against the warden, trying desperately to free herself and gabbling that her grandmother was at home, but he was having none of it.

'Some folk are too old to get to safety, but there's no sense in both of you risking your lives,' he said breathlessly as Suzie continued to struggle with all her might, but in the end he was too strong for her, and would have got her into the shelter had it not been for a bomb falling close by, knocking them both off their feet. Seizing her opportunity, Suzie was up and off down the road before the man could stop her.

Racing towards Crooked Lane, Suzie gave a cry of triumph. She would get her grandmother out, and they would deal with her father the next day when he'd had time to calm down. As she ran she wondered whether he might have had a change of heart and gone back to fetch his mother. She shook her head; when her father made his mind up to do something, there was no changing it. She had just reached Mercer Court when the second bomb fell. She closed her eyes instinctively as the phosphorous white fire engulfed the coal merchant's. Putting her hand up to protect her eyes from the fierce flames, she tried to make out their home, but the flames had consumed the entire building.

Tears streaming down her face, she turned her back on the disaster which met her eyes. She couldn't bear to think of her grandmother left to die because she had spoken the truth. Suzie stood rooted to the spot, unable to move, then started as someone placed an arm around her shoulders. She looked up into the face of Mabel's mother, Elsa Johnson.

'Good God, Suzie, what on earth are you doing out here?' she said, quickly guiding Suzie back to the shelter. 'You're lucky you weren't in there ...' Seeing Suzie's tear-stained face, she put a hand to her mouth. 'Where's your grandmother and father?'

Suzie erupted into yet more tears. Her shoulders shaking, she managed to stammer out, 'Gran was still at home ... she's gone.'

Mrs Johnson knew better than to question a Haggarty on their life choices. It was plain to see that Suzie had been going to fetch her grandmother, but why she hadn't either been in a shelter or with her gran in the first place was anyone's guess. Even if she asked the question, it was highly unlikely she would find out the truth. 'I'm sorry, luv, but it's dangerous for us to be out here, and I daresay your gran wouldn't want to see you riskin' your life for summat you can't do nowt about.'

Feeling dead to her core, Suzie allowed herself to be propelled into the shelter. The warden, a different one from the man who had tried to bring her into the shelter before, shook his head in disbelief. 'You're damned lucky to be alive! You can't afford to dilly-dally when there's a raid on ...' He fell into silence under Mrs Johnson's warning gaze. Realising that something was terribly wrong, he changed his tune. 'Go to the back of the shelter and see if you can't get your head down for a bit, it's quieter down that end.'

Suzie did as she was told, a multitude of thoughts running through her mind. Perhaps her father had had second thoughts and gone back for her grandmother after all, but even if he had, he'd never have had time to get her down the steps before the bomb fell. This in turn led her to another thought. If he had gone back, then Suzie hadn't just lost her grandmother, but her father as well. She sat down on one of the benches and curled up into a tight ball. Tears trickled down the side of her nose and she wondered how she would cope on her own. For the first time since Roz's departure, she thought of the other girl. If Roz hadn't been so deceitful, she would still be living with them, and Callum would've made Roz guard the jewellery and not his mother. Roz didn't have any parents or siblings, so had nothing to lose. Her tears drying, her thoughts turned to revenge. She hoped with all her might that Roz would never find her parents, and that Felix would leave her, because as far as Suzie was concerned Roz didn't deserve to live happily ever after.

*

Callum had seen the flames reach into the sky from the house he had been searching. His jaw dropped as the enormity of his actions sank in. No one could survive a fire like that. His mother was now gone and all because of his temper … He swallowed hard. Just like his wife … Snapping out of his thoughts, he looked towards the shelter where Suzie was sitting, safe. At least he had got her out before the bomb hit. Another thought entered his head – his treasure. He wondered if he would be able to retrieve it, because if he didn't, it would be found in time, and there wasn't a doubt in his mind that the police would be able to trace many of the belongings back to the victims of the bombings, and no one in their right mind would believe that Lilith, an old lady, unable to make it down the stairs to the shelter, would be capable of looting bombed-out buildings. He grimaced. He would have to go back there at first light to see what he could salvage, because if they found the belongings of the person he had left to die, they would soon put two and two together.

Roz and Bernie, having finished the milk round as best they could given the bomb damage, returned to Hollybank Farm, where they called out for the others to join them.

As always, Bernie's mother, Helen, had been busy making sandwiches and flasks of tea, ready for the workers to take into the city to give to the volunteers, as well as a helping hand wherever they could.

Roz and Joyce joined Arthur, along with some of the land girls from neighbouring farms, and they climbed up into the cart and waited for Bernie to take the reins. Roz had been pleasantly surprised by Joyce's offer to help out the morning after the first raid.

'I know I said I'd never go back,' Joyce sighed, 'but this is different. It would be selfish for me not to help.'

Now, as they headed into town, Bernie and Roz quickly told the others what to expect. 'It's bad,' said Roz, 'much worse than we've had so far, so brace yourselves. A lot of what you once knew has gone, and much of what's left is badly damaged, but you have to look past that, because we have to carry on.'

They spent the morning helping to clear sites and assisting those who were searching for missing loved ones, as well as supplying refreshments to those in need.

'Is it alright if I go and check on my friend's family?' Roz asked Bernie, as he prepared to lead the others deeper into the city. 'I won't be long, and I'll soon catch up.'

'I could come with you if you like?' he suggested, but Roz was shaking her head.

'You have to drive Goliath, but I promise I won't go into anything that looks dangerous. I just want to check that they're alright.'

Joyce came forward. 'What's happening? I thought we were going into the city.'

Roz nodded. 'I'm just going to check on my pal's family.'

'It's pretty rough out there,' said Joyce. 'Are you sure you should be going alone?'

Roz smiled. 'Not you too! I'll be fine, but thanks for the offer.'

Heading off as quickly as she could, Roz wasn't surprised to see that the docks had taken the brunt of the bombing, and as she neared Mercer Court she began to worry that the Johnsons had been hit, but to her relief she saw the court was untouched. She was knocking a brief tattoo against the door when a voice hailed her from across the way.

'They're down at Crooked Lane,' said a man peering at Roz from around the door of the communal latrine.

Waving a hand in acknowledgement, Roz hesitantly made her way towards her old home. She was wondering why on earth the Johnsons would be at Crooked Lane when she saw the answer to her question. The old coal merchant's where Roz had once resided was still aflame. She stared in horror until a familiar voice called out.

'Mrs Johnson!' cried Roz. 'It's so good to see you! How is everyone?'

Elsa hugged Roz tightly before the two women turned to look at the warehouse as firemen desperately tried to tackle the blaze.

'We're all fine, which is more than I can say for the Haggartys,' Elsa said darkly.

'You don't mean ...' Roz began, but sensing her question Elsa nodded.

'Lilith. We don't know about Callum yet, but Suzie's alive.'

Just like Mrs Johnson with Suzie, Roz knew it was silly to ask the whys and wherefores when it came to the Haggartys, so she left the matter alone, asking only where Suzie was.

Elsa shrugged. 'Last I seen she was down the shelter. As far as we know, Callum's okay, so perhaps he came for her and they've gone to find somewhere else to live.'

Roz grimaced. She didn't like the Haggartys one bit, but the thought of the old woman trapped alone inside the building sent a shiver down her spine.

Having seen his former home still up in flames, Callum had scrapped the idea of looking for his loot. He would have to wait until the fire had been put out before chancing that, so he had gone to the shelter where he'd left his daughter. The warden, his head heavily bandaged from the blast, looked up as Callum approached.

'I'm looking for my daughter Suzie,' Callum said. 'I brought her here last night, she didn't want to go in ...' he elaborated, for better identification.

The man lowered his gaze. 'I tried me best ...'

Callum gripped the other man by his collar and pulled him so that they were within inches of each other. His eyes flashed dangerously as he snarled the words. 'You let her go?'

The man shook his head then winced as the pain seared through his skull. 'Of course not! Only a ruddy bomb fell, knocked us both off us feet. I smacked me noggin on the pavement and your Suzie took off like a hare. She was gone before I had a chance to stop her ...'

The man cried out in vain as Callum stormed away, but Callum had no intention of turning back. His daughter had perished in the fire along with his mother, and it was all his fault. He knew he had been wrong to leave his mother on her own, but he was too bloody-minded to listen to Suzie's warnings, and as a result he'd lost his entire family. He was alone, and he had no one to blame but himself. First his wife, then his own flesh and blood. With these images clouding his thoughts, Callum headed for the Old Swan district, where nobody knew him.

The air raid warden stared after the man who had taken off in such a hurry. If only he'd given him the chance, he'd have been able to tell him that the young girl had been brought back to the shelter and was currently in the school hall with everyone else who had been made homeless last night. He touched his bandages. If it hadn't been for that wretched girl he wouldn't have a lump the size of an egg on the side of his head. He wondered whether the man would find his daughter then reassured himself with the thought that he was probably running to the school hall to see if she was there. After all, it was common knowledge that those made homeless headed for the nearest public building that was left standing. Telling himself that this was more than likely what the other man had done, he got back to the business of tidying out the shelter.

After ten relentless nights of bombing the Luftwaffe turned its attention to the Russians, but the aftermath had taken its toll. Those who had been down shelters when their houses had been bombed now found themselves homeless, and others were without jobs if their place of work had been hit, but with these miseries came a glimmer of hope. Hollybank Farm had opened its doors to anyone in need of a bed or a job. Even if they weren't enlisted in the land army, Helen and Arthur had reasoned that it was just as helpful for them to work for room and board.

Roz could sense that Joyce had been dubious at first, believing that they would be more of a hindrance than a help, but after seeing the worn out faces of those who came seeking sanctuary, she had soon changed her mind.

'They're like lost souls,' she had said to Roz as yet another family turned up, adding 'poor little wretches', as two children no more than six years old stood barefoot before her, their clothes tatty and their eyes white against their dirt-smeared faces.

They had rehoused the carts and heavier machinery in the Dutch barn, then used the stone barn as temporary accommodation. People had donated beds where they could, but when they fell short they had made makeshift mattresses out of straw, something which the children found to be a great adventure. It had taken a while to get everyone equipped with wellingtons and suitable clothing, but once they had, everyone who was able was put to work on the farm, whilst those who were too old had been set the task of darning clothes and keeping an eye on children too young to work.

Bernie had proved to be an absolute marvel. Every day after finishing his rounds, he would come back, unload the empty churns then go straight back to the

315

city and ask anyone who needed a bed for the night to jump on board. Roz couldn't help but be impressed by his generosity when it came to those who had nothing.

'He's such a big heart,' she told Joyce as she watched Bernie taking some of the little children for a ride on Goliath's back. 'Those kids must have thought their world had come to an end, but Bernie soon showed them that life goes on.' She glanced at Joyce. 'He's going to make some woman a terrific husband and he'll be the best father.'

'Oh?' said Joyce. 'Does that mean you're beginning to have more than a physical attraction towards him?'

Roz sighed heavily. 'I should, because I'd be a fool not to, but there's something missing, although I don't know what.'

Joyce smiled kindly. 'There's nothing missing, luvvy. Your heart belongs to someone else, simple as that.'

'I do think a lot of him though,' said Roz. 'He's such a dear, kind man, and I know that most women would think me a fool to turn him down.'

'They're not you, and it's you what counts, so if it's not meant to be, then it's not.' Joyce spied some people wandering into the yard, looking rather lost. 'Come on, let's see to this lot.'

Joyce and Roz's morning tasks now included taking the names and old addresses of the people who had found their way to the farm.

The bombings had had a sobering effect on Roz. Even though Felix was miles away from Liverpool she had developed a sense of unrest, and a strong desire to be with him. She knew that she always felt this way when she thought Felix was in danger, but this time it was far stronger – so much so that she had approached Helen and Arthur to ask if she could be excused for a short weekend break so that she might visit him. Bernie had been present when she had put her request in, and it was clear to see how disappointed he was. Roz had felt a real heel, almost as if she was betraying him, but she knew this was something she had to do.

Bernie caught up with her outside.

'Are you sure it's a good idea to go and see him when we've been through such a traumatic event? Surely that will only cloud your judgement?'

Roz levelled with him. 'All I know is I won't rest until I've seen him.' She shrugged helplessly. 'I know it's silly, because I know he's alright, but it's almost like a magnet drawing me to him. I shan't be able to think straight unless I see him for myself.'

Even though every part of him wanted to try and stop her from leaving, Bernie stood to one side so that Roz could get by. He looked after her as she entered the cottage. How typical was it that the only woman who had been of interest to him was in love with another man? He could try and kid himself that this wasn't the case, but deep down he felt sure that as soon as Roz saw Felix she would realise her true feelings. He sighed heavily. What could he do? Not a damned thing.

*

August 1941

It was late summer when Roz arrived at Lincoln station. Her tummy fluttered with nerves as the crowded train on which she had travelled came to a halt. She scanned the platform for any sign of Felix, and realised as she did so that she was very much looking forward to seeing him. *You've missed him*, she thought, her heart beginning to fill with joy, until nagging self-doubt caused her to wonder if Felix had missed her. Her heart thumped in her chest. What if he'd found someone else? What if he no longer found her attractive? What if he realised he was only with her because he had empathised with her predicament? She drew a deep breath. If any of those scenarios were correct, then there was nothing she could do about it. In fact she considered it a bit rich that she should have such fears when she herself had been drawn to another man.

Shuffling along behind the queue of people waiting to dismount from the train, Roz wondered how she could ever have doubted her feelings for Felix. When it was her turn to descend from the carriage, she looked into Felix's upturned face. He looked exactly as he had the day she had said goodbye to him at the Betwys-y-Coed train station. She corrected herself. He didn't look exactly the same: where once his face had been smooth he now had slight lines, no doubt caused by the stress and worry which war brought. Holding his hand, she stepped lightly down from the carriage, but before she could put both feet on the platform he had lifted her up into his arms and was kissing her tenderly. In that very moment Roz chastised herself for ever doubting the strength of their relationship.

Felix was the man for her, always had been and always would be.

Lowering her gently to the ground, he slid his arms from around her waist and smiled down at her. 'Gosh, how I've missed you,' he said softly. 'I've been so worried hearing about the blitz, and knowing you're not too far away from the city.'

She smiled as he kissed the tip of her nose. 'We're three miles away, Felix, hardly round the corner, and the blitz was months ago, thank goodness.'

'But you go in every day to deliver the milk,' said Felix. 'There could still be unexploded bombs, incendiaries, grenades, who knows?'

'Grenades?' Roz echoed, puzzled. 'Aren't they handheld?'

He shrugged. 'The mind imagines all sorts, but I suppose grenades might be a tad unlikely.'

'I'm sorry to hear that I've caused such worry,' she said, studying the frown lines now prominent on his brow.

He placed his arm around her shoulders and gave them a squeeze. 'You're safe and sound and that's all that matters.'

She laid her head against his shoulder as they walked away from the station. She felt terrible knowing that she had once considered their future to be in question, especially since he had clearly been worrying about her. She glanced up at his chin, flecked with stubble. Another new thing, she thought, but Felix was looking fully a man now.

'I've booked you in at the Adam and Eve,' said Felix. 'It's not far from the station, and I've eaten there a few times, and the food is always good.'

319

'I've just thought of something,' said Roz. 'This is my first sort of holiday, and I'll be spending it with you!'

He chuckled softly. 'I do have to keep working, but I know what you mean. It'll be lovely to spend some time together. They've a nice park here, and the river makes for a pleasant stroll. How's things at the farm?'

'Busy,' said Roz. 'We've been housing people who have lost their homes or their jobs due to the bombing, so there's plenty of help, but that can come with its own set of problems.'

He looked down at her in surprise, his eyes twinkling as they gazed into hers. 'Really? I'd have thought the more hands the better.'

'They don't know what they're doing, so have to be taught,' Roz explained, 'and some people aren't natural when it comes to livestock, and others have children who think it's alright to run in circles around animals.'

He winced. 'Dangerous!'

'It certainly is,' agreed Roz. 'It's a miracle no one's been kicked or bitten yet, although I daresay it's just a matter of time.'

'Farms are a brilliant place for children to grow up but they come with their hazards, and the livestock's just one of them. I hope their parents have enough sense to keep them away from the plough and harvesting machines.'

'So far,' said Roz, 'but then again, they're all kept in the Dutch barn where the children can't get at them.'

Felix stopped outside the public house where Roz would be staying and motioned for her to go in ahead of him. 'Here we are, let's get you checked in.'

Roz looked around to see where she should go, then turned to Felix with a helpless shrug.

'Check-in's at the bar,' said Felix. 'Come with me.'

Roz followed him through to a warm and cosy-looking bar. The ceiling had black beams running from one side to the other, and each one was decorated with various brasses. 'It's lovely!' said Roz approvingly.

A woman's voice came from below the bar. 'Thank you, dear, we try our best.' She emerged into view, a friendly smile etched on her cheeks, her blue eyes twinkling at Roz, but as soon as her eyes fell on Felix, the friendly smile turned into a broad grin. 'Felix!' She turned to Roz. 'And you must be the beautiful Roz!'

'She certainly is!' said Felix. He turned his attention from Roz to the woman and back again. 'Roz, meet Celia, she serves the best pale ale in Lincoln.'

After the two women had exchanged hellos, Celia chattered happily away to Roz. 'We've heard ever so much about you, dear, our Felix thinks the world of you. I'm so glad you could make it.'

Her blush deepening, Roz felt as though she were positively glowing.

'Oh, I can see I've embarrassed you.' Celia waved a dismissive hand. 'Let's get you a nice cold drink to cool them cheeks of yours down.'

Smiling shyly, Roz asked for a lemonade, and after taking a sip, she decided to steer the conversation away from herself to her host.

'You seem to know a lot about me, yet I don't know much about you, save that the food here is excellent according to Felix.'

It was now her host's turn to glow, as she waved a tea towel at Felix. 'He likes his grub and no mistake, although I'm not sure that it could be described as excellent ...'

'Nonsense,' said Felix, pushing the required amount of money into the landlady's outstretched palm. 'You serve the best lamb hotpot I've ever had.'

With Celia giggling like a schoolgirl, it occurred to Roz that Felix had the same effect on this woman as Bernie did on the housewives in Liverpool. She tilted her head to one side, as the landlady went off to fetch the key to Roz's room. 'You've turned into a real charmer, Felix Ackerman.'

He took a sip of his beer, then wiped the froth from his top lip. 'I've always been charming,' he said, a cheeky grin playing on his lips.

'That's true.' She took another sip of her lemonade. 'Do you hear much from Bill and Alan?'

He nodded. 'Heaps. They're having a rough old time of it down the docks, but they keep on going.' He nudged her foot playfully with the toe of his boot. 'What about this Bernie you told me about? I've not heard you mention him much recently?'

Roz could have dropped on the spot. The last thing she had expected was for Felix to mention Bernie. Did he know? Pretending to make light of his question, she looked down as she nudged him back. 'Nothing to tell, that's why I've not mentioned him.' She assured herself this was sort of true. 'Why do you ask?'

He shrugged. 'Only natural, I suppose. You're a very attractive young lady, any man with eyes in his head can see that ...' He stopped short as the landlady reappeared, holding out a key, which Roz took, grateful for the interruption.

'You're in room two, luvvy,' she pointed to the door on the far side of the bar, 'go through there and it's the second on your left.'

Placing her lemonade on the bar, Roz picked up her rucksack. 'I shan't be long.' Disappearing through the door which had been indicated, she thanked her lucky stars that Celia had appeared when she did. She opened the door to her room and placed her rucksack on her bed. She knew that she was only suspicious of Felix's question because she felt guilty. Of course it was only natural for him to ask; she would do the same if the boot were on the other foot. Praying that he hadn't picked up on her uneasiness, she closed the door behind her and went back to Felix, who was reading a paper which someone had left behind. Seeing her enter, he folded the paper and placed it back on the bar. 'Ready for a wander?'

Roz nodded and slipped her arm through his outstretched elbow. 'Where are you taking me?'

He smiled down at her. 'How does a boat trip on the lake sound?'

She smiled. 'As long as you're the one doing the rowing, it sounds fine by me.'

They walked to the lake and Felix paid the owner of the rental boats before asking Roz to choose a vessel.

Roz chose a blue and white painted rowboat, informing Felix that her choice was based entirely on what she felt would be most visible should they get into difficulties.

'Oh ye of little faith,' laughed Felix, holding the boat steady whilst Roz placed one foot then the other into the boat, which wobbled slightly under her weight. Once she was sitting on the bench, she nodded to Felix to say that she was ready for him to join her. Felix wasn't as graceful or well balanced as Roz, and the boat swayed alarmingly as he got in and sat down rather clumsily. Giving her what he hoped was a reassuring smile, he gripped the oars as though his life depended on it and began to row them towards the centre of the lake, a destination that Roz felt they weren't quite ready for, so she asked if he would mind if they stayed a little closer to shore, just to be on the safe side.

'Your word is my command,' said Felix, but Roz could see he was relieved that she didn't fancy going so far out. It took a while for him to get the hang of rowing, and after repeatedly bumping into the banks of the lake whilst ducking under low branches, he eventually got into the swing of things, although Roz still insisted they stay within a few feet of safety.

'It's not that I can't swim,' she said conversationally, 'I just don't want to – not fully clothed, at any rate.'

Felix grinned. 'Surely you're not suggesting skinny-dipping?'

Roz shot him a withering look, although a smile twitched the corners of her lips. She had never heard the expression skinny-dipping before, but the suggestive look which crossed Felix's face was enough for her to know that it was inappropriate. 'No, I am not, whatever that is,' she said wryly, 'although I'm pretty sure I can guess.'

'Each to their own,' chuckled Felix. 'Skinny-dipping is what you see the boys doing down the pools of the Tate and Lyle factory.'

Roz had seen those boys on several occasions. It was hard not to, considering they'd hoot and holler for you to watch them jump off the pipe into the warm water. 'I thought as much.' She looked into the inky water. 'I daresay this won't be as warm as the pools.'

Felix dipped his fingers in and gave them a wriggle. 'You're right. I've been swimming in the pools, and they're a lot warmer than this!'

He watched her, his eyes brimming with affection. 'I seem to remember you saying your dad liked boats?'

A faint smile played on Roz's lips. 'Dad used to take us when I was little. He'd do the rowing, saying that Mum and I were the queen and princess of the lake, and he the king.' Her eyes flicked up to meet Felix's and she felt a surge of affection towards him as he gazed lovingly at her. 'He used to pretend the small island in the middle of the lake was our kingdom. He'd take us there and we'd have a picnic. When I was little I thought we were the only ones to visit the island, and maybe I was right, but whether I was or not doesn't matter. It felt like the most magical place on earth because it really did feel as if I was a princess with my own island.' A giggle escaped her lips. 'I bet that sounds silly to you.'

Felix held her gaze, gently shaking his head. 'Not at all, it sounds idyllic, and your father sounds like a wonderful man.'

'He is,' said Roz, then, averting her gaze to look into the depths of the lake, she added, 'or at least he was. I still don't know whether he's around.'

Felix stopped rowing and allowed the boat to drift for a while. 'Do you think about them much?' He shook his head hastily. 'That was a stupid thing for me to ask, of course you think about them a lot. What I meant to say was do you often wonder about what's happened to them?'

Roz shook her head. 'I daren't because I never imagine anything good. I still can't understand how we got separated. I know they'd have done everything they could to keep us together, so something really bad must have happened after the accident. If I try not to think about it, it's as though none of it ever happened – does that make sense?'

He nodded. 'Perfect sense.' He waited until their eyes met before continuing. 'My mother would love you; she'd be pleased as punch that I've found myself such a wonderful girl.' He chuckled incredulously. 'I still can't believe I've found such a perfect woman, and I thank my stars every day that you agreed to be my belle, because I know you can't be short of offers.'

Roz laughed. 'They must be keeping these offers to themselves, because I've not had any of them.' Which was true: whilst Bernie had made it plain that he liked her, he'd never made a move, although she considered that this was probably because he was a gentleman and he knew Roz was spoken for. The fact that she was uncertain of her feelings didn't come into it.

'They must have rocks in their heads,' said Felix. Another thought seemed to be playing on his mind. 'And you've never been attracted to anyone else?' He added hastily by way of explanation, 'It would be understandable considering the distance between us. It's not as if we get to see each other much, especially with me being on the ack-acks.'

Roz could have told the truth – it would have been the perfect opportunity – but what was the point? She was certain of her feelings, and it wasn't as though she'd been unfaithful to Felix. The annoying voice of her conscience spoke out: only he's on about distance, and that isn't the reason why you've questioned your relationship. If you tell him you've doubted your love for him, then that might shed a whole new light on things, make him feel uneasy, maybe even cause him to question his own feelings, and you don't want that. So instead she shook her head. 'Absence makes the heart grow fonder,' she said, and the blush which tinged her cheeks was because she knew it had been an untruth. Luckily for her, Felix took it as shy embarrassment.

He rested the oars in their locks and leaned forward. He had meant it to be a romantic moment, but instead they ended up clutching the sides of the boat as it rocked violently. Tentatively, he slowly leaned back before gripping the oars once more.

'Kissing is an experience to be enjoyed on terra firma,' he said with conviction.

Seconded by Roz, who was glad he hadn't persisted with his romantic notions. 'It'll certainly be a lot drier,' she said, and they both started to laugh.

'Perhaps a boat trip wasn't my best idea,' said Felix reflectively, but Roz was quick to put him right.

'I think it was a wonderful idea. I've enjoyed every second of it, even the hairy parts.' She smiled at Felix, who flashed her a dazzling grin.

'You're certainly a game lass,' he said, much to Roz's amusement.

'You're starting to sound like one of the locals.'

He nodded. 'I spoke good English before coming to Britain, but since living with Alan and Bill, then joining the army, I've picked up a lot of the lingo.' His features turned stern. 'I've not forgotten how to speak German, but it will be a cold day in hell before I do it again.'

'I know what you mean,' said Roz. 'It's a life I'd rather forget ever existed, but I can't because it's the only memories I have of my parents, and I never want to forget them.'

'And you won't,' said Felix sincerely. 'No one can take that away from you, and when all this is over, I will buy us a cottage, somewhere by the sea, we'll have pigs, and chickens and cows, and enough room for your parents to come and live with us. We'll be one big happy family, and we'll never set foot in the fatherland again.' He shook his head angrily. 'Fatherland! Makes it sound caring, nurturing, but it couldn't be farther from the truth.' He had managed to bring the boat to the shore, and it was currently gently bobbing against the pier. As he spoke, the boat rental owner came over and helped Roz and then Felix back onto the pier. Thanking him briefly for their trip, Felix slid his hand into Roz's. 'Britain is my home now, and as far as I'm concerned I'm British,' he paused before correcting himself, 'I'm a Scouser, because they're the only ones who have ever really accepted me for who I am.'

Roz smiled. She felt exactly the same way, and the future Felix had described was her ideal. She looked up into his dark eyes which glittered passionately down at her. How could she ever have doubted her feelings? Felix was the man of her dreams, her rescuer, her friend, and one day, when they were married, he would be her lover.

They only had one more day together, but they were both determined to make the most of it. They repeated their experience on the lake, but this time, when Felix tried to kiss her, instead of the boat moving, it was the sensation in Roz's heart, when he cupped her face in his hands, and the two of them melted into a long and amorous kiss. As Felix rightly commented, there was no island, but that didn't mean to say that Roz wasn't the queen of the lake and he the king.

From the lake they took a stroll around the city of Lincoln. It was a far cry from Liverpool with its old winding roads, and the castle which stood proud above the city. Roz had never seen an English castle before, so Felix took delight in showing her round. Standing on the battlements, he stood behind Roz, his arms around her waist, and kissed her neck. At that moment she felt as though the Luftwaffe could do its worst and she'd still be safe, because she was in Felix's arms. Sighing happily, she imagined that they were indeed the king and queen and Lincoln was their city. Turning, she kissed his cheek. 'I wish the war was over, and we were living in the cottage you spoke of yesterday.'

'We'll have to get married first,' said Felix. He pulled her closer so that there wasn't the slightest glimmer of light between their bodies, and they looked at the city below them as Felix spoke softly into her ear. 'Your dress will be fit for a queen and your father will walk you down the aisle.'

Tears shimmered in Roz's eyes. 'If my father gets to walk me down the aisle you will have made me the happiest woman on earth.'

He kissed the side of her cheek and his breath tickled her neck as he spoke, sending delightful shivers through her body. 'I don't know if you believe in miracles, but I do, and I won't marry you without your father's consent.'

Twisting in his arms so that they were face to face, Roz melted into his embrace. As Felix kissed her, tears of happiness ran down her cheeks. Breaking away, he kissed the tip of her nose, causing her to giggle. 'Do you think your parents will approve of me?'

Roz nodded fervently. 'You've looked after their little girl when they were unable to. Believe me, Felix, my parents will love you.'

Even though the blitz was over, it wasn't the end of the bombing in Liverpool. Although not as devastating, houses were still lost, and people still homeless.

The majority of the first families who had come to Hollybank in search of help had now found permanent places of their own to live, whether it be with relatives, or somewhere outside Liverpool. That didn't mean to say there wasn't a steady stream of newcomers, all of whom were grateful for a meal and somewhere to lay their head, where they could get a decent night's sleep in relative safety. However, new people meant Joyce's time was taken up teaching them how to milk and muck out, and what food to give to which animals, which meant that Helen had taken over welcoming newcomers, making sure they were settled in and accounted for. It was typical, Joyce thought to herself, that as soon as Roz went away, however briefly, everything changed at the farm. They were now so full that Helen had said they would have to start putting people in with Roz and Joyce.

It was the morning that Roz was due home, and Joyce had just come back from overseeing the morning's milking, when Helen met her halfway across the yard.

'Another new girl has arrived, and this one's a real land girl,' she said, hoping this would diminish the disgruntled look on Joyce's face. 'So you've proper help again, and Roz is back today, so even better.'

'Has this girl worked on a farm before, or are we her first?' asked Joyce, a definite hint of scepticism in her voice. She added as an afterthought, 'Has she met Bernie yet?'

The older woman flashed a toothy smile. 'Yes, she has, and she's not gone weak at the knees so you needn't worry about that. Besides, I think our Bernie's carrying a torch for Roz. I know she's off with this Felix, but I can't see it lasting, not with our Bernie showing an interest. He's got a lot to offer, and it wouldn't surprise me if Roz has gone to break things off with Felix so that she and Bernie can be together.'

Joyce tried to avoid eye contact with the older woman. She knew how keen Bernie's mother was to see him settled and wed with a family of his own, but Joyce had spoken at length with Roz about Felix and if she was right, she thought Bernie and his mother were both in for a big disappointment.

*

331

Roz made her way up the long drive leading to Holly-bank Farm. Her days with Felix had been the best in her life, and she had left content in the knowledge that her relationship with him was based on love and not circumstance. He was the man for her and she was totally and utterly in love with him. For a long time all she had thought about was how dreadful everything was, but since reuniting with Felix, she actually saw hope for her future, something which she never thought she would do. She knew that Joyce would be eager to hear her news, and Bernie disappointed, but she hadn't promised him anything, and even though she suspected he hoped that she would become his belle, she had been honest with him from the start so her conscience was clear. She thought of Mabel, in whom she had always confided her thoughts and doubts, but when it came to Felix she had kept quiet. Walking into the yard, she saw Joyce and Helen deep in conversation outside the door to the cottage. Joyce waved in greeting, followed a second or so later by Helen.

'So? How was Lincoln?' said Joyce, eager to hear the news, but Roz, who didn't feel like discussing her private life in front of Bernie's mother, waved a dismissive hand.

'Plenty of time for that later. How's tricks here?'

'Helen's just been telling me how we're finally getting a proper land girl, someone who knows what she's doing!' said Joyce, beaming with delight.

'When?' asked Roz, eager to know when their real help would arrive.

Mrs Lewis nodded towards Rose Cottage. 'She's already arrived.' She glanced at Joyce. 'She came when you were showing the others how to do the milking.'

Roz looked interested. 'Another batch of new recruits, I take it?'

Joyce rolled her eyes. 'I welcome the help, and I know you do too, but sometimes it feels like I'm trying to teach a blind man to bowl – half the time you'd be quicker doing the work yourself.'

Helen grimaced apologetically. 'And I was just going to tell you that another stray's turned up.'

'Oh blimey,' sighed Joyce. 'Any good?'

Helen shrugged. 'Hard to tell, she doesn't say much. The feller that brought her here said she's hardly spoken nor eaten anything since losing her family in the blitz.'

Joyce and Roz exchanged surprised glances. 'But that was months ago!' said Roz. 'Where's she been all this time?'

'They think she's been wandering around like a lost soul,' Helen said. 'I told the feller to leave her with us, and we'd see what we could do.'

'Perhaps she'll begin to come out of her shell once she starts working with the animals,' said Roz, 'they normally do.' She hefted her rucksack onto her shoulder. 'Let's get inside and meet the new land girl.'

Joyce smiled. 'And whilst we're at it, you can tell me all about your trip to Lincoln.'

They entered the cottage where they saw a young woman with her back to them. As she turned to face them, Roz's jaw practically dropped on the spot.

333

'Adele!' she cried, before dropping her rucksack to the floor and running across the short space and enveloping her friend in a hearty embrace. 'What on earth are you doing here ...' she began, before remembering Helen's words. Thrusting her friend away from her, she studied her face carefully, searching for any signs of distress or discontent, but Adele was beaming back at her.

'You inspired me to join up! I couldn't believe it when I got my posting; I was going to write but then I thought it far better to surprise you.' She looked at Joyce, 'I know Roz, so I'm assuming you must be Joyce?'

Joyce nodded. 'Guilty as charged.' She cast a glance between the two women. 'Obviously you two know each other, but how?'

Tucking her arm into the crook of Adele's elbow, Roz explained how Adele had escaped Germany on the Kindertransport with her and Felix, and that they'd all stayed together in Dovercourt.

'I was the first to leave,' said Roz, 'then Adele went to Norwich, and Felix of course came to Liverpool.'

'How is he?' said Adele.

Roz was beaming from ear to ear. 'You'd best take a seat whilst I explain everything.' She nodded at Joyce. 'I'll fill you in on my trip whilst I'm at it.'

The three women sat round the table as Roz regaled them with tales of boat rides and trips around Lincoln. When she had finished, she fixed Adele with an inquisitive gaze. 'Now I've finished filling you in with the details of my trip, how about you tell me what you know? Have you met Bernie yet?'

'The drop-dead gorgeous farmer? I should say so!' chuckled Adele. 'What a corker!'

'He certainly is,' agreed Joyce, 'and what's more he's got the hots for our Roz here. Question is, who will she choose? Felix or Bernie?'

'Decisions, decisions,' Adele laughed sarcastically. 'Two gorgeous fellers vying for my attention! I wish I had your problems!'

Giving her friend a playful swipe, Roz tried to swallow her grin, as the other two sat on the edge of their seats with anticipatory excitement. 'Well?' said Joyce. 'Don't keep us in suspenders!'

'Felix!' cried Roz, to the others' delight. 'I knew it from the moment I saw him. How on earth I could ever have doubted my feelings for him is beyond me.'

'Does Felix know you had your doubts?' asked Joyce.

Roz shook her head. 'Not a clue, and I'd prefer it if we kept it that way. What the head doesn't know the heart cannot grieve over. I'm in love with Felix, and that's all that matters.'

'Well, we won't say anything, will we?' said Joyce.

Adele nodded heartily. 'I've a rule of thumb to stay out of other people's relationships. It only causes grief in the long run, no matter how good your intentions.' She leaned back in her chair. 'Do you ever hear anything from that rotten family you stayed with in Liverpool?'

Joyce raised her brow in surprise. 'You never told me anything about a rotten family?'

Roz grimaced. 'To be honest, I'd rather forget about them, although from what I've heard ...' She suddenly fell silent as a familiar and unwelcome face appeared in the doorway behind Joyce. 'You!' hissed Roz. 'What the hell are *you* doing here?'

Suzie rolled her eyes. 'Just when I thought things couldn't get any worse ...' She stopped abruptly, as Joyce turned to face her.

Standing up so fast that her chair toppled over, Joyce stared at Suzie, her hands clasped across her mouth.

Suzie stared back, her eyes wide, all colour having drained from her face as if she'd seen a ghost. Tears brimming in her eyes, she spoke quietly, as though she couldn't believe what she was about to say. 'Mam?'

Chapter Eight

For a moment Roz thought she must be dreaming, so she pinched the skin on the back of her hand to confirm that she was indeed awake. She had heard what Suzie had said, but she was having difficulty in believing her own ears, and indeed would have thought she had misheard if it wasn't for the fact that both Suzie and Joyce were staring at each other as if there was no one else in the room.

Without waiting to hear what Joyce had to say, Suzie ran out of the cottage, slamming the door behind her as she went.

Joyce stared wide-eyed at Roz and Adele. 'I – I ...' was all she could manage before sinking back into her seat.

Roz stared at the shut door before turning her attention back to Joyce. 'Now I understand why you don't want to go back to Liverpool. It's not the bombings you're afraid of, it's *him*. Am I right?'

Joyce nodded slowly. 'I realise how this must look, but it's complicated. I didn't run away from Suzie, and I very much wanted to see her again, of course I did, she's my daughter, but not like this. She didn't deserve to see me like this ...' A confused frown furrowed her brow, and she looked at Roz. 'How do you know them?'

Roz sank down in the seat opposite Joyce's. 'They're the horrible family that I lived with; it was Callum who threw me out.' She took Joyce's hand in her own. 'Lilith ...'

Wiping her nose on a handkerchief that Adele had passed her, Joyce muttered, 'That old bag ...'

Roz pulled an awkward grimace. 'She died in the blitz ... I know because Mabel's family, the Johnsons ...'

Joyce's head snapped up. 'Donald and Elsa?'

Roz nodded. 'You know them?'

'Elsa was the one who helped me run away from Callum in the first place; she even got me a job working for an elderly lady down south.'

Roz gaped at her. 'So Suzie didn't know, and that's why she thought you were dead ...'

Joyce stared back, horrified. 'What on earth would make her think that?'

The cottage door opened and Suzie stood in the doorway. 'Because you disappeared without a word. When we woke up the next morning I seen your bed was empty. Dad was already up, and looking proper shady.'

'You thought your father had done me in?' said Joyce, scarcely able to believe the words that were leaving her own mouth.

Suzie shrugged. 'He's got a temper, everyone knows that, and none of us knew where you were. We couldn't even mention your name without Dad losin' his rag. I asked Gran about it, and I could tell she thought the worst.'

'I can see why,' Joyce admitted. 'He was always giving me a thick ear for one reason or another; sometimes it seemed I only had to breathe and it was the wrong thing to do.' Her eyes locked with Suzie's, and it was clear to see the remorse which lay within. 'I'm sorry that you thought the worst, luv, but I couldn't come back, else he really might have done me in.'

'So you left me with him and Gran,' said Suzie accusingly. 'Thanks for putting me first!'

Rising from her chair, Joyce attempted to put her arm around her daughter's shoulders but was instantly shrugged off.

'I couldn't take you with me,' said Joyce reasonably. 'I couldn't look after myself, let alone a child.'

'I'd have been better off with you than I was with them,' said Suzie, her bottom lip trembling.

'I know you think that, Suzie, but your father wouldn't have laid a finger on you, and he could put a roof over your head and food in your belly, and that's more than what I could have done at the time.'

But Suzie wasn't in the mood for listening, especially with Roz hearing every word. 'Instead you've been out here living it up with your pals,' she snapped, 'a terrible place for a child to grow up, I must say.'

Joyce shook her head slowly. 'I haven't been here all this time. At first I was working as a lady's maid in Norfolk.'

Suzie wrinkled her nose in a disbelieving manner. 'A likely story! How would you get a job somewhere you'd never been?'

'Elsa Johnson made all the arrangements,' said Joyce. 'She was friends with—' She got no further – apparently this was more than Suzie could stand.

'That cow Mabel!' she shrieked. 'That total utter bitch, she knew where you were but she never said?'

Joyce hastily shook her head. 'No, luv, Mabel didn't know a thing about it, just her mam and me, it was our secret. I didn't want your father getting wind of where I was ...'

'Don't patronise me, Mother!' cried Suzie. 'Mabel's mam will've told her, and I bet she told *you*, didn't she?' She pointed an accusing finger at Roz. 'I bet you all had a good laugh at my expense.'

Looking like a rabbit caught in the headlights, Roz held her hands up in a placating manner. 'Not me, I knew as much as you ...'

'Liar!' screamed Suzie before flouncing out of the room.

'I'm so sorry about all this,' gabbled Joyce to Roz and Adele as she hastily moved to run after her daughter, 'you must think me awful.'

Roz caught her by the elbow and stared her straight in the eye. 'I most certainly do not. I lived with that man and his mother, so I know full well what he's like, and believe you me, the day he threatened to kill me?' She shook her head. 'He wasn't joking. If you ask me you've had a lucky escape, and I think Suzie knows, it's just going to take time.'

'What a bloody mess,' said Joyce. 'Do you think I should go after her?'

Roz looked at Adele, who looked doubtful. 'It's a lot for her to take in; she might be better if left on her own for a while.'

When Roz spoke next, even she was surprised by the words which left her lips. 'I could go and talk to her if you like? I know I'm not exactly her favourite person, but at least I know Callum and Lilith.' She tilted her head to one side as another thought occurred to her. 'Elsa said that Lilith was a victim of the bombings, of that they were certain, but what they didn't know for sure was where Callum was. I wonder if that's why Suzie has been wandering around Liverpool – perhaps she was looking for her father?'

'Poor kid,' said Joyce, her voice thick with tears, 'she didn't deserve any of this.'

Roz opened the door. 'All I can do is try. If she won't speak to me, I'll see if she wants to speak to you.'

Joyce gave her a rather wobbly smile. 'Thanks, queen, you're a star.'

Roz headed into the yard and looked around to see if she could spot where Suzie had got to. Hearing quiet sobbing noises coming from the feed shed, she took a deep breath and stole over to the door, which was ajar, and knocked gently. She wasn't expecting Suzie to invite her in, so she went in anyway.

'I've come to see how you are,' she said by way of explaining her presence.

Suzie was sitting in the corner hugging her knees to her chest, her face hidden from view. 'Well, you needn't have bothered, so you may as well sod off,' came the muffled response.

Ignoring Suzie's advice, Roz continued, 'You've just had some pretty shocking news to say the least. Your . . .' she hesitated, as she was still getting her own mind around the thought of Joyce being anyone's mother, let alone Suzie's, '... mum's worried about you.'

Suzie raised her head to look at Roz, her face wet with tears. She viewed Roz through narrowing eyes. 'Tell her she's about six years too late!'

Roz sat down on the floor beside Suzie. 'I think she's always worried about you. I understand if—'

She got no further before Suzie erupted in an angry torrent of abuse. 'Understand? *Understand?* How can you possibly understand anything about me or my life? You know nothing about me, you've no idea what my life was like before you came along, but let me tell you, it was a lot better before you arrived. You may not like my gran and dad, but at least they looked after me, not ran away and left me on my own.' Standing up, she flapped her hands in despair. 'For God's sake, we've lived for years thinking my dad is a murderer, and he isn't! He didn't do anything wrong! It's my mam's fault that things were fraught at home, all of us treading on eggshells, my dad because he knew what everyone was saying behind his back, and me and Gran because we thought the rumours were true!' Her lips wobbled as she tried to fight back the tears. 'And I don't know where he is so I can't even tell him I'm sorry!' she cried, before storming out of the shed.

Roz quickly got to her feet, but by the time she was out of the door, Suzie was already halfway down the drive and running fast. Roz headed back to Rose Cottage where she found an anxious Joyce being comforted by Adele. Seeing Roz walk through the door, Joyce looked up hopefully, but Roz was shaking her head.

'She took off like a hare. It seems the rumours of your death have affected her a lot. She's blaming you for the discontent between her father and herself.' She braced herself, then recounted the conversation she'd just had with Suzie.

Joyce thought for a moment. 'There's always been discontent between the three of them, because that's what it's like. Callum likes to play the blame game, and he has no respect for himself or ...' seeing Roz nodding her understanding, she paused before finishing, '... I keep forgetting that you know him, so you already know all of this. But I still don't understand why Suzie thinks I'm to blame.'

Roz grimaced. 'Deep down, she probably doesn't, but she's understandably confused and angry, and you're the only one she can take it out on.'

'Where is she?' said Joyce and was getting to her feet when Roz put a hand on her shoulder.

'About halfway to the city by now judging by the way she took off,' she said. 'I think you're best leaving her to get it out of her system. Besides, if she's hell-bent on blaming you, it's not going to matter what you say or do at the moment, because she'll still hold you responsible.'

Adele spoke quietly. 'If it's any consolation, it sounds as though she was in a bad way even before she knew you were here. I think this is more grief talking than anything else. She's seeing her relationship with her father and grandmother through rose-coloured spectacles, because she's grieving.'

'So what do I do?' said Joyce. 'Carry on like nothing's happened?'

Roz shook her head hastily. 'No, no one's suggesting you do that.'

Adele butted in. 'You have to carry on, and hope she comes to her senses, and she will – maybe not today, or tomorrow, it could even be months – but she will one day, and when she does she'll come to you.'

'So keep my fingers crossed and hope for the best?' said Joyce.

Roz placed her arms around her friend's shoulders. 'That's all you can do, that and be here for her when she comes back.'

Joyce sniffed loudly. 'You really think she'll be back?'

Roz nodded with certainty. 'Not a doubt in my mind.' Although privately she thought that Suzie would be back more through necessity than forgiveness.

As Suzie reached the bottom of the drive she looked along the road. To the left was Liverpool, but what was to the right? Suzie knew nothing of life outside the city because the only time she had ever ventured further than their neighbourhood had been when she went to Dovercourt, and that had been with the security of her grandmother and father by her side. She looked doubtfully at the road which led away from the city. For all she knew she could be walking for days before she got anywhere, and what would she do for food and shelter? She looked in the other direction. At least she knew Liverpool, so that was one advantage. She envisaged her old home before it had been burned to the ground, then Mercer Court where that dreadful Mabel and her family lived. Her jaw tightened as an image of Elsa

Johnson appeared in her mind. If it hadn't been for her, Suzie's mother would most likely never have left home, and they would still be a happy family. She immediately quashed a tiny voice which tried to protest that they hadn't been happy before her mother left. *We may not have been blissfully happy,* Suzie reluctantly admitted, *but I was happier with Mam there than when she'd gone, and not just because of the knowing looks and whispered conversations between the neighbours, but because Mam was the only one who ever gave me cuddles, made me think I was worth summat, that Dad wasn't always right, and that I wasn't useless.*

Her breathing quickened as the memories washed over her. Whenever Callum had accused Suzie of doing something, it was only Joyce who had stuck up for her, told him to leave her alone and to stop being a bully. She would then take Suzie to one side, wiping away her tears and telling her that it wasn't Suzie that was in the wrong, but her father, and to ignore him. But after Joyce left all that had stopped, and it seemed to Suzie that she had taken her mother's place, always bearing the brunt of the blame for anything and everything. She had hoped that when Roz came along, Callum would switch his accusations to her, but instead he had given Roz most of Suzie's jobs saying that Roz was better at them than Suzie. She wiped her tears away with the heels of her hands. She never thought she would see the day when she would be jealous of someone doing the degrading job of begging for leftovers in the market, because they were deemed better at it than her. Roz had made Suzie feel worse about herself than she already did, and to cap it all, she had the effrontery to get herself a boyfriend and a better life despite everything she had lost, leaving Suzie with a disgruntled father, and a grandmother whose mobility was going downhill fast. She shook her head. How dare Roz enter their lives and turn everything upside down before swanning off into the sunset?

She gave an exclamation of disbelief as she remembered the conversation she had overheard before entering the room. Roz didn't just have one lad but *two* vying for her affections, and she had sat there like Lady Muck deciding who she liked the best when Suzie couldn't even get one. She wondered if they knew about each other, then remembered something Roz said about not wanting to rock the boat. It had sounded to Suzie as though Bernie knew about Felix but not the other way round. She tutted disapprovingly. Everyone seemed to think that Roz was some wonderful girl who'd had such a hard time, but Suzie didn't see things that way. She thought that Roz had a much better life than she, and it was high time someone did something about it, but how?

She leaned against the boundary stone wall whilst she weighed up the pros and cons. If she went back now, she would at least have somewhere to lay her head and food in her belly, and she would also be in a position to get her revenge on Roz, even if she didn't know how as yet. The downside was that she would have to confront her feelings, because she couldn't possibly avoid her mother when they would be living and working practically cheek by jowl. On the other hand, if she left she wouldn't have anywhere safe to stay, and food would have to be obtained when and wherever she could pinch it – not only that, but she wouldn't be in a position to keep an eye on Roz whilst working out the best form of revenge. The only pro to leaving was not having to be near her mother. She sighed heavily before a slow, evil smile spread across her cheeks. Her mother had left her alone, not given two hoots about what happened to her, and got away with it scot-free! If Suzie stayed she would be able to give her mother a taste of her own medicine, because try as she might to make amends, Suzie would not forgive her for what she'd done. Her jaw jutting out in satisfied determination, she made her way back up the drive.

Joyce and Roz were about to show Adele round the farm when the door to the cottage opened. Standing in the open doorway, Suzie stared coolly at her mother. 'Don't think I'm back to rekindle our relationship, because I'm not. As far as I'm concerned there is no relationship, and I am *not* your daughter, and I'd appreciate it if you didn't go telling people otherwise—' She stopped speaking as Roz spoke over her.

'Oh, don't be so ridiculous! You can't deny your mother – whether you like her or not she's still your mum.'

Her eyes flashing angrily at Roz, Suzie continued, her voice cutting through the air like a knife. '*I* can do what *I* want. As far as *I'm* concerned my mother died six years ago, because the woman who I used to live with would never have turned her back on me. I don't know who this woman is,' she said, nodding her head at Joyce, 'but she's not my mother.'

Roz went to speak again, but Joyce spoke before she had the chance. 'Suzie's right, I can't expect to walk back into her life as though nothing has happened.' Her eyes levelled with her daughter's. 'I'll play this any way you want to.'

'I won't be sleeping in this cottage for a start,' said Suzie. 'I know Mrs Lewis said there was no room in the barn, but I don't care, I'll sleep on the floor if need be – not only that but I don't want any of you teaching me what to do.'

Roz folded her arms across her chest; this was typical Suzie. 'You can't just sit around doing nothing all day, that's not the deal. Everyone who comes to the farm has to pay their way through the sweat of their brow.'

Suzie shot her a scathing look. 'I didn't say I wouldn't work, I just said I didn't want any of you teaching me.'

Roz glanced at Adele, then back at Suzie. 'What about Adele? Surely you can't object to her teaching you what to do?'

Suzie gave an exasperated sigh. 'Is she a friend of yours?'

Roz nodded.

Suzie rolled her eyes, then shot Roz a withering glance. 'In that case I don't want anything to do with her either.'

Roz felt sorry for Suzie, she really did, but there was only so much she could take. 'Then *who* is going to teach you?' she said, waving an arm around the otherwise empty room.

A wicked glint entered Suzie's eye. 'Bernie,' she said, a calculating smile playing on her lips.

Roz gave an incredulous laugh. 'Don't be ridiculous! Bernie doesn't teach anyone; he does the hard labour and the milk round, that's it.'

Suzie turned a meaningful gaze on her mother. 'Either he teaches me or I'm off, and you'll never see me again!'

Roz wanted to point out that this was blackmail, and that in her view it was hardly a threat but something to be welcomed, but Joyce had already agreed. 'I'll speak to him, but I'll have to tell him who you are, because he'll want to know why you're refusing to let any of us teach you.'

Suzie's jaw flinched as she mulled this over briefly before nodding sharply. 'Very well, you can tell him he can find me in the barn.'

As she left the room, Roz exclaimed, 'He won't go for it, he'll say she's acting like a spoiled brat – which she is – and that will be the end of the matter. She's just going to have to swallow her pride and let one of us tell her what to do.'

Joyce gave Roz a pleading look. 'He'd do it for you.'

Roz waved her hands in front of her. 'Oh no, it's going to be bad enough when he hears that me and Felix are together, he won't want to do a thing for me then.'

Joyce swallowed. She didn't want to speak her thoughts, but she had no choice. 'Do you have to tell him?'

Roz gave her an incredulous glance. 'Are you asking me to lie?'

Joyce shook her head hastily. 'Not lie so much, just omit the truth.' She shrugged helplessly. 'You don't have to go into details if he asks you how the trip went, just say it was good, and that Felix was well. If he probes any further just tell him you don't want to talk about it – that way you're not lying ...'

'Yes, I am!' said Roz. 'Because I know that me and Bernie don't stand a chance, because I'm in love with Felix, speaking of whom, Felix would be furious if he thought I was leading Bernie on.'

'He'll never find out,' said Joyce. 'It's not for ever, you'll be able to tell him the truth ...'

Roz pointed an accusing finger, cutting Joyce off mid-sentence. 'The truth! So you admit I'd be lying!'

Joyce shuffled awkwardly in her seat. 'Fibbing, or if you prefer, a white lie,' she said, keeping her eyes averted from Roz's, 'but one little fib might mean I get my daughter back, because once she's learned the ropes, she'll have had time to calm down, and she might even forgive me.' A tear rolled down her cheek. 'Please, Roz, I know it's not the right thing to do, but it really is only a little fib, and Felix will never find out. What can be the harm?'

'Bernie,' said Roz simply. 'It would be unfair to lead him on when I know there will be nothing between us, deceitful even.'

Adele looked at Joyce, then Roz. 'It won't be for long, and think of the good that could come of it. That poor girl has lost everything, her grandmother, her father. She's only just got her mother back – does she really need to lose her too?'

Hearing Suzie being described as a poor girl would normally not sit well with Roz, but under the circum-stances? Sighing heavily, she nodded, causing Joyce to clap her hands with joy. 'Only I'm not promising anything,' said Roz. 'I'm no liar, nor a fibber, and if he sees through me it's not my fault, never mind the fact he might not even go for it!'

Leaping up from her seat, Joyce went round the table, gripped Roz in a firm embrace and kissed her on the cheek. 'All you can do is try.'

Nodding ruefully, Roz walked into the bedroom. 'I'll put my things away, then get straight on to it.'

Outside Rose Cottage, Suzie beat a hasty retreat before she was caught eavesdropping. She had wondered how she might get her revenge on Roz, and the answer had fallen straight into her lap. She wasn't too sure what she would do with the information yet, but hearing how upset Felix would be if he knew Roz was lying to another man about their relationship was certainly a good starting point.

Knowing that Bernie would be on his way back from the milk round, Roz walked down the drive to greet him. If she was going to fib, she'd rather nobody else witnessed it. Hearing the familiar clip-clop of Goliath's hooves against the tarmacadam road, she peered round the corner. Seeing her watching him, Bernie called out as he waved enthusiastically. 'Did you miss me?'

She smiled. 'Whatever gave you that idea?'

'You're waiting for me, so I'm guessing you just couldn't wait to see my handsome face,' chuckled Bernie.

Roz gaped at him. It simply hadn't occurred to her that this was giving the wrong impression. She had just wanted to make sure she wouldn't be overheard when she spoke to him.

'So?' said Bernie, looking expectantly at her. 'How did it go with Felix?'

Roz wanted to tell him the truth, but she had made a promise to Joyce. 'Good. Felix is doing well; I feel a lot better about the situation.'

He glanced down at her ring finger which remained bare. 'I see there was no proposal of marriage?'

Roz looked alarmed. 'Is that what you thought he was going to do?'

He clicked Goliath on with his tongue. 'I would if I was him, and you were my belle.'

'Oh,' said Roz quietly, 'well no, there was no proposal.'

'His loss,' said Bernie, winking at Roz, who was looking as though she had the weight of the world on her shoulders, probably because she did. This hadn't gone unnoticed by Bernie, who furrowed his brow in concern. 'Is everything alright?'

She went to nod then shook her head. 'The new girl, Suzie, she's the one I lived with when I first arrived in Liverpool ...'

Misreading her statement, he glared ahead of him. 'Then she can sling her ruddy hook,' he said angrily. 'If I'd known who she was—'

Roz placed a hand on his forearm, to quell his anger. 'That's not the problem, there's been a revelation ...' She explained about Joyce, Suzie's reaction and her request for Bernie to teach her. 'I wouldn't normally ask,' Roz continued, 'but it would mean a lot to Joyce, and I can't help but feel sorry for Suzie knowing that I, too, thought the worst of her father.'

Bernie's eyes twinkled at her from under thick lashes. 'And what about you? Would it make you happy?'

Feeling rotten to the core, she nodded.

Placing his hand over hers, he smiled. 'Then I shall teach her all she needs to know. Would you like to come out with me for a meal tonight? To celebrate you coming home?'

She knitted an eyebrow. 'I've only been away a couple of days!'

He smiled. 'It felt an awful lot longer to me, and I rather hope that now you've made up your mind we might spend a little more time together.'

Roz stared at him. How on earth had he come to that conclusion? She hadn't said anything about her relationship with Felix, yet from what Bernie was suggesting, it sounded as though he thought them to be apart. The urge to tell him the truth rose uncontrollably, but he spoke before she had the chance.

'Unless you think that I need to spend the time with Suzie? Because if that's the case perhaps I should take a rain check, make her see she's being unreasonable, and that she should allow one of the land girls to show her what's what. It might even do her some good ...'

Hating herself for the outright lie she was about to say, Roz shook her head. 'No, that's not it at all, I'd love to go out for a meal.'

Bernie beamed. 'I shall call for you at seven. We can take a stroll across the fields, it's not far that way.'

Roz looked up. 'And Suzie?'

He waved a hand. 'If you untack Goliath I'll take Suzie round the farm, get her acquainted with everything, but I won't teach her owt until tomorrow morning when I show her how to feed the stock.'

Roz nodded miserably. Somehow she had ended up practically telling Bernie that she and Felix were over, or at least she hadn't said anything to correct him. Feeling thoroughly ashamed of herself, she began to untack Goliath. To her surprise, Bernie pecked her on the cheek before heading to the barn to fetch Suzie. When she had finished untacking the horse she walked back to Rose Cottage where she unburdened herself to the girls.

Joyce placed her head in her hands. 'I'm so sorry, Roz, I didn't realise he'd blow it out of proportion. I don't blame you if you want to tell him the truth.'

Roz ran her hand around the back of her neck, which was tense. 'It's not going to be for long, but after he's taught her, I'm telling him I've had a change of heart.' She shook her head. 'I'm going for a lie-down, I've a thumping headache.'

Lying on her bed, she wondered what Felix would say if he knew what she'd done. Would he understand, or would he say that Roz had acted inappropriately and have nothing more to do with her? She wouldn't blame him if he did. Closing her eyes, she tried to get some rest. She would have to hope that Suzie was a fast learner, and that Felix never found out the truth.

October 1941

Having read Roz's letter aloud, Mabel turned to Gethin, who was listening with great interest. 'You Scousers don't half live entertaining lives!'

'Hmmm,' said Mabel, lost in her own thoughts she stared at the letter in her hands.

'What?'

'There's something Roz isn't telling me,' she said, rubbing her chin betwixt forefinger and thumb.

'Really? You actually think there's more?' said Gethin, who was finding it hard to believe that Roz could be omitting something even worse than what she had already written.

Mabel placed the paper down on the table and stared at Gethin. 'I do, only not to do with Suzie per se, more Roz herself. There's something she's holding back on, although I don't know what, but if I'm right, it must be bad for her to feel she can't tell me.'

Heulwyn, who was making vegetable soup, gave the spoonful she was about to test a gentle blow before gingerly tasting her cooking. Nodding with approval, she replaced the lid and wiped her hands on the tea towel which was tucked into the belt of her apron. 'I didn't hear her mention Felix, but I thought she'd been to see him?'

Mabel clicked her fingers. 'Spot on, Heulwyn! Why didn't I notice that?'

'Because I should imagine you were still reeling from the news that Suzie's just been reunited with her mother, who turned out to be Roz's friend – heck, I'm still reeling from the news and I don't even know any of them!' said Gethin.

But Mabel was only listening with half an ear, because Heulwyn was right, Roz hadn't mentioned Felix, yet he should've been the majority of her letter, so why hadn't she? She looked at Heulwyn. 'Would it be alright if I went home for a week?'

Heulwyn nodded. 'Of course it would. I take it you won't want to leave until Gethin goes back?'

Mabel grinned. 'You guessed correctly.' She closed her eyes as the delicious smell of simmering soup wafted in her direction. 'It may only be a week, but I won't half miss your cooking!'

When Roz got Mabel's letter her heart sank into her boots. She waved it at Joyce. 'Mabel's coming to visit. She's going to stay with her mum but she wants to meet up.'

Joyce smiled. 'That's wonderful news, why aren't you happy?'

'Because I've not told her about Bernie and our little arrangement, and I don't like the idea of lying to her – I've done enough of that already.'

Adele shrugged. 'Tell her the truth then. If she's a good friend she'll understand.'

Roz knitted her eyebrows. 'She can still be a good friend but disapprove of what I'm doing, and I should think she probably will. She likes Felix, they get on like a house on fire. She won't like the idea that he's having the wool pulled over his eyes.'

'In that case don't tell her,' said Adele as though this was an easy thing to do.

'That would be lying, and she's bound to ask me how Felix is and how my trip went, and ...' Roz clasped a hand to her forehead. 'I didn't even mention my trip in my letter because I felt a real heel. How am I going to be able to lie to my bezzie?'

Joyce shook her head. 'This is all my fault. You shouldn't have to lie to anyone. I think enough is enough.'

Roz got to her feet as Joyce tried to head out of the door. 'Don't! I can't undo what's been done, so what's the point in backing down now, especially when Suzie's doing so well?'

'Because it's making you miserable,' said Joyce, her hand on the door handle, 'and it's not fair. I saw your face when you returned from that meal – you looked miserable, but you still smiled your way through it. I had no right to ask you to do this in the first place, and now I need to put things right.'

'So what are you going to do?' said Roz. 'Go out there and tell Bernie that I've been stringing him along?'

'No, of course not!' said Joyce, horrified that Roz would think such a thing.

'Then what are you going to do?' said Roz simply.

Joyce released the handle and sat back down, her head in her hands. 'I don't know, I wasn't thinking.'

'Too right you weren't,' said Roz. 'I'm in this charade up to my neck; if I don't see it through it will have all been for naught. Let me do things my way and I might come out of this unscathed. I'll deal with Mabel when she gets here.' She glanced at Adele. 'You're right in one way, because whether Mabel agrees with me or not, she's a good friend, and friends stick by each other.'

They had seemed such simple words at the time she said them but now, as Roz made her way to Mercer Court, telling Mabel suddenly didn't seem to be as easy as it sounded, because even if Mabel did forgive her, Roz couldn't forgive herself. It had been different with Adele, because whilst she liked Felix very much, she knew how much it had hurt Roz to carry out the plan. Knocking tentatively against the door to Mabel's house, she smiled as she heard Mabel's familiar voice calling for her to enter.

'Long time no see!' said Mabel, sliding down from the bench next to the cooker.

'Too long,' agreed Roz, adding, 'you look fabulous – I can see Heulwyn's hearty food is giving you a waistline.'

'She could feed the five thousand, that one,' agreed Mabel. Indicating that Roz should take a seat by the table, she put the kettle on to boil before asking the question which Roz feared the most. 'How's Felix, and why didn't you mention him in your letter? Or, to put it another way, just what aren't you telling me?'

Roz's jaw dropped. 'What makes you so sure I'm holding out on you?'

Mabel quirked an eyebrow. 'You're trying to tell me you're not?'

Roz took a deep breath before letting it all out with a whoosh. 'You know me too well, Mabel Johnson.'

Mabel nodded wisely. 'I do, and that's why I've been so worried. You wouldn't keep quiet unless something was really wrong, so is it Felix?'

Roz ran a nervous tongue over her bottom lip before answering, 'Not exactly.'

Seeing the look of impending doom written all over her friend's face concerned Mabel greatly. 'Roz, what on earth has happened?'

Looking miserable, Roz told her everything. By the time she had finished, she was too ashamed to look her friend in the eye.

'Oh golly,' sighed Mabel, 'this really is a rough row to hoe.'

'Do you think I'm horrid?' said Roz, still hanging her head in shame.

'No!' snapped Mabel, adding, a little more softly, 'I think your heart's in the right place, maybe a little misguided, but your intentions are good.'

Roz looked at the ceiling, blinking back tears of embarrassment. 'It started as a little white lie to help a friend, but Bernie got hold of the wrong end of the stick and since then it's just got worse, and I feel terrible. As for Felix, I've considered ending our relationship, I feel so bad about lying to him.'

Walking over to Roz, Mabel put her arms around her friend's shoulders. 'Don't be daft. There's no need to go that far – it's not as if you and Bernie are in a relationship, or kissed or ...' She hesitated. Roz wasn't agreeing with her. 'Roz?'

Roz hastily shook her head. 'I haven't kissed him, but he does peck me on the cheek every now and then, and he takes me out for the odd meal and he doesn't do that with anyone else.'

Mabel pulled an awkward face. 'Oh dear, it sounds as if he's taking things slowly, which means he's serious about you.' She squeezed Roz's shoulders.

Roz looked even more miserable. 'He is, and that's what makes this even worse. He's just assumed that me and Felix are over and that he's the only suitor around.' She sighed heavily. 'What am I going to do, Mabel?'

'Christmas!' said Mabel.

Roz looked up, confused. 'Sorry, what?'

'Come and stay at the farm for Christmas – Felix can come too if he likes. Heulwyn said I should ask you both before I left, she said it would be fun, like last year, only this year Gethin will be there too. It'll give you time away from Joyce, Suzie and Bernie, and when you go back you can tell Bernie that I invited Felix without your knowledge and you and Felix got reacquainted and as a result you're now back together.'

Roz brightened. 'That would be perfect, and it would look natural too.' She smiled thankfully at her friend. 'I knew you'd come through for me, you always do, just like Felix.'

Looking shy under such praise, Mabel gave a dismissive wave. 'Don't be daft. It's easier to think when you're on the outside looking in.'

'Do you want to come to Hollybank and meet everyone?' said Roz, feeling better about the situation.

Mabel laughed as she shook her head. 'I think seeing me might just be the straw that breaks the camel's back as far as Suzie's concerned.'

Roz grimaced. 'I hadn't thought of that. It's a shame, though. Have you told your mum about Joyce?'

Hearing the kettle boil, Mabel got to her feet. 'She was thrilled to hear that Joyce was alright, but worried about Suzie, especially after the bombings.'

'I can understand why, it was terrible. I saw the coal merchant's the morning after and it was still burning fiercely.' Roz shuddered. 'Do you think there was anything left of Lilith?'

Mabel gave a horrified gasp. 'Roz! The thought hadn't entered my mind, and I rather wish it hadn't yours, because now I shan't stop thinking about it ...' She stirred the tea in the pot, transfixed by the tea leaves. 'What on earth made you think something so gruesome?'

'Because if there was, then surely they'd know if she'd been on her own, because by all accounts Suzie wasn't certain of her father's whereabouts.'

'Don't you think that's odd?' said Mabel, eyeing her friend quizzically. 'Why was Suzie certain that her gran was at home, but not so sure about her dad? And why was she down the shelter on her own? Surely her gran should've been with her?'

'Do you think she's lying?' said Roz, although she couldn't imagine why Suzie would lie about such a thing.

'Knowing the Haggartys, anything's possible.'

Roz shook her head as the image of Suzie, tears pouring down her face, accusing Roz of being the reason that her family were dead, washed over her. 'She's not lying. Not even Suzie can act that well.'

'Then where was Callum? Because it sounds to me as though Suzie thinks he was out, but couldn't be certain.' This question was answered by Elsa, who had overheard her daughter's words as she entered the house.

'Because Callum saw Suzie down to the shelter, that's what old Bill Parkins reckons. He said he'd seen Callum practically dragging Suzie to the shelter, then legging it when the warden took over.'

Roz's brow furrowed as she tried to picture the scene. 'So Suzie didn't want to go down the shelter?'

'Not by the sound of things, and I think I know why. I saw Suzie moments after the bomb exploded. She was standing watching the flames, crying because her grandmother was inside.'

Roz asked the question uppermost in her thoughts. 'Who's this Bill Parkins?'

'He's one of the locals down the Pig and Whistle. He recognised Callum as soon as he saw him; he was making his way to the shelter when the first bomb hit, it was him that went to the warden's rescue. Terrible business.' She looked at Roz as though only just realising she was there for the first time. 'Hello, luv.'

'Hello,' said Roz, her voice distant as she tried to think where Callum had got to, and why Lilith had been left on her own. Without any answers springing to mind, she voiced her thoughts to Elsa.

'Who knows when it comes to that lot?' said Elsa. 'It seems awfully strange to leave his mother like that, but he obviously had.'

'This is the Haggartys we're talking about,' said Mabel. 'I wouldn't put anything past that lot.'

Roz, however, knew the Haggartys better than anyone in that house. If Lilith was on her own, then it was for a reason, and if she was right, and Callum knowingly left his mother during an air raid, then he had as good as killed her. She said as much to the other two women.

Elsa looked haunted. 'It's the only thing that makes sense. I know Lilith is old, but I do believe she could make it down those steps if she had to, so there must've been another reason for her to stay behind – and one that Suzie didn't agree with if Callum was having to drag her to the shelter.'

'He might not have murdered Joyce,' said Roz, her tone leaden, 'but if we're right, he sure as hell killed his own mother.'

*

362

December 1941

Suzie was beginning to enjoy her new life at Hollybank. Seeing her mother desperately trying to appease her had pleased her no end, and whilst she would never admit it to the others, she very much enjoyed working with Bernie on the farm, although how she had managed to hold her tongue and not let him know the truth behind Roz and Felix's relationship showed just how determined she was to twist the knife when it would have the most impact. She didn't even feel sorry for Bernie – why should she? She knew he had only agreed to teach her so that he would win favour in Roz's eyes; as far as Suzie was concerned Bernie deserved everything he got.

Hearing voices coming from the yard, she peered round the corner of the milking shed. Roz was back, although Suzie hadn't the foggiest where the other woman had been. However judging by the look of elation on her face she had imparted goods news which was greeted with gusto by Joyce and Adele, who were looking extremely pleased for their friend. Suzie racked her brains. What on earth could have caused Roz such happiness? Determined to find out, she sauntered slowly towards the group of women, forcing her lips into a smile.

'Someone's happy? Care to share?' she asked, in what she hoped was a carefree manner.

Roz was guarded; she really didn't want Suzie knowing anything about her or her plans. The girl had barely spoken more than two words to her since she had agreed to remain in Hollybank, which was fine by Roz, so why the interest now?

'Roz is going away for Christmas!' said Joyce, who was grateful that her daughter was making an effort.

Roz shot Joyce a warning look to keep quiet, but Joyce wasn't paying her any attention. This was the first time Suzie had approached any of them in a friendly manner, and Joyce was determined to make the most of it.

'Oh, how lovely!' said Suzie. 'Anywhere nice?'

Knowing that Suzie would only be interested for the wrong reasons, Roz decided to nip the conversation in the bud. 'I'm going to stay with Mabel.'

Assuming that Roz meant she would be staying in Mercer Court, Suzie immediately lost interest and returned to her usual sulky demeanour. Shooting her mother a scathing look, she arched an eyebrow. 'I suppose you'll be going too?'

Before Roz could stop her, Joyce let the cat out of the bag. 'Gosh, no! Mabel's living on a farm in Betwys-y-Coed!'

'Is she now?' said Suzie, her interest reignited. 'I daresay I wouldn't know, as nobody bothers to tell me anything.'

Roz eyed Suzie with deep suspicion. 'Why would you care where Mabel is? I thought you hated her?'

Suzie shrugged in a nonchalant manner. 'Maybe I've decided to let bygones be bygones, life's too short to dwell on the past.'

Joyce threw her arms around her daughter and hugged her tight. 'Oh, Suzie, that's wonderful to hear! I'm so glad you've decided to forgive and forget.'

Roz continued to stare at Suzie who wasn't returning the warmth of her mother's embrace. Keeping her eyes on Roz, she spoke softly. 'Forgiveness is one thing, but forget? That might take time.'

The air between Roz and Suzie, could have been cut with a knife, and Roz was flummoxed as to what was going through the other girl's mind. Suzie was regarding her smugly, as though she knew something which Roz didn't, but what could she know? Roz made sure she kept her cards close to her chest when it came to the other girl, but looking at Suzie with her face full of malicious intent, Roz knew she was up to no good. A chill ran down her spine. There could only be one answer: Felix!

Never breaking eye contact, she tried to keep the anxiety out of her voice as she spoke. 'Bernie says you've learned just about everything there is to know at the farm; he says you're doing really well.'

A knowing smile flickered on Suzie's lips. 'Bernie's a good teacher, a lovely man. You're a lucky girl, Roz, he's obviously very keen on you.'

Roz swallowed. Damn and blast it, she was certain Suzie knew about Felix, and that Roz wasn't being honest with Bernie.

'Shan't be a mo,' said Roz, before walking as quickly as she could without raising suspicion towards the hay barn where she knew she would find Bernie.

As she walked through the open door, she turned to look at Suzie, and was not surprised to see that the other girl was watching her with interest whilst listening to her mother who was chatting away happily. Roz would have to hope and pray that Joyce didn't let slip about Felix also going to Glasfryn for the holidays.

'Hello!'

Roz was so lost in her thoughts, she started when Bernie greeted her. She drew a deep breath as she turned to face him. 'There's something I need to tell you.'

'Oh?' He rested the pitchfork against the wall. 'Sounds ominous!'

'I've been thinking about our relationship an awful lot lately, and whilst I know you had hopes that our friendship might develop into something more, I've decided that I need to concentrate on finding my parents, or at least doing all I can to find them.' She eyed him sympathetically. 'I'm sorry.'

'Oh, right,' said Bernie in a subdued fashion. 'There's not a lot I can say to that.' He hesitated. 'Has this anything to do with Felix?'

The question had come out of the blue, nearly knocking Roz off her feet, so she said the first plausible thing that came to mind. 'I was uncertain about Felix because I had too much going on in my life, and I don't want to make the same mistake twice.'

'That's fair enough.' He gripped the pitchfork. 'I hope you find your folks soon, because it's a shame that this is stopping you from moving forward.'

Smiling gratefully, Roz thanked him for his understanding, adding. 'If things had been different...' before turning on her heel and hastening back to the cottage.

Watching her go, Bernie wondered if someone had said something to change Roz's mind. If so, he couldn't think what. He knew that she had been confused about her relationship and feelings towards Felix when she came to Hollybank; perhaps she felt the same thing was happening between herself and Bernie, as she had suggested. He cast his mind back over the last few weeks. Before Suzie's arrival he had spent all his time with Roz, but since Suzie had come on the scene they had spent little time together. Had this caused distance between them? He'd taken Roz out for a couple of meals, and evening walks, and even though she smiled, she always seemed distracted. He had deliberately taken things slowly so that he could be sure she was genuinely keen on him and that she wasn't with him on the rebound.

He looked over to where Suzie stood talking with her mother, something which he had never seen her do before. It looked very much as though the two had finally put their differences aside and made amends. Could that have anything to do with Roz's decision? He felt his stomach drop into his boots. Had Roz only shown interest in him so that he would agree to teach Suzie? *Surely not!* Unable to believe that Roz was capable of something so heinous, he immediately dismissed the thought from his mind. He was adding two and two together and coming up with five. He knew that Roz had been to see her old pal Mabel, so perhaps the other girl, who had known Roz when she was dating Felix, had warned her friend to take things one step at a time. He felt a sense of relief. That must be the answer. Relieved that he hadn't got Roz wrong, he headed back into the barn, to carry on with his work.

Roz watched Suzie chatting merrily with Joyce. She didn't blame her friend for not questioning Suzie's motives, but Roz knew better and this was all part of the act, only Suzie was in for a surprise if she thought she was going to set the cat amongst the pigeons as far as Roz and Bernie were concerned.

Suzie beamed at her mother, who was talking about their future with enthusiasm. Only she wasn't beaming because she actually wanted a future with her mother, but because she knew her suspicions to be right. Roz had been moping around the farm ever since she had begun the charade with Bernie. So, if Roz's plan to visit Glasfryn had filled her with euphoria it could only mean one thing – Felix must be going too, which was why Roz had gone over to dampen her relationship with Bernie. Suzie had seen the way he was watching Roz from the hay barn; he had clearly just received some unwanted news. So that was Roz and Bernie's friendship at an end; all she had to do now was find a way to destroy Felix and Roz's relationship, and she thought she had the very idea.

Even though she was no longer officially under Bernie's wing, Suzie had asked if she might join him on the milk round, claiming she had had a dream the previous night in which she had seen her father walking along one of the streets where they delivered milk.

From everything Roz had told him, Bernie very much believed Suzie's father to be dead, but he had agreed, not wishing to be the one to dash her hopes.

As they neared the end of their rounds, Goliath came to a halt of his own accord, outside one of the houses where he always received a treat or two. Suzie jumped down from the cart and greeted the woman with a cheery smile as she took the jug and filled it to the brim.

They each set about filling various vessels, taking money or, in the case of some of the poorer households, accepting a knitted scarf or whatever it was they could spare in exchange.

With their customers content, they mounted the cart and Goliath moved on.

'So much for me thinking that I'd had some kind of premonition!' said Suzie, not sounding quite as disappointed as Bernie would have expected her to sound.

'War's a terrible thing,' said Bernie. 'You lost your gran and Roz lost her mam and dad. You only have to see the waifs and strays that come to Hollybank to realise the dire straits some folk are in.'

Suzie had to stop herself from grinning. She had hoped the ruse of hoping to see her father – which had been the stuff of nonsense – might prompt a conversation about Roz's parents, but she hadn't dreamed it would be as easy as this. She paused before speaking. In order to appear believable, she would have to appear truthful, which might not be so easy.

'I'll admit I wasn't at all sympathetic when Roz first came to live with us, but since being in her position I can quite see how hard she's had things. She's been very lucky to have friends like you and my mother in her life.'

Bernie raised an eyebrow. 'Am I to take it that things are good between not only you and your mother but Roz too?'

This was the part where Suzie would have to mix truth with fiction. 'I'd say they were better with Roz, and things are looking more positive between me and me mam, but we've still a long way to go, and I find it difficult to look her in the eye at times.'

Bernie seemed impressed with her maturity. 'I think being at Hollybank's done you the world of good.'

She gave a half-smile. Not because he had complimented her, but because he had fallen for the nonsense that things were better between her and her mother, because that was the fictional part. Suzie hadn't forgiven her mother, and she doubted she ever would.

'It seems that everything's coming up roses,' she agreed, before adding, 'although I can't help but notice that you and Roz don't seem to be spending as much time together any more, which is a shame because I think you'd make a lovely couple.'

To her delight, she saw his jaw flinch. 'Roz has decided she needs to concentrate on finding her parents – I'm sure you can relate to that?'

'Of course,' said Suzie. She knew that Roz had quelled her relationship with Bernie, but she hadn't known the reasons that Roz had given, not until now. She pressed on. 'I must say, I'm rather surprised, especially after what happened between her and Felix. I'd have thought she wouldn't want to make the same mistake twice.'

Bernie eyed her quizzically; he very much doubted Roz would confide that she'd had second thoughts with Felix, but Suzie obviously knew something. 'What do you mean?'

'I overheard her telling my mother that she and Felix would probably be betrothed by now, if it weren't for his absence.'

Bernie sat up with renewed interest in what his travelling companion had to say. 'What do you think she meant by that?'

Suzie savoured the moment. He was falling for it. 'I'm not really sure, but Mam said summat about faint heart never won fair lady, whatever that may mean.'

'It means he should have fought for her harder, instead of accepting it was over,' said Bernie.

'Oh!' said Suzie, pretending that this was news to her. 'So, she wants someone to fight for her affection?' He nodded, and Suzie could tell he was giving the thought much consideration. She only had one more move, the rest would be up to him. 'What time is it?'

Suzie knew that the milk round always took the same amount of time; they were always back around eleven.

Bernie really should have wondered why she had asked what time it was, but he was so lost in his thoughts it never even occurred to him to question her. 'Eleven, maybe ten past, why?' he said, gazing at Rose Cottage as Goliath plodded past.

'Just thinking that Roz is probably at the station by now.'

He looked at her with blank incomprehension before the penny dropped. If he was to win Roz he would have to act fast. He turned to Suzie. 'Can you put Goliath away for me?'

Her heart pounding in her chest, she smiled pleasantly. 'Of course I can, is something wrong?'

He grinned at her and said. 'Faint heart never won fair lady!' before disappearing into the house, only to reappear with his father a few minutes later, carrying a small holdall and jogging across the yard towards the Morris Oxford that they only ever used for emergencies.

As they drove past Suzie, he rolled the window down. 'Thanks, Suzie, you might have just done me the biggest favour!'

Watching them leave, Suzie couldn't keep the smile off her face as she imagined him turning up at Lime Street Station, because she knew for a fact, after talking to her mother earlier that morning, that Roz had agreed to meet Felix there!

Seeing Felix waving to her from further up the platform, Roz hurried towards him. The past few months had been awful and she couldn't wait to be back in his arms, safe in the knowledge that she didn't have to pretend to anyone, not any more. Taking her in a passionate embrace, he swept her off her feet and turned her full circle before gently placing her back down. Breaking apart but keeping their foreheads together, he spoke softly. 'You don't know how much I've been wanting to do that.'

'Me too,' murmured Roz, before his lips locked with hers once more. Aware that there were others on the platform, she was the first to break away. She had decided on the way to the station that even though she didn't have to, it would only be right for her to tell Felix of Joyce's plan for Suzie to stay on the farm. She knew that if she were the one to tell him, she could do it on her own terms and in such a manner that he might understand the reasoning behind her actions. 'I've so much to tell you,' she said quietly, 'but I'd rather wait until we were somewhere a little more private.'

Smiling, he kissed the tip of her nose. 'Sounds intriguing!'

'It's not something I'm proud of ...' Roz began, only to be interrupted by a squeal of the train's brakes as it pulled into the station. 'I think this might be us,' she said. 'Let's see if we can get ourselves an empty carriage.' She glanced around the platform which was much emptier than she had expected, and by the looks of some of them, they were here to greet people rather than board the train.

Felix followed her gaze. 'I reckon we stand a good chance,' he said, picking up first his luggage, then hers. 'Come on.'

Roz followed in his wake. She was not looking forward to the journey, especially with the news she had to impart, and she did wonder if he might be angry at her for telling him on the train where he would be trapped, rather than before they boarded, when he would still have had the chance to walk away if that's how he felt.

Standing back from the carriage door, he indicated for her to go before him. 'Ladies first,' he said, and Roz dutifully boarded the train. Turning to take her luggage from Felix so that he might be able to board himself, her heart sank. There, not twelve feet away from them, stood Bernie, a holdall in his hands, with a look of utter disbelief on his face. It was obvious why he was there. Feeling her mouth go dry, she hastily took her luggage from Felix and ushered him aboard, mumbling that she wouldn't be a minute. She stepped down from the carriage and hurried to where Bernie stood glaring at her. His eyes moved to Felix who was watching with interest from the carriage doorway.

'Nice of you to tell me you were going to Glasfryn with your *boyfriend*,' he muttered with disgust. 'How long has this been planned? Only I'm taking it that he must be Felix, unless you've a string of us ...'

In an effort to try and keep his voice down, Roz placed a finger to her lips. 'Please, Bernie, not here. I promise I'll explain everything when I get back, but not now.'

Bernie, who had been glaring jealously at Felix, turned his attention back to Roz. 'Why not, Roz? What's the big secret?' Jolting his head backwards, he clapped his forehead with the palm of his hand, and continued to strike it with each word. 'Stupid, stupid, stupid!' Shaking his head, he eyed her with disbelieving amusement. 'I must be a right idiot, 'cos you've played me like a fiddle!'

He looked at Felix, who, sensing the tension, had come to see what was going on. Pointing at Felix, Bernie continued, 'Does he know? About me, I mean? Or was that not part of the plan?' One look at Felix's face gave Bernie the answer to his question. 'Of course he doesn't know. You've played the two of us, him because you never told him about me, and me because you led me on just so that your pal's daughter would stay.' He shook his head. 'What's worse is I questioned your motives, but guess what, Roz? I didn't believe it, I never thought you could be so cruel.'

'Not here,' pleaded Roz, but Bernie wasn't listening; instead, and to her horror, he was now addressing Felix.

'Just so you know, I'd never go for a woman in a relationship. I was only ever interested because she told me that she doubted her feelings for you. I kept away until she came back from visiting you in Lincoln.' He shot Roz a withering glance before turning his attention back to Felix. 'She made out that you and her were over, and when I said as much she never put me right.'

The tears which filled Roz's eyes were now falling freely down her cheeks. She wanted to deny everything, but how could she? She turned to Felix, who was looking at Bernie as though the other man had just punched him in the face. His eyes turned to Roz, a look of pleading deep within them. 'Please tell me it's not true, please tell me he's lying.'

Swallowing hard, Roz turned first to Bernie. 'Please believe me when I say I'm sorry, and that I didn't mean to hurt anyone.'

Giving her a slow, sarcastic round of applause, he shook his head. 'I wouldn't believe a word that left your lips,' he said, before turning back to Felix. 'You're welcome to her.' With that, he turned on his heel and walked away.

She looked at Felix, her eyes searching his for a clue as to how he felt. 'It's not as it sounds,' she said quickly. 'If you just give me a chance to explain, I know you'll understand.'

Felix's jaw flinched. 'I don't see that there is much to understand. That feller had a lot to say for himself, and you never denied any of it. I know what it's like to love you, Roz, and if you can treat him like that ...'

'Only I don't love him,' said Roz quickly, trying desperately to convince Felix of the truth.

'Nor me, from what he's just said,' said Felix evenly.

Roz shook her head. 'When I first got to the farm, I questioned my feelings for you and yours for me. He knew from the start that I wasn't single.'

'You just weren't sure whether you should be,' Felix added sarcastically.

Roz looked helpless. 'No, I wasn't sure. I was really mixed up, I can't tell you why because I don't know myself, but when I came to see you there wasn't a doubt in my mind that we were meant to be together, and that I loved you with all my heart. It was only when I got back to Liverpool and the whole thing with Suzie and Joyce blew up that things started to get complicated.' She hastily explained Suzie's ultimatum, and Joyce's plan. 'I didn't want to do it, but I didn't want to see Joyce lose her daughter, nor Suzie lose her mother.'

'Oh, so you did it for Suzie?' said Felix, his voice heavy with incredulity.

'No!' snapped Roz. 'I did it for Joyce,' she hesitated, 'but now you mention it, then yes, I also did it for Suzie. I know she can be spiteful, horrid, vicious even, but I also know what it's like to lose your parents, and if I had the slightest chance of finding mine I'd be over the moon, but Suzie's too immature to know what's good for her, which is why I stepped in, because I knew that given time she'd change her mind but we're at war, so it might be too late by then...'

'When are you going to stop thinking of others and start thinking of yourself?' said Felix. 'And what about *me*?' he added bitterly. 'Did I even cross your mind, or didn't I matter?'

Roz stared at him aghast. 'Of course you crossed my mind, and you matter more than anyone else!'

'Well, you've a funny way of showing it ...' Felix began, before the guard calling for all passengers to get aboard cut him short. With an exasperated sigh, Felix headed for the carriage, with a relieved Roz following close behind. At least he was still coming to Betwys-y-Coed, and she could explain everything in greater detail once they were on board.

They entered the carriage and Felix stowed her luggage beneath the seat before taking his own bag and slinging it over his shoulder. Seeing the look of despair on her face, he shook his head. 'I'm sorry, Roz, but I can't come with you, not under the circumstances.'

Fresh tears brimming in her eyes, Roz pleaded with him. 'Please, Felix, don't do this. I love you.'

Smiling ruefully, he cupped the side of her cheek with his hand. 'And I love you too, that's why it hurts so much to know you ever doubted your love for me.' He kissed her on the top of her head, the tears shining in his eyes. 'I get why you did what you did, but I have to ask myself whether you'd have done that if you *really* loved me.' He placed a finger to her lips as she opened her mouth to protest. 'I have to make sure in my heart, Roz, and I can't do that if I'm with you.' He kissed her softly on the lips as the tears rolled down her cheeks. 'I'll be in touch' were his final words as he left the carriage.

Roz immediately went to grab her case, but no sooner had the guard shut the door behind Felix than the train jerked into motion. For a brief moment she contemplated jumping off the train before it gained momentum, but Felix must have pre-empted her thoughts because as she looked out of the window, he was gazing back at her, slowly shaking his head. Nodding her understanding, she slumped into her seat and placed her hands over her eyes, then let the tears flow freely.

Back at the farm, Bernie climbed out of the taxi and called out to Adele who was crossing the yard. 'Where's Suzie?'

Adele pointed to the milking shed. 'She's washing down. Is everything alright?'

Without bothering to answer, Bernie strode to the shed, where he found Joyce on the hose whilst Suzie brushed the slurry down the drain. 'You evil little bitch,' he said, pointing an accusing finger at Suzie.

Flabbergasted as to what had made Bernie, usually a mild-mannered soul, speak in such a fashion, Joyce stared at him. 'What on earth's happened, Bernie?' She looked at Suzie, who was feigning innocence, but only a fool would have believed she didn't know exactly what Bernie was talking about. 'Suzie?'

'Don't give me that!' snapped Bernie. 'You're as bad as your daughter, if not worse. I know all about your little plan for Roz to woo me just so that I would teach Suzie.' His jaw flinching angrily, he turned his attention back to Suzie. 'You could've just told me – there was no need to humiliate me in front of a station full of people.'

Joyce's hand flew to her mouth and she stared pleadingly at her daughter to tell her it wasn't so, then spoke thickly through her fingers. 'You didn't?'

Ignoring her mother, Suzie turned to Bernie. 'And you'd have believed me? Besides, don't you think Felix deserved to know the truth?'

'Not like that!' growled Bernie. 'He's in the same position as me – we're the innocents in all this – not that that bothered you! All you thought about is your damned self. Well, I won't have a backstabber working on my farm. You can take your things and leave.'

Suzie's eyes widened. 'You can't throw me out! It's your parents who own the farm, and I should think they'd be grateful that I've shown Roz's true colours.' Tutting with disbelief, she added, 'If that's what all the Jews are like, you can kind of see why Hitler …' She got no further. Joyce, who had been bending over backwards to make amends with her daughter, spoke her piece.

'Enough! People have laid everything on the line for you, done all they could to mend our relationship, and why? To help you, that's why! Yet you were hateful to Roz from the word go, because you were jealous of her.' She gave an incredulous laugh. 'Jealous of a girl hounded out of her own country in fear of her life, jealous of a girl who doesn't know whether her parents are dead or alive, who's lost everything …'

'What about me?' snapped Suzie, hot tears of anger forming in her eyes. 'Haven't I lost everything?'

'You hadn't,' said Joyce reasonably. 'When Roz came to live in Crooked Lane you still had your father and grandmother …'

'But I didn't have *you*!' Suzie exclaimed. 'And it's you I wanted! You were the only one who ever stood up for me; I lost everything the day you disappeared.'

'And you've not forgiven me for that, that's plain to see,' said Joyce through thin lips.

'Why should I? You could've stayed for my sake!'

With a look of sympathy, her mother's voice softened as she spoke. 'Do you not remember the beatings? I was black and blue half the time, and it was never going to get better. You know how scared I was of your father; even Lilith feared for my safety – not that she'd have admitted it, of course, because she didn't want Callum's anger to turn on her.'

'I know,' said Suzie sulkily, 'that's why it was so easy to believe he'd gone too far.'

'I know you love him, your gran too, and that's only right, but you have to see, I had to leave for my own safety, otherwise he really might have killed me, by accident or otherwise.'

Suzie whimpered as the truth behind her mother's words resonated in her soul.

'Suzie?' said Joyce. It was obvious by her daughter's hunted look that she was hiding something.

Looking up, Suzie spoke thickly through her tears. 'That night when the air raid siren sounded, he made Gran stay home as punishment.' Gulping back the tears, she continued, 'He forced me to go to the shelter. I ran back as soon as he'd gone, but I was too late ...'

'Bloody hell,' said Bernie, all thoughts of Suzie's vicious revenge temporarily forgotten.

Joyce enveloped her daughter in a tight embrace. 'I'm so sorry. You shouldn't have had to go through any of that, but surely you must see why I had to leave?'

Suzie nodded, her face buried in the crook of her mother's shoulder. 'I know he's bad, he steals from the dead and loots people's houses during raids, he's the lowest of the low, but he's still my dad, or at least he was.'

Joyce stroked the back of Suzie's head. 'I take it you're wondering whether he went back to the loft to save your gran?'

Suzie gave a little nod.

Joyce breathed a deep sigh. 'Even if he'd had the time, do you really think he'd have gone back for her?'

Suzie gave the tiniest shake of her head, then leaned back. Wiping the tears from her eyes with the back of her hands, she faced the truth. 'He'd never have had time to get back home, let alone up the stairs. I left the shelter seconds after him and I ran all the way. I might be younger than Dad, but I'm faster too.'

'You've been taking your anger out on the wrong people,' said Bernie. 'Although I can see why you're so angry.' His jaw twitched. 'Given the circumstances, I think you've been punished enough, so you can stay, but one more stunt like that and you're out of here.'

'I won't,' said Suzie her voice dripping with relief. 'I'm sorry, I really am.'

Raising his hand in acknowledgement, Bernie left the two women to talk.

'Roz is going to hate me,' said Suzie quietly.

'She will, but it's my fault, so I'll take the responsibility,' said Joyce. Much to her surprise, Suzie shook her head.

'It's Dad's fault. If he hadn't been faster with a punch than a kiss, then none of this would have happened, but it's me who really put the cat amongst the pigeons, so it's me that'll sort things out with Roz, as best I can at any rate.'

'How?' said Joyce.

'I'll go to the farm – Glasfryn, wasn't it? Set the record straight and see if I can undo any of the harm I've caused.'

Joyce smiled fondly at her daughter. 'I'm proud of you, Suzie Haggarty.'

Her lips wobbling, Suzie smiled back. 'I wish I felt the same.'

'You've been to hell and back, but you're putting right your wrongs now, and it takes courage to do that,' said Joyce.

Suzie gave a small laugh. 'You're telling me – my stomach's doing somersaults at the very thought!'

Felix watched the train until it was out of sight before heading toward Alan and Bill's. He hadn't seen either of them since his posting to Lincoln, and if he counted anyone other than Roz to be his family in Liverpool it was them. As he walked he replayed the last twenty minutes – which felt like hours – in his mind.

Roz had said she wanted to tell him something before Bernie had arrived at the station, yet it was obvious that she hadn't expected him to turn up, so she wasn't about to tell him the truth for fear of getting caught out. He mulled this thought over for a moment or so. If that was the case, then it meant that Roz, despite not having to, was going to tell him the truth because she thought he should know. Another thought crossed his mind. If she'd doubted her love for him once, what's to say it wouldn't happen again? He didn't think he could stand to have his heart broken for a second time, because finding out that the woman he loved most in the world had been spending time with another man, no matter what the reason behind it, had cut him to the quick. He might love Roz with all his heart, but sometimes love just wasn't enough.

Roz watched the fields roll by, the trees bare of leaves, the skies grey and threatening rain. The scenery matched her mood. It was just her luck that an old lady had decided to share her carriage, meaning that Roz couldn't wallow in self-pity and cry the journey away. She ran through the scene on the platform for the umpteenth time, wondering how she could have handled things differently, what she could have said or done that would have led to a better outcome, but nothing sprang to mind, not that it mattered now. Her actions had come back to haunt her, and even if Bernie *hadn't* turned up, and she *had* managed to tell Felix whilst on the train, she very much doubted the outcome would have been different apart from the fact that they would have had to spend a very uncomfortable journey together, with Felix probably leaving the train at the first station they stopped at.

The lady leaned forward in her seat and held out a bag of sweets to Roz. 'Here you go, duck, you have yourself a sherbet lemon, that'll make you feel better.'

Forcing a smile, Roz politely took one of the sweets. 'Is it that obvious?'

Taking a sweet for herself, the woman popped it into her mouth and stowed it inside her cheek whilst putting the paper bag back in her handbag. 'Not that I meant to pry, but I couldn't help noticing the fracas on the platform.'

Roz grimaced. 'I should imagine half the station saw that.'

'When I were a girl, I thought that I'd meet a wonderful feller, fall in love, get married and have me a gaggle of kiddies.' She sucked the sweet thoughtfully before continuing, 'It was only when I'd been married for a few years that I realised that marriage ain't a bed of roses, and you have to work hard to stop yerself from throttlin' the bugger.'

Roz laughed.

'That's better!' chuckled her companion. 'You've got a pretty smile.'

'Thank you,' said Roz, adding with an embarrassed grimace, 'I hope we didn't make too much of a show of ourselves.'

The woman waved a dismissive hand. 'No more than most, and it'll give the passengers summat to talk about on a long journey, so you've done them a favour – it's just a pity that it's come at your expense.' She smiled kindly at her. 'Want to talk about it? It's a long way to Betwys-y-Coed, and sometimes talking to a stranger can help sort things out, and I don't like to see someone so upset, not this close to Christmas.'

'By trying to please others I hurt the most important man in my life,' said Roz simply. 'He's the one who took his luggage off the train.'

The woman gave a knowing nod. 'I see. Do you think he'll change his mind once he's had the chance to simmer down?'

'You tell me,' said Roz, and she went on to tell her travelling companion about Hollybank and the circumstances that had led up to that moment.

'He's a silly beggar if he doesn't,' said the woman who finally introduced herself as Edith. 'But they say that pride comes before a fall, and men are proud creatures. Is that what your Felix is like?'

Roz shook her head. 'I wouldn't say so. He has a heart of gold and is very kind – he's never struck me as the sort to be proud, far from it. If anything, he's quite humble.'

'Affairs of the heart are different,' said Edith, 'especially when there's another suitor involved, and Bernie sounds quite the catch.'

'He is, but not for me,' said Roz. 'Felix is my kind of man. I just wish I'd stuck to my guns and stayed out of it all.' Tears began to well in her eyes so she took a handkerchief from her handbag and blew her nose.

'Well, he obviously loves you, else he'd not have reacted the way he did. I reckon he'll come back after he's had a chance to lick his wounds.' Edith smiled kindly at Roz, who wasn't looking so certain. 'It's just going to take time, that's all.'

Roz nodded, but in truth she feared she had severed Felix's trust completely. Sometimes love just wasn't enough.

Chapter Nine

Callum stood on the crowded platform. Since leaving Crooked Lane he had been living rough, but other than that nothing had changed. He still headed into the city when the sirens sounded, ready to loot houses abandoned for fear of the bombs, then flogged his wares down the Pig and Whistle. He had, however, diversified his talents, and was now pickpocketing as well. Train stations were particularly good for this; with people concentrating on when the train would arrive, they rarely paid attention to who was standing behind them.

He had been just about to slip his hand into the blazer pocket of the man in front of him when someone placed their hand over his. He turned to tell them to bugger off and mind their own business then stopped, his jaw dropping as he found himself staring at his daughter.

'Suzie!'

Nodding, Suzie tapped the man in front of her father. 'Keep your hands on your valuables, there are pickpockets on this platform.'

Hastily the man plunged his hands into his pockets, smiling gratefully at her. 'Thanks for the tip.'

Suzie turned her attention back to her father, who was scowling. 'What do you think you're playing at?' he hissed angrily.

'That man probably works hard for his money, which is more than what you do!' She gave him a scathing look as she eyed him from head to toe. 'When was the last time you had a bath?'

He adjusted his shabby clothing, looking past her. 'Some of us don't have them luxuries ...' He cast an eye over her appearance. 'I see you've persuaded some mug to take you in ... Seeing as you've landed on your feet, how about you persuade them to take me in too? It could be just like the old days, you going down the market, me ...'

Stunned that her father thought they could carry on as before without so much as mentioning her grand-mother, Suzie spoke through pursed lips. 'You seriously think I'd ask someone to take *you* in when you left your own mother to die?' Her voice cut through the air like a knife as she continued, 'And do you really think I'd want to go begging again, whilst you run riot robbing bomb victims of anything they have left?' Her voice rose higher, causing several people to glance over their shoulders, but Suzie didn't care. 'You're a thief, a liar, and a rotten father.'

'At least I never beggared off like your mam did!' snapped Callum. 'Because despite what you think, I never done her in. If you ask me, she left because she couldn't stand the sight of you no more and I can't say as I blame her.'

Her eyes flashed with fire as she put the record straight. 'Shows what you know! I've seen me mam and she told me she left because she'd had enough of your kicks and punches, not to mention anything else which came to hand. You cause nowt but misery and destruction wherever you go.'

Callum stared at her in horrified disbelief. 'Liar. You ain't seen your mam!'

Suzie folded her arms across her chest. 'I have, and what's more I see her every day.'

He threw her a look of pure hate. 'You're like two peas in a pod, the pair of you, only out for your own gain, not giving a rat's arse about anyone else!'

She eyed him back with equal disgust. 'All these years I blamed Mam for everything going wrong, when I should've been looking closer to home. It was your fault Mam left and your fault Gran died. What kind of son forces his own mother to stay behind during an air raid?'

Fearing his daughter would be overheard, Callum clapped his hand around her neck and over her mouth. 'Shut your filthy, lyin' ...'

From behind, someone gripped Callum's wrist, forcing him to release Suzie. Twisting it painfully, his assailant pulled Callum so that they were nose to nose. 'You don't remember me but I know all about you, Callum Haggarty,' said Felix. 'Your daughter's correct. You're a thief and a liar, and a bully to boot.'

'Who the hell are you?' said Callum, fearful that this man appeared to know a lot about him.

'I'm Felix, Roz's boyfriend, she's told me all about you,' hissed Felix, 'and from what I've just heard, I think we need to have a word with the police, don't you?' Callum tried struggling, but Felix's grip was like iron. Turning pleading eyes to his daughter, he begged her to tell Felix to let go, but Suzie shook her head.

'If stealing off people in a raid isn't bad enough, I just caught you red-handed trying to pick pockets.'

By now, and with Callum restrained, even more people were turning to face them.

'Someone's nicked me wallet,' cried one man, 'somebody check 'is pockets!'

Suzie deftly picked both her father's pockets before he could move to stop her.

'You sneaky little ...' Callum began, but Suzie silenced him with a withering glance.

'If I am, it's only because I learned from the best.' She examined the three wallets and watch which she had removed from his pockets. The man who claimed to have had his pocket picked pointed at a brown leather, rather tatty-looking wallet.

'That's mine,' he said, holding his hand out.

Suzie handed it over and waited for the man to check its contents. As he did so, the crowd parted to let a policeman come through.

Recognising the policeman, the man whose wallet had been returned spoke to him directly. 'This good-for-nothin's stole me wallet, Charlie, and I daresay the other two ain't his neither, nor that watch.'

The policeman took the remaining stolen goods from Suzie and asked the people around them to check to see if they had anything missing, before turning to Callum. 'Well, well, if it isn't Callum Haggarty, can't say I'm surprised.' He looked at Suzie, 'I see you've turned it into a family day out.' Shaking his head, he added, 'The apple hasn't fallen far from the tree, has it?' Taking some handcuffs from his person, he indicated for Suzie to hold her hands out, but was immediately met with an outcry from the crowd, as well as Felix and Suzie.

'She didn't do anything wrong,' said Felix, 'it was Suzie who caught him.'

The policeman shot Felix a patronising smile. 'Sorry, son, but she's pulled the wool over your eyes good and proper. They're in cahoots together, well known to the police, the pair of them.'

'No!' said Suzie. 'I'm not here with my dad. I came here ...' She got no further before the man whom she had warned about pickpockets spoke up on her behalf.

'She really isn't, officer, it was this young lady who warned me of pickpockets. I overheard the whole thing.'

Looking confused, Charlie cocked an eyebrow as he studied Suzie's face for any sign of trickery. 'If you're not here with him then why *are* you here? Bit of a coincidence, don't you think?'

Suzie nodded. 'I know how it looks, but I was going to get a train to see a girl I know. Her name's Roz, and this ...' she jerked her head at Felix, '... is her boyfriend. She's staying on a farm in Betwys-y-Coed.'

'That cow!' sneered Callum. 'What the hell do you wanna see her for—'

He broke off as Charlie rushed to stop Felix from giving Callum a well-deserved clout. 'Now, now, we'll have none of that.'

'He shouldn't talk about her like that,' growled Felix.

'Maybe not, but I'd rather concentrate on the matter in hand, so if you don't mind ...' The policeman turned to Suzie. 'Am I to believe that you don't live with your father any more? I know your …' he paused whilst he tried to find the right words to describe the room which the Haggartys had occupied, '… home was bombed, but I took it for granted that you'd all moved elsewhere.'

She shook her head. 'I haven't got a clue where he went, and Gran died in the bombing.'

'Where were you?' said Charlie, wrinkling an eyebrow.

Drawing a deep breath and taking no pride in what she was about to say, Suzie began to tell the policeman everything that happened that fatal night.

Callum paled, and he was starting to back away, hoping to make a run for it, when he inadvertently stepped on the toes of the man behind him, who cried out and pushed him forward into Charlie who, realising his intentions, swiftly cuffed him.

'Oh no you don't,' said Charlie. Holding Callum by his elbow, he continued to talk to Suzie. 'Go on.'

Callum lunged at his daughter, in a bid to silence her. 'Shut your bleedin' trap!' he roared, before turning to those gathered around. 'She's lyin'! I wouldn't do that …'

'Then why was the old woman on her own?' called a voice from the back of the crowd.

Callum's eyes darted around as he tried to think of a reasonable excuse as to why he'd left his mother on her own, but with nothing coming to mind, and the hangman's noose looming, he fought desperately to break free from Charlie. But Charlie, being both stronger and younger than Callum, merely tightened his grip, and called to Cyril – another policeman – for assistance.

Realising he had no hope of escape, Callum spat at his daughter's feet. 'You ain't no Haggarty,' he said, his voice full of venom.

'Good!' said Suzie. 'Because I wouldn't want to be.'

Charlie looked at Suzie. 'I know it's a big ask, but we need you to come down to the station and make a statement.'

Suzie looked at her father, who was glaring fiercely at her in the hope that she would refuse, but Suzie had had enough.

'I lost me mam and me gran because of you – everything you touch turns rotten.'

Callum hissed a warning. 'You do this and we're through – you're on your own.'

She gave a mirthless laugh. 'I'm better off without you. You never approved of me anyway, always having a go, saying I never did nothing right, but I wasn't the one who drove Mam away, and I wasn't the one who left Gran on her own in the middle of an air raid.' Angry tears trickling down her cheeks, she shook her head. 'I told you she couldn't get down them steps on her own, but you were more bothered about the stuff you'd been nicking from other people's houses than you were about your own mother.'

The truth hit Callum like a hammer. His face fell as the enormity of her words struck home. 'How was I to know they'd hit our place?' he said wretchedly. 'You can't blame me ...'

'Only I do,' said Suzie frankly. She turned to Charlie. 'I was catching the train to Betwys-y-Coed, but I'll have to give that a miss, this is far more important. Can I just have a quick word with Felix?'

Nodding, Charlie indicated the steps that led to the station. 'We'll wait for you out there.'

Thanking the policeman, she spoke hastily to Felix as the train pulled into the platform. I'll be brief. 'Bernie told me what happened. All I can do is apologise. I was so jealous of Roz, and I blamed her for everything.' She shook her head impatiently. 'I haven't got time to explain why, but I set out to destroy everything she had, and I can see I succeeded, because you're still here, yet you should be in Glasfryn with Roz.' She heaved a heartfelt sigh. 'I'm going to make this right. I don't know how, but I am.'

He shrugged. 'You were only the messenger; everything you said was true, you just went about it in a spiteful manner.'

Suzie shook her head fervently. 'If it hadn't been for me, Roz would never—'

'Roz doubted her feelings for me,' said Felix plainly. 'That had nothing to do with you, and that's the part that hurt the most.'

Suzie stared at him. 'Good God, Felix, we all have doubts! I gave my father the benefit of the doubt for years, always trying to please him, kidding myself that he was a good man really, and it was other people that pushed him over the edge.' Seeing the platform emptying, she threw her hands up in an exasperated fashion. 'You can't hang someone for having second thoughts. You need to be sure in life – no wonder she had insecurities, just look at what she's been through!'

She hesitated. 'Only you're here, so you must be going to Glasfryn ...'

Felix pulled a rueful face. 'I'm afraid not ...'

'Why on earth not?' squeaked Suzie. 'Didn't you hear a word I've just said?'

He nodded. 'I'm here for the Lincoln train. It was due in over an hour ago, but what with the war and Christmas and everything, the railways are pretty shocking when it comes to timekeeping.'

Suzie gave him a blank stare. 'I never took you for a fool ...' She hesitated as she saw Charlie appear in her line of sight. 'I've got to go, but you'll do well to remember that only a fool cuts his nose off to spite his face, and that's what you'll be doing if you let Roz slip through your fingers.'

Chapter Ten

It was Christmas Day, and Roz, unable to sleep, looked out of the bedroom window at the thick snow which was falling was so fast it had already covered the ground outside. When she had arrived at Glasfryn some days previously, the first question on everyone's lips had been, where was Felix?

She had had no other option than to tell them the truth.

'Oh dear,' said Heulwyn, 'what a tangled web!'

'I wish I'd kept out of it,' Roz had agreed miserably.

'At least it wasn't in vain,' said Mabel reassuringly, 'because if it wasn't for you, Suzie might never have made up with her mam.'

'That's the only thing that makes this whole thing bearable,' said Roz wretchedly. 'I just wish Felix would see things the way you do.'

'He will,' said Heulwyn. 'He's a grand lad is your Felix, and he worships the ground you walk on. His pride's taken a bit of a knock but it'll heal.'

This conversation had taken place just after she'd arrived on the farm, and Roz had hoped that Felix would appear at the door to the cottage full of forgiveness and everything would go back to how it was before the incident at Lime Street Station. But as the days had rolled by, her hope faded.

Now, as she watched the snow whirl around in little eddies, she held the small bar of Lifebuoy soap, which she had bought Felix as a Christmas present, up to her nose and gave it a tentative sniff. Given the circumstances, it may have seemed silly for her to wish that Felix would turn up for Christmas, but she couldn't help hoping, even now, that he would appear. She turned to see Mabel shuffling over, her eiderdown wrapped around her shoulders as she joined Roz by the window.

'Merry Christmas, Roz,' she said, holding out a small paper bag.

Taking the bag, Roz looked inside and smiled. 'Everton mints! Where on earth did you get these?'

Mabel winked. 'I have my ways.'

'You mean you've got Gethin,' smiled Roz.

'He has his uses. Do you realise this is going to be our first Christmas together?'

Keen to steer the subject away from boyfriends, Roz handed her friend a bar of Fry's Chocolate Cream.

'Ooh,' said Mabel, 'I shall have one piece a day, to make it last.' She followed Roz's gaze to the yard. 'You still hoping?'

Roz nodded. 'Hope is all I have.'

Mabel stretched out her arm and snuggled Roz into the eiderdown with her. 'Maybe they've stopped the trains due to the snow,' she suggested. 'It can get really bad here in the mountains.'

'Either way, he's not here,' said Roz. 'I don't wish to be a wet blanket, but I'd rather get on with the chores – it's better than dwelling on the ifs and maybes.'

Nodding, Mabel made her way back over to her bed, put her slippers on, and swapped her eiderdown for her dressing gown. 'I'll go and fetch some hot water, so we can have a wash.'

Roz nodded, but continued to look out of the window. 'Where are you, Felix Ackerman?' she said quietly. 'I need you.'

It was much later that morning by the time Roz, Mabel and Gethin had finished seeing to the animals.

'I think my toes have turned to ice,' said Mabel as she removed her wellies and headed for the fire. 'I'm going to have chilblains on chilblains at this rate.'

'It wouldn't have been so bad had you not jumped into that drift,' said Roz, wagging a reproving finger, although she was smiling as she did so. 'How old are you?'

Mabel grinned. 'Young enough to have a bit of fun, but too old to get this cold!' She glanced at Gethin who had come into the kitchen, stamping his feet to get rid of the snow, something which Heulwyn strongly objected to.

'Do that outside the house, not in!' she exclaimed. She was carrying a tray containing three mugs of cocoa.

Roz grinned as she saw Mabel hastily stowing her wellingtons out of sight.

Heulwyn placed the tray on the table and instructed them to help themselves to a mug. 'The chicken'll be another half-hour yet, so you've time for a wash and change before I serve up.'

'Cocoa first, though,' said Mabel. Taking a long sip, she smacked her lips with satisfaction. 'Ooh, that hits the spot.'

'Best cocoa in Wales,' agreed Gethin. Sitting down on one of the chairs which flanked the fireplace, he gestured for Mabel to sit on his knee.

Taking the seat opposite, Roz held her triple-socked toes up to the fire. 'I wonder what Felix is doing right now.'

Mabel was about to speak when someone knocked on the door. Grinning, she jumped off Gethin's lap and headed over to the small window at the side of the parlour door, lifting the curtain slightly so that she could see without being seen. The smile instantly vanished from her lips. 'It's a woman! I've never seen her before.'

The woman knocked again.

'Are you going to open the door, or do you want me to?' said Gethin, as Mabel continued to peer through the gap in the curtains. 'It's hardly in keeping with the Christmas spirit to leave someone on the doorstep.'

Roz got to her feet. 'We're never going to know who she is if we don't answer the door. Honestly, Mabel, there are easier ways to find out who's calling ...' As she spoke she opened the door. The woman, who looked as though she was about to walk away, turned to face her.

Much to Gethin and Mabel's alarm, Roz staggered back from the door, her hand clasped to her mouth.

'What's wrong?' said Mabel. 'Is it summat to do with Felix? Is it ...' She got no further, for Roz, to Mabel's astonishment, had rushed forward, taking the stranger in a tight embrace.

Tears flowing down her cheeks, they heard her say just one word: 'Mama!' before collapsing.

When Roz came to, she was surprised to find herself lying fully clothed on her bed, with Mabel looking down at her, with concern.

Sitting up on one elbow, she spoke to her friend. 'What happened? Last I remember I was in the kitchen ...' She frowned as she tried to make sense of it all. She had been in the kitchen when someone had come to the door; no one seemed keen to answer it, so Roz had ... She looked at Mabel. 'I had a dream, that my mother ...' She fell silent as her mother appeared over Mabel's shoulder.

'Not a dream ...' said Inge.

Roz gaped at her mother, then at Mabel, who nodded, her lips trembling as she smiled. 'And that's not all ...'

Roz craned her neck to see who else was there, keeping her fingers crossed that it would be her father.

'Felix!'

Smiling, Felix too entered the room.

Still staring expectantly at the bedroom door she spoke softly. 'Where's Dad?'

Inge sank down beside the bed and cupped Roz's hands in hers. 'We got separated when we were leaving France, the Resistance thought it would be best ...'

'France?'

She nodded. 'That's where we've been all this time. You see, the man your father had swerved to avoid was a German soldier. As you can imagine, the accusation would have been that we had tried to hit him on purpose, so we had to think quickly. You had been thrown clear of the car, so everyone thought we were on our own and it

400

was better that way. I couldn't just leave you though so I asked a woman nearby to take you into the station. That's when we made our escape. We knew it wasn't safe to stay where we were so we made our way to France, where we worked on various farms for our keep.

'We wanted to come to England, of course we did, but it was too dangerous. I wanted to write to let you know we were safe, but Papa said no in case the letters were intercepted. When France fell to Germany I really thought we were done for, but there's a band of heroes who call themselves the Resistance, they're like a secret army, and they're fighting Hitler. The farm we were hiding in put us in touch with their leader, and that's when things started to get better for us. They said if we helped them, they could arrange safe passage to England. It was the best news we'd had in a long time and of course we jumped at the chance.'

'So where's dad, and why isn't he with you?' Roz held her breath as she listened to her mother's explanation.

Inge sighed ruefully. 'We decided it would be best if we travelled alone, under false identities. Your father was meant to board the same train as me but not at the same time, only when I got off in Holland there was no sign of him. I searched the platform, but nothing.' Inge gave her daughter a reassuring smile. 'The Nazis are always pulling people off trains, just to be awkward, which is why we had a backup plan. If either of us got left behind they would return to the farm, whilst the other continued on to England.'

Roz breathed again. 'So what now?'

'He'll lie low for a few days then try again.' She smiled. 'Wild horses won't stop him from seeing his

401

bubala. You mark my words, your father will be with us before the year is out.'

Roz nodded thoughtfully. 'I see, only how did you meet Felix?'

'The plan was to head straight for Liverpool, so that's what I did. It was in Lime Street Station that I met this one.' She smiled at Felix.

Felix locked eyes with Roz. 'I was waiting for the train when I thought I saw you standing a little further along the platform, only instead of being in wellies and dungarees you were dressed in a smart suit. I walked over to get a better look, and it was you, just a few years older. I couldn't believe what I was seeing. Then it struck me, either you had a doppelgänger, or I was looking at your mother.'

Inge placed her arm around Felix's shoulders. 'He came over and asked if I was Mrs Sachs. At first I was reluctant to answer, for obvious reasons, but there was something so honest about him and he spoke with such urgency and concern, I decided to be truthful, and what a good job I did, because Felix knew exactly what to do. He took me straight to the Liver Building, where we spoke to Mr Garmin. He was wonderful. A real godsend. He said he'd keep an eye out for your father and let him know where we were, should he turn up.'

Felix took up the rest of the tale. 'Seeing as we'd missed the train for Wales, he arranged for us to get a lift with a pal of his, and here we are.'

It was at this point that Heulwyn called them down for their dinner. As the others left the room ahead of them, Felix held a hand across Roz's path, his brow raised. 'A quick word?'

She nodded. 'Me first. I'm so sorry, Felix ...' She hushed as he placed a finger to her lips.

'Let's not dwell on the past. If anyone should be sorry, it's me for letting my stupid pride get in the way.'

Hooking her arm through his, she smiled up at him. 'You had every right, but like you say, let's forget the past, and concentrate on the future.'

Leaning down he kissed her softly.

Mabel called up from the bottom of the stairs. 'Are you two coming or what?'

Sliding his hand into hers, Felix led Roz down the stairs, and Roz sat in the seat next to her mother's. Placing her hand over Inge's she gave it a squeeze. 'I thought this Christmas was going to be rotten. Just goes to show how wrong one can be.'

Smiling, Inge squeezed her daughter's hand in return. 'Next year will be even better, just you wait and see.'

Feeling happier than she had in some time, Roz turned her thoughts to those she had left behind at Hollybank. She couldn't help thinking that Joyce and Suzie would not be having a merry Christmas, and said as much. 'I hope Joyce and Suzie manage to have a good Christmas, because when all's said and done, they've only got each other.'

'I forgot, you don't know, do you?' Felix clapped a hand to his forehead as he relayed his encounter with Callum and Suzie and all that had transpired as a result of their meeting.

'I knew it!' hissed Roz. 'Didn't I say, Mabel?'

Mabel nodded. 'We may have got it wrong about his wife, but we hit the nail on the head when it came to his mam.'

'Poor Lilith,' said Roz, 'as if things weren't bad enough, knowing that your own son had left you like a sitting duck!'

'Well, Callum's going to get all that's coming to him now,' said Felix, 'and I have to admire Suzie for the way she stood up to him. It can't have been easy.'

There followed a chorus of ohs and ahs as Heulwyn placed the chicken on the table, ready for Howell to carve.

'Tuck in, folks!'

They didn't need asking twice. All the excitement had created quite an appetite, and when they felt they couldn't eat another morsel the men retired to the parlour whilst the women did the dishes.

'You're going to have to tell me more about your work with the French Resistance,' said Roz as she took a plate over to the sink.

'I'm afraid I can't discuss my time with them,' said Inge, 'you know what they say ...'

She stopped speaking as Felix entered the room. 'Can I have a word?' he said, looking directly at Roz.

'Of course!' Roz followed him out of the kitchen through to the parlour. 'Where are we going?' she said, as Felix handed her her coat.

'For a walk,' he said, pulling on a pair of Gethin's old wellingtons.

Roz looked round at Gethin and Howell, both of whom seemed to be avoiding her gaze.

Once outside she pulled her hat firmly onto her head and lifted the collar of her navy blue coat. 'Do we have to go for a walk? It's freezing out here!'

Felix placed his arm around her shoulders and pulled her close. 'I wanted to ask you something.'

'Couldn't you have asked me inside?' said Roz, adding, 'Where it's warm.'

'It's warm in Zeus's stable,' reasoned Felix, opening the door.

She entered the stable and patted Zeus's neck, giggling as he snuffled at her for treats, something which Roz always had in her pockets.

Felix was eyeing her with great affection. 'Do you remember what I said to you when we were at the top of Lincoln Castle?'

Roz cast her mind back and nodded slowly. 'You said lots of things, but the one I remember the most is when we were talking about the future, about how we'd live on a farm and have our own animals.' She smiled dreamily. 'You made it sound so wonderful.'

Coming forward, he placed his arms around her waist. 'Do you remember me saying how I'd not ask you to marry me until I'd had your father's permission?'

She nodded slowly. 'Only my father's not here.'

'Granted, and whilst I may not have your father's consent, your mother was thrilled to bits when I said I was eager to meet him so that I could get his approval. So much so, she has given permission in his place. She said he'd be over the moon to know his daughter had a man like me looking after her.'

Tears shining in her eyes, Roz managed a small nod. 'He would.'

Without hesitation Felix sank to one knee. 'So how about it, Rozalin Sachs? Will you agree to be my wife?'

Roz gave a small squeal of delight. 'Yes, of course I will!'

He stood up and his eyes twinkled as they gazed into hers. 'I'm so glad I missed the train, because it gave me the chance to do something.' Pushing his hand into his pocket, he pulled out a small box and opened it for her to see.

Roz looked down at the small circle of silver. 'It's beautiful,' she breathed, as Felix pushed the ring onto her finger.

'Just like the woman who's wearing it.'

She placed her arms around his waist and smiled dreamily up into his face. 'All we need now is my father and your mother, and this will be the best Christmas ever ...' She hesitated, for Felix was shaking his head sadly.

'I don't understand,' said Roz.

He kissed the top of her head. 'I'm afraid my mother won't be joining us.'

She wrinkled her brow. 'You don't know that, you can't ...' She stopped speaking. Tears had formed in Felix's eyes. Fearing the worst, Roz spoke hastily. 'Felix? What haven't you told me?'

He held her close so that she might not see his tears. 'My mum's gone, Roz, she passed away not long after we left for England.'

Roz pushed herself away from him. Tears streaming down her cheeks, she shook her head, refusing to believe such sad news. 'You can't possibly know, you must've got it wrong ...'

He smiled kindly down at her. 'I wish I had, but I haven't. The rabbi who helped me escape got in contact with Reggie Jones, and he got in touch with me.' He heaved a jagged sigh. 'In short, my mother died in one of the camps. He didn't say how, just that now she's in a better place.'

Roz could hardly believe what she was hearing. 'When?'

'I found out the day before you came to Lincoln.'

Roz cast her mind back. 'That can't be right. We were in Lincoln when we were talking about the house in the country ...' She stopped speaking as she ran through the conversation in her mind. She buried her face in his chest. 'You said your mother would be ... '

Felix rocked her in his arms. 'I didn't want you to worry. I'd had my hopes dashed, and I couldn't – wouldn't see that happen to you.'

She allowed her tears to melt into his jacket. 'I was too wrapped up in my own affairs to see that something was wrong ...'

He lifted her chin with his finger. 'You can't know what someone doesn't want you to,' he said reasonably. 'I said it at the time and I'll say it again: my mother would've been pleased as punch to know that I had found myself such a wonderful woman.'

'And I shall do everything I can to make her proud by being the perfect wife and mother.' She hesitated. 'What were your parents' names?'

'Belinda and Archie.'

'Then if our firstborn is a boy we shall call him Archie, and if it's a girl we shall call her Belinda, and we shall tell them who they are named after and how brave your mother was.'

'And once again you remind me why I love you so much, and even though I have your mother's approval I want us to wait until your father can be here to give you away. So I'm going to do all I can to find him.'

Roz gave lovingly at him. 'I know you will, because you're Felix Ackerman, the most wonderful man in the world, and I'm lucky to have you as my fiancé.'

'I'm the lucky one,' murmured Felix. Holding her tight, he brushed his lips against hers, before kissing her with a love and passion that took her breath away.

READ IT NOW

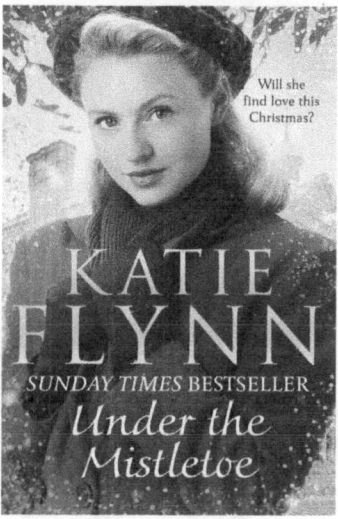

Liverpool, 1940

When war comes to Britain, Jessica Wilson and her friend Ruby seize the opportunity to leave behind the orphanage they grew up in and start new lives in the NAAFI. With only forged papers as identification the girls expect to be turned away but are delighted with an offer of work.

For the first time in their lives they experience real independence and it isn't long before they're spending their evenings enjoying the delights of Liverpool.

When Jessica meets the handsome Tom, she feels as though her life is complete, but after a chance encounter with a friend, she soon learns that not everything is as it seems.

As Jessica begins to uncover the truth, she unravels a web of lies, starting with the night of her birth . . .

AVAILABLE IN PAPERBACK AND EBOOK

arrow books

KATIE
FLYNN

If you want to continue to hear from the
Flynn family, and to receive the latest news about
new Katie Flynn books and competitions,
sign up to the Katie Flynn newsletter.

Join today by visiting
www.penguin.co.uk/katieflynnnewsletter